PASSION

Tender Loving
PASSION

DONNA HILL

HARLEQUIN® KIMANI ARABESQUE®

Recycling programs
for this product may
not exist in your area.

TENDER LOVING PASSION
ISBN-13: 978-0-373-09152-2

Copyright © 2014 by Harlequin Books S.A.

The publisher acknowledges the copyright
holders of the individual works as follows:

TEMPTATION AND LIES
Copyright © 2009 by Donna Hill

LONGING AND LIES
Copyright © 2010 by Donna Hill

Printed in U.S.A.

CONTENTS

To all my readers old and new. I thank you for the continued love and support. Enjoy the ride!

TEMPTATION AND LIES

Chapter 1

The October sun peeked through the slats in the vertical blinds, throwing a soft glow across the state-of-the-art kitchen. Mia Turner loved to cook and considered herself something of a gourmet chef, always willing to try new recipes. And she firmly believed that a good meal opened and soothed the soul. The best conversations, confessions and gossip could be had over a good meal.

With her piping-hot mug of imported Turkish coffee on the left, her sparkling pearl-handle .22 on the right, she snapped open the *Daily News* and immediately turned to Page Six. She circled several high-profile items about celebs and business tycoons spotted in and around the Big Apple as she sipped her coffee. The smooth blend had been a gift from one of her grateful clients. She made a note on the pad next to her saucer to call Paul Han and thank him for his "thank you."

Page Six aside, she turned her attention to the egg-white omelet that she painstakingly prepared every morning. It was stuffed with mushrooms, tomatoes, green peppers and cheddar cheese. She took a forkful and sighed with pleasure.

There were two things that were paramount in Mia's life: great food and paying clients. Well, three things—order, too. No, make that four—Steven.

The last item on her must-have list made her smile and she thought about the incredible lovemaking session they'd had just that morning, in this very chair. She wiggled her plump bottom as images of her and Steven played behind her partially closed lids.

Her best friends, Savannah Fields and Danielle Holloway, teased her about her neurotic obsessions, but they had to agree that Steven Long was certainly worth being obsessed about.

Mia was the last of the trio to find someone special in her life. Savannah and Blake had been married for seven years and had just had their first child—Mikayla—the most gorgeous baby girl the world had ever seen. And Danielle had finally allowed her heart to open and let Nick Mateo in, and they were now living together and engaged!

For a while Mia believed she'd always be the fifth wheel, until she actually took a second look at Steven Long.

They'd known each other casually for years: Blake and Steven were best friends and business partners at their architecture and development company.

But it wasn't until Mia had hosted a party at her

house about ten months earlier that they actually saw each other as more than "the best friend of their best friend."

Since that night, Mia and Steven had been pretty much inseparable, only allowing the pressing business of their respective livelihoods to keep them apart.

Mia closed her paper, finished off her omelet and washed it down with the last of her coffee.

She took her dishes to the sink, rinsed then placed them in the dishwasher.

This part of her morning ritual completed, she took her gun from the table and walked the short hallway that led from the front of the two-bedroom condo to the back where the master bedroom and reconverted second bedroom were located.

She and Steven used that second bedroom as their combined office, so she would never risk him discovering the contents of her "kit," as Danielle's lover Nick had done.

A minor disaster like that would take more explaining than she was willing to do. So being the orderly and forward-thinking type-A personality that she was, Mia had cut out a little panel behind the top shelf of her clothes closet, hidden behind boxes of very expensive shoes.

She removed the panel and pulled out her TLC "beauty kit." Mia smiled as she ran her hand across the smooth pink leather carrying case with the TLC logo emblazoned across the front.

Taking the case to the bed, she turned the latch to review the contents: burglary tools, computer-scanning disk, listening and recording devices, chloroform and a fingerprint dusting kit and, of course, the container that held the bath beads that were actually specially designed tranquilizer bullets for her .22. All the contents were ingeniously camouflaged as bath oil, body lotions, eye shadows, blush, perfumes and lipsticks. She smiled.

Reassured that everything was in order and accounted for, she lifted the top tray and replaced the gun in its cutout compartment below. She knew it was risky to take the gun out each morning after Steven had left for work, but the thrill of seeing it right next to her, where she could admire and stroke it—even though it only held tranquilizer bullets—still gave her a rush.

Mia had become an official member of the Cartel seven months earlier, although she'd been a fringe member since Savannah's first case a little more than a year ago, which turned up an ugly land deal that would have destroyed an ancient African burial ground right in downtown Brooklyn.

As the owner and CEO of MT Management, Mia's schedule, though hectic, was her own. That flexibility lent itself to her sideline as an undercover operative for TLC.

Mia returned her kit to its hiding place and checked the time. Jean Wallington-Armstrong, the head of the Cartel, had asked Mia to come to the Harlem brownstone to discuss a new assignment that Jean felt Mia was perfect for.

From there it would be off to her real job—the one she could tell everyone about, she thought with a smile.

Event management was the perfect occupation for Mia. It gave her the opportunity to arrange every aspect of an event, down to the most mundane detail, and she loved every minute of it.

Ever since she was a little girl, growing up in Bedford-Stuyvesant in Brooklyn, she'd had a knack for arranging things. As a preschooler she had a precise time and location for all her doll tea parties and all the accessories had to match and be placed "just so" on the tiny pink plastic table.

The most traumatic incident in her young life was when she went to place the teacups on the saucers and discovered that one of the handles was broken and there were no more in her collection that matched. "You see, the tablecloth, paper napkins and the dolls' outfits were all color-coordinated," she'd explained to Savannah and Danielle many years later, who'd both given her sympathetic looks.

She'd become so hysterical that her mother had to promise to replace the entire set the following day. Mia was only five at the time, and her obsession with detail and order only grew and crystallized as she got older.

Of course, now she didn't collapse into tears and fits when things went awry, but her entire demeanor would become one tightly wound band of tension that was terribly uncomfortable to be around.

That aside, Mia Turner was your everyday, ordinary kind of woman unless, of course, you counted her other life.

She squinted at her appearance in the oval hall mirror. Her smooth, shoulder-length hair haloed her face in soft waves. The slight touches of makeup—bronze lip gloss, mascara and a little powder to keep the shine off her nose—kept her lovely features from being overshadowed. She cinched the belt on her knee-length dress, took her coat and purse and headed out, checking the locks three times before she felt comfortable.

* * *

Twenty minutes later she pulled onto 135th Street in Harlem. She parked her midnight-blue Lexus two doors down from the brownstone. The luxury car was a recent present to herself for having achieved a stellar year of profits from her business. In these tight economic times, everyone was cutting back, but her business continued to flourish. Big business, celebrities and the well-off were always having conventions or hosting parties to sell something, impress others or remind everyone else how important they were, and MT Management was the one they invariably called.

Mia slid off her glasses and tucked them into her purse. She was terribly nearsighted but refused to wear her glasses in public and was adamant against "sticking something in her eyes" as she put it, referring to contact lenses. So vanity won out and she went through life squinting, which often gave her a severe appearance that was totally contrary to her open and warm personality. In business, however, it often worked to her advantage: in her dealings and negotiations, her steely gaze gave the impression of a no-nonsense businesswoman.

She gathered her purse and hopped out, her chocolate-colored Milano ankle boots hitting the pavement with a soft pop.

She grabbed her ecru-colored swing coat from the hook in the back of the car and quickly slipped it on. Although it was early October and the sun was high in the sky, the weather had already begun to grow cool.

Setting the alarm on the car, she headed to the brownstone and rang the bottom bell.

Within moments, Claudia, Savannah's mother, came to the door.

"Hello, darling," Claudia greeted her, enveloping Mia in a warm hug. The soft scent of Chanel floated around her.

Claudia Martin was in her early sixties, but she didn't look a day over forty-five. Class and style always exuded from Claudia. She kept her auburn-tinted hair in a fierce cut that mimicked the early Halle Berry look. Her cinnamon complexion was flawless and she rarely wore much makeup, save for a dash of lipstick and mascara to accentuate her incredible hazel eyes. St. John was her designer of choice and she wore it well.

Claudia had been a member of TLC for several years and had recruited her daughter, Savannah. And all those years that Mia, Savannah and Danielle had seen Claudia toting around her TLC carryall and saying she was going to meetings, they'd always believed what she told them: that she was selling beauty products. Ha!

The joke between them, now that Savannah had a daughter of her own, would be that she would recruit little Mikayla when she came of age. Knowing her already feisty infant, Savannah had said Mikayla would probably launch her own division of TLC Tots!

"Looking good as always, Claudia. Bernard must be treating you well. You're glowing."

Claudia laughed lightly. "That he does, my dear. Nothing like a good man to get the kinks out." She winked at Mia and walked inside.

"Have you two finally set a date?"

"Actually, I wanted to talk to you about that." She clasped Mia's arm and her diamond ring flashed in the late-morning light. "Now that Savannah had the baby and can fit into something 'fabulous,' as she said, we wanted a December wedding. Do you think you can put something together in time?"

Mia stopped short, propped her hand on her hip and gave Claudia a look of mild reprimand. "Claudia, this is me. If you said your wedding was this afternoon and you wanted it in Paris, I would make it happen. It's what I do."

Claudia laughed in response. "Chile, what was I thinking? Go on," she said, still chuckling. "Jean is upstairs in her office."

"We'll make an appointment to talk," she promised before heading off.

Mia went up the stairs and down the "hall of fame" as it had been dubbed. The walls on either side were lined with portraits of all the Cartel members who had been affiliated for at least a year and had successfully completed their assignments. She smiled as she spotted Savannah's photo and then two photos down was one of Danielle. Claudia's was at the beginning of the row, right next to Jean. Mia drew in a breath of resolve. One day soon her photo would grace the hall of fame, too.

Mia knocked lightly on the closed door.

"Come in." Jean looked up from her computer screen when Mia entered. "Have a seat. I'll be right with you."

Mia did as instructed, taking in the room while she waited. As with all of the brownstones in Harlem and in Brooklyn—which had not been cut up or converted— the rooms were enormous; *grand* would be a better word. Vaulted ceilings, crystal chandeliers, parquet floors, mahogany sliding doors, massive mantelpieces, stained-glass windows and working fireplaces. Some even had the claw-foot bathtubs and original porcelain sconces.

She'd grown up in a brownstone on Putnam Avenue in Brooklyn. Not quite as big as this one, but large enough. So any time she came here she felt right at home.

Mia crossed her legs.

"Thank you for coming," Jean began, bypassing any pleasantries.

Mia merely nodded, knowing from experience that Jean wasn't one for chitchat.

"I have an assignment that is perfect for you, especially with the business that you're in."

Jean took a sealed manila envelope from her desk drawer. "All the details are inside. I'll briefly give you some background. This was handed to me from a personal contact at the FBI. There are some extremely high-profile individuals involved and before the lid gets blown off, they need to be absolutely sure." She cleared her throat and removed her red-framed glasses, setting them gently down on the desktop. "There is a major, very elite, very exclusive escort service operating in New York City. Although that's nothing new, what is new is that it appears to be run by Avante Enterprises. You need to find a way to get inside the organization, and get the evidence that the Feds need to shut it down."

For an instant, Mia couldn't move. She hoped that Jean couldn't read the distress on her face, or hear the escalated pounding of her heart. Avante Enterprises had been one of her clients, and several years ago she'd broken a cardinal rule and had a short but fiery affair with its CEO, Michael Burke.

Chapter 2

Mia managed to get through the rest of the briefing without screaming. When she got behind the wheel of her Lexus, she wasn't quite certain she'd heard anything Jean had said after she'd dropped her Michael Burke bombshell.

By rote she turned the key in the ignition. The engine purred to life, along with the sounds of Marvin Gaye's classic, "What's Going On."

That was the question of the day, she mused. She put on her glasses, drew in a long steadying breath and slowly pulled off in the early-afternoon traffic.

In the privacy of her business office, a ground-floor rental in SoHo, Mia closed and locked the door on the off chance that her new assistant, Ashley Temple, might decide to burst in—as she was prone to do—to update her on the latest TMZ news (a celebrity online and off-line news outlet). She was relieved that Ashley wasn't up front when she came in and she was able to get to her office undetected, at least for the time being.

Mia depressed the Do Not Disturb button on her phone, then removed the manila envelope from her purse.

She placed it on the desk and stared at the innocuous-looking envelope. It looked like millions of others, but she knew better. The contents had the potential to turn her life inside out.

The affair between her and Michael had been discreet. No one knew about it, especially within the business circles they traveled in. Not even Savannah or Danielle had any idea that anything had transpired. They'd always believed that she simply hadn't found the right man and, until she'd met Michael, she hadn't.

When they broke up, it was a long three years before she started intermittently dating. But she'd never found anyone who could measure up—until Steven Long.

Mia ran her manicured finger across the smooth surface of the envelope.

If she broke the seal and opened it, there was no turning back. She'd have to carry out the assignment. Her type-A personality wouldn't allow her to give up or turn the reins over to someone else.

Drawing in a long breath, she exhaled her doubts and trepidations and broke the seal.

The documents detailed Michael's rise up the business ranks to eventually running his own management company. He was considered one of the best in the management consulting business.

Her pulse pounded in her temples when she scrolled down to review his personal information.

Marital Status: Divorced

Reflexively, she gripped the pages tighter between her fingers. Her heart thumped as her breathing shortened.

Divorced. He was free. At least on paper.

He was married when they'd met. Guilt had riddled her each time they'd made love until her conscience had no longer allowed her to do that to another woman. Michael had literally begged her not to leave him. He'd promised to get a divorce—just give me some time, he'd said.

But time and promises were things she could not depend on, nor did she want to.

"I can't do this anymore, Michael," she recalled saying to him, the agony of speaking the words making her voice paper thin, sounding weak and without conviction.

He turned onto his side. His dark brown eyes moved slowly along her face. His thumb brushed across her bottom lip. "Do what?" he asked, his voice husky and taunting. "This?" His large hand slid between her damp thighs and gently caressed her there.

Mia drew in a sharp breath as the powerful sensations rippled through her.

"Michael…" Her hips arched. She gripped his shoulders and he rose above her, bracing his weight on his forearms.

"I love you so much, Mia," he said on a ragged breath as he pushed slowly inside her.

Mia wrapped her body and her heart around him,

giving him all of her because she knew that this could never happen again.

And it didn't.

Mia ran her hand along the length of her hair and for a moment shut her eyes, wishing the images of the past away.

She looked down and read further. Michael had been under surveillance for a while. He'd come under suspicion during a routine audit of his company's finances. There were several discrepancies, which had apparently been cleared up, but he remained a blip on the radar screen.

Apparently, deposits of three to five thousand dollars were routinely placed in one of his secondary accounts, then were quickly transferred to an offshore account in the Cayman Islands.

The more she read, the more ill she became.

The Michael Burke she knew was ambitious, and he could be manipulative if it would land him an account. But this man on paper was not the man she remembered and had once loved.

She closed the folder and knew that shortly the ink would disappear, as if the damning words had never existed.

The knock on her door snapped her to attention. She shoved the envelope into her desk drawer, removed her glasses and went to unlock the door.

"Hi. Come in."

Ashley's updated Angela Davis fro bounced in a cinnamon-brown halo around her openly expressive face.

Every time she looked at Ashley, Mia thought of a

highly energetic, inquisitive child, even though Ashley was easily in her early thirties.

Ashley was a godsend after Mia lost her last assistant to marriage and happily ever after. Ashley was bright, totally efficient and loved the event-planning business. She was so good, in fact, that Mia had given Ashley two of her own accounts to manage, and her clients loved her.

"Hey, boss," Ashley greeted her, her warm brown eyes sparkling, as always. Her deep dimples flashed.

"What's up?"

"A couple of calls that I thought you'd want to handle personally." She handed Mia a slip of the company's teal-colored message paper.

They walked toward the small circular table in the far corner of the office and sat down.

Mia squinted at the words on the page until they came into focus. "Sahara Club?" she asked.

Ashley read from a sheet in her hand detailing all the particulars about the Sahara Club, which catered to married couples who wanted to plan quick romantic getaways. The club management wanted to put together an event to promote their business, inviting previous guests to give testimonials about their experience.

Mia's brows rose as she listened.

"I did an Internet search on them," Ashley offered in response to the question that hovered on Mia's lips. She handed over her research material. "I also have a short list of some of their clients. I can have them checked, if you want."

Mia took the notes and briefly scanned them, the words blurry around the edges.

"This one is for the grand opening of a boutique in

Tribeca," she went on reading her second set of notes. "They want something really upscale. They'd like to come in and talk with you. Should I schedule it?"

"Why don't you take that one?" Mia said absently. "I'll sit in on the initial meeting if you need me, but I think you can handle it."

"No problem." She paused a moment. "Are you okay? You seem really out of it."

In the six months that Ashley had worked for Mia, they'd grown rather close, sharing stories and giving each other advice on things like clothes, cars, best deals, politics, religion. Mia had even invited Ashley to join her, Savannah and Danielle for their weekly girls' brunch at their favorite hangout, The Shop. Over time Mia had grown to respect Ashley's judgment and clearheaded opinions, which she often sought out. But her current dilemma she could not share.

"I'm fine. Just a little headache."

Ashley leaned forward. "Maybe if you wore your glasses to read and move around in the world, your head would stop hurting. It's probably eyestrain."

Mia made a face. It was her personal pet peeve. "I'll be fine. I'll take something for it."

Ashley huffed. "Suit yourself." She pushed up from the desk. "I'll give these ladies from the boutique a call and get that set up."

"Thanks."

Alone now, Mia's thoughts reluctantly turned to her most pressing situation: in order to complete her assignment, she was going to have to see Michael again. And she wasn't sure how she was going to handle that.

What she needed was some advice. Savannah was

totally out of the question. She was a devout believer in the sanctity of marriage. She'd had her own scare with her husband, Blake, and she didn't look favorably on the "other woman," which is what Mia had been.

Danielle, though much more open-minded, had mellowed since she'd settled down with Nick. And although she might be more understanding, Dani's quick, sharp tongue was not something she wanted to deal with, either.

Those were the reasons why she'd never told her two best friends about what had gone on between her and Michael. It went against everything they believed in. She'd cringe every time the topic of adultery and cheating came up during their chats. She never wanted to disappoint them or see that appalled look in their eyes. She knew they'd demand an explanation as to why, and she wouldn't be able to provide one, because she didn't know why.

Sounds of Ashley singing a very bad rendition of a Mary J. Blige tune drifted to her ears. Mia smiled. Oh, to be carefree, she mused.

Her phone rang.

"MT Management, Mia speaking."

"Hey, baby. Caught you at your desk."

"Hi, sweetie. This is a surprise. To what do I owe the pleasure?"

"I have a couple of hours and I thought I'd swing by and take my favorite girl to a late lunch. If you haven't eaten already."

"I'd love to."

"Great. See you in about twenty minutes."

"Okay." Mia hung up the phone. Spending some time with Steven was just what she needed.

* * *

As promised, twenty minutes later, Steven came walking through the door.

Mia's heart skipped a beat when she saw him. She stood and came from behind her desk, her body warming with every step.

"Hi," she whispered as she came to a stop in front of him.

Steven Long was, for lack of a better word, gorgeous. His complexion was the color of polished mahogany, he had a hard square jaw and chocolate-brown eyes with silky brows and lashes to die for.

Two years in a row *Jet* magazine had listed him as one of New York's most eligible bachelors. That was before he'd hooked up with Mia. Now he was off the market—permanently, if Mia had any say in the matter.

His gunmetal gray suit fit every inch of his six-foot frame, and damn if she didn't love a man in a good-looking suit. His pearl-gray shirt and burgundy-and-gray-striped tie set off the suit and his skin to perfection.

Steven snaked his arm around Mia's waist and swept her into a deep, lingering kiss that took her breath away. When he released her, she felt shaken and hot with desire.

"You're going to have to stop by more often," she said, stroking his cheek with the tip of her finger.

He grinned. "If only I could, gorgeous. How's your day been so far?"

Reality slammed into her. Her heart thumped. "Uh, not bad. We may have two more clients."

"That's great. Congrats."

"Good for business, but not great for relationships.

It means that I'll be even busier," she said, knowing that in the coming weeks she would need time away from Steven.

He took her hand and massaged the center of her palm in sensuous circular motions that sent shivers running through her.

"If anyone can multitask and make it look like child's play, it's you, babe." He pecked her softly on the lips. "I ain't worried," he said with a grin. "Come on, let's go before we spend all our free time talking about what time we won't have."

"Lead the way."

"How did you manage to get time away from the office?" Mia asked as they were seated in a back booth at Brothers Bistro, a great health-food eatery within walking distance of her office.

"Blake is in the field taking some sketches of the renovation project in Brooklyn. This morning I put the finishing touches on the blueprints for the town houses in D.C. and realized I actually had some breathing room for a change."

It was amazing how far Steven and Blake had come in just over a decade. They'd built their business from a two-man company, working out of a storefront, to one of the major players with a staff of ten, an office in midtown and contracts that were expanding their business from its Manhattan locale to the capital.

"If business keeps growing this way, any midday getaway would be wishful thinking," Steven said.

"Are you and Blake planning to hire more people?"

"We may have to, just to handle the volume. But my fear is, as I've explained to Blake, at some point the bottom is going to drop out. Builders are going to stop building because no one can afford to buy."

Mia nodded in agreement. She knew all too well the fragility of the current economy and how it had wreaked havoc on countless American businesses, not to mention the thousands who'd lost their homes.

"I don't want to have to hire new people and realize in six months or a year that we have to let them go."

"What does Blake say?"

"You know Blake, Mr. Optimistic. But I think I'm getting him to see my point."

"So what's plan B?"

"Work our asses off," he said with a chuckle.

Mia raised her water glass. "To working our asses off."

As she sat there laughing and talking with the man she loved and who loved her back, she knew that it was only a matter of time before the lies began. And she could only pray that he never found out—not so much about the Cartel, which would be devastating enough—but about her and Michael.

Savannah's censure she could live with. Danielle's sharp tongue she could handle. But the hurt and lack of respect that she knew would be in Steven's eyes would kill her inside. She would do whatever it took to keep that information from him. She'd get through it.

But the true test would come when she saw Michael again for the first time. She knew it would be soon.

Much too soon.

Chapter 3

It had been three days since Mia received her assignment and she had yet to do anything about it. She felt frozen, torn between what she had agreed to do—the oath she'd sworn—and the possible repercussions if she did what was necessary.

"Mia."

She glanced up from the files on her desk and was surprised to see Ashley standing in front of her.

"I…didn't hear you come in," she muttered.

"I know. I knocked three times, but you didn't answer. I've been standing here for a good thirty seconds and you didn't budge. Is everything okay? You've been totally distracted for the past few days. That's so not like you."

Mia sighed heavily and leaned back in her chair. She'd been debating about sharing some of her dilemma with Ashley—an abridged version—in hopes of getting an objective view. But because of the sensitivity of the issue, she'd balked at airing her dirty laundry. But holding it in was driving her crazy.

She was a person of action, one who dealt with issues head-on. This inertia was maddening.

"You want to talk?" Ashley gently nudged. "I'm a pretty good listener," she added with an encouraging smile.

Mia pressed her lips together in thought. Finally, she spoke. "Have you ever been in a situation when an old flame came back into your life?"

"Sure. Why?" She sat down on the chair beside Mia's desk.

"What did you do?"

"Well, we had dinner, talked about old times, the way things were. I spent the night at his place and we woke up the next morning and realized that it was truly over—you can't go back. At least Dave and I couldn't."

"Hmm." Mia's gaze drifted away. Spending the night with Michael was not an option. She couldn't do that to Steven in a million years.

"Is that what's going on?" Ashley tentatively asked.

Mia turned her gaze on Ashley. "Something like that. I'll put it this way, seeing him again is inevitable."

"And you don't know how to handle it."

"It's been a long time," Mia admitted. "But a lot was left unresolved."

"Well, I'd never be one to tell somebody what to do, but the one thing I do know, unless you resolve whatever it is that's eating at you, it will always jump up and get in your way." She smiled softly. "You'll work it out."

Ashley hopped up from her seat. "My bill is in the mail," she teased, drawing a chuckle from Mia. "The meeting with Verve Boutique is still on for noon."

"Right. The ones from Tribeca."

"Yep. They should be here soon."

Mia nodded. "Buzz me when you're ready."

"Sure." She headed for the door then stopped. "Mia…"

"Yes."

"As I said, I don't give advice often, but if I can offer this one piece—just think with your head and not with your heart." She tossed up her hands. "That's it." She grinned and sauntered out.

Ashley was right, Mia thought. She was thinking and projecting based on pure emotion and old memories.

Michael was more than over her by now. She was sure he'd moved on and was probably involved with someone else.

She was getting bent out of shape about nothing. What she needed to concentrate on was finding a way to get the information she needed.

That thought was like a knife to the chest. The idea that Michael could be behind an escort service still stunned her. It seemed impossible. But the reality was that people change. And if that adage was true, then Michael Burke was definitely not the man she remembered.

Think with your head.

That's exactly what she was going to start doing. She swiveled her chair toward the flat-screen computer monitor that sat on the right-hand side of her desk. She did a quick search of Avante Enterprises. Within moments a list of choices came up on the screen. She chose the link that opened the company Web site.

Michael's handsome face greeted her and her breath caught in her throat as a flood of memories rushed to the surface. *Think with your head.* She pushed the images back and started taking notes.

Before she knew it, she'd filled three pages and Ashley was buzzing her about their noon appointment. She shoved the notes in her desk. At least she'd done something concrete, she thought, mildly satisfied with herself.

She closed the file, got up from her desk and went to join the ladies in the conference space.

Felicia and Linda Hall were sisters and the proud owners of Verve. They'd been in business for about a year, but had never had the grand opening that they really wanted. Now, with some experience under their belts and a solid customer base, they thought it was time.

Felicia was the talker of the two, and wasted no time laying out what they wanted: a full weekend with music, entertainment, food and plenty of media coverage, she'd said.

"What kind of budget do you have to work with?" Mia asked.

"Five thousand dollars. Six max," Felicia answered. "But we're really hoping you can do it for four." She flashed a hopeful smile that revealed a tiny gap in her front teeth.

On cue, Ashley and Mia stole a glance at each other. Five would barely cover their expenses, not to mention putting on the event.

Ashley's look clearly said, *It's your decision, but I like them.*

"Why don't I have Ashley put some ideas together for you and what we think is feasible and we'll get back to you with a proposal by the end of the week. How's that?"

The sisters smiled in unison. The gap mirrored on their faces.

Felicia stuck out her hand toward Mia. "Thank you so much." She shook Mia's hand, then did the same with Ashley.

"I really hope you'll consider taking us on," Linda said, the first time she'd spoken since they'd arrived.

Ashley stood. Her notebook pressed against her small breasts. "By the way, I meant to ask, how did you find out about us?"

"Oh, a friend of ours who helped to get our business up and running," Felicia offered.

"Michael Burke," the sisters sang in harmony.

"He recommended you very highly," Felicia added.

Mia held back a yelp of surprise. Her pulse pounded so loudly that the voices faded into the background. She wasn't sure if she'd even said goodbye.

The sound of the front door closing snapped her to attention. She was alone in the conference room.

Recommended by Michael Burke. Coincidence or just her luck? Manhattan, for all its pomp and circumstance and worldwide notoriety, was nothing more than an island jam-packed with people and buildings. Sooner or later paths were bound to cross.

So he hadn't forgotten about her and even thought

enough of her to recommend a possible client. She didn't know if that was a good or a bad thing, but it *was* one thing—the opening that she needed.

Chapter 4

Michael Burke tugged off his suit jacket and tossed it on the back of the couch before heading across the gleaming wood floor of his condo to the minibar on the far side of the living room.

He took out a bottle of brandy and poured a short tumbler full—no ice. It was a habit he'd picked up over the past few years. The years after his divorce, the years after Mia.

He took a long swallow, closed his eyes and let the smooth, warm liquid work its way down and hopefully soothe the constant ache that had found a home in the center of his gut.

Absently, he put the glass on the top of the bar counter and went to the window. Lights flickered in apartment windows and in offices inhabited by the lone employee working overtime to impress the boss.

Michael braced his palm against the frame of the window. The sky suddenly lit up, followed by a loud crack of thunder.

The rain would come soon, Michael thought. On nights like this, when he could get away, he remembered walking through the city with Mia, laughing and hugging as they darted under the eaves of buildings and into doorways, stealing kisses like teenagers.

His jaw clenched reflexively. He had many memories of Mia. But the one that stood out in his mind was the day she walked out of his life.

They'd spent a glorious night together at the Hilton on Avenue of the Americas. His wife, Christine, was visiting her mother in Philadelphia, her childhood home. She'd been gone for a week and was due back the following day. Michael intended to make the most of his last night of freedom.

"I can't do this," she'd said. He remembered teasing her about what she'd meant before making love to her, pouring his heart and soul into her.

When he awoke the next morning she was gone. He called and called. He went to her apartment and got no answer. Her neighbors said they hadn't seen her.

She was working for a small management company at the time, and when he inquired about her, he was informed that she'd taken a leave of absence.

For weeks afterward, he couldn't sleep, and he barely ate. Every time his phone rang, he knew it would be Mia, but it never was.

Then about three months later a letter came to his office, no return address.

Dear Michael,

I know I took the coward's way out. But if I didn't I would have never found the strength to leave you.

No matter what it is that we feel for each other, it was wrong. We were wrong. And if I could do that to another woman, then what kind of woman did that make me?

I hurt. Every day I hurt. But I know in time it will get better. And you will find a way to be the husband Christine deserves.

I wish you all good things, my love, now and always.

Please don't try to contact me. It's best for all of us.

Mia

He still had that letter. He'd kept it all these years. Memorized every line. He would recite it to himself whenever the overwhelming urge to call or see her would consume him.

Most ironic, less than a year after Mia walked out of his life, Christine filed for divorce. She'd found someone else.

He supposed it was what he'd deserved, and he'd agreed to the divorce uncontested.

Michael turned away from the window, just as the rain began to fall. He was a free man now, a wealthy man who could have whomever and whatever he wanted. He wanted Mia Turner. And he was going to have her, no matter how long it took or what it took to achieve his goal. He'd honored her wishes not to contact her, until now.

He picked up the remnants of his drink and finished it off. It was just a matter of time, he thought as the golden-brown liquid heated his insides. A matter of time.

"Whew, it's pouring out there," Steven muttered, shaking himself off as he crossed the threshold of the apartment that he and Mia shared.

He'd given up his tiny one-bedroom apartment when he and Mia decided that they wanted to be with each other exclusively. That was six months ago, and he hadn't regretted a day of it.

He'd often envied the stability of Blake and Savannah's marriage, although he would never admit that to Blake, even though they were best friends. Blake and Savannah were a team and the union had grounded and matured Blake in a way that nothing else had. Savannah and now their new baby were his life. And the business that he and Blake had built from the ground up, which had been his number-one priority, now took second place to his wife and daughter.

Steven had often teased Blake about how square he'd become since his marriage: no more hanging out with the fellas, dating, chasing women, or even talking about them. Steven couldn't imagine himself with the same woman day in and day out—tied down. The thought often chilled him. Until he met Mia. She turned his world on its ear and he was still pleasantly reeling from the aftershocks. Never in his wildest imaginings did he think he'd be looking forward to coming home to his woman at night.

He shook his head in wonder as he dropped his umbrella in the stand by the door.

Sounds of the evening news drifted from the television set in the living room, mixed with the tantalizing aromas of something distinctly Italian.

Steven grinned. Mia sure knew the way to her man's heart—knockout sex and a mouthwatering meal.

Mia poked her head out from the archway leading to the kitchen. Her face was scrubbed clean of makeup and her skin seemed to glow. Her hair was pulled up into a ponytail, revealing the soft angles of her brown sugar-toned face. She greeted him with one of her heart-stopping smiles. God, he loved her.

Steven moved in her direction until he was right next to her. His gray-green eyes moved like a trained masseur's stroke across her face.

"Hey, baby." His tone was low and very intimate—just for her.

She slid her right hand around the back of his neck and took the last step that separated them. Her body melded with his like putty, molding itself to the hard lines of his from the broad expanse of his chest to his muscular thighs.

Mia tilted her head slightly upward and brought her mouth to his.

Steven groaned deep in his throat when the softness of her lips connected with his. He maneuvered her so that her back was against the frame of the archway to the kitchen.

The sweetness of her tongue set off a firestorm in his gut. His erection was electrifying and so suddenly powerful that the world receded and an uncontrolled need took its place.

Her long, slender fingers grazed along his body, stoking the growing fire of desire. She reached up and pushed down the fragile spaghetti straps of her thin top and tugged it down, exposing her bare breasts.

Steven nearly hollered. Instead, he feasted on one then the other, as Mia's short nails dug into his shoulder blades and her whispers of "Yes, yes, yes," rose in concert with the thunder that boomed in the night.

He dropped to his knees, pulling down her cutoff shorts and pink thong in the process, until he came face-to-face with her hidden treasure. Like a moth to a flame he was drawn to her, taking the tiny pearl between his lips and teasing and stroking it with his tongue until her inner thighs began to tremble and her knees grew weak.

Steven rose, unbuckling his belt and unzipping his pants in one smooth motion, freeing himself, his phallus hard and pulsing. He lifted her off the floor and she wrapped her legs tightly around his waist and locked her arms around his neck.

She was hot and wet when Steven pushed up inside her and he nearly exploded with that first thrust.

Their coupling was hard and fast, the need between them so intense that fulfillment was the one and only goal.

And when it came, their cries of ecstasy rose above the drumroll of thunder and was more brilliant than the lightning that kept silhouetting the Manhattan skyline.

Mia sat behind the closed doors of her office, reviewing the data that she'd collected on Michael and Avante Enterprises. He was currently the management company for Mercury Entertainment, which groomed and produced new R & B stars. She did a check of the client list and found it to be impressive, to say the least. She recognized more than a few of the names. According to the information that she had, Avante was in the process of planning a major red-carpet event to debut its new artists.

She smiled. She had what she needed. Although Avante oversaw the operations, they subcontracted out all the work.

Mia turned on her shredder and one by one she slid the pages through. Couldn't be too careful.

All night, even after that incredible erotic romp with Steven, her thoughts continued to drift back to Michael and the job at hand. She knew how weak she could be when it came to Michael. She had maintained her strength by staying away from him all these years. That was about to end.

She knew that she was tempting fate by opening a door that would best be left closed. However, she'd sworn an oath to the Cartel: not only would she uphold the tenets of secrecy, but she would execute her assignments to the best of her ability for the ultimate good of society, without regard to personal interest.

Mia believed in the mission of the Cartel to right wrongs and to protect the welfare of the innocent, as an aid to law enforcement. She took it all very seriously, and she could not allow her personal issues to hamper her ability to get the information that she needed on the escort service.

Besides, she was a big girl. She could handle herself with Michael. Plenty of time, space and other people had passed between them—enough to make what she had to do strictly business.

Strictly business, she counseled herself, as she dialed the offices of Avante Enterprises.

"Good morning. My name is Mia Turner, MT Management. I'd like to speak with Mr. Burke."

"Please hold."

Mia squeezed her eyes shut and sucked in a breath. She wondered if the receptionist could hear the uncontrollable pounding of her heart that was surely vibrating through the phone.

Another voice, more controlled, less perky came on the line.

"May I help you?"

"Yes. I'm calling to speak with Mr. Burke."

"Mr. Burke is very busy at the moment. Maybe I can help you."

She hadn't realized that Michael had risen to the point of having two screeners for his calls.

"Perhaps if you let him know that it's Mia Turner…"

There was a moment of deafening silence.

Ms. Control cleared her throat. "He really cannot be disturbed, but I'll be happy to take a message."

Mia's slender neck jerked back. She was about to blurt out, "Say what?" but remembered who she was—a professional.

"Why don't I do this—I'll call him on his cell a bit later. Perhaps he won't be so busy then," she said, playing the power game. Of course, she didn't have Michael's cell-phone number, but this chick didn't know that. "And who am I speaking with?"

"Brenda Forde. I'm Mr. Burke's executive assistant."

I'll just bet you are. "Thanks so much for your help… Brenda." She hung up.

Mia sat back and tugged on her bottom lip with

her teeth. She could have left a number for him to call her back, but that would have defeated her purpose of pretending to have the upper hand. Besides, she wasn't quite ready for Michael to have a direct connection to her.

But now that she'd lied and said she'd reach him on his cell phone, she'd have no logical reason to call back.

While she was pondering her next move, Ashley buzzed her on the intercom.

Mia stabbed the flashing red light. "Yes."

"There's a Michael Burke on the line for you."

Mia nearly choked. "Who?" she asked with all the calm she could summon.

"Michael Burke. Could that be the Michael Burke of Avante Enterprises—the one that Felicia and Linda said referred them?"

"I…suppose so." Her heart was galloping at breakneck speed.

"He's on line two."

"Thanks," she managed. "I'll take it."

For several moments she stared at the flashing red light. Would he sound the same? What did he want? How would she respond?

The unanswered questions rushed through her head. Finally she picked up the phone.

"Hello?"

"Mia…"

The deep bass of his voice rolled through her in waves. For an instant nothing stood between them, but then she remembered what she had to do.

"Michael, how are you?"

"Actually, quite well."

Silence. Then they both spoke at once.

"You first," Michael conceded.

"I wanted to thank you for the referral. I must admit I was surprised when they told me it had come from you."

"Why?"

The one-word question was suffused with a melancholy tone. Although it was asking the obvious, the inflection of his voice was asking her for an answer she couldn't give.

"I...had no idea..."

"What, that I've followed your career?"

He had? "Well...yes."

"I have. I know all about your business, that you're doing very well. I have friends who have seen you around the city. They tell me that you're still beautiful," he said softly.

She shut her eyes and a Technicolor image of Michael bloomed behind her lids.

"So now that we've gotten the formalities out of the way, was that the only reason for your call today?"

Mia cleared her throat and tried to clear her mind, but it was pointless.

"Yes. Why else would I call? I mean, it was very generous of you and I wanted to thank you."

"I think you know that I've always wanted the best for...my clients and myself. And that's what you are."

Why couldn't she get her brain to work and her lips to move? She felt like an idiot. Concentrate.

"I took a look at some of the projects that you're working on," she finally said, taking the first step into the land of no return. "And I was wondering if you'd contracted with anyone for the upcoming red-carpet event for Raven, the new R & B artist."

"I have two outfits that I'm considering, but if you wanted to handle it, I can call them off right now."

She laughed nervously. "Just like that?"

"Why not? You are the best at what you do?"

She drew in a breath.

"Why don't we meet and talk about it?"

This was going better than she'd hoped. "Sure, I can come to your office." She needed to get access in order to plant some listening devices and perhaps a small camera.

"I thought we could discuss it over drinks. I can have a car pick you up at your office about six."

"Six? Tonight?"

"No time like the present. You do want the assignment, don't you?"

"I don't even have a proposal prepared."

"We can discuss it when we see each other. Six o'clock. A black Lincoln will be out front. I've got to go. I have a meeting in a few minutes. I'll see you later." He disconnected the call before she could come up with a reason not to.

Slowly, she returned the handset to its cradle. Six o'clock. Absently she glanced up at the clock on the wall. Four hours. She had four hours to prepare to see the man her heart would not let her forget.

There would never be enough time.

Chapter 5

Mia walked to the front of the office. Ashley was just hanging up from a call. She looked at Mia curiously.

"You okay? You look…shaken."

Mia pressed her lips tightly together, as if the action could somehow hold back the words she needed to say. She pulled up a chair next to Ashley's desk and slowly sat down.

"Remember the other day I asked you if an old flame had ever come back into your life?"

"Yeah," she said, drawing out the word into two syllables.

Mia glanced away. "Well, my old love asked me out for drinks."

Ashley's finely arched brows rose. "Oh. Okay. Was this your idea or his?"

"His!" she said much too quickly. The guilt already getting to her.

"Why don't you start at the beginning? Maybe that would help."

The beginning. Yes, she could do that. Perhaps it was time.

Mia looked directly at Ashley. "I've never told this to anyone. No one. Not even Savannah and Danielle," she said with a new pang of guilt for having kept her two best friends in the dark for so long. She drew in a long breath and as she released it, the illicit love affair spilled out on a rough tide of emotion.

Nearly an hour later, Mia blinked back the past and her gaze rested on Ashley, waiting for condemnation, a look of reprimand. Instead, she saw tears welling up in Ashley's eyes.

Ashley sniffed and dabbed at the corner of her almond-shape eyes with the tip of her index finger. "Wow," she sputtered. "A true-life, tragic love story." She folded her hands together. "And now he's single?"

Mia bobbed her head.

Ashley pressed her hands flat on the desktop and leaned forward. "Do you love Steven?"

The question taunted her, tugged at her heart.

Of course she loved Steven, she told herself again as the black Lincoln navigated in and out of midtown Manhattan rush-hour traffic.

That's what she said to Ashley, who told her simply, "Keep that at the forefront of your thoughts and then when you see Michael everything will fall into place."

Mia certainly hoped so.

* * *

The driver gave her no indication where they were going. He'd only told her that Mr. Burke had arranged for dinner.

Dinner! That wasn't the agreement, she'd worried. Drinks were impersonal. Dinner was intimate. It raised this meeting to another level.

When she next looked out the window, she realized that they were leaving the city. She grabbed her glasses from her purse and the directional signs came into focus. The driver had taken the exit to the FDR Drive.

She tapped on the Plexiglas partition. The window slowly whirred downward.

"Yes, Ms. Turner?"

"Where are we going?"

"To dinner."

"You said that already."

"That's all I know, Ms. Turner."

"You must know where you were told to drive," she pressed, trying to control her rising temper, which was being overshadowed by her rising panic.

The partition whirred back into place, cutting off any further communication.

It was just like Michael to dream up something elaborate. But how in the world would she be able to explain what would certainly be a late night to Steven?

Sighing, she settled back against the plush leather. There wasn't much that she could do other than wait it out. It's not as if she could jump out of the car and make a run for it.

She'd deal with Michael when she saw him. She folded her arms and silently fumed, even as part of her bloomed with a macabre sense of excitement.

Forty minutes later, they took the exit to Sag Harbor. Mia jerked up on her seat and peered out the window.

The historic and quaint seaside town was elegantly quiet. The shops that were reminiscent of a postcard ad for weekend getaways were closed. The boats were docked and bobbing gently in the water.

The driver continued through the commercial section of town and drove to the outskirts, where the stately home of the wealthy African-American elite lived.

Finally, the driver turned into a cul-de-sac and pulled onto a gravel driveway.

Mia's door was pulled open and the driver extended his hand to help her out of the car. She stepped out and reflexively inhaled the heady scent of the sea and brisk night air. The sky had just begun to fill with stars and the half moon seemed to hang perfectly above a two-story, sprawling white house that overlooked the ocean.

It was breathtaking.

"This way," the driver said, leading Mia up the path to the front door.

As she took the first of three steps, the door opened. Her gaze rose. Her heart leaped in her chest. She thought she was prepared to see him.

She wasn't.

Michael descended the stairs like a fantasy hero out of a dream.

Mia couldn't move, and before she could pull herself together, Michael was taking her hand and saying something to her, but she couldn't make out the words: they were being drowned out by the pounding of the pulse in her ears and the electricity that was surging through her from his touch.

"I'm glad you came."

Those four simple words stripped away the past, all the lost years and misgivings, and suddenly she was glad she'd come as well.

Michael could barely contain all that he was feeling inside. When he laid eyes on Mia, those words he spoke were no more than a smoke screen. He didn't want to make polite conversation. He wanted to take her and make her remember what it felt like to have him inside her, her body wound around his, her soft moans yielding to screams of release. That's what he wanted to do, but of course he couldn't. Instead, he apologized.

"Sorry for all the cloak-and-dagger," he began, guiding her into a foyer the size of her entire condo. "But I knew if I told you where you were going, you would have refused."

"Still trying to make up my mind for me, I see."

That had always been a bone of contention between them. Michael wanted what Michael wanted, and he could never fathom why everyone didn't go along with him all the time.

He turned to face her and laughed lightly. "You're right. I should have given you the option. But now you're here." His chestnut-brown eyes meandered over her, taking in every inch.

He was still a gorgeous man to behold, Mia thought, an older, more mature version of Blair Underwood—a cool combination of boyish charm, dangerous sexuality and a ruthless streak that made for a lethal combination. The tinge of gray at his temples and the tiny flecks in his shadow of a beard only added to the dazzling package.

Michael was eight years her senior, but he was as fit as a man half his age. At forty-five, he had achieved what many only dreamed of and, knowing Michael, he'd only just begun.

Mia forced those thoughts to the back of her mind. He was a prime suspect in an illegal operation and she could not allow the intoxicating scent of his cologne, the glimmer in his eyes or the electricity of his touch to make her forget that.

"Please come in and sit down. I've had dinner prepared. But if you'd like that drink first—apple martini, right?" His smile lit up the room.

"You remembered."

"There isn't much about you that I've forgotten." His gaze held her.

Mia swallowed. "A drink will be fine, but I really can't stay for dinner."

Disappointment creased his eyes. But just as quickly the look was gone. He lightly ran his tongue across his lips and a shiver ran down Mia's spine.

"I see." His right brow flicked. "Then let's have that drink for old time's sake."

He walked ahead of her and stepped down into the sunken living room, which was something right out of *House Beautiful.* The shimmering teal-colored marble floors gave the illusion of walking on Caribbean water. Low contemporary furniture in a mix of fabrics and textures, all in cream and sandy-brown hues, dotted the space. Three-quarters of the room was wrapped in glass. The panoramic view looked out onto cliffs and oceans beyond. One wall encased a fireplace that would be perfect on a winter night, watching the powerful waves crash against the shore.

Mia set her purse on the glass coffee table while Michael fixed drinks. "You have a beautiful place."

Michael turned to her. "I had it built for you."

She couldn't have been more stunned if he'd slapped her. "For me?"

He offered a sad smile. "I'd always told you we'd have a place of our own one day." He lifted the bottle of vodka and poured some in a silver tumbler, followed by the apple martini mix and crushed ice. "I'm a man of my word." He capped the tumbler and shook it vigorously. "Got my divorce, too." His piercing look at her from over his shoulder held her in place.

Mia was speechless. A divorce. A house. It was everything she'd wanted. But it was too late. She was in love with Steven. And she couldn't let Michael's powers of persuasion or his unrelenting charm, this fabulous house or the fact that he was a free man dissuade her.

He crossed the room and handed her the drink.

"Thank you."

He raised his glass. "To old friends."

Cautiously, she touched her glass to his.

"I wanted to thank you for the referral," she said, needing to break the invisible hold he had on her.

He shrugged dismissively, walked a few paces and sat opposite her in the armchair that matched the couch, both covered in a butter-soft ecru-colored fabric that was so lush, the cushions so thick and soft, you could sink into it and never get up.

"I'm sure you didn't need the business. But I thought you'd be perfect for what they wanted."

"How would you know?"

He offered a slight smile. "As I said before, I've

followed your career. I've even attended some of your events. Incognito, of course."

That confession shook her. "Why?"

He took a short swallow of his drink, studied the contents for a moment before speaking. "It was my way of staying in your life."

The answer was delivered so softly, so sincerely that it twisted her heart.

This couldn't be the man that Jean claimed might be behind an illegal escort service. This was the man she'd once loved. Standing before her was the man she'd prayed he would one day become. There was no way that the two could be one and the same.

"What are you thinking about?"

The gentle nudge of the words drew her back from her thoughts.

"Just that I never thought I'd see you again, especially like this, and that you've been following my career." She shifted her glass from her right hand to her left. "Which events did you attend?" she asked, the beginnings of a smile flickering around her mouth.

Michael chuckled. "The one on the yacht last year."

A flash of that event ran through her mind, along with the fact that the clients had turned out to be behind an identity theft ring that Danielle uncovered.

"How come I didn't see you? Why didn't you say anything?"

There was that shrug again. "I made sure that you didn't. I can blend in when I need to. Besides, there had to be at least three hundred people there and you were pretty busy."

"You could have said something."

"I thought it best not to. The last thing you wrote

to me was not to contact you. So I figured the last thing you wanted was for me to show up at one of your events."

That bit of truth stung. She remembered the letter and the weeks that it took to compose it and finally mail it. She glanced away.

"How have you been, Mia?" he asked gently. "Without me. How have you been?"

What could she say? That she struggled to get him out of her system for nearly five years? That there were still times when she thought of him, remembered how they were together, the emptiness that she felt when she walked out of his life? Of course she couldn't say that.

"I've managed. My business keeps me busy."

All of a sudden, she looked up and he was standing over her. He took her glass from her hand and put it on the table, then took her hands and pulled her to her feet.

"I've missed you. Each and every day I've missed you. Everything that I do, dream or plan—you are in my thoughts. I want you back, Mia."

Her heart thundered. Her entire body was on fire. She could feel his energy wrap around her, draw her in, break down her will. And then his mouth was on hers and she couldn't move.

His mouth was warm, all-encompassing and incredibly sweet. She remembered those lips, the feel of them against her own. But when his tongue tentatively glided across her lips, then into the recesses of her mouth, she began to shake and he held her—held her firmly against him and she felt his longing, his need press hard and heavy between her thighs.

Her thoughts spun in a million directions at once, then crashed.

She pulled away, turned her head and stumbled back. "I can't do this." She shook her head.

He reached for her but she held up her hand to stop him.

"Don't."

Michael stepped back. "I'm sorry. I shouldn't have done that."

She dared to look at him. All she saw was longing and sincerity in his expression.

Michael exhaled. "Can we start over?"

She sat down before she fell down and clasped her hands together atop her weak knees to keep them from shaking.

What she wanted to do was run as far as she could. But she couldn't do that and she couldn't alienate him. She needed to get inside his business, inside his life. But what was she willing to do to accomplish that?

Mia forced a tight smile. "Sure."

Michael seemed to sigh in relief. "Great. And to show you I really mean it, I'm gonna sit right here and not move a muscle until you're ready to go." He sat down on the lounger, folded his hands, pressed his knees together and plastered a contrite look on his face. The visual effect was hysterical and Mia burst out laughing.

Michael grinned. "That's how I like to see you, with that pretty smile on your face."

Mia smothered the rest of her giggles. "Can we talk about business now?"

Michael leaned back, then stretched out on the chaise longue. "Absolutely." He gave her the Reader's Digest version of Raven, the star he was hired to debut. She was nineteen for the public, but she was really twenty-two. Great voice, painfully shy, inked a major deal with Atlantic Records and her CD was scheduled to "drop" in two months. All the industry execs were to be invited, the cable stations, media and selected guests.

"Sounds simple enough. So why do I hear a *but* in there somewhere?"

"Our star doesn't want to do it."

"Oh… Why?"

"As I said, she's incredibly shy. She just wants to make music. So even though the studio wants a blow-out event, we…you still need to make it feel intimate, so that our star doesn't freak out."

Mia nodded.

"Venue and setting are going to be crucial to make all parties concerned happy."

"Do you have a date in mind?"

"Three weeks."

Mia's eyes widened.

He shrugged. "My hands are tied on that one." He waited a beat. "You still want to do it?"

"Sure. I'll make it happen. No problem."

"Great. I'll have Brenda put all the information to-gether for you and have it sent to your office."

She needed to get inside his office. "Hmm. I can pick it up. I'd like to see where you work."

He grinned. "Whenever you're ready."

"Tomorrow."

"A lady who doesn't waste time."

"As you said, no time like the present."

He put his feet on the floor and stood up. "Let me show you the rest of the house." He extended his hand to help her up.

"How long have you had this place?" she asked as he guided her with a hand at the small of her back to the kitchen.

"I was having it built when we were together. It was going to be my big surprise."

What! Her stomach did a somersault. He'd never said a word.

Michael turned on the light and the magnificent kitchen was suffused in soft track lighting. Racks of stainless-steel pots hung from the ceiling. And in sharp contrast to the modern feel of the living room, the kitchen was pure country. Glass-paneled French doors led to the back and would undoubtedly provide great lighting. Oak covered the floors and they gleamed. Freestanding hutches and corner cupboards provided plenty of storage space. A huge oak island sat in the center of the enormous kitchen and this is where the modern came in. Somehow, Michael had managed to have a wok, a grill and running water built into the island. A table for four was placed near the French doors and the open-faced cabinetry exhibited a chef's dream of condiments, pastas and spices. Another extraordinary touch was the restaurant-size refrigerator/ freezer and built-in range. The meals she could fix in this space, she thought.

"I had you in mind when I had the kitchen done," he said softly, stepping up behind her.

She spun toward him, nearly colliding with him he was so close. She took a step back and drew in a sharp breath.

He angled his head to the side. "Maybe you'd like to come up one weekend and try out some of the stuff."

Mia swallowed over the knot in her throat. She

turned away. "What about the rest of the house?" she said instead of responding to his offer.

"This way." He led her to the connecting room, which was the formal dining room. Then onto a small home theater that sat at least fifteen.

He opened another door. "I work in here whenever I come up for the weekend."

The room had two computers, shelves of books, a fax, a phone and what appeared to be a scanner.

"How often is that?"

He closed the door. "At least twice a month."

She made a mental note. "I see you still keep your computers on even when you're not using them."

"Old habits, I guess. Back here are the two guest rooms, and baths." He flung open two doors that were side by side. "This is the master bedroom." He opened the door.

It was totally Michael. Rich, lush, completely masculine with bold browns and bronzes, a king-size bed and a television that was almost as big. She glanced across the room and was stunned to see a framed photograph of the two of them on the dresser.

She remembered the day they'd taken it. It was the week before Christmas and the first snow had fallen. Michael had gotten tickets to see *The Nutcracker* at Radio City Music Hall. When they came out, a photographer who was hawking his wares offered to take their picture. She was staring up into his eyes with a bold smile and his look showed total adoration.

"We were happy," he said gently.

She flinched. It was as if he'd read her mind. "Michael…"

"I know, I know…I'm sorry." He held up his hands in supplication.

"I probably should be going."

He nodded. "I'll get Carl to bring the car around."

They went back up front. She needed just a few minutes alone. She picked up her purse. "Uh, I'm going to use the restroom."

"Sure. Straight back, left then right."

She left him in the living room and found his office. Listening for any footsteps, she quickly went inside, opened her purse and took out a CD. She silently prayed that he was actually logged on so that she wouldn't be stymied by a password.

She hit the Enter key and the desktop opened. She released a sigh of relief, put in the CD and listened to it whirr while it planted a tracking program onto the hard drive. The CD popped out. She tucked it in her purse, hurried out then headed back up front.

Michael looked up when she entered the room. "Carl is out front. He'll take you home." He walked her to the door.

At the door he asked, "Are you sure you want to work on this project? We'll have to see a lot of each other."

She looked directly at him. "I'm a big girl, Michael. And this is business. Right?"

He leaned down and gently kissed her cheek. "Get home safely, Mia," he said, avoiding her question.

She looked at him for a moment before turning away and walking toward the waiting car.

It's business. I love Steven. It's business. I love Steven. She repeated that mantra all the way back to the city.

Chapter 6

By the time Mia turned the key in the lock of her front door, it was nearly eleven. She'd wracked her brains trying to come up with some plausible explanation as to where she could have been until now. Nothing sounded remotely legitimate.

When she stepped in, she fully expected Steven to be sitting on the couch waiting for her. He wasn't.

She walked through the front of the condo to the bedroom in the back. Even in the moonlight she could tell that the room was empty. She switched on the light and looked around.

The bed was still made. Absently, she put her purse down on top of the dresser and walked to the bathroom. Empty. Where was Steven?

She made an about-face, returned to the front of the

apartment and went into the kitchen. That's when she saw the note on the fridge.

She snatched it down and read it.

Hey, babe, decided at the last minute to have a boys' night out. Hanging with Blake, Nick and Bernard. We're celebrating one of the guys on the job's birthday. Tried your cell. Went straight to voice mail. Don't wait up. Luv ya.

She didn't know whether to be relieved or pissed off. She took the note and tossed it in the trash. On the one hand, she didn't have to explain her own late night. On the other, if she'd known that Steven would be late, she might have stayed longer. What did that mean?

She frowned, thinking of the note again...*went straight to voice mail.* Ohhh, of course. She'd turned her phone off in the event that Steven did call while she was with Michael. That way she wouldn't have been caught in the uncomfortable position of talking to her current lover while her ex-lover listened to every word.

Well, at least this time she was off the explanation hook.

This time.

Mia retrieved her cell phone from her purse on the hall table and turned it back on. Sure enough, there were three missed calls. She dialed into her voice-mail service and listened.

The first message was from Steven, pretty much saying what the note did. The second call was from Danielle, checking in with her, and the third was from Ashley.

"I hope everything went okay. If you want to talk tomorrow, I'm here."

She hit the delete code and pressed the phone to her chest.

Did it go okay? The minute she saw Michael, she'd lost control of her senses. She'd let him kiss her and she'd kissed him back. And what about her feelings when she realized that Steven wasn't home and that if she had known he was going to be late she would have stayed longer?

Mia walked into the bedroom. Did all that equal *okay?* She caught a glimpse of herself in the oval mirror above the dresser. If she didn't know better, she'd swear she could see *Scarlet Woman* plastered across her forehead. At the very least *Guilty.*

She stepped out of her shoes and put them in the rack in the closet.

She'd betrayed Steven. She'd betrayed their relationship. She massaged her temples. How could she have been so weak?

The sensation of that kiss snuck up on her and a sudden heat suffused her body.

Vigorously she shook her head. It was the first and the last time, she vowed. She had a job to do. Michael Burke was an assignment, and that was it. She was in love with Steven. And she could not allow herself to forget that ever again. No matter what.

With that determination at the forefront of her mind, she went to the closet, took out the shoe boxes and opened the panel where she kept her kit. Quickly she removed it.

Meticulously inventorying the contents, she removed the eye-shadow case, the pressed-powder compact and a tube of mascara. She would need all these items when she met Michael at his office. The eye shadow concealed a minirecording disk that could stick to any surface. The compact doubled as a camera, and the mascara was actually a memory stick that she would use to download files from his computer—if the opportunity presented itself. She put all these items in her tote bag.

Before Steven came home, she wanted to sync her PDA with Michael's computer. Although he didn't go to the Sag Harbor house often, he did mention that he used that computer for work. It was worth a shot.

Mia turned on her PDA and scrolled to the *Find Me* program that would allow her to look inside Michael's computer, see his files and actually open them remotely. She keyed in the access code and after several moments the screen read that she was connected.

Her heart thumped in concert with the opening of the front door. Her head jerked up from the information in front of her.

"Mia!"

She took a quick look around to be sure she hadn't left anything out, then turned the PDA off and dropped it in her tote. She darted into the bathroom and turned on the shower.

"Hey, babe," he called out over the rush of water. "Sorry I'm so late."

Mia peeled off her clothes, tossed them in a pile on the floor and ducked into the shower.

The bathroom door inched open and Steven stuck his head in. "Hey, sweetie, mind some company?"

Mia pulled the shower curtain partially back and smiled in greeting. "Love some."

* * *

Later that night, as Mia lay curled in Steven's embrace and their racing hearts had settled, she thought with alarm that it was the very first time that Steven had not satisfied her.

Chapter 7

Mia was totally distracted at work the following day and as hard as she tried she couldn't concentrate on the monthly financial report. The numbers seemed to jump all over the page just to torment her.

Frustrated, she pushed the pages aside and stared blankly at the screen saver on her computer. She glanced up at the clock above her office door.

Still two hours before she was due to be at Michael's office. Maybe she'd get lucky and not have to see him. But that, of course, would defeat the whole purpose of her going. She needed access to his office, his phone and his computer.

But what troubled her most was what had happened—or had not happened—last night between her and Steven. Not to mention this morning. She and Steven always had sex in the morning, and at the very least a stimulating touching and kissing session as they prepared for their day, leading to heightened anticipation at night.

But this morning she wasn't in her usual playful, teasing mood, and although Steven had given her several long, lingering kisses, he didn't pursue anything further.

Had he realized that she hadn't climaxed last night? Did it bother him? Did he care? And then an awful thought leaped into her mind. Was he seeing someone else?

The sharp knock on her door jerked some sense into her. It was her own guilty conscience, she knew, that had her conjuring up dalliances about Steven. She shook her head.

"Come in."

Ashley stepped through the doorway. "I worked out a preliminary plan for the boutique. If you want to take a look at it, I put it in New Projects on the shared drive."

"Thanks." She forced a smile but couldn't look Ashley in the eye. She'd done everything short of taking in dirty laundry from a stranger to keep herself busy so that Ashley wouldn't ask her about last night. For the better part of the morning, she'd been able to avoid her. Until now.

"I'll, um, look at it, but I'm sure it's fine." She studied the first line of a memo she held in front of her as if it could block out reality and what she was certain was Ashley's inquiring gaze.

"Look, I want you to know that it's okay to talk to me and it's okay to look at me. If you don't want to discuss last night or our conversation yesterday—ever— it's fine. Seriously." She took a step closer. "I won't judge you. I thought I was your friend. And I value the confidence you put in me." She drew in a breath and stood straighter. "That's my spiel for today."

"I'm meeting him at his office today," she blurted out and looked up at Ashley with something akin to fear in her eyes.

"Why?" she softly asked.

Mia curled her fingers into fists on her desk. "I have to." She struggled with the words, the burning in her stomach.

Ashley frowned in confusion. "You. Mia Turner never *had* to do anything, especially something that she is obviously having an issue with." She tentatively sat down, reached across the desk and put all the phone lines on hold. She turned to Mia. "If you want to talk, I'm listening. And there is no one to disturb us." She waited.

Dozens of thoughts raced through Mia's mind. *Last night, seeing Michael again, the kiss, the sex with Steven, her guilt, her assignment, the Cartel, her oath.* They all ran together until her head began to pound and panic seized her. Her life and emotions were suddenly out of control and she didn't know how to handle it.

Finally, she released her clenched fists, raised her gaze and focused on Ashley. There were obviously things she could not disclose, which would make her having to see Michael difficult to explain. She cleared her throat.

"I'm going to tell you some things. Some are not going to make any sense because of the things that I *can't* tell you. Understand?"

Ashley blinked in confusion. "Not really, but go ahead. I'll piece it together."

"Well, you already know about me and Michael's past…"

Ashley nodded.

"Last night he didn't take me for drinks. He had his driver take me to his home on Sag Harbor, the home he said he'd had built for me and him."

Ashley sucked in a breath of surprise, but didn't interrupt.

Mia swallowed. "He kissed me. And I didn't stop him."

From there the rest of the story poured out: how she felt, her confusion, even what happened between her and Steven, her guilt.

She rubbed her forehead as if the action could rub away the thoughts and images that tramped through her brain.

"Wow," Ashley murmured after Mia had finished. "And I guess the reason why you have to go see him is the part you can't tell me."

Mia nodded.

"Why not let me go with you?"

"I wish I could but I can't. All I can say is that it's bigger than me and you and I promised that I would do this."

Ashley blew out a breath. "I respect that. But can I offer some advice?"

"I could use some."

"Be clear about the why. Be sure that you're doing this because you have no choice and not because you subconsciously want to rekindle your relationship. Because if you do, you owe it to Steven to be honest with him about your feelings."

How could she explain that it was a combination of

both? A part of her felt duty-bound and another part wanted to see what life would be like again with Michael. In addition to which, she wanted to prove that he couldn't be capable of the things he was suspected of. And she hoped that her own misgivings would not cloud her judgment.

Ashley pushed up from her seat. "If you change your mind, I'm free all afternoon," she said with a soft smile. She turned to leave.

"Wait!"

Ashley turned back around.

Mia stood. "If I take you with me, you have to promise not to ask any questions, no matter what happens."

"Gee, Mia, you sound like some kind of spy or something."

Mia snatched up her purse and tote bag. She looked Ashley in her eyes. "Or something." She headed for the door, leaving Ashley pinned in place by her declaration. "Coming?"

Ashley hurried behind her boss and wondered what she'd gotten herself into.

Chapter 8

"No point in circling the block again," Mia groused, looking above and below car tops and along the tightly packed street as she inched down 56th Street. Michael's office on Madison Avenue was in the heart of Manhattan. But parking on Madison was out of the question. "It's mostly either No Parking Anytime or For Commercial Traffic Only."

"There's a garage about a block down on your right," Ashley pointed out.

Mia signaled then eased into the right lane in front of a yellow cab and zipped across the intersection before the light changed. The Quick-Park parking garage was franchised throughout the city. Their trademark black-and-gold signs were like beacons of salvation for harried drivers.

Throughout the thirty-minute drive, Ashley had refrained from asking questions, basically making small talk or keeping quiet, which totally went against her grain. This entire scenario had Ashley deeply concerned about Mia. Mia had said there were things she couldn't tell her, and heaven only knew what that meant. She just hoped that whatever Mia had gotten herself involved in was not going to get her hurt, and she didn't mean physically.

During the months that she'd spent working with Mia, she'd come to admire and respect her. Mia was forthright, professional, loyal to her friends and able to charm the most difficult clients. She ran her business with precision, and she conducted her life with the same kind of order and attention to detail—all without breaking a sweat. Which was why it was so unsettling to see her like this—totally distracted, edgy and, for lack of a better word, scared. Those were words Ashley would have never associated with Mia, and Ashley vowed to stick by her side and see things through.

Mia unsnapped her seat belt, pulled down the overhead mirror and reapplied her lipstick, which she'd pretty much chewed off during the trip.

For an instant she froze. The look in her eyes that was reflected back at her was one of uncertainty and confusion. And she knew that it had more to do with her twisted feelings for Michael than her ability to do her job. Yet both were intricately intertwined, and she couldn't see one without the other. But she had to.

She felt Ashley staring at her and turned. "I may need your help."

Ashley's honey-brown eyes widened ever so slightly. "Sure. Whatever you need."

Mia offered a tight-lipped smile, flipped the mirror back in place, grabbed her purse and tote and hopped out.

The attendant handed her a ticket and asked how long she would be.

"No more than an hour." She turned and walked up the ramp and out onto the busy street.

Michael's offices were on the five-hundred block of Madison Avenue, surrounded by the headquarters of all the major banks both domestic and foreign and the leading financial institutions, Schwab, Deutsche Bank. His office was at 554-11 Madison on the twenty-second floor.

The duo pushed through the glass-and-chrome revolving doors. They were stopped at the security check-in desk, and asked to produce identification and sign a logbook.

Ever since 9/11, all the major New York City office buildings had instituted this procedure. Mia often wondered what possible good it would do and what kind of deterrent it was for someone who really wanted to do harm. There was no way to prove that anyone's ID was legitimate.

Her friend Danielle's last Cartel case was a perfect example of what people could do with ID. Dani's identity theft case even added an additional element of finding famous look-alikes who were used to gain access to parties, offices and homes with the purpose of stealing unsuspecting victims' identities. The successful outcome was all in the news, with no mention of Danielle or the Cartel, of course.

No matter how careful you were and no matter how many safeguards were put in place, someone, somewhere, was working to breach your defenses. The Ladies Cartel was a testament to that truth. Besides, she reasoned, if someone intended to get in and blow up a building, the logbook would be destroyed in the process. It was all quite arcane and silly in Mia's mind, but if it offered some sense of security, she supposed it was useful.

Mia and Ashley walked side by side to the second bank of elevators after signing in.

Mia watched the dial of the elevator as the lights did a countdown. "I may need you to keep his executive assistant—and possibly Michael—busy," she said without looking at Ashley.

"Sure. No problem. Busy I can do."

The elevator doors slid open and deposited a half dozen people into the lobby. Mia and Ashley were the only two to get on.

"If I say I want to use the restroom, I'm going to need you to keep everyone occupied. At least for five minutes. If we get to sit in Michael's office, I'm going to need you to get him out of it."

"How?"

"We'll think of something."

The bell dinged and the doors slid open.

"This would be so much more fun if you told me what you couldn't tell me," Ashley said under her breath.

Mia tossed her a look and stepped off the elevator. The directional signs indicated that the Avante Enterprises offices were to the right. They turned toward a set of glass doors.

A receptionist looked up at their approach. "May I help you?" Her perky voice came through the intercom embedded in the wall. Mia recognized it from the phone call. She stepped closer to the intercom.

"Mia Turner. I have an appointment with Mr. Burke."

The door buzzed, along with the sound of the lock disengaging. Mia grabbed the large chrome handle and pushed the door open.

"If you will have a seat, I'll let Mr. Burke know you're here."

"Thank you," Mia murmured and took a seat with Ashley right next to her.

"Nice digs," Ashley said.

"Hmm." Interesting, she thought, as she took in the décor of the reception area. The colors were in sharp contrast to the house on the harbor. Here black dominated, with gray and burgundy accents. The colors and coordinating décor spoke power, style and control. All nouns easily associated with Michael Burke.

Moments later, a woman of about thirty with a cap of silky black curls outlining a perfectly made-up face approached them. Mia instinctively knew this was Ms. Executive Assistant.

The woman's chocolate chip–pinstriped suit jacket hugged her narrow waist, fanned out ever so slightly to caress her hips, and the above-the-knee-length skirt showcased the legs of a dancer—long, lean, perfectly formed and strong. She seemed to instinctively know one from the other and extended her hand to Mia.

"Ms. Turner. I'm Brenda Forde. I believe we've met via phone." She directed intense honey-colored eyes at Mia, all the more disconcerting because of their lightness against her flawlessly brown skin and the fierceness that hovered in them.

Real or contacts, Mia wondered in a comedic moment.

"Yes. We have met, haven't we? Always good to put a face with a voice." She released the butter-soft hand and turned to Ashley. "This is *my* executive assistant and business manager, Ashley Temple."

Ashley extended her hand. "Nice to meet you."

Brenda gave a short nod of her head. "If you'll follow me, I'll get you settled in the small conference room. Michael...Mr. Burke is on a business call. As soon as he's done, he'll join us."

There goes that *us* again, Mia thought. She smiled and followed Brenda down the short hallway and was led to a room with, unfortunately, a glass door and walls.

"Please make yourselves comfortable. Would you like something to drink while you wait?"

"Some water for me," Mia said.

"Water is fine," Ashley added.

"I'll be right back." She picked up a remote from the table and pointed it at a television mounted onto the wall. The CNN studio filled the screen. "Michael likes CNN," Brenda said with a smile that held a challenge.

"I remember," Mia tossed back, unable to help herself and secretly delighted in seeing Ms. Executive Assistant flinch before she walked out.

"Meow, meow," Ashley sang. "At least let me know when to duck out of the way of the claws. What was that about?"

Mia quickly gave her the rundown of her earlier conversation with Brenda.

"You think they're seeing each other?"

Mia gave a slight shrug. "If not, she certainly wants to. Not that it's any of my business," she added quickly.

Ashley bit back a smile.

Mia reluctantly pulled her glasses out of her purse. She took a good look around the room. The conference table took up most of the space, surrounded by eleven chairs, five on each side and one at the head. Two computer stations braced one wall. With her growing knowledge of electronics and technology, she noted that there were microphones built into the table, which let her know that conversations here were recorded. The wall panel that controlled the television also controlled the screen that could be lowered from the ceiling. She was pretty sure it included teleconferencing, which would account for the video camera in the back of the room.

Her instincts told her this room was used for meetings much more sensitive than who would be the next R & B star, which gave her even more reason to want to tap it. What solidified her resolve was the camera that she'd spotted hidden between the panels on the wall. It was no bigger than a quarter and to those who were none the wiser it looked like an imperfection in the wall. A hidden camera would certainly limit what she could get away with in this room. The ideal situation would be to find Avante's control room.

Mia glanced toward the door. Brenda and Michael were coming in. Mia couldn't miss the adoring look that Brenda gave Michael as he held the door open for her. Mia took off her glasses and returned them to her purse.

Ashley stole a look in Mia's direction as the doors swung open.

"Mia." Michael came right to her, braced her shoulders and kissed her cheek. "Had to bring backup, huh," he teased, whispering in her ear. He stepped back and looked her in the eye, as if she was the only person in the room.

Mia swallowed over the tightness in her throat. The intoxicating scent of him momentarily clouded her thoughts. "Michael, my executive assistant, Ashley Temple."

"My pleasure, Ms. Temple," he said, finally focusing on something other than Mia. He shook Ashley's hand, then turned back to Mia. "Would you prefer to talk here or over lunch?"

"Here is fine. Ashley has prepared a PowerPoint presentation for our proposal. Then we can have lunch. If that works for you." She smiled sweetly.

"Not a problem."

Ashley took the printed copies out of the leather folder she carried, along with the CD of the presentation. She handed out the literature.

Mia's heart pounded. She hoped that Michael would allow them to use the computer to run the program and not just the projector.

"All this technology is not my thing," Michael admitted. "That's Brenda's area of expertise." He tossed his hands up in the air in a gesture of exasperation.

"Is your computer linked to the video screen?" Mia asked.

"Of course. I'll get you set up." Brenda went to one of the computers and turned it on. She lowered the lights then depressed a button on the wall panel and the screen descended. "You can load your CD."

Ashley went to the computer and inserted the CD.

Mia's heart was pounding. If there was one glitch in the program that she'd embedded on the CD, they were toast. After Ashley had completed the Power-Point proposal, Mia had volunteered to put it on the CD. Later that evening, Mia wrote a code—with the help of Jasmine at Cartel headquarters—that would track the activities of the computer and was activated when the PowerPoint was shown.

What it gave Mia the opportunity to do was look inside the computer files in addition to mirroring every keystroke.

The screen filled with MT Management's logo and its tagline, "Your dream event is our reality."

For about ten seconds the screen froze then flickered. Mia held her breath. Jasmine had warned her about this and advised her not to panic. She'd been meticulous about entering the code. She'd gone over it three times to be sure she'd typed in the correct HTML string.

The first screen finally opened and Mia exhaled as Ashley's voice gave the text and images verbal support.

While everyone was engrossed in the presentation, Mia felt around inside her tote bag, which she held on her lap beneath the table, and unzipped her "go bag"— her little carryall that held some of her tools of the trade. It looked like a makeup pouch. She felt around for the recording disk that looked like an eye-shadow pot. She had to unscrew the cap and lift the disk out. It was no bigger than a dime and nearly slipped from her fingers. One side was sticky and would adhere to any surface, virtually inconspicuous. She pressed the sticky side underneath the table, felt it to be sure it was secure then dropped the circular pot back into her go bag.

Ashley had about three more minutes. Mia began to breathe a little easier.

"I'm impressed," Michael said when the screen went blank.

Brenda turned on the lights.

"How soon can you get started?"

"Michael—" Brenda cut in.

He held up his hand.

Mia and Ashley glanced at each other.

"As soon as you're ready," Mia answered.

"That's what I like to hear." He stood. "Let's seal the deal over lunch."

Mia tossed a triumphant grin in Brenda's direction. Triumphant in more ways than one.

As they walked out, Mia hesitated. "I need to use the restroom."

"I'll take you," Brenda offered.

"That's fine. Just tell me where it is. I'm sure I can find it myself."

"I'd love to see the rest of your space," Ashley chimed in, hearing her cue.

"Sure," Michael agreed. "Mia, we'll meet you up front."

"Down the hall, make two lefts," Brenda reluctantly instructed Mia.

"Thanks. I won't be a minute." She walked in the general direction of the restroom. She decided it would be pointless to try to get in the control room, but Michael's office was a different story.

She hurried down the hall, passing a few employees along the way, who didn't pay much attention to her. She glanced at the nameplates on the doors. The offices were set up like a maze: short hallways that led to different departments, quick turns and dead ends. She felt as if she should have left bread crumbs so she could find her way back.

Finally, she found Michael's office after following a sign for administration. She hoped that it wasn't locked. She tried the knob and the door opened. Taking a quick look left then right, she stepped inside and shut the door behind her.

Mia was pretty certain that if Michael were involved in anything, the last place he would have microphones and cameras would be in his office.

The rectangular office screamed masculine. Brown leather furnishings, vertical floor-to-ceiling blinds in a bronze color that gave the room a warm glow. An antique oval rug covered the center of the wood floor. His desk was pure Michael—rich and dark. His mantra screen saver crawled across the monitor: *"I'm dreaming of great things and doing them."*

She went directly to his desk. The first thing she did was insert a recording device into his phone, then she took a CD out of her bag and put it in the computer. After it loaded, she hit the Enter key and the disk whirred then exited.

Mia checked her watch. She'd been gone a little more than five minutes. Hopefully, Ashley was running her mouth and asking a zillion questions. She took one last look around, went to the door and cracked it open. The hallway was empty. She stepped out and shut the door behind her.

Briskly she walked down the hallway, turned right and ran smack into Brenda.

"Oh, I'm so sorry," Mia sputtered. She pressed her hand to her chest.

Brenda stared at her. "This isn't the way to the ladies' room."

Mia smiled and shook her head. "I got totally turned around. I should have taken you up on your offer."

"It's this way," she said with quiet deliberation. She extended her hand in the opposite direction.

Mia clutched her purse tighter in her hand and secured her tote on her shoulder. "Thanks." She followed Brenda to the door with the image of a woman emblazoned on the front. Mia pushed the door open.

"I'll wait for you so you don't get lost again."

"'Preciate that." Mia stepped inside and nearly collapsed against the door. Another minute and Brenda would have seen her coming out of Michael's office.

She walked to the sink, turned on the cold water and looked at her reflection. "This is only the beginning," she said to the reflection, "so get it together."

Mia ran her wrists under the cold tap water to slow down her racing heart and lower the heat in her body that was making her light-headed. She dried her hands then took her lipstick from her purse and touched up her mouth.

Brenda was leaning against the wall when Mia stepped out.

"All done!" she said with a cheery smile.

Brenda stepped up to her, so close that Mia noticed she was wearing individual false eyelashes and a couple of them had come out.

"I don't know what your deal is," Brenda said with chilly calm. "But stay away from Michael." With that she spun away on her two-inch heels before Mia could digest the veiled threat and deliver a comeback.

Stirred but not shaken, Mia followed the scent of Brenda's perfume and joined the trio at the receptionist's desk.

Brenda Forde was going to be a problem.

Chapter 9

"You've been pretty quiet today," Blake Fields said to Steven as they reviewed the blueprints for a co-op they were helping to develop. "Everything cool?"

In Steven's circle of friends, Blake was at the center. They'd been tight since college. Steven was Blake's best man when he married Savannah and was godfather to their daughter Mikayla. They'd shared a great deal through the years, the good and the bad, and they never lied to each other, no matter how much the truth might sting. That was the cornerstone of their friendship. If there was anyone that he could talk to about what may be going on with Mia, it was Blake. It helped, too, that Blake's wife was Mia's best friend.

Steven put down his drafting pencil and looked across the table to Blake, who was rerolling the blueprints that needed to be stored.

Blake turned from the pigeonhole where the blueprints were kept and focused on Steven. His brows
drew together in concern. "I'm listening."

Steven linked his fingers together while his tum-
bling thoughts settled down. "It's about Mia."

The frown line deepened. "Is she okay? She's not
ill...pregnant?"

Steven released a short chuckle. "Naw, none of the
above."

"Oh, cool. So what is it?"

"Man, I don't even know where to start or if I'm
making something out of nothing."

"Start at the spot that's buggin' you the most."

He ran his tongue across his lips and blew out a
breath, leaning slightly forward. "Me and Mia have
this bangin' sex life, no pun intended. Anyway, lately
she hasn't been there, ya know what I mean?"

Blake nodded.

"I know my woman. I know her body and I know
when she's faking."

Blake's eyes widened.

"She acts like she's into it but I can tell she's not.
And last night..." His voice drifted off. He wasn't sure
that he was ready to tell his buddy that he couldn't satisfy his woman.

"Have you talked to her?"

"I'd feel like an idiot. It's probably just in my head."

"If it's in your head, it got there for a reason."

Steven was silent for a moment, trying to pinpoint
the date and source of his unease. "I guess it started
about two weeks ago. She's been distracted and kinda
secretive. I mean, I've walked in on her a couple of
times and she shuts the computer off or abruptly ends

a call. And she's been evasive when I ask what she was working on. Then the whole sex thing." He looked away.

Blake was quiet for a moment. He'd been in Steven's shoes, or at least his wife, Savannah, had been in Steven's shoes. Tristan Montgomery—a client—had decided that she wanted Blake as an addendum to their business contract, and she made life very difficult for him, to a point that he seriously considered ending the contract, returning the money and moving on. The tension played havoc with his marriage and Tristan's tireless come-ons could wear down the best of men. But he couldn't imagine that someone was hovering in the background of Steven and Mia's relationship. Unfortunately, however, anything was possible even in the best relationship.

"Look, man," Blake said, straddling a chair and bracing his forearms along the top. "You know the mess I went through with Tristan. The only thing that saved me and Savannah was talking. Once I let Savannah know what was really going on, it removed her doubts, it gave me strength and then as a team we dealt with it together."

"I guess the thing that shakes me the most is that it's always been me who was holding all the cards, the one who raised the questions, the one who got to walk away."

"Hey, hold on. That's taking it to the extreme, don't you think?"

"I know, I know, I'm just saying…I feel out of my element. I've never let a woman get this close to me. And move in with a woman!" He snorted. "I took a big chance with Mia. If she messes over me…" He shook his head.

"We all thought we were playas until the right woman came along. Even you couldn't outplay me until Savannah came along," he teased.

That drew an appreciative chuckle from Steven. "So whatcha sayin'? I'm your wingman?"

"And a damn good one, too," Blake said, laughter rumbling over his words. "Bottom line, my brother, you have to admit that your playa card had been pulled. And the sooner you accept that and give in to what you feel for her, all that other macho BS about being in control and in charge won't mean jack. But you gotta talk to her. Tell her how you feel, what's been on your mind."

The waning afternoon light played on Steven's eyes, turning them a darker shade of grayish green.

"Yeah, guess I'm gonna have to. This just isn't my thing, spilling my guts."

Blake gave a crooked smile. "You'll get used to it."

"Do me a favor."

"Sure."

"See if you can pick Savannah's brain. Maybe Mia might have said something to her."

"I'll try. But haven't you heard of the girlfriend oath?"

Steven frowned. "The girlfriend oath?"

"Yeah, no boys allowed."

When Steven arrived home, he had every intention of talking with Mia, as Blake had suggested. But the truth was, talking about insecurities and being vulnerable to a woman didn't sit well with him.

He lived by the example set by his father. A man was a man. Men didn't cry, show fear or give in to their emotions. You never let a woman get beyond those defenses, no matter how much you loved them. If a woman could get to you in that way, then your enemies could get to you through her.

His father, Frank Long, had been a street hustler since his early teens and carried the mantra of the street deep in his soul. Although Steven knew that his father loved his mother, there were never open displays of affection or words of love tossed freely around. Frank showed his love through things. They had a stunning home on Sugar Hill in Harlem. His mother had more jewelry than she would ever wear, and he and his brother and sister never wanted for anything.

It was his mother, Grace, who provided the affection, some softness in their lives, but his father's lessons and the way he lived his life were heavily ingrained in Steven.

He knew he felt deeply for Mia, more than any woman he'd been with. She anchored him and he didn't want to be with anyone else—this was a first for him. Having more than one woman at a time had been a way of life for him. It kept him from becoming too involved, caring too much. Steven Long was a playa to his heart, but as Blake had clearly pointed out, Mia had pulled his card.

Did that mean he was in love? Or in deep like? It must be something, he thought as he tugged off his tie en route to the bedroom. He'd given up his bachelor pad and moved in with Mia. That had to mean something, which made how Mia had been acting all the more unnerving for him.

He flicked on the bedroom light, took off his jacket and tossed it on the lounge chair near the window. He pulled the curtain back and gazed out at the street below.

Twilight was settling over the city. That in-between time of day and night when your eyes played tricks on you and things weren't quite as they seemed.

Just as he was about to turn away, he saw Mia's Lexus pull up in front of the building. He waited for her to exit. He loved to see her walk. When she didn't get out, he grew curious. He peered a bit closer and the outline of her body was defined by the streetlights. She had her head down on the steering wheel. And several times she hit the wheel with her palm.

Finally, she sat up, flipped down the mirror and checked her appearance. Then sat for a couple of minutes more before she gathered her things and got out. He watched her approach the building; the usual bounce and sway in her step was missing. Mia usually walked as if she was ready to take over the world— head held high, long smooth strides, determination etched on her face. But tonight her body language shouted defeat.

He turned away from the window once he saw her enter the building. Something must have happened at the office or with a client or with one of her friends. Mia never got rattled, so it had to be something major. Whatever it was, they'd deal with it. He heard her key in the door and went up front to meet her.

She came in and when she glanced up and saw him standing there, a smile to light up Broadway bloomed across her mouth.

"Hey," she greeted him. She pranced over to him

and kissed him softly and briefly on the lips. "How was your day?"

"Fine," he murmured, totally confused by the woman he'd seen outside only moments ago who was obviously upset and the woman standing in front of him who acted as if the world was hers for the taking.

She brushed his cheek with her fingertip and moved past him. "Hungry?" she called out over her shoulder.

"No. I'm good. Late lunch." He followed her into the bedroom. "So how was your day? Anything exciting happen?"

"Not really." She gave him the benefit of a quick look before sitting on the side of the bed to take off her shoes.

Whatever was on her mind, she apparently didn't want to share it with him. He turned abruptly and headed back to the living room.

Moments later Mia heard the sound of the evening news coming from the living-room television.

Briefly she let down her guard and the weight of her day consumed her. The tension she dealt with at Michael's office while she planted the devices, followed by a two-hour lunch with him, Brenda and Ashley, all came closing in on her at once. They'd been seated in a booth for four and Michael took the liberty of sitting next to Mia.

Although lunch was very businesslike and aboveboard, she couldn't mistake the intermittent bump of thighs beneath the table or the brush of fingertips as they reached for the same item.

She could barely concentrate on the conversation going on around her and then as they left Michael was right behind her and whispered, "I want to make love to you, and I will."

The words were as much a promise as a threat. Michael Burke never said he would do anything without fully intending to do it.

When she and Ashley returned to their office, Mia was unusually subdued, but that didn't stop Ashley from voicing her opinion.

"I can see why you and a hundred other women would be attracted to Michael Burke," she said, taking a seat opposite Mia's desk without being asked. "And I also see that he still cares about you. But the only thing that really concerns me is that I see the same thing in you for him."

Mia's eyes flashed in Ashley's direction. She started to debate the point, but it was useless. She did have feelings for Michael. What they were she wasn't sure, but they were there just beneath the surface. She covered her face then finally found the courage to look at Ashley.

"I don't know what to do," she finally said.

"Look, I can take over this account so you won't have to deal with him."

"If I could have you do that, I would in a heartbeat."

"This is the part you can't talk about." It was more of a statement than a question.

Mia nodded.

"Then I'm fresh out of suggestions." She pushed up from the seat. "But whatever I can do to help, let me know."

"Thanks."

"Is something bothering you?"

Mia's head snapped up. She turned toward the doorway. Steven was standing there.

"Just a little tired, I guess. Kinda busy day at work. Nothing that a hot bath and a good night's sleep won't cure."

"You sure that's it?"

"Yes. Why?"

He rocked his jaw a minute. He started to tell her that he'd seen her in the car and had been standing in the doorway while she sat motionless and totally unaware of him. But he didn't want to hear her lie to him anymore.

"Nothing. Just asking. Look, I'm going to run out for a while."

"Oh." Mia focused on him as if seeing him for the first time. "Out?"

"Yes. Out. I'll see you later." Without further explanation he turned and walked away.

Mia sat there for a moment, too drained to react. It was probably best that Steven did go out for a while, she reasoned. She needed some time to push away Michael's words, wash away the heat of his breath on the back of her neck, the touch of his hand at the small of her back and the look in his eyes that said, *I'm coming for you.*

Her cell phone chirped. She dug it out of her tote and immediately recognized the number.

"Hello, Jean."

"I'm calling to remind you that I'm going to need an update from you by the end of the week."

"Of course."

"How much progress have you made?"

"I've made contact and I've established an opportunity to get inside the company."

"Excellent. I knew you would be the perfect one for

this assignment. I'll expect a complete update." She clicked off without so much as a goodbye.

However, as much as Mia didn't want to admit it, Jean's call was just the kick start that she needed. With Steven out of the house, it was the perfect time to check and sync all the devices. If she got really lucky, she might hear something worthwhile.

Chapter 10

Steven got in his BMW and headed off with no particular destination in mind. Driving usually cleared his head, especially when he was working on a difficult design problem. He usually didn't take evening drives to get his head right regarding relationships. If he drove somewhere, it was either home or away for good.

This was different. But everything about his and Mia's relationship was different. He was treading in brand-new territory and he had no idea where the land mines were.

He took the exit to the West Side Highway and headed south toward the Chelsea Piers.

The area had been totally revitalized over the past few years with bike and roller-skating lanes, benches and trees. The set for *Law & Order* was inside the pier as well, just off 23rd Street.

He slowed, pulled into one of the parking areas and got out. If there was one thing that could always be counted on in New York, it was that there was guaranteed to be people out doing something no matter the time, day or the weather. Truly, the city that never sleeps.

Steven set the alarm on his car and began to stroll along the docks. Anchored crafts bobbed in the water and the masts of the massive, once-military vessels, jutted toward the darkened skies.

A young couple Rollerblading streaked past him, followed by several joggers. A stiff fall breeze blew in from the water. He drew up the collar of his jacket around his neck. Lights ahead drew his attention and he walked toward them.

On one of the commercial strips was a small restaurant and bar located next to a bowling alley that was also still open for business. He decided to go into the restaurant.

"Good evening," said a young woman dressed in black. "Will you be having dinner or would you prefer to sit at the bar?"

"The bar is fine. Thanks."

"Up the stairs to the left. Enjoy your evening."

Steven walked toward the bar and found an empty seat in the middle of the horseshoe-shape counter.

"What can I get for you this evening?"

Steven glanced up.

"Steven? Steven Long?"

He focused on the attractive face and tried to place her. "I'm sorry…" he said helplessly.

"Michelle Dennis. You used to date my friend, Renee McDonald."

Recognition popped in his eyes. "Wow." He shook his head in embarrassment. "I'm sorry. Spaced out for a minute. How are you?"

"I'm great. Doing a little moonlighting," she said with a smile, giving an expansive look around.

"You were modeling, if I remember correctly."

She laughed a sweet sound. "That, too. In my real life I work at the post office. So how have you been? I think the last time I saw you was about two years ago."

"I've been doing well. Business is booming. Can't complain."

"That's a good thing."

"How's Renee?"

"Renee is married and working on her second baby."

Steven let out a burst of surprised laughter. "You're kidding. Renee?"

"Yep." She bobbed her head.

"'Scuse me, can I get a little service down here?" a man called out from the other end of the bar.

Michelle made a face. "Sorry. Be right back."

Steven took a brief look around. For the middle of the week, the place was fairly crowded with a combination of the straggling after-work patrons and the locals stopping in.

It had been a while since he'd been out alone at a bar. Since he and Mia had gotten together, he'd shut down that part of his life. Funny how a bar was the first place he'd ventured to. He supposed old habits die hard.

Michelle returned. "So what brings you out?" she continued as if they'd never been interrupted.

He shrugged slightly. "Needed some air."

She leaned forward, exposing ample cleavage that Steven could hardly ignore.

She lowered her voice. "Unfortunately, if you're going to sit here, you have to order something. If you don't, my boss will kill me."

"Sure. No problem. I'll take a Coors."

"Coming right up." She turned and bent into the fridge to retrieve the bottle, giving Steven a good solid look from the back. She turned and set the bottle down in front of him, along with a glass and a napkin. "Out for some air, huh?"

He looked at her. When he and Renee had been together he'd seen Michelle several times. She'd always been with a guy, so he hadn't paid much attention to her. Now he did. She was a good-looking woman. Not necessarily a showstopper, but there was something appealing and sexy in her open expression, engaging smile and inviting eyes.

She wore her hair natural in short spirals that took years off her age—middle to late thirties—and her skin looked soft and supple to the touch, with a body that you wouldn't toss out of bed.

"Something like that," he finally said, responding to her question. He took a swallow of the icy-cold beer. "How many nights do you work here?"

"Just two and every other weekend. Helps keep the bills at bay." Her gaze drifted over him. "I get off at ten." She turned and walked a few paces away to serve a customer. She tossed Steven a last look.

Steven looked up the overhead clock above the bar. Ten. He could keep himself occupied until then. Maybe a diversion was just the thing he needed to get his head right. He sipped his beer and relaxed to the music.

* * *

Mia had her laptop open on the bed. She'd con- nected it to her PDA and logged in using the TLC access codes. Within minutes a string of programs opened. She keyed in the necessary information and soon she was inside Michael's office computer.

She did a cursory search of his files and didn't find anything that struck her as out of place, which could mean that there was nothing for her to find or that she would have to open each and every file.

However, after considering her options she thought that if Michael was involved in the escort business, he would minimize any trail from his office. More than likely anything incriminating would be on his home computer or gathered from her phone taps. But if he was using company funds to pay people, there might be something in these files.

She took a second look at a folder labeled Accounts and opened it. At least one hundred files filled the screen. She groaned and began looking at them. The majority of them were businesses, many of which she was familiar with, at least by name. Others were for in- dividuals. As she took one last look, a file marked Log caught her attention. She clicked on the file and a mes- sage opened requesting a password. Her heart thumped.

Password. During her training, Jasmine, the head IT person at TLC, had been very clear about passwords. *If you weren't certain that you knew it like your own name, do not try to access the information. If the file is somehow encrypted, then whoever did it would know if attempts had been made to hack into the file.* In cases like that, Jasmine was to be contacted.

Maybe it was nothing, Mia tried to convince herself

as she stared at the flashing request for a password. She was probably jumping the gun. Most likely this file was no more than an employee list, or his personal banking information.

What if it wasn't? Was she trying to blow it off because she really believed it was nothing or because she *wanted* to believe it was nothing?

Reluctantly, she picked up her cell phone and dialed TLC headquarters. An automated service answered.

"Welcome to Tender Loving Care beauty products for today's woman. Please enter your ID number now."

Mia pressed in her ID.

"Thank you. If you know your party's extension, please dial it now. To order supplies, press 1; to schedule training, press 2; technical support, press 3. If this is an emergency, please enter your emergency code."

Mia pressed "3."

"Jasmine speaking."

"Hey, Jazz. I have something that I need you to look at. It's encrypted and needs a password."

Jasmine laughed. "Piece of cake. Send me the file."

"Actually I can't. I'm in the subject's computer remotely."

"Go head, girl! Okay. I'm going to take over your computer. Give me your IP address."

Mia did as instructed and seconds later she watched her cursor move around the screen, open and close files and type in strings of code. For an instant the screen went black. When it came back on, Mia was looking at some sort of client list with payment schedules and amounts. All the names were women.

Mia began to feel ill.

"I'm going to take a screenshot of this and e-mail

it to you, close the file and then I'll release your computer back to you," Jasmine was saying through the cell phone's speaker. "Got everything you need?"

"Yes, thanks," she said absently.

"Well, good night."

"Night." Mia disconnected the call.

Moments later her computer beeped, indicating a new arrival. She clicked on her in-box and saw the e-mail from Jasmine. She forwarded the e-mail to her office account. She'd print it out there.

Little by little she shut everything down, trying to put a positive spin on what she'd seen.

After putting everything away, she realized how late it had gotten. It was nearing midnight and Steven had yet to return. The fact that he wasn't home was bad enough, but what was more damning was that she hadn't noticed until now.

Steven waited for Michelle to finish her shift. Good sense dictated that he should simply get up and leave. But old habits kicked in and he hung around. He needed some positive reinforcement and his gut instinct told him that Michelle would be more than willing to do just that.

"Finally," she breathed, coming up to the table where he'd been relaxing for the past hour.

Steven glanced up from his drink. He pushed up from the seat. "I know it's late, but have you eaten?"

"I'm starved."

"Come on. There's a great place about three blocks from here. If we hurry we can catch the kitchen before it closes."

"Lead the way."

They walked out into the brisk evening air.

"Getting cold," Michelle said, pulling her short jacket tighter around her. She slipped her arm through the crook of Steven's and moved closer to him.

"We can take my car if you want."

"No. The air will do me good. I've been cooped up in there for four hours." She walked next to him quietly for about a block. "So tell me what's been going on with you."

A half smile moved across his mouth. "Business has been great. We've expanded some of our developments out to D.C.—"

"That's not what I mean," she said, cutting him off.

He glanced at her.

"I could run an Internet search on you if I wanted to know about your business life."

He chuckled.

"Men don't usually come into a bar alone unless they're looking to meet someone or they have something heavy on their minds. What's your story?"

"Is this the counseling bartender talking?" he teased, avoiding the question.

"No. Just someone who's interested in knowing why a brother like you is out alone at a bar in the middle of the week."

"Maybe I needed a change of scenery."

Michelle stopped walking. Steven stopped short and faced her.

"What?"

Michelle glanced downward then looked him in the eyes. "I want to be honest with you and I hope you'll be honest with me. I like you. I always did, from back when you were dating Renee. But I would never move on my friend's man." She drew in a long breath. "But Renee is married. I'm not seeing anyone and you're out alone."

When he looked at her and took in what she was saying, what she was offering, he had a sudden, sick sensation of guilt. What the hell was he doing? He wasn't that guy anymore. He wasn't on the prowl. He didn't want to retreat to the days when he called all women "sweetheart" because he didn't care or couldn't remember their name.

Had this been a year ago, he probably would have taken Michelle up on her offer.

"Look. It's only dinner with an old acquaintance. Nothing more. If I gave you that impression then I'm sorry."

She pressed her lips together and smiled. "Now that we're on the same page, let's go before the kitchen closes."

Chapter 11

Mia wasn't sure if she should pretend to be asleep when she heard the key in the door or if she should let him know that she was up and was concerned about where he'd been. She peeked at the digital clock. It was nearly 2:00 a.m.

The bedroom door opened. Steven moved quietly around the room, taking off his clothes before going into the master bathroom.

Moments later, Mia heard the shower water running. She stared up at the ceiling. She tried to regulate her breathing and slow down the beating of her heart. This was a new place that she and Steven had entered. Since they'd been together, they'd never been out for most of the night separately. They'd never walked out on each other with friction hovering between them.

She knew part of it was her fault—the secret she was

carrying around with her about her conflicting feelings about Michael, and her TLC assignment. She had to get a handle on it before things got worse between them.

The bathroom door opened. For a moment, Steven stood in the lighted doorway before turning off the light.

Mia felt the side of the bed sink from his weight and the covers shift as he got in beside her.

Steven turned on his side and draped his arm across her waist. He kissed her ear. "I know you're not sleeping," he said softly. "Can we talk?"

"Okay," she said softly, while trying to keep her own guilty thoughts from giving her away.

"Something almost happened tonight."

Her heart slammed in her chest. Then Steven was silent for so long she began to believe that her punishment for her own indiscretions was to never know what Steven had "almost" done.

"Look," he finally said. "This whole baring my soul thing is not me. It never has been. But what happened tonight—that can't go on between us."

She was too afraid to move, to breathe.

"I walked out of here tonight because I didn't want you to lie to me anymore."

Oh, God, she was going to faint.

"Are you seeing someone else?"

Her relief burst from her lips. "No! Of course not." She turned on her side to face him. "I wouldn't do that. Never."

From the dim light of the moon sliding in between the blinds, she saw the worry in those incredible eyes, felt it in the rapid beat of his heart and heard it in between the words he did not say; he loved her and was afraid he was losing her. What could she say to prove him wrong when she felt deep in her soul that he might be right—losing her to memories, possibility and unanswered questions.

What she wanted from Steven, she suddenly realized, was more than great sex, nice things and a guaranteed date on Saturday night. She wanted a man who was willing to give every ounce of himself to her, who wanted her so much that he was willing to build a house for her even if they weren't together. She wanted someone to say the words *I love you, Mia* without the prompts, without it only coming as an echo of her own words.

"When things get so that they're not working for you, you need to tell me," Steven was saying, drawing her back and away from her cascading thoughts.

"I can't imagine that happening." But fear and doubt knotted her stomach. She cuddled closer. He tenderly kissed the top of her head. "You want to tell me what almost happened?" she tentatively asked.

"It didn't. That's what's important. Didn't come close, only the suggestion—if I'd been willing."

Mia listened intently for words between the lines and beneath the surface. She found none. Only the simple truth.

Mia gently draped her leg over his. Their toes touched and played. She smiled inside.

Steven pressed his lips against the sensitive spot between the space of her neck and her collarbone. She trembled. He ran his hand down and along the curve of her body's right side, covering each inch like the brush of a master painter.

Mia spontaneously arched her body into his. The

pulse of his growing erection pressed between the juncture of her thighs. She moaned softly as he brushed his thumb across her nipple before cupping her breast in his palm and caressing it. Her body became infused with heat.

Steven eased her onto her back. He stared down into her eyes. He looked as if he was on the verge of saying something. Instead he kissed her long, deep and slow. And she gave in to the kiss, the feel of his hands on her body, the weight of him pinning her beneath him.

Mia closed her eyes, wrapped her arms and legs around Steven and let the sensations take over her mind, body and soul.

The following morning after Steven left for work, Mia set up the tools of her trade and spent the next hour watching the computer screen for activity and listening to the phone taps for something worthwhile.

Just as she was about to pack up and head to the office, Michael received a call on his Sag Harbor phone.

She sat up straighter.

"Hi, it's Michelle. I need some extra hours. Slot me in for any upcoming openings. Thanks."

Mia frowned. What did that mean? Was Michelle one of the alleged women in the service or nothing more sinister than an employee who needed some O/T or the cleaning lady?

She looked at the incoming call for the number. It read like a cell phone. She made a note to give it to Jasmine to see if she could get a last name and maybe an address.

Mia checked the time. It was nearly ten. She needed

to stop by the cleaners on her way to work and drop off a few things. She had a conference call at noon.

She put everything away, shut off the computer and stashed her PDA and cell in her tote, along with her go bag. She collected the clothes that she'd tossed on the side chair in the bedroom. She added the two pairs of slacks and a dress shirt that Steven had hung on the back of the bathroom door.

One last look around to ensure that she hadn't left any telltale signs of her clandestine activity and she hurried out.

"Good morning, Ms. Carol," Mia greeted her.

Carol Bennett was the matriarch of the Bennett Dry Cleaning family. Mia had been bringing her clothes to them for years. And although there was a more modern cleaner closer to her condo, she preferred the personal touch, and it gave her a sense of pride to support a black-owned business.

"Mia, how are you, sweetheart?" Carol slipped on the glasses held around her neck by a beaded chain.

"I'm fine, Ms. Carol. How is the family?"

"The children—" she shrugged "—they wish they had a different business to inherit. But it's like I tell them all the time—baby doctors, morticians and cleaners will always have business."

Mia chuckled. "You are so right."

Carol held up each garment and jotted them down on the slip. "Okay, one ladies' suit, two blouses, two dress shirts and two slacks. When do you need them back?" She peered at Mia from above the top of her glasses.

"Hmm. Tomorrow? Can I pick them up around six?"

"Sure."

"Great. Thanks. I gotta run. Have a good day." She picked up her purse from the counter.

"You, too, dear." She gathered the clothes up into a bundle with the intention of putting them in the basket when some change fell out of one of the pockets.

Mia stopped. "I'm sorry. I should have checked the pockets."

Carol picked up the change from the floor. "A whole sixty-two cents," she said with a smile. "Not enough to retire on, so you keep it."

Mia grinned. "Thanks."

Carol went through each item to check the pockets. "This is yours, too." She gave her a business card.

Mia took it and stuck it into her tote.

"That's it," Carol concluded.

"Good. If anything else turns up, just leave it with the clothes. Bye!" She hurried out. Hopefully, she wouldn't get caught in traffic. She probably should have left home sooner, but she'd let her quest for answers—or vindication—consume her morning.

Once behind the wheel of her car, she dug her cell phone out of her tote and gave the voice command to call Ashley.

"Hey, Ashley," she said through the speakerphone. "I'm running behind schedule. Hopefully, I should be there in about forty minutes."

"No problem. I have everything covered."

"Any calls?"

"Just one." Ashley paused. "Michael Burke. He plans to stop by later."

Mia's brakes squealed as she nearly rear-ended the driver in front of her. She had about ten seconds to pull herself together before the cars behind her demanded her head on a platter for holding them up.

"Thanks," she managed, easing her foot off the brake and onto the gas. "Did he say what time?"

"I told him we had an early-afternoon appointment. He said it would be around 2:30. He had some information on the event that he wanted to deliver personally."

Mia's heart skipped a beat. "Okay. I'll see you soon." She pressed the speakerphone button and disconnected the call.

What could he have to bring that he hadn't turned over already? Ideally, she wanted to limit her face time with Michael to the bare minimum. Obviously, he had other ideas.

Chapter 12

Michael strolled into his suite of offices, feeling better than he'd felt in months. Since connecting with Mia again, his life seemed to take on a new purpose. He wanted more than the next big contract, a fatter bank account, more houses and more cars than he could live in or drive.

When Mia had left him, he had fallen apart, piece by piece, with the final straw being his divorce. He'd fallen into an abyss of not caring, of only wanting women in his life whom he could control. He drew a macabre pleasure out of getting them to do what he wanted when he wanted. But after five years, he'd grown even more restless. Nothing satisfied him. Not women, clients or money. And then the opportunity to get back in Mia's life presented itself and the dark world into which he'd descended suddenly grew brighter. He walked down the hallway toward his office.

"Good morning, Michael," Brenda greeted him, as she stepped out of her office into the corridor.

"Morning."

She quickly looked right then left. "I thought you were going to call me last night," she said in a hard whisper.

"Not now, Brenda."

She flashed him a tight look, her mouth turning into a single line. "Then when?"

"I'll let you know. Do you have details on the Chrysler account?"

She lifted her chin, unwilling to take the verbal smack he'd given her. "On your desk."

"Thanks." He continued toward his office, certain that if Brenda had daggers they'd be deep in his back. He opened the door to his office, then shut it behind him. He took off his navy-blue Armani jacket and hung it on the rack by the window.

For a moment he stared out onto the street below. Cars, trucks, buses and strings of yellow cabs filled the blacktop. Harried businesspeople darted around a casual slow-strolling, camera-toting tourist.

This was his city. The pulse and rhythm of it beat in his veins like nourishment, but he'd let it all go to get Mia back.

He slung his hands into his pants pockets. Of course, it wouldn't be easy. There were many people who depended on him. He'd miss the excitement, the challenge, the danger and especially the money. But he'd do it for her. If she'd only give him the slightest indication that she still had feelings for him.

He sighed heavily and turned from the window. Before he got that far, there were still a lot of things he was going to have to settle and exorcise from his life. One of them was Brenda.

It was a mistake taking the boardroom into the bedroom. He knew it the moment he'd reserved the hotel suite at the Ritz Carlton. But his wounds were so deep after losing Mia, then his marriage and the endless series of faceless women, that the comfort Brenda offered was what he needed.

They'd fallen into a discreet routine, talking by phone in the evening, meeting for the weekend at his house in Montclair, New Jersey, or for short getaways to Vegas, the Bahamas, the Poconos and even the West Coast, on occasion.

The relationship worked for both of them. At least Michael thought it did. The scene that Brenda had put on after the meeting with Mia and Ashley was worthy of YouTube.

She'd stormed into his office, her eyes full of fire, and marched straight up to his desk.

"What is going on between you and her?"

"I don't know what you're talking about."

"Like hell you don't! I saw how you look at her. I hear how you talk to her. It's more than business. Don't BS me." Her chest heaved in and out as her agitation grew. "I love you, Michael. You're not going to do this to me."

It took everything he had to control his rising temper. Had they been in a more private setting, things would have been entirely different. When his dark, brooding gaze pinned her, he saw her involuntary withdrawal, the moment of alarm that widened her eyes.

His tone was bitter cold. "I suggest that you leave my office. Please."

She opened her mouth to speak. He held up his hand to stop her.

"Leave, Brenda, for both our sakes. We'll talk later."

The bluster with which she'd barged in had dwindled to a barely noticeable breeze.

She straightened her shoulders, then turned and walked out.

He'd said they would talk. But the truth was he really didn't want to deal with her. She'd crossed the invisible line by telling him she was in love with him. Love couldn't work between them. Ever.

He cared for Brenda. But he wasn't in love with her and never would be. He released a long, slow breath. He had to handle this delicately. She didn't deserve to be hurt, but he certainly had no intention of ruining this chance with Mia.

Mia got through her morning working hard to keep thoughts of Michael at bay. But what concerned her most was her on-the-fence feelings about Steven.

Before Michael reappeared, she'd been so certain that Steven was "the one." Now she was filled with doubt.

The chirping of her cell phone drew her attention. She looked around for it on top of her desk to no avail. The chirp continued and she realized it was still in her tote.

She hurried across the room to her bag, which was on the side table, reached inside, turning the bag over in the process. "Dammit." She retrieved the phone from the floor just as it stopped ringing and went to voice mail. "Double dammit." She bent down and picked up her belongings from the floor and was in the process of sticking an errant business card in her wallet when she stopped. Frowned.

Last Call Bar & Grill. The address was on Pier 23. Hmm. She didn't recall ever having been there. And her business hinged on her knowing about the businesses in the city to best serve her clients. She flipped the card over and her heart felt as if it actually stopped.

Michelle Dennis. She stared at the number, unable or unwilling to let the numbers make sense. But she couldn't deny what was right in front of her. It was the same number that had showed up on Michael's phone. The same first name—Michelle. She knew this wasn't one of her business cards. It must have fallen out of Steven's pocket at the cleaner. This was where he'd been last night. This was what "almost happened."

Her stomach rolled.

What the hell did it mean? Was this some ugly coincidence? God, how was Steven involved? Was he seeing some woman who might be part of this escort service?

Mia was suddenly so hot she couldn't breathe. The implications of what might be going on she didn't want to think about.

Then pushing its way past the suspicions, the doubts and fears was a surge of jealousy that shook her with its intensity. How far did things really go between Steven and Michelle? How long had he known her? Was she someone from his past?

Her gaze shifted to the neatly written name and phone number.

Mia, Ms. Organized, Ms. Anal-Compulsive, felt like she was coming apart. She couldn't focus on anything beyond calling that number and demanding to know who Michelle Dennis was and what she had to do with Steven.

Mia reached for the phone, just as it rang in her hand.

"Your conference call is on line two," Ashley said.

Mia's hand shook. The room came back into focus. What in the world was she getting ready to do—"go hood" on this Michelle? She'd never argued or fought over a man in her life. What was wrong with her?

"Mia?"

She breathed deeply. "Thanks."

"You okay?"

"Yes, I'm fine. I'll, uh, take the call." Focusing on business would help to clear her head and get her thoughts back on track. She pressed the flashing light on the telephone base.

"Sharlene, hi… Yes, we're in the final stages of the plan…"

Fortunately, the conversation was with a client she'd worked with on an annual basis because, as hard as she tried, she really hadn't been paying attention.

Steven. Michael. Steven. How were they connected?

Ashley knocked lightly on the door and stuck her head in. "Got a minute?"

"Sure."

Ashley came in. She stood in front of Mia's desk. "I wanted to know if you need me to be here when Michael comes."

Mia's gaze rose slowly and settled on Ashley. "Would you?" she asked and her voice broke. Her eyes filled.

Ashley came around the desk and knelt down beside Mia. "What is it? What happened?"

Mia was incredibly torn. She desperately needed to unburden herself. Normally she would tell Savannah or Danielle. But they knew nothing about Michael, and Ashley didn't know about the Cartel. And Mia was trapped in the middle.

What she needed was an ally. She needed someone she could depend on. She tugged on her bottom lip with her teeth. It was wrong. It went against her promise and it could very well put an innocent person in danger.

But protocol had been broken more than a year ago when Savannah made up her own rules and involved her and Danielle. Mia was about to break it again.

"I think you should sit down…"

About a half hour later, Mia had spilled her guts about the Cartel without divulging its location or naming names. She told Ashley about her assignment, the card she'd found and her confusion about what to do next.

Mia sat back, emotionally spent, expecting to hear words of disbelief, laughter, something. She got none of those. What she got was an expression on Ashley's face that she'd never seen before—hard, piercing, no-nonsense. And she instantly knew she'd made the biggest mistake of her life.

"I'm not really from Los Angeles. I'm from D.C."

Mia frowned.

"I didn't just happen to be the lucky one to fill the job opening as your assistant. I was sent here."

Mia pushed her chair back a bit. Her gaze darted toward her tote. In her go bag the sample-size "body mist" was a bottle of mace. If she could get to it…

"I was sent by the D.C. office when I asked to be relocated."

Mia blinked several times. Ashley was out of focus. What the hell was she talking about?

"I was assigned to be here, by Jean."

Oh...triple damn.

Chapter 13

Mia had every intention of saying something, but she couldn't find the words. Ashley was one of the Cartel operatives? Right under her nose? What kind of member was she if she couldn't spot one of her own right in front of her face, day in and day out?

Then again, that was the whole point of being part of the Cartel. They were all regular, everyday women who could blend in and not draw attention to themselves.

"All the new recruits with less than two full years under their belt have a shadow," Ashley was saying. "Even if they don't know about it. I'm sure you remember what happened with your friend Danielle. Bernard was her shadow."

Yes, Mia remembered. Danielle had been assigned an identity theft job and, shock of shocks, Bernard Hassell, Savannah's stepfather-in-law-to-be was an agent for Homeland Security and a personal friend of Jean's. He wound up being Danielle's shadow, and it was with his help that they were able to bring down the ring that had stolen hundreds of identities and millions of dollars.

"I still can't wrap my mind around the fact that you've been a part of TLC and I never suspected."

Ashley smiled. "Then I guess I'm pretty good, huh?"

"So how badly have I been doing?"

Ashley settled into her seat. "Not bad at all. I will tell you this. Jean knows everything. Don't think for a moment that she didn't know that you and Michael Burke had a past. It's the main reason she selected you for this assignment. If his hands are dirty, he would never suspect that you were the one who was going to clean them."

A sick sensation rolled through her stomach.

"That's why it was more important than ever that you have a shadow—to prevent you from compromising the assignment."

Mia's throat tightened. "So all that pretending to be my friend, listening to all my personal…stuff…it was just all part of the job, too, I suppose."

Ashley's stern expression slowly softened to the one that Mia recognized. She leaned slightly forward. "No. I listened and advised because underneath all this spy stuff, I really like you. I want us to be friends. And everything I told you about me, it was real." The right corner of her mouth lifted to a hopeful smile.

Mia breathed a bit freer. "So now what?"

Ashley straightened. "This is your case. I'm only here to help, not direct. You tell me what you want me to do. That's how this is going to work. I have no intention of taking over."

"Then I guess, since we're on the same side, I should bring you up-to-date on everything I have so far."

They spent the next half hour going over what Mia had recorded from Michael's home and the information she'd accessed on his office computer. And Jasmine, over at tech support, was able to download the list of names and payments that Mia had found on his office computer. She pulled up the information she'd stored on her PDA and shared it with Ashley.

"Pretty impressive set of names and numbers," Ashley said, studying the list.

"Exactly. But to give him the benefit of the doubt, he is a businessman and his business is to know people, make deals and make money in the process."

Ashley flashed Mia a sharp look. "Do you really believe that's what this list is or is it what you want to believe?"

Mia flinched. "I guess a bit of both," she quietly conceded.

"I can't impress upon you enough the importance of separating your feelings from the reality of what is going on. If you don't, you're going to make some major mistakes that could be very costly…and I don't mean monetarily."

"I know. I can handle this."

"Good. So how do you want to proceed? How can I help? Like I said, I'll be more than happy to take over the project with Avante if that would make it easier for you."

"No." There was a new fierceness in her eyes. "You're right about what you said earlier. He would never suspect me. And that's going to be the key to everything. I can get close to him."

"Okay. This is your show." She checked the clock that hung over the door. "He should be arriving shortly."

Mia's heart thumped. She nodded.

"I'll be up front." Ashley got up to leave.

"Ashley…"

She stopped and turned. "Yes."

"Thanks."

Ashley smiled. "That's what spy friends are for."

"Listen, there is something you can do for me."

"Sure."

Mia explained what she wanted.

"I'll have the info for no later than tomorrow."

Mia nodded.

Mia slumped back in her chair after Ashley left, then covered her face with her hands. She was still in a mild state of shock, although she shouldn't have been. Everyone said that Jean Wallington-Armstrong was a brilliant manipulator and had an uncanny sixth sense about people, not to mention her resources in finding out everything about each and every member of her team. She should have known that if anyone would have an inkling about her and Michael's torrid past, it would be Jean.

That fact made Mia more determined than ever to bring the assignment to a swift and satisfying conclusion, no matter which way it turned out. Certainly a part of her hoped that all the signals about Michael were wrong, but if they weren't, she'd deal with it.

Her intercom buzzed.

"Yes?"

"Mr. Burke is here with his client."

Mia was caught off guard. She hadn't expected him to bring anyone, but that was probably a good thing. They wouldn't have an opportunity to be completely alone. She got up from her desk and walked up front to the small reception and file area.

"Michael."

"Mia, you look great, as always."

She merely smiled in response. Then she directed her attention to his guest and walked toward her. Mia extended her hand. "You must be Raven."

The stunning young woman stuck out her hand and limply shook Mia's. She offered a dazzling smile. And Mia immediately saw why crowds would swoon over her.

Raven was at least twenty, a stunning combination of Japanese and African-American ancestry, which gave her a sleek, exotic look. She had dark, silky hair that reached her waist, large almond-shaped eyes that curved ever so slightly at the corners, and a body like Halle Berry covered in a butter-smooth caramel complexion. She was about five foot five but she gave the appearance of being much taller.

"Raven, it's a pleasure to meet you. Michael has told me a lot about you, and the Internet is full of stories. Please, have a seat." She waited until Raven and Michael were seated. "Michael told me that you're very shy, which must be very difficult in your business."

"It is. I'm trying to deal with it," she said softly.

"We plan to make this event spectacular and as easy on you as possible." She buzzed Ashley.

"Yes?"

"Would you mind bringing in the details we've worked out so far for Raven's red-carpet event?"

"Sure. I'll be right in."

Several moments later Ashley came in with a thick folder.

"Ashley, this is Raven. Ashley is my event coordinator and is going to be responsible for logistics."

For the next few minutes, Mia explained the layout and how they planned to use video and audio clips throughout the night in lieu of Raven having to be engulfed in the throngs of people. Ashley gave a video presentation, detailing how they were going to lay out the space.

"The highlight of the evening will be your performance, which will happen toward the end of the night. Right after you finish, a limo will be waiting to take you back to your hotel. We are creating the image of untouchable for you and I think it will work. It will keep the media guessing and keep you out of the spotlight." She took a breath. "So what do you think?"

Raven beamed in delight. "I love it."

"Wonderful. We'll work out the final details, get the invitations out, handle the RSVPs and then set up the interior." She turned to Michael. "Any questions?"

"I think you've covered everything." He turned to Raven. "I told you she was the best." He stood. "I'm going to head back to the office. I know you ladies are busy and I...*we* appreciate your time. Mia, I'll be in touch. Good seeing you again, Ashley."

"You, too. I'll walk you both out." She spoke to Mia over her shoulder. "I'm going to take care of that errand. If I get finished in time, I'll be back."

Mia nodded.

She slumped back into her chair. Her day had been exhausting, to say the least, and it wasn't over yet.

While Ashley was on her assignment, Mia made a call to the girls.

Chapter 14

Steven and Blake were closing up shop for the night and walking to their respective cars.

"So how are things going with you and Mia? Ever have that talk?"

Steven shrugged slightly. "Sort of."

"Okay." He dragged out the word. "What does that mean?"

"We talked. I told her how I felt…kind of. I mean, damn, she's my woman. She's supposed to know how I feel."

Blake chuckled. "Listen, my good brotha. Here is a lesson in Women 101. Whatever you think you know, you don't. Did you tell her how you feel, what was bothering you?"

"Yeah…kind of."

"Man." He laughed full out. "You sound like you

have communication issues, which equals a brother's biggest downfall, not being able or willing to communicate."

"It's just not me, man. The words are in my head, I feel 'em, I just can't get them to cross my lips." He chuckled without humor. "But she has to know how I feel about her. Would I have given up my carefree life, my own crib, if I didn't want to be with her?"

"I know to you it seems obvious. But a woman doesn't always see the surface things. She needs to feel it, she needs to hear it."

Steven blew out a long breath. "I did ask her if she was seeing anyone."

"What did she say?"

"She said no."

"Did you believe her?"

He hesitated for a moment. "Yeah."

"Well, that's something. A start. You just have to talk to her, man. Once you get started, it gets easy. I swear." He grinned, seeing the pained looked on his friend's face. He slapped him on the back.

"I almost hooked up with this woman I met the other night."

Blake stopped in his tracks. "Say what?"

"I don't know. I was angry, confused, so I went for a drive and found myself out by Chelsea Piers. Stopped in this bar and grill. Remember when I was dating Renee McDonald?"

"Vaguely. They were coming and going so fast and furious it was hard to keep up," he teased.

"Very funny. Anyway, she had this friend, Michelle Dennis. Well, that's who I ran into the other night— Michelle. She was working the bar."

Blake's brows rose. "And…"

"And she made it clear that if I was willing, so was she."

Blake lowered his head and shook it slowly. "But good sense prevailed…"

"Yeah, that's not what I'm looking for. I'm not on the prowl anymore, don't want to be."

"Hey, none of us can afford to be. Black folk have the highest rates of HIV/AIDS and the numbers aren't coming down. These days you play, you pay, and it could be with your life. It ain't worth it, man."

"Humph, who you telling? I had my scare just before I met Mia. Don't plan to go down that road again."

"So where are things with you and Mia? You two on the same page or what?"

"I think so, man. I know I have work to do. It's just gonna take some time."

Blake draped his arm around Steven's broad shoulders as they walked across the underground parking lot. He leaned close. "If it's in your heart, man, just say the words." He grinned. "It feels almost as good as great sex."

Steven chuckled. "Yeah, okay."

They parted ways and Steven got in his car and sat there for a few moments as he watched Blake drive off.

Tonight he'd make a special effort. He'd show Mia how much he cared.

When he arrived at their condo, Mia hadn't gotten in yet. It was a little after six, plenty of time to plan a romantic evening in New York.

He walked into the bedroom, tossed his briefcase

and jacket onto the lounge chair then went to the phone by the bed.

He knew it was too last minute for any of the high-end restaurants in the area, but there was a local Italian place, totally family-owned, that Mia swore by. He placed an order with special instructions for delivery.

With that task out of the way, he went in search of some candles. In moments, the air was filled with the soft scent of vanilla. Mia's favorite. He checked the time. If Mia stayed true to form, she should be getting in between eight and nine, although lately it had been closer to nine. That gave him close to two hours to find the right music, break out the special dinner-ware, put the chocolate-colored satin sheets on the bed and still have time to run out for some flowers and take a shower before she got home.

Steven smiled as his plans for the evening began to take shape. He may not say the right words all the time, but he knew how to put on a grand party.

Mia was the first to arrive at The Shop. The trio—Savannah, Danielle and she—had been coming to the little West Village bistro for years, Mia having discovered it during one of her canvassing jaunts of the city in search of venues for clients or possible events. She was so pleased with the atmosphere, the service and the food that she made it a permanent stop and the girls adopted it as well.

She secured their booth in the back. By the time she got settled, she looked up and Danielle, stunning as always in an exotic kind of way, was walking through the door, with Savannah, still holding on to the lush postbaby curves, right behind her.

The moment Mia saw her two dearest friends walking through the door, the tightness that had lived in the center of her stomach for days and days began to ease. These were her girls, her friends. She needed them now more than ever, but if they were to be in any kind of position to help her, she would first have to come clean. She drew in a long breath of resolve and let out a breath of determination.

"Hey, girl," Danielle greeted her, buzzing Mia's cheek with a light kiss.

"My turn," Savannah said, the glow of happiness brimming in her eyes as she followed Danielle's greeting.

They both settled down into the worn leather booth seats.

"Dinner on you," Danielle asked, "since you convened this soiree?"

"Sure, and drinks, too."

Savannah's wide brown eyes widened even farther. "Must be serious with you springing for dinner *and* drinks. Do I need mine now?"

Mia's expression pinched for a moment. "You might."

Danielle raised her hand to signal for the waitress. "I'll have a cosmo," she said upon the waitress's arrival.

Savannah ordered a daiquiri and Mia an apple martini.

"So what's up, sis?" Savannah said. "I don't think I can wait for drinks." She lowered her voice. "Is it about your assignment?"

"Partly."

Danielle and Savannah leaned closer, their expressions open and expectant.

"I don't even know where to begin," Mia said.

"Wherever you feel comfortable," Savannah offered in that soft way of hers.

Mia lowered her gaze, trying to organize her thoughts. She looked into the eyes of her friends. "I've never told either of you this before. For that I apologize, but I think after I tell you everything you'll understand why. At least I hope you will." She swallowed. "When Jean gave me the assignment, it wound up being about investigating someone I knew…intimately…"

Mia poured out her story, from her shock at finding out that Michael was the suspect of the investigation, then traveling back to how they'd met, their torrid affair, his being married, him being her first true love, the guilt she felt about their affair, the breakup. She told it all: her visit to his house in Sag Harbor, the one he said he'd had built with her in mind, her growing feelings of uncertainty about her and Steven. She told them everything—up to and including the fact that Ashley was a Cartel operative and was at the moment tracking down Michelle Dennis.

By the time she'd finished, they'd consumed two drinks each and their dinner was halfway eaten. During the entire time, neither Danielle nor Savannah said a word.

Mia sat back, looked from one stunned face to the other, waiting for the verdict.

"You could have told me," Savannah said, surprising Mia. She thought Savannah would have been appalled that Mia would have taken up with a married man. "I know I might come across as all straight-laced and whatnot, but those are *my* rules. I don't put them on anyone else, especially my friends. Love comes in all kinds of packages and at all different times. I may not agree with what you did, but I admire how you finally took care of it." She reached across the table and took Mia's hand, which was balled into a fist.

"Girl, I would never have thought you had it in you," Danielle said with her usual sarcasm. "But the real deal is not what happened then, but what is happening now. Do you still have feelings for him?"

"That's just it. I don't know. I'm not sure if the feelings are real or some kind of residue of the past."

"You know you have to get that together," Savannah said. "First, for the sake of your relationship with Steven and then for the Cartel. We both know what it's like trying to manage a relationship and these assignments. We've been there."

Danielle wholeheartedly agreed. "And so Ms. Girl is a TLC lady." Danielle grinned. "I knew I liked her."

"Jean is something," Savannah said. "It's really kinda scary how much she knows and how she puts people exactly where they need to be. She knew it was going to be Blake's company that would be involved with the Tristan Montgomery investigation, and she knew that Dani and Nick's relationship was going to be put to the test with her identity theft assignment."

"She puts us in these kinds of emotional tugs-of-war situations to test our loyalty to the organization," Danielle said. "I guess when she realizes that we won't compromise ourselves, our relationships or the organization, we are truly Cartel-worthy."

Savannah lifted her glass then put it back down. "Can I just say this? I've seen you and Steven together. I see how he looks at you and how you look at him. I hear how you talk about him—the joy in your voice."

She took a breath. "One thing I've learned is that you can't go back. If Michael could cheat on his wife, what makes you think that if it was just the two of you he wouldn't wind up doing the same thing to you?"

"And bottom line," Danielle cut it. "If he's under suspicion by Jean and the Cartel and you have come up with your own suspicions, chances are there's something to it, sis. If you're going to hinge old feelings onto this assignment, you'll never see clearly and it could really get you hurt in more ways than one."

"I don't know Michael," Savannah said gently. "But if you loved him, I'm sure at his core he is a decent man. You are the only one who can make the right decision. You know your heart and you know both of them. I know that you'll do what is best for everyone involved, because I know *you*."

"Exactly, sweetie. We love you and don't want to see you hurt, but you know we got your back no matter what choice you make," Danielle added.

Mia sniffed back tears of relief. These were her friends, her sisters in spirit through good and bad, and she should have known that they would understand and not judge her. Such a weight had been lifted from her soul after finally being able to share with them what she had been through and the situation she currently found herself in.

And, like the dear friends and fellow Cartel members they were, they were willing to help with the case in any way that they could.

As she drove home, Mia thought about everything that was said during their impromptu get-together. Of course they were right. Deep in her soul it was something she already knew. She could not remain torn. Too much was at stake, specifically her relationship with Steven.

Her heart twisted just a little in her chest. She was being so unfair. She'd begun to compare Steven to Michael. That wasn't right. They were two different kinds of people and they showed their affection in different ways. Simply because Steven didn't shower her with words of love did not mean that he didn't love her. He *showed* her how he felt.

No more sitting on the fence. No more questioning her feelings and her relationship. She pulled into a parking space across the street from her condo. She loved Steven. True, she'd loved Michael, deeply. But *loved* was the operative word. *Past tense.* She must live in the now. And that was exactly what she intended to do.

When she put her key in the door, the soft scent of vanilla wafted to her nose. The living room was dim, apparently illuminated by candlelight.

Slowly she put down her purse on the hall table and closed the door. She distinctly heard the Luther Vandross classic "A House is Not a Home," crooning softly in the background. What was going on? And was that veal parmesan she smelled?

"Steve? Honey…I'm home," she said, and almost laughed at the oft-used one-liner.

Steven emerged from the bedroom, clad only in black silk boxers that hugged his chiseled chocolate skin. Her heart thumped along with the tiny bud between her thighs as he came toward her. Steven held their circular silver serving tray perched up on one hand with two long-stemmed wine glasses filled with something clear and bubbly. He had a white towel draped across his other arm.

"Good evening," he said in a low voice, the inkling of a smile hovering around the corners of his mouth.

Mia moved in closer, her eyes full of questions. That's when she spotted the huge bouquet of flowers in the center of the living-room table, bursting with color.

"What is going on?" she asked with a girlish giggle in her voice.

"You are being served," Steven said. He waved his hand toward the dining area that was an extension of the living room closer to the window. "Please have a seat." He went to the rectangular cherrywood table that sat six, set down the tray and pulled out a chair for her.

She looked up at him as he placed a glass of champagne in front of her. "Whatever you have on your mind, I'm loving it so far."

"That's the plan." He winked then disappeared into the kitchen.

Mia thoughtfully sipped her champagne. What in the world had gotten into Steven? He was always sweet and willing to help out: cook, clean, whatever was needed. But this—even for Steven, this was taking it to the next level.

When she heard his footsteps approaching, she turned toward him and her mouth dropped open. He was rolling in their food cart, laden with piping-hot dishes of veal, linguini, shrimp marinara, hot buttered rolls and steamed vegetables that made her mouth water. Forget the fact that she'd just had a large Caesar salad and two drinks. Suddenly she was starving.

"Dinner is served," he said with a slight bow, bringing the cart to rest next to her. He lifted one of the plates from the tray and placed it in front of her.

She looked across at him as he took a seat opposite her, and her heart filled with love and lust for her man. "Steven…I'm speechless." Her eyes sparkled and her voice kept getting caught in her throat. "What…a beautiful surprise. I…don't know what to say."

"Don't say anything. Just enjoy." He smiled at her and she saw something in his eyes that she couldn't describe.

She nodded, her lips pressed tightly together to keep from crying.

He'd set the CD player to play all her favorites, from Luther to Kem, Barry White to the Dells, Marvin, Teddy, the Manhattans, some old-time Ella with a little Miles mixed in. Steven was the music aficionado. He could talk about music from every genre and era and not miss a beat, no pun intended. And if he was coaxed enough, he'd even play a little alto sax when they had their get-togethers. Truth be told, he didn't have to be coaxed hard at all.

And that's what he did tonight. Standing right in front of the window, with nothing on but those silk boxers and satin skin, he brought the sax to his lips and blew out a soulful tune that vibrated through her insides, made her want to weep with the purity of the sound, the sweetness of it as he serenaded her.

She wasn't sure how they made it into their bedroom, because the loving started from the moment she'd walked in the door, through dinner and a bubble bath that awaited her, to the satin sheets that they only used on "special occasions."

Steven toyed with and played with her body as expertly as he played the sax, with artistry and precision, awakening every nerve ending until her entire body vibrated and trembled with desire.

When he parted her thighs and tenderly drank of her essence, she knew heaven. The roar and rush of sensations that jettisoned through her made her head spin. Her body was no longer her own. It belonged to him. She knew that. And when he slowly, deliberately, inch by taunting inch, eased deep inside her, tears of exquisite joy seeped from her eyes as they moved to the rhythm that was uniquely their own.

Steven's heart and soul seemed to merge with Mia's. When he was inside her, he felt protected and safe, believing that nothing could ever compare to what he experienced and felt when he was with her.

Women had always been a part of his life, yet more of an afterthought than an integral piece. But Mia was different. Since they'd been together, his world revolved around her, revolved around making her happy. He knew he still had that hard edge, still had that part of him that he was leery of exposing and releasing— his gentle side—the side that his mother nurtured but was beaten back by his father.

But Mia had cracked that door open, pushed it ajar, and he could see possibility on the other side and it scared him with its intensity—the valley of the unknown. Yet he knew deep in his soul that if he dared to cross the threshold, Mia would be there waiting for him on the other side, willing to embrace him so that he would not fall. She'd lead him out of that dark place and into the light of her love.

He felt all those things, one on top of the other as he

moved within her and she held him, stroked his back, cried his name, wrapped him in her love.

And suddenly the words burst from his lips as the explosion fired in his belly.

"I love you," he groaned in agony and ecstasy. "I love you."

And when he said the words, the world seemed to open, but maybe it was his heart. The happiness that rushed through him made him dizzy and he shook violently with the force of verbal and physical release.

Mia held him, took him in, rocked him to greater heights and she cooed in his ear, "I know, baby, I know." And she did.

As they held each other, drifting in and out of the sleep of the totally satiated, Mia heard the distant chime of her cell phone. Whoever it was would have to wait until morning, she thought, drifting deeper into sleep. Her man loved her, and for now that was all that mattered.

Chapter 15

The following morning, after Steven had left for work, Mia busied herself cleaning up from the dinner of the night before, then settled down to her own morning ritual. She'd sent Steven off to work with a Kool-Aid smile on his face, as she'd decided that what was needed to get their morning off on the right foot was a little change of venue.

Before the sun came up, like two kids, they took the elevator of their six-story building up to the top floor and locked it. Then they totally reenacted the elevator scene from *Fatal Attraction*.

Giggling like two teens, they returned to their apartment, to the glaring stares of a couple who'd been waiting for the elevator.

Amused, she thought about that as she checked out Page Six, circled some interesting articles and dug in to her omelet. Just as she was about to take her second bite, she heard the distinctive sound of her cell phone and suddenly remembered the unanswered call from the night before.

She hopped up from her chair and hurried out into the hallway, where she'd left her purse. She dug out her phone. Her heart thumped when she saw Ashley's number come up on the caller ID.

"Hello?"

"Hi, did you get my message?"

"Actually, no. I haven't checked. What did you find out?"

"I think we need to talk in person. What time will you be in the office?"

"I should be there within the hour." Her chest tightened. "How bad is it?"

"Bad enough. Let's just say that by the looks of things, Michael Burke is in deep. I'll see you at the office."

A sick sensation ran through her, souring her stomach. A part of her hoped that all the bad signals that they were getting about Michael would be wrong. She sighed heavily, stared at her omelet, her paper and her gun.

She could no longer push the inevitable aside. She had a job to do, and if Michael got caught up in the net, then so be it.

"It appears that this Michelle Dennis is on the payroll. She may be moonlighting at the bar but she definitely has another sideline," Ashley was saying. "We got to talking while I nursed my drink. I told her that I sure could use some extra income and had been trying to find something. She told me if I was really interested and was willing to be friendly with some really wealthy men from time to time, she might be able to set something up for me."

The more Ashley talked about her meeting with Michelle, the sicker Mia felt.

"I asked her what she meant by *friendly.* She was quick to tell me that you never had to do anything you didn't want to. Mostly it was to be dates for businessmen, make them feel good and important, be seen with them at functions, things like that. And it paid very well. Now it was up to each girl what they were willing to do beyond that.

"Anyway, she gave me a number and told me to give this guy a call. The guy is Michael."

Whatever hope Mia had that this was all some ugly mistake, some strange mixup, was now gone. She nodded solemnly.

"Okay," Mia said on a breath. "Now we know. The next step is to get the goods on him and everyone he works with, and turn it over to Jean."

"Exactly. But I think we're going to need some help. Michael has already met me. No way can I turn up as a potential escort to get behind the scenes."

That much was true. Mia thought about it for a minute. Now that both Savannah and Danielle knew about Michael and were both part of the Cartel, she might be able to call on them for assistance. Especially since Michael had never met either one of them.

"First things first. We have the red-carpet event for Raven. That will be a perfect opportunity to check out everything up close," Mia said.

"Do you really think that he would risk something like that at a major event?"

"I know Michael. The challenge of pulling it off would be enough to make him do it. With the list of who's who in attendance, I can pretty much guarantee that some of his ladies will be there."

"Okay. We start there. Of course, I can't chance being at the party now. If Michelle shows up, we'll have a problem."

That reality struck Mia and momentarily dimmed the light in her eyes.

"As a matter of fact, now that I'm thinking about it, I know she will be there. While we were talking, she mentioned a major event coming up—something to do with some new singer, was the way she put it. She intimated that Michael might be willing to use some extra help."

Mia was thoughtful for a moment. "We'll find a way to work it out. We're not superspies for nothing."

Ashley grinned.

For the next few days it was a constant whirlwind of activity for MT Management. Putting in place all the intricate pieces for hosting this major blowout event took up all their time and energy, not to mention the other clients they had as well.

While Mia tried to stay focused on the red-carpet event, Ashley worked on the boutique grand opening. They barely had enough time to talk to each other in the office, between the phone calls, meetings and endless errands that they had to run in addition to dealing with the long list of vendors for each of the events.

Mia was seriously considering hiring a new assistant because the long hours were really beginning to take a toll. But as Steven had told her over lunch several weeks earlier, the last thing you want to do is hire someone only to find out in six months that you have to let her go. Perhaps she could advertise for a temporary position or just use one of the agencies. At least a temp could take calls and even do some of the running around.

She thought about it as she looked at her computer screen, which displayed the layout of the venue. With her luck she'd probably wind up hiring yet another Cartel member. She chuckled at the thought.

"It's always good to see you laughing."

She jerked up in her seat. Her eyes went to the door.

"Michael. What are you doing here?"

He stepped fully into the office and Mia silently cursed the fact that she didn't have that third hand. Ashley was with the two sisters going over the menu for their opening, which left her alone in the office.

"No one was out front, so I wandered in."

"Wandered in from where? Your office is on the other side of town."

He grinned. "I know, but I suddenly got this overwhelming urge to see you and I couldn't seem to stop myself."

She swallowed over the sudden dry knot in her throat. The sultry, manly scent of him drifted to her nose, short-circuiting her thoughts.

"That's really nice, but I'm so busy."

He came around behind her. She could feel the heat of his body. She held her breath.

He reached over her shoulder and pointed to the screen. "Is that the venue for Raven's event?"

"Yes." Her voice shook. She wanted to get up, but he had her trapped in her chair.

"Michael…I'm really busy…"

His hand drifted down, first resting on her shoulder. Her heart was hammering so hard she could barely breathe. His fingers grazed the top of her right breast and she gasped.

"Don't you remember how it was? Just let me touch you, Mia," he crooned in that tone that always made her do things she shouldn't. "I can make you remember." He cupped her breast in his palm and moved it in a slow circle. She saw stars an instant before reality struck.

She pushed back in her chair with all the force she could summon, making him stumble backward. She leaped up from her seat and whirled toward him. With her back to the desk, she gripped the edge to keep herself from falling as her knees had turned to jelly.

His eyes were dark, hungry and filled with lusty need. Her chest rose up and down in rapid succession as she tried to breathe to clear her head.

"I want you," he groaned. "I want you so badly that I ache every minute of the day. Can't you understand that?" In an instant he was right upon her and with nothing but air to separate them he pressed his body up against hers and she felt his need grind into her.

Oh, God, she remembered.

He snaked his arm around her waist and pinned her to him.

"Feel that?" he said against her neck.

Her thoughts were turning like a merry-go-round. Her body was on fire.

Michael reached for the hem of her skirt and pushed it up toward her hips.

"I love you." But it wasn't Michael's voice that she heard. It was Steven's.

His large hand went under her skirt. Reality slammed against her. She grabbed his wrists with all her strength.

"Don't do this, Michael. Don't!"

The front door opened. Michael moved back, looking toward Mia's partially opened office door. Mia pushed down her skirt just as Ashley's voice called out that she was back.

"I need you to leave. Please."

"I'm…I'm sorry. I know I shouldn't have done that." He reached out to her. "I'm sorry."

She pushed his hand away. "Please…"

Ashley tapped on the door and stepped in. All at once she took in the torrid scene. To the untrained eye it would appear harmless enough; Mia leaning slightly against the edge of her desk with Michael looking handsome and oh-so-casual. But beneath the surface the air was hot, the heat of sexual tension so high that it could suffocate you. And if you looked very close, you could see the tiny line of perspiration that ran across Michael's hairline, Mia's quicker-than-normal breathing and a look that almost resembled panic in her eyes.

Ashley's eyes bounced from one to the other. She came fully into the room. "Good to see you again, Michael. Is everything okay?" She looked to Mia. "With the plans," she qualified.

Mia glanced away for a second. "Yep, Michael was just leaving, actually."

"You ladies are doing a fantastic job. I know it's going to be a great event." He started to move from behind Mia's desk. "She was just showing me the layout of the venue on the computer." He grinned. "Damn computer programs can do just about anything." He headed for the door then stopped, slapped his palm against his forehead. "I almost forgot why I stopped by." He reached into the breast pocket of his jacket and pulled out an envelope with the Avante Enterprises logo on the front. He handed it to Mia. "That's the other portion of your payment. And as we agreed, if it is as successful as I know it's going to be, there'll be a fifteen percent bonus on the total cost." He pulled the door open, stepping past Ashley. "Have a great day, and see you both on Friday." He walked out.

Mia slowly eased herself into her chair.

"Mia, what's going on? What did I almost walk in on?"

"Nothing," she managed to say.

"It didn't look like nothing and it's hot as a sauna in here. Did he try something?"

"No," she lied, because if she admitted the truth, she'd have to admit that she almost let him and she couldn't admit that. She wouldn't. "Nothing more than his usual, let's-get-back-together talk." She forced a smile. "It's fine. Really. How did everything go with the sisters?"

Ashley looked at her and decided to let it go. Mia was a grown woman. Hopefully, she knew what she was doing. But one thing was certain: Ashley was not going to stand by and let Mia screw up this assignment over a man she very well may still have the hots for, a man who was their prime target. Not on her watch.

Michael returned to his office. What he needed was a cold shower. What had he been thinking? That's just it. He hadn't been thinking, at least not with the head on top of his shoulders. He'd been totally blinded by lust. That wasn't like him. But Mia had that effect on him—she always did. And the years that they'd been apart had not dampened his need for her. If anything, it had intensified. He had to get himself under control before he really blew it. If there was any chance of them getting back together again, what almost happened in her office wasn't the way to make it happen.

His stomach twisted with regret when he remembered the look of fear in her eyes. He would never hurt her. He prayed that she understood that. Somehow he'd find a way to make it up to her.

He continued down the corridor to his office and walked inside. Before he had a chance to get settled, there was a knock on his door.

"Come in." He took off his jacket and tossed it on the back of his chair. He looked up. It was Brenda.

"Hi," she said tentatively. "Can we talk for a minute?"

"Sure. Come in and close the door." He sat down.

Brenda came in and sat opposite him. "I, um, I just want to tell you that I was wrong for flipping out on you the other day. From the beginning you never lied to me about what this relationship was. You never led me on or tried to make me believe that it was more than what it actually was. That's all on me."

"Brenda…look, you don't have to—"

She cut him off. "Please…let me finish before I lose my nerve," she said with a shaky laugh. "I know how I feel about you, Michael, and I accept the fact that you don't feel the same way about me." She lowered her gaze then looked directly at him. "I wish things were different, but they aren't." She drew in a long breath. "So I'm going to back off. If you want to be with someone else, I understand. I won't stand in your way. But if you ever change your mind or things don't work out… well, you have my number." She stood.

For the first time Michael saw Brenda, really saw her for the strong, intelligent, pretty woman that she was. She'd been there for him when he didn't know if he was coming or going. She'd helped run his business when he'd lost all interest. She'd listened to him, she'd counseled him. She loved him purely. And somewhere beneath all the rubble of his emotions, he knew that he truly cared for her. True, not in the way that she wanted and certainly not in the way he felt about Mia. But he cared for her. And the sad part was he'd been so absorbed in himself and his business and making deals and money that he'd never given her the chance to be all that she could be in his life. He'd taken her presence and her body for granted, as if it were some kind of entitlement of his rather than a gift.

Brenda turned to leave and her always proud shoulders were slightly bent, as if she'd been defeated by some unseen force.

"Brenda, wait."

She turned to him. He smiled softly. "How about dinner tonight? It's been a while. We could leave early and go to my place out on the Harbor. What do you say?"

She hesitated. Thought about the implications, what she really wanted and what she knew she could get. She loved him so deeply and so strongly that she'd been willing to settle for whatever he was giving. What kind of half life was that? She deserved more. She was a good woman and she deserved a man who loved her as much as she loved him. And until Michael purged his soul of that woman who'd bewitched him, he could never be that man for her.

"I don't think so, Mike. But thank you for asking." She opened the door, stepped out and closed it softly behind her.

"I've been thinking about hiring a temp for the office," Mia was saying as she and Ashley finally found time to scarf down a salad and some diet soda. "I was looking at our calendar for the next four months and I truly cannot see how we are going to be able to manage without some help."

"I'd been thinking the same thing. And with the shaky economy, temp is definitely the way to go."

"Would you mind checking with a few of the agencies and see if they can send some potential candidates over?"

"Sure. Not a problem. I'll take care of it right after lunch. Listen, have you thought any more about what you want me to do about this Michelle chick and the phone call that I have yet to make to Michael?"

Mia took a swallow of her soda. "Yes, and I've tossed ideas around in my head. I was thinking that we're going to have to bring in some help. You can't be on scene Friday night. I'm going to ask Savannah and Danielle to step in."

"Makes sense. Have you talked with them yet?"

She thought about the confession she'd made to her two best friends the night before. A soft smile framed her mouth. "Yes. And I told them everything…finally," she admitted.

Ashley nodded. "Good. They should know. They're your friends. How did they take it?"

"Much better than I could have ever imagined. They were totally in my corner, as they've always been. I do have to ask them if they're free Friday night," she said, laughing lightly.

"I'm sure they will be." Ashley got up from the small circular conference table in Mia's office and collected the remnants of their lunch. "I'll start making those calls to the temp agencies. If we're lucky, maybe we can get someone before the end of the week."

Ashley turned to walk out just as the front door to the office opened. Both she and Mia's brows rose in unison.

Chapter 16

"Brenda," Ashley said before looking over her shoulder to Mia. "What can we do for you?"

Today was definitely the day for uninvited guests, Mia thought in a rush. She stood up and came toward the door.

"Actually, I came to see Ms. Turner." She looked past Ashley at Mia's approach. "I know I should have called first but I took a chance that you would be here. Do you have a few minutes?"

"Of course. Come in."

"I'll, uh, start making those calls," Ashley said before closing Mia's door.

"Please, sit. What can I help you with? If this is about the event on Friday, everything is taken care of."

"No, it's not the event. As Michael said, he only hires the best, so I'm sure everything is fine." She slipped out of her lightweight coat and draped it across her lap as she sat down. "It's about Michael."

Oh, damn. What now? "Michael?"

"Yes." She paused. "I'm not sure how to even go about this. This is so out of character for me."

Mia waited. Was this going to be one of those *Jerry Springer* episodes?

"I know that Michael is in love with you."

Mia flinched inside.

"And I'm in love with him." She sputtered a laugh. "Unfortunately, he doesn't feel the same way. But I know he cares about me. At least as much as he can." She studied her folded hands then stared Mia straight in the eye. Her expression suddenly hardened. "I know things—things that could ruin him."

Mia's heart started to kick up a notch. Aw, damn, this was the woman-scorned episode.

"I know who you are and what you do."

Mia laughed nervously. "Of course you do."

"That's not what I mean." She reached into her purse and took out a tiny black disk. She placed it solidly down on the table.

Mia nearly had a heart attack. It was the listening device that she'd planted in Michael's office.

"Look familiar?"

Mia frowned, going for her Oscar for best actress. "Haven't got a clue. It looks like a black quarter or something. What is it and why should I care?"

"I've used them before. Plenty of times. It may have been dark in the room while you and Ashley were doing your song-and-dance routine the other day, but I was watching you. I saw you when you placed it under the table. I went back to check after you left. I recognized it right away. I should have dumped it, but I didn't want you getting suspicious about what happened to it. But I thought for the purposes of this meeting I should bring it so that you'd know I wasn't bluffing."

Yep, she was going to have a heart attack. Right this minute and then this nightmare would be over.

"I have no idea what you're talking about."

"Let's not play games, okay? I was a member about eight years ago."

"Member?" she echoed.

"Yes, of the Cartel. I was based in Chicago until I moved here and wanted to get out of the business. That's when I met Michael. Jean Wallington-Armstrong sound familiar?"

This was a test. Jean was obviously up to her tricks again.

"No, it doesn't. And to be honest, I'm really busy, as you know, so please get to the point of your impromptu visit so that I can get back to work."

Brenda dug in her purse again; this time she took out her cell phone. She dialed a number. "Yes, 258643," she said to whomever answered. She kept her gaze on Mia. Moments passed. "Hello, Jean, it's Traci."

Traci?

"I knew if I used my old code all the red flags would go up and it would get you on the line. I'm here with Mia. I think I have information that you can use." She listened before passing the phone back to Mia.

"Hello?"

"Listen to me carefully. Just agree with everything I'm saying."

"Sure, of course."

"I'm going to send Bernard over there right now.

Keep her talking. Bernard will bring her in. I'm going to send an alert to Ashley immediately so that she will know what's going on. Subdue her if she tries to leave."

"Great. I understand. Thank you. Yes, I'll check in later." She swallowed and handed the phone back over to Brenda. Mia forced a crooked smile. "Guess you're the real deal. Seems to be raining secret agents lately," she said, more to herself than Brenda or Traci—whatever her name was. "So what is it that you know that you think I should?"

"First of all, I'm not crazy. That's what Jean is going to try to convince you of. I left the Cartel because I couldn't deal with the double life, the havoc that it was wreaking on everything I did. I spent all my time lying to my friends, and in my relationships. I couldn't take it anymore. The thrill, the excitement was gone. I went to Jean and I told her. She tried to make me stay. Said I was the best operative she'd seen in years, but I told her I couldn't do it anymore, I needed a life—a real life." She paused. "So she essentially erased me from existence. Any association that I had with the Cartel was deleted, all traces of my connection to them were removed. You could get the best computer hackers in the world and they'd never be able to find a shred of information on my being part of the Cartel."

Mia got a sudden chill.

"She made me disappear." She glanced away for a moment. "Once I knew that I was finally free, I left Chicago and came here to New York. I got a job with Michael's company as Brenda Forde. Traci Bennett was gone, buried. Until now."

"I can't believe that Jean didn't know you were here, that you worked for Michael."

Brenda smiled smugly. "As I told you in the beginning, even Jean had to admit that I was the best. I wanted to cover my tracks, and I did. She had no idea who I was."

So Jean wasn't infallible after all, Mia thought. She didn't have a sixth sense, at least not in this case. "You still haven't told me what you came here to say."

"Michael has another business, a very secret but lucrative one. He has no idea that I know about it. But simply because I'm no longer a card-carrying member of the Cartel doesn't mean that I've lost my skills." She stared at Mia. "I'm sure you've met Jasmine in operations."

Jasmine was the computer whiz.

"Yes, of course."

"I trained her."

If there was any truth to Brenda/Traci's story, she was definitely a force to be reckoned with. Jasmine could do things with a computer that most geniuses never even dreamed of. So if Jasmine had been taught by the woman in front of Mia, then Brenda/Traci's skills were phenomenal.

"Now I am impressed. *If* what you're saying is true."

"You don't have to believe me. I know what I'm capable of and I'm pretty sure that once you and Jean have that little chat she will verify everything that I've said. Now back to Michael. He's running an elite escort service. He's raking in millions a year."

Mia felt a wave of nausea surge up to her throat.

"His list of clients could cripple the city if their names were ever exposed. It includes everyone from politicians to Fortune 500 executives and bank presidents, and not only here but out-of-state as well."

"How do you know this?"

"I know because I've been to the parties. I've seen the women. It's all very discreet, mind you. Unless you were really looking, you would never know. I didn't for a while. But then I started seeing some of the same women's faces with different men at different private events. I've never said a word to him about it. He has no idea that I know. But once I became suspicious, I tapped into his computer. I found the file."

It was probably the same file that she'd found, Mia thought.

Mia's door opened.

Brenda twisted in her seat. Before she could react, Bernard had a handkerchief over her mouth and she crumbled in her seat.

"I'll take it from here. Jean wants to see both of you within the hour."

He picked Brenda up, braced her against him and put his arm around her waist to keep her on her feet. "Hand me her coat and purse."

Mia numbly did as she was instructed.

He half dragged, half walked her out. Mia rushed to the front of the office and saw the black Ford Explorer parked at the curb. If she didn't know better, she'd swear that was Claudia, Savannah's mother, on the other side of the tinted windows behind the wheel.

Bernard settled Brenda into the backseat, got in beside her, and the SUV pulled off.

It was a scene right out of a James Bond movie.

Mia pressed her hand to her chest. She needed a drink.

"You want to bring me up to speed?" Ashley asked, snapping Mia out of her trance.

Mia blinked, bringing Ashley into focus. For a moment, Mia was disoriented—nothing made any sense. But in the next minute she was pissed. What the hell was going on? First Ashley was right under her nose and now Brenda. She suddenly didn't know what was real and what wasn't. And the in-her-mind relationship with Michael was a perfect example of how she was no longer able to separate fact from fiction.

She turned on Ashley. "Is Ashley even your real name?" she railed. "What other secrets do you have that I should know about? Are you really here to spy on me, make me crazy? What did Jean do to her to make her want to have a whole other life? My God, what have I gotten myself into?"

Burning tears of anger and frustration filled her eyes and spilled over her eyelids.

Ashley stepped toward her gingerly. She put her hands on Mia's stiff shoulders. "Mia, calm down. Okay? I know all this seems too much right now, but it's going to be all right. I promise."

Mia slapped her hands away. "Just leave me alone." She held up her hands. "Leave me alone!"

Ashley took a step back. "Fine. Let me know when you're ready to see Jean. I'll be out front."

Mia spun away. On wooden legs she went to the love seat in the corner and collapsed into it. She pressed her head against the back of the couch and wept. What she needed right at that moment were the strong arms of her man wrapped tightly around her, telling her that it was going to be all right. But if she knew nothing else, she knew that, at best, that little desire was hours from fruition.

* * *

They took Ashley's Infiniti for the drive uptown to Harlem. The first few minutes of the ride were done in silence. The only sounds were the intermittent street noises.

Finally, Mia spoke. "I'm sorry for going off on you earlier. There was no excuse for taking my frustration out on you." She turned halfway in her seat. "I apologize. Really."

"No problem. If anyone understands how this whole thing can get to you, I do. So forget the apology. Chalk it up to stress."

Mia faced forward. "Will you be honest with me?"

"Sure."

"Did you know Brenda or Traci?"

Ashley shook her head. "No. She was gone before I came along. I'd heard about one of the members leaving, but it was always very hush-hush. No one would talk about it."

"Hmm." She was thoughtful for a moment then frowned. "How come your picture isn't up on the hall of fame?"

Ashley laughed. "It is. It's not in the main corridor to Jean's office. It's on the top floor. Most newbies don't have access. In addition to which, when Jean assigned me to you, she intentionally moved it. Even if you had seen it you probably wouldn't have recognized me without my Angela Davis fro." She patted her halo of naturally spiral curls.

Mia chuckled. "I can't imagine you without it."

"There was a time," she singsonged.

"What about Brenda?"

"As I said, I'd never met her before. My guess is that

once she'd left the agency—and not under the best of
circumstances and with Jean literally erasing her out of
existence—Jean would have taken the picture down."

"You're probably right. Does Jean scare you?"

"Scare me? What do you mean?"

"It's like sometimes she doesn't have a soul and everyone is expendable in her life. It's all about the job,
at any cost."

"For her, it is. She's really not as coldhearted as you
think. Jean…Jean has had a real rough time of it in relationships and in the career path that she chose. She
was screwed over in the CIA by people less qualified
than her and badly hurt by her husband."

"Husband? I didn't know she was married."

"She isn't now, but she was. What happened between them changed her a lot. She only refers to him as
Mr. Armstrong. Look, I really shouldn't be telling you
this. Maybe one day she'll tell you all about it. Maybe
she won't. All I can say is that beneath that cold, hard-
ass exterior is a real decent human being. Even if she
does act like a machine," she tossed in with a smile.

"I'll try to keep that in mind."

"Let me put it this way. She changed my life when
it desperately needed changing, and I will always be
grateful to her for that."

"Changed your life? How?"

She turned her head to look at Mia. "I was at the
bottom of the food chain, strung out, living on the
street…she rescued me, gave me a life. But that's another story for another day."

Mia rested back against the leather seat. The last
person on earth she thought had a caring bone in her
body was Jean Wallington-Armstrong. This little bit

of information forced her to look at Jean from a different perspective. There's always more to a person than meets the eye. No truer adage had even been written, especially when it came to the Ladies Cartel.

They pulled up in front of the brownstone.

Showtime.

Chapter 17

Claudia met Ashley and Mia at the front door when they rang the bell. Her expression was somber. "Jean is upstairs."

Mia and Ashley walked inside behind Claudia.

"Where's Brenda or Traci whatever her name is?" Mia asked.

"She's here. Jean will explain everything," Claudia replied.

After Mia and Ashley were seated, Jean didn't waste any time getting to the point.

"I'm sure you are both aware that there has been a serious breach in security." Her gaze darted in Brenda/Traci's direction, who only sat up straighter in her seat, as if challenging Jean in her own way.

"So that we are all on the same page," she began again. "Brenda Forde, known to me as Traci Bennett, was a former member of the Cartel who was decommissioned of her own accord five years ago. To my knowledge—" she cleared her throat "—Traci was off the radar and living her life, apparently much closer than I ever realized. For reasons that she has explained to me, she is willing to help us get as much inside information as necessary in the Avante Enterprises case. I'm sure that the both of you understand that because of the way she approached you we had no recourse but to take her in as quickly and as quietly as possible for questioning.

"To reassure you both, we are running a thorough check on her, using all our resources to guarantee that she will not be in a position to compromise us in any way. When the report is back, which I suspect will be shortly, I will give the clearance so that we can proceed as planned and whatever help Traci can offer will be accepted at that point."

"How can you be sure that this isn't some kind of setup to infiltrate the Cartel?" Ashley asked.

"I can't. At least not right now, which is why she was drugged and blindfolded before she was brought here." She stole another look at Traci. "She has no idea where she is."

Mia was certain this was some weird out-of-body experience. The whole scene was surreal. Right down to the characters, the dimly lit room and the manipulating head of operations moving people around like a grand puppeteer. At that moment, she wanted to jump up and run the hell out as fast and as far as she could. She wanted to have the nerve that Traci did and get out before she got dragged down so far that there was no way out. But who was to say that she wouldn't wind up just like Traci, right back in the place she was trying to get away from?

A knock on the door drew everyone's attention. Jasmine stepped inside. She spotted Traci sitting off to the side and there was the flash of recognition, followed by a look of admiration that quickly passed. "I have that report." She handed over a manila folder to Jean. "I sifted through all the intel and took out the extraneous information. Only the relevant data is included."

Jean snapped her gaze up from the papers in front of her. "The next time that I ask you to compile data on a potential rogue I want all the data! Not only what you think is important. *I* make those decisions. Understood?"

The entire room froze in shocked disbelief. Jean never lost her cool, and certainly never lost her temper. But it was clear that this mini-explosion was an indication that she was rattled.

Jasmine visibly recoiled from the verbal assault. "Yes. Of course. I'll recompile the data." She turned to leave, keeping her gaze focused on her Reeboks.

"Jasmine."

She stopped with her hand on the knob and turned halfway. "Yes?"

Jean lifted her chin ever so slightly. "That won't be necessary," she said in what must be her apologetic tone. "I'm sure this will be sufficient. I can look at everything at a later time. If I think I need more, I'll let you know."

Jasmine only nodded and walked out, closing the door quietly behind her.

Jean took a seat behind her desk, slipped on her red-frame glasses, flipped open the folder and began to read. You could hear a pin drop in the room, the rhythm of heartbeats, the turn of a page. For a solid fifteen minutes, no one dared to move or breathe out loud. Finally she closed the folder, removed her glasses and turned to Traci. "It appears that everything you've said regarding your whereabouts, your activities since leaving the Cartel checks out."

Traci's features, which had remained taut through-out this ordeal, slowly began to relax. She gave Jean a barely there nod of her head.

"Although Traci will not be given full access to or privileges of the Cartel, she says that she is willing to help us bring down Avante Enterprises and Michael Burke. As you know, Avante is a front for an illegal escort service. We have names and amounts, but what we don't have is irrefutable proof. We don't have trans-actions taking place, photographs, audio or locations. This is where Traci can be of assistance."

"I know Michael," Traci began, "and, more impor-tantly, I know how the legitimate end of the business works. I have access to the files, the computers and all the people Michael knows and associates with." She zeroed in on Mia. "The red-carpet event that you're running on Friday for Raven…I know that many of the women will be there. I can point them out."

"I'd like to bring in Danielle," Mia said.

"Explain," Jean said curtly.

"We can use the extra hands, especially when it comes to perhaps photographing the attendees, over-hearing conversations."

Jean was thoughtful for a moment. "Fine, bring her in." Jean exhaled. She looked from one to the other. "Anything else that you can think of?"

"No."

"We'll talk again the morning of the red carpet to ensure that everyone is in place and you have what you need, Mia."

Mia nodded.

Ashley stood up and Mia followed suit. They took one last look at Traci and walked out. Bernard was right behind them.

"I still don't know if I can trust you," Jean said, once they were alone. She turned to face Traci. "You left once before, nearly ruining a case as a result. How do I know that you won't suddenly have a change of heart for this man you claim to have fallen for and just tell him everything?"

"I wouldn't do anything to risk exposing the Cartel or an operation. You know that."

"It seems that lately I don't know much of anything anymore. I thought I did." Her tone sounded uncharacteristically weak, sad almost, as if for the very first time she was faced with the knowledge of her own vulnerability. "But until I can be sure about you and your real motives, I want you to stay in the background and if you can't, I'm sure you know that I can make that happen."

"There's no reason to threaten me, Jean. I'm not here to hurt you or the organization. I want to see Michael brought down."

"Because you're a woman scorned or because you really believe what he's doing is wrong?" she taunted.

Traci's jaw clenched. "Maybe a little of both."

"But why come back now?"

She glanced away. "I've known that Michael didn't

love me, but I thought he at least cared for and respected me. When I stumbled across those files, everything that I thought about him began to crumble. I didn't want to believe it. I wanted to be wrong. And then Mia shows up and I can see in an instant where his heart is and has always been. I guess something inside me snapped and when I found the listening device and knew the source, whatever kind of fleeting hope or desire I may have had regarding me and Michael vanished. I realized that what I'd found had merit and it wasn't my imagination because the Cartel was already investigating him."

"You disappointed me, Traci," she said, her voice leaden with regret. "You were the best. You were more than a Cartel member, you were like my own child." She turned sad eyes on Traci, eyes begging to understand what she'd done that had prompted Traci to run away.

"I guess I can tell you now."

"Tell me what now?"

"The truth about why I really left the Cartel when I was in Chicago. I can finally tell you about that scumbag you married," she said, her voice hard with emotion.

"What! What the hell are you talking about?"

"Your husband tried to sleep with me. Not once, not twice, but every chance he got, which was many, since I was always at your home."

Jean's face blanched. "W-what are you saying?"

"Yes, Eric Armstrong. He went so far as to blackmail me into sleeping with him."

Jean flinched. "Why are you lying? He wouldn't do that!"

"Of course he would. Eric was as manipulative as you are. It's why you both got along up to a point. But Eric was manipulative for his own greedy reasons." She crossed the room then walked back, talking as she did. "To this day I don't know how he did it. He had an audiotape of my voice—calling him, telling him…things. Talking about how great it was between us, what I wanted him to do to me the next time we were together." She rubbed her hands up and down her arms as if she'd suddenly gotten a chill. She stopped walking and turned to look straight at Jean. "He told me that he was going to give you the tapes if I didn't sleep with him. I couldn't let him do that." She shook her head, her gaze looking back to that ugly time in her past. "You were so in love with him. Happy for the first time since I'd known you. I mean, really happy. I knew if he gave those to you, it would kill you inside, ruin our relationship. I couldn't let him do it. So I left. I left the Cartel and my whole life so that I wouldn't ruin yours."

Jean's face was so pale it became translucent. She didn't move. She didn't speak. Slowly she lowered herself into her chair. With what appeared to be almost painful understanding, she leveled her gaze on Traci.

"Giving you this information and helping is my way of making up for walking out on you and not telling you what kind of bastard you were married to." She pressed her fist to her mouth then moved it away, drawing in air through her mouth. "When I found out what Michael was doing, it brought it all back—women being used—even if they are getting paid."

"I…think I always knew," Jean said, her words barely above a whisper. "I knew he saw other women, but I turned a blind eye because I loved him." Her throat worked up and down. She blinked several times. "But never this. Not what he tried to do to you. I'm so sorry, Traci." She slowly shook her head, her eyes pleading for forgiveness.

They moved simultaneously toward each other and embraced, erasing all the years that had separated them.

Chapter 18

Mia and Ashley left Bernard at the brownstone and started back to the office.

"So what do you make of everything that happened back there?" Mia asked as they pulled out into the late-afternoon Manhattan traffic.

"I think the thing that freaks me out the most is to realize that Jean is not infallible. That she really doesn't know everything and that there was actually someone out there who had outsmarted her—for years. That scares me because Jean scares me. But Traci is the real deal."

Mia nodded in agreement. "I know exactly what you mean. Not to see Jean in total control was a reality check, to say the least."

"So it looks like we're going to be working with Traci. How do you feel about that?"

"You mean because of her relationship with Michael?"

"Yeah."

"Hmm. I don't feel anything one way or the other. Whatever illusions I may have had about Michael have been crushed. To be truthful, I feel bad for Traci. Michael is a charismatic man. His aura can overwhelm you and before you know it you're totally mesmerized by him, doing things you never would have thought you would do. And when your heart and emotions are all tied up in it, it's that much more devastating. But from what I've seen so far, Traci is a strong woman. She'll be fine."

"Damn, I was looking forward to the catfight!"

Mia poked her in the arm and they both laughed.

"We still need to figure out what we're going to do with my Michelle connection," Ashley was saying as they left the car and walked into the office.

"That's where I think Danielle can play a role."

"How?"

Mia opened her office door; the soft winter white and creams instantly soothed her. Ashley came behind her.

"I'm thinking that since you obviously cannot be at the event on Friday, in case Michelle is there and recognizes you, Danielle could be a potential candidate."

Ashley frowned. "Color me slow. I'm not getting you."

Mia grinned. "Sorry, it's in my head and not making it out of my mouth." She leaned against the edge of her desk and folded her arms. "I want you to contact Michelle. Tell her that you have a friend who would be interested in her offer. You want to bring her by the bar to meet her and see what she thinks. That someone is going to be Danielle. We need her on-site on Friday, and that will be the perfect way to do it. Michael has never met her. There would be no reason for him to suspect anything."

A slow smile of understanding moved across Ashley's mouth. "Gotcha."

"I'll call Danielle and bring her up to speed. You get in touch with Michelle."

"I'm on it." Ashley walked out and went up front.

Mia went behind her desk and sat down. Maybe this whole mess would come together after all. She dug in her bag and pulled out her cell. The glitches and surprises were seriously attacking her orderly state of mind. She dialed Danielle.

"Hey, Dani, got a minute?"

"Just barely. I'm in the middle of a photo shoot. What's up?"

"I'm going to need your help to pull this assignment off."

"What do you need me to do? Something exciting, I hope."

Mia chuckled. "Let's just say you'll have to get dressed up and be fabulous."

"Right up my alley. Sounds easy."

"Well, it's a bit more complicated than that. I'm going to need you to be available to go with Ashley to meet Michelle at the bar. You're going to apply for one of the 'extra income' positions."

"Ohh," she said, understanding dawning. "When?"

"Ashley is trying to contact Michelle now. As soon as she can set up a time, I'll let you know. Obviously, it needs to be sooner rather than later."

"No problem. I'll work it out. Look, I gotta run. Call me."

"Thanks, sis."

"Of course. Later."

With that done, she pulled out her PDA, connected it to her computer and put on her headset. She set her computer and PDA to the communications program that was continuously recording Michael's phone calls at his office and home in Sag Harbor. Although she had access to both locations at any given time, the past few days and the information that she'd uncovered had been more than she had been prepared to handle. Hearing anything more incriminating moved down on her agenda. However, she was supposed to report her findings to Jean and the last thing she wanted Jean to think was that she was slacking off in her role because of residual feelings that she may still have for Michael.

The radio frequency grid came up on her screen in two panels—one attached to his office, the other to his home. At the moment, both were flat, meaning that he wasn't on either phone. She clicked on the Archives link to recover anything recorded in the past five days when she noticed the flat green iridescent line in the second panel on her computer screen. He was on his office phone. She adjusted her headset and pushed up the volume.

"It's Mike. I need to make some transfers from here to the Caymans."

"When?"

"Today. You have all the information."

"Today?"

"I think this game has run its course. I want to protect what I've gained so far. Then I'm getting out."

"Don't tell me anything you don't want me to know. That's our agreement."

"Fine. Just get it done, Andy. Okay. Call me when you have it taken care of."

"Do you want everything moved?"

"Everything."

"I'll call you tonight with the confirmation numbers."

"Thanks."

The call disconnected.

Slowly, Mia removed the headphones and set them down on the desk. She frowned in concentration. What was he doing? Of course, if he was talking about the Caymans, she knew it had to be a money transfer. He'd also mentioned getting out. Was he getting out of the escort business, taking the money and running?

Then that voice that was in the back of her head started talking to her. The voice that kept telling her that she still had feelings for Michael. The voice that would whisper to her and tell her that this was all some ugly mistake.

If he was given enough time and space, maybe he could get away before the law came swooping down on him. It was still hard for her to imagine that when this was all over, Michael would go to jail and she would be responsible for putting him there. It was a weight of guilt that she, deep down in her soul, didn't want to carry. Maybe if he just had some time, the voice whispered. No one has to know, it urged.

Mia jumped up from her seat, banishing the urgent whispers from her head. She needed to ground herself, clear those traitorous thoughts from her head. She reached for the phone on her desk and dialed Steven.

After being told that he was out of the office for the rest of the day, she felt bereft, and she knew herself. When she got in this unattached, disorganized space in her head, she began making mistakes and getting tense.

She drew in long, slow, deep breaths from her diaphragm and exhaled through her nose, as her tai chi instructor had told her years ago, when she'd taken up the relaxation art. It helped to soothe her, as it did now. After about ten minutes, she could feel her jangled nerves evening out, the racing of her heart beginning to slow and her thoughts starting to line back up. She opened her eyes. Everything was going to be fine. She was going to make this work. She checked her computer again to make sure that she'd saved the file she'd just listened to, then downloaded all the recordings to date on a flash drive ready to hand over to Jean at their next meeting.

With Cartel business out of the way, she turned her attention to running her business.

"Hey, Michelle, it's Ashley. Remember me?"

"Of course. How are you? Did you make that call like I told you?"

"Actually, no. And only because I know I'm going to be out of town for a while. But that's not the reason I called. I got the impression that you sort of have an in with that guy Michael. Well, I want to give a very good friend of mine an opportunity. She could definitely use the extra money. She's gorgeous and would look good on any man's arm. I was hoping that you might have some time to meet her, see what you think."

Michelle was silent for a moment. "How close is this friend to you? I mean, this is not something that you tell everyone you know. If you can't be discreet… Look, forget we ever had a conversation. This isn't cool."

"Wait, listen. This woman is cool. I've known her since high school. I didn't give her any details, other than she may have a chance to make some extra money just for looking good for a few hours. She was all for it. But that's all she knows. You meet her, feel her out. If it seems good to you, then make a decision then." Ashley held her breath. She couldn't blow this now.

"Can you be here at the club around seven tonight?"

"Not a problem."

"Okay. And listen. No more recruits. That's my job."

Ashley's brow rose. "See you at seven." She hung up the phone and breathed a sigh of relief, just as Mia approached.

"Did you make contact?"

"Just got off the phone with her." She explained what had happened and how they had almost lost that connection.

"Good thinking on your part," Mia said. "We definitely can't let her get suspicious or say anything to Michael."

"Exactly. Guess you should give Danielle a call and let her know about tonight. We need to figure out where to meet up."

"Here's her cell number. I spoke with her a while ago and gave her a heads-up. She's actually on location right now. Leave a message on her voice mail. Makes more sense for you to call with particulars than me."

"True." She took the number. "I'll call her in a little."

"Okay. I'm going to run over to check on the venue for tomorrow night. When I get back, we'll go over the final punch list. If you can touch base with the videographer and the lighting people to let them know we want to do a run-through tomorrow at 10:00 a.m., that would be great."

"I'm on it."

Mia returned to her office, grabbed her bag and tote then headed out.

Ashley had arranged to meet Danielle on Chelsea Piers at six-thirty to go over the strategy. They were best friends since high school. They both attended Boys & Girls High School in Bedford-Stuyvesant in Brooklyn, and now both of them worked for Mia's firm. Neither of them were married or currently involved. And they needed the extra income to get out of debt and breathe a little easier.

Once their stories were in sync, they headed over to the Last Call Bar & Grill.

As usual, Danielle was totally the fashion diva. Her naturally wavy hair fell in soft cascades around her face, over her shoulders and halfway down her back. She was a solid size 10, full and curvy, and she kept her body encased in only the best. Today she wore an M. Preston two-piece pantsuit in crimson, with bold bulky silver jewelry at her throat and wrist. A silky white camisole peeked out from the top of the jacket. And to complete the ensemble, she wore a pair of black alligator ankle boots.

When Ashley saw her, she was amazed at how stunning Danielle was. Of course, she'd seen her on several occasions at the TLC headquarters and was always impressed with her natural beauty. But she'd never really seen Danielle put it all together as she did now. No way could Michelle not be impressed.

"Do you go to work dressed like that?" Ashley asked as they approached the bar.

Danielle took off her dark shades as they stepped into the dim interior. "No, I ran home and changed. Didn't think I'd make a good impression with my sweaty T-shirt and jeans."

"There she is," Ashley said under her breath. "The one with the pink tank top."

They approached and took seats next to each other at the end of the bar. They had that end to themselves. Several moments passed before Michelle came over.

"How are you ladies doing this evening? What can I get you?"

"I'll take a coke with lemon," Ashley said.

"Same for me."

Michelle looked at Danielle for a long moment. "Be right back."

"I think she's trying to play it real cool," Ashley said. "When we met for the first time, she was Ms. Chatty Cathy."

Michelle returned with their sodas. "My boss is working the bar tonight," she said in a pseudo-whisper. "He'll be here for another hour. Can't really talk until then."

"No problem. We can wait," Ashley said. "What do you have on the menu?"

Michelle handed them a menu and they ordered a plate of buffalo wings with blue cheese and celery sticks.

"Coming right up. You can have a seat at one of the tables if you like. Or you can eat at the bar. Your choice."

Danielle turned to Ashley. "Table sounds good."

They took their drinks, got up and headed to an open table.

"Looks like it's going to be a long night."

Ashley pursed her lips as they sat down. "Unfortunately. But it will give us a chance to get to know each other. How did you get involved in the Cartel?"

"Through Savannah. I guess you probably know that her mom, Claudia, recruited her." She laughed lightly. "Well, Mia and I actually helped Savannah out on her first assignment. When she got her next assignment, she couldn't take it on, the pregnancy was kicking her butt. Oh, you have got to meet her baby girl, Mikayla. She will steal your heart and then the show." She smiled, thinking of her. "We're all her godmothers. Anyway, when Savannah couldn't take on the job, she asked Mia and me. Well, Mia was going to be out of town so I got the job. Almost blew it, but it all worked out."

"It usually does."

"Can I get you ladies anything to drink?" a waitress asked.

"No. I'm good," Ashley said, holding up her glass of soda.

"Me, too, thanks."

"Your order should be ready shortly."

"What about you? I mean, I thought I knew you, but obviously I didn't. Do you have anyone special in your life?" Danielle asked.

"No. Not at the moment. A long moment," Ashley added with a short laugh. "But I'm always hopeful. I'm sure there's someone out there who would be interested in a quirky, blues-loving, former homeless woman turned secret agent. I mean, after all, this is New York."

"You have a lot going for you. You'll find the right man at the right time. I never thought I'd actually settle down with one man until I met Nick. It was a struggle at first, but we worked through it. Both of us came into the relationship with a lot of emotional baggage. But the load is much lighter now."

The waitress appeared with their platter of buffalo wings and they dug in. They spent the next hour talking about everything from the upcoming presidential election to women's rights and the sagging pants on young boys. The more they talked, the more they realized all the things they had in common.

Danielle really liked Ashley and could see why Mia liked her so much.

They were engaged in a hot debate about Star Jones's miraculous weight loss when Michelle came up to their table. She took a seat next to Ashley.

"Sorry. Never can tell when the boss is going to show up." She looked around. The club was relatively empty. "I guess it's okay to talk here." She focused her attention on Danielle. "So your friend tells me that you're interested in making some extra money."

"Yes, I am. She also told me that you're the one who can make that happen."

The corner of Michelle's wide mouth quirked upward. "Something like that. But the final decision is not up to me. I can only make recommendations. So why don't you tell me something about yourself."

Danielle gave her the spiel that she and Ashley had gone over.

Michelle nodded as Danielle spoke. She looked at

Ashley once Danielle was finished speaking. "I think she might be okay. I like her." She leaned forward. "There's a major party coming up Friday night. Some blowout red-carpet event. I'll introduce you to Michael then. Are you available?"

Danielle casually flipped her hand. "Sounds perfect. I'll make myself available."

"That's what I like to hear." She wrote down the address for the party on a napkin, then pushed up from the table. "See you on Friday."

Ashley and Danielle walked toward their car.

"Looks like we're in," Ashley said, opening the door.

"Yes, indeedy."

Chapter 19

The stretch limos, luxury sedans and chauffeur-driven SUVs lined up along Park Avenue as one after another of the icons of the music industry, accompanied by their entourage, strutted onto the red carpet and into the grand foyer of the hotel.

Flashbulbs popped in rapid succession as every news outlet vied for the money shots of the glitterati who sparkled in the night like the diamonds that adorned their wrists, necks, ears and fingers.

Every time a new car pulled up in front of the venue, the media went wild, hoping to get a shot of the elusive Raven.

Reps from TMZ, BET J, Page Six, *Entertainment Tonight, Access Hollywood,* photographers from all the hip-hop magazines, and A&R execs from the major labels were in attendance, from Arista to J Records, Atlantic to Bad Boy and everything in between.

The dons and divas of hip-hop were also in attendance: Jigga and his new bride, Usher, Mary, Diddy, Alicia, John and even old-school royalty made their presence felt with Eddie Levert, Pattie and Gladys.

The walls had been covered in voluminous sheer draping with silver thread running through them. Lighting came from behind the draping, giving the impression that the event was floating on clouds. Waiters and waitresses in white and silver worked the crowd with trays of appetizers that included stuffed clams, grilled shrimp, caviar, an assortment of cheeses and sushi. Huge jumbo monitors hung from the ceiling, displaying videos of Raven in concert, rare interviews and other footage. An eight-piece band played underneath the rumble of soft and deep voices and squeals of delight.

Mia was so thrilled with the turnout and the presentation of the venue space that she was almost nervous. She checked and rechecked every element of the evening so many times that the staff began to give her dirty looks.

Savannah took her by the arm the tenth time she flew by.

"Mia, you have got to relax, girl. You're going to break a vessel or something. Everything is perfect." She squeezed her hand. "Seriously. And if you took a breath, you'd realize it yourself."

"Oh, am I really that bad? I'm just doing my job. My company's reputation is on the line. Not to mention—" she lowered her voice "—the other thing we have going on. Have you seen Danielle yet?"

"No. But as we planned, she will be coming with Michelle."

Mia drew in a breath. "Right. Right." She squinted around the room. There had to be more than two hundred guests. She'd hired some temps to help with the check-in, and security was tighter than the Pentagon.

"Fabulous job," a woman singsonged as she passed Mia and Savannah.

"See? Told you."

Mia chuckled. "Okay, okay. Blake has the baby?"

"Yep. It's a father-daughter night. I told him to give Steve a call to come and keep him company. So they will be occupied for the evening."

"Thanks, sweetie. Oh, there are Michelle and Danielle."

"Gotta act like we don't know them."

Danielle caught Savannah's and Mia's eyes and casually indicated the square-shaped catch on her purse by tapping it as they moved through the crowd into the main ballroom.

Mia nodded in acknowledgment. She turned to Savannah. "Let me go mingle and make sure everything is running smoothly. Traci is hand-holding Michael, and Ashley insisted on being part of the operation. She's out there on the street somewhere, posing as media."

"That'll work. We're going to need all the photos we can get. Is she going to be able to come inside?"

"I thought it was too risky. On the off chance that Michelle might recognize her—or Michael, for that matter. But she said she could pull it off. And with a crowd this size, it should be fine. But keep your eyes and ears open. I'll check back with you later." She headed over to Brenda/Traci and Michael.

"Hi. So what do you think so far?" Mia asked, her eyes flitting around the room as she tried to keep it all in focus. She wished she could put her glasses on, but vanity prevailed.

"Looks like you've outdone yourself, Mia," Michael said. "The spread is fantastic. The band is great and the entire décor is spectacular."

"I couldn't agree more. I've been eavesdropping on some of the guests and everyone is blown away." Mia pressed her hands together at the center of her chest. "After the first hour, we'll move inside and the entertainment will begin."

Michael nodded. He turned to Traci. "Brenda, will you excuse us for a minute?"

"Sure, I'm going to mingle."

When Traci was out of earshot, he turned to Mia. "I knew I'd made the right decision when I asked you to take on this project." He stepped a little closer. "You look beautiful tonight." He ran his hand across her bare shoulder.

She fought not to flinch at his touch, beating back the memories. "Thank you. We worked hard."

"Where is Ashley, by the way? I didn't see her around."

"She was here earlier getting everything set up."

He nodded. "Maybe you and I can get together after the event."

"I don't think so. It's going to be a long night."

"We need to talk."

"About what?"

"Us."

"Michael—"

He held up his hand. "Not now. But we will. There's so much I want to tell you."

The look of warmth and sincerity in his eyes set her stomach fluttering. She glanced away. She couldn't be dragged back into the abyss of charisma again.

She looked at her watch. "I need to make the rounds."

He nodded as she walked away.

"Michael!"

He turned toward the sound of his name being called. Michelle was walking toward him with a woman so stunning it took away his breath for a moment. This must be the woman Michelle had spoken to him about, he thought. At least he hoped so. She would be perfect.

"Michael, this is Danielle Holloway. Danielle, Michael Burke, CEO of Avante Enterprises and the driving force behind this event."

Michael shrugged off the accolades and zeroed in on Danielle. He extended his hand. "Ms. Holloway, a pleasure to meet you."

"Thank you. I've heard great things about you from Michelle."

"Michelle is better than paid advertising." He paused, looked Danielle over, taking in her champagne-colored sheath gown, which dipped to a delicious low in the front and a dangerous plunge in the back. The silky fabric glided over her curves, the color so perfectly matched to her skin tone that upon first glance it gave her the illusion of being a naked Venus. Her dark mane of hair was piled on top of her head, reminiscent of the goddesses of Greek mythology.

"So what do you do, Danielle?"

"I'm a freelance writer," she said.

"Really. I'm sure you could find plenty to write about tonight."

She cocked a brow. "True. But, unfortunately, assignments like these usually go to the regulars. We freelancers may get the leftovers, or if someone bows out. It's a tough life."

"I can imagine." He placed his hand on her arm. "Let's talk." They walked over to a semi-quiet corner near the bar. "Can I get you a drink?"

"No, thank you. I'm fine." She pressed the button on the catch on her purse.

"So, Michelle tells me you're looking to make some extra money."

"Yes, I am. And she also said you were the one to make that happen." She looked up at him from beneath smoky lashes.

Michael grinned.

"So, tell me, what is it that I would be doing?"

"I have associates, very important associates, who sometimes…need attention. They may be in town, unfamiliar with how to get around, or simply want a beautiful woman to accompany them to an event."

"I see. Sounds simple enough. How do I make money doing that?"

"Depending on the event, the amount of hours of your time will determine your fee. Every now and then a gentleman may want you to accompany him to one of the Caribbean islands. That ups your fee, of course. And they are responsible for all expenses."

Danielle nodded and hoped that the recording device was catching every word.

"So how does that sound?"

"I'm interested, if that's what you want to know. My time is my own—no ties." She shrugged sexily.

"I was hoping that's what you would say. Let me introduce you to some of my associates. People you will certainly get to know much better. Then I'll have Michelle introduce you to some of the ladies."

Traci and Mia walked through the crowd.

"See the woman in the black Vera Wang near the caviar?" Traci asked.

Mia squinted until the woman came into focus. "Yes."

"She's a regular. She's at every event and usually goes off with one of the guests by night's end." She jutted her chin in the direction of a couple talking over glasses of champagne. "That's the CEO of Bankers Union, one of the largest bank conglomerates in the country. The woman next to him is Dina. She's been on the payroll for a while."

As Traci scoped the room, she pointed out nearly a dozen classy, highly attractive women who were on Michael's list of eligible escorts.

"Do you have any idea where they all live? Are they from New York?"

"That I don't know," Traci admitted.

"Ms. Turner."

Mia turned behind her. "Yes?"

"Hi, I'm a reporter from *The Times* Entertainment Section. I was hoping to steal a few minutes of your time."

"Me?"

"Yes, you were responsible for putting this together, correct?"

"I am. Yes."

"I wanted to ask you about your business, how you built it, got to this point. Things like that. A short profile. It will only take a few minutes. Promise. I know how busy you must be."

"I can give you about five minutes. I need to get ready for the entertainment portion of the evening."

"I'll catch up with you later," Traci said, then walked off to talk with a group that included one of the A&R execs from Atlantic.

"Jean sent me," the woman said, as soon as they were alone.

Mia's open expression froze. "Excuse me?"

"Jean sent me. She said to be sure that you don't try to take Michael down tonight. You are only to gather whatever information you can. It's too open and there's too much media. And she doesn't want your name and business tied into this at all. She wants everyone involved to meet at the brownstone tomorrow morning at ten."

Before Mia could respond, the woman walked away and out. For several moments she didn't move. Suddenly she was chilled, and rubbed her hands up and down her bare arms.

"I'm sure I can find a way to warm you up," a deep voice whispered from behind her.

Her heart thudded. She turned around. "Michael."

He kissed her cheek. "I've been hearing nothing but good things all evening. Congratulations."

"Thanks." She was still rattled by the visit from one of Jean's operatives.

Michael frowned. "Is everything okay?"

She swallowed. "Yes. I'll settle down once the night is finally over."

He rubbed her arm. "I've never known you to be nervous," he said, looking at her curiously.

"Just a very hectic night." Her eyes darted around the space. "I need to get ready for the entertainment, check with the sound men and the video." She checked her watch. "Raven should be here in about an hour."

Michael nodded.

"She's going to show up, right?"

"That's what her people promised me."

It was the only piece of the puzzle that she couldn't guarantee.

"I've really got to go." She started to move away.

Michael clasped her wrist. "Wait. I want to talk to you…about another event. A lot less people, more intimate, at my place in the Poconos. I want to put something together for some close friends."

She was ready to turn it down, but Jean's directive stuck in her head. This might be another opportunity to get more information. "Can we talk tomorrow?"

"Over lunch." It wasn't a question.

She hesitated. "Fine." She hurried away.

Raven's performance went off without a hitch, just the way it was planned. The crowd loved her. The media was frantic that they didn't get a chance to interview her. But her mystique stayed intact and Mia had a friend for life.

Tomorrow was another day and another meeting with Jean.

Chapter 20

With all the ladies having other lives, they'd agreed before leaving the party the night before to meet at the brownstone by eight. Hopefully, it wouldn't take too long and they could return to their livelihoods.

Mia, Savannah, Traci, Danielle and Ashley all arrived within minutes of each other and gathered together in the main room on the ground floor.

It had turned decidedly chilly overnight and the warmth of the brownstone was a welcome relief. They'd all dressed for the weather, sporting everything from lined leather jackets to jazzy cashmere car coats. Mia, always one to show off her long legs, wore a short ink-black wool skirt and black leather pumps topped with a winter-white silk sweater and a fire-engine red shawl, draped dramatically around her neck and shoulders. Savannah, relishing the fact that she could finally fit into her clothes after the baby, was fashion-ready in a two-piece, camel-colored suit with bold bronze-colored buttons and three-inch Jimmy Choo chocolate-brown heels. Ashley, always elegantly casual, wore gray suede pants with an oversize black cowl-neck sweater, accessorized with silver at her wrists and dangling from her earlobes. Danielle, who always looked as if she'd just stepped off the cover of a magazine, wore denim as only Danielle could, the short battle jacket and matching jeans accented with chunky jewelry and her signature ankle boots. Not to be outdone, Traci was corporate sharp in a hunter-green, two-piece skirt suit, cinched at the waist to subtly accentuate her hips.

To a casual observer it looked like a gathering of heads of the fashion or entertainment industry.

Jean had set out a continental breakfast, anticipating their early arrival and need for expediency.

As they sat around sipping herbal tea and imported coffee, and munching on croissants and muffins, Jean came in, followed by Jasmine.

"Good morning, ladies. I know we don't have much time so this will be as brief as possible. Mia has sent over all the footage from last night and Danielle provided the recorded conversation she had with Michael Burke. At first blush, it appeared that we had enough to go on. But after reviewing the audiotape and running it past the attorney general, there is not enough on there to bring an indictment. A good lawyer would tear what we have apart. We need concrete evidence."

Low groans bounced around the room.

"That is not anyone's fault. There wasn't anything that could have been done better," she said, directing her comment to Danielle. "The most important thing was that we couldn't appear to be entrapping anyone. Then all of your hard work would have been for nothing." She paused and looked around the room. "We're going to have to get more to nail him."

"We might have that chance," Mia offered. "He wants me to put together a private party for some close friends."

Jean nodded. "I see."

"I'm sure those private friends will be some of the men who were there last night," Traci said. "And I can guarantee that the women will be there as well."

"When is this party?" Jean asked.

"I'm not sure. I'm supposed to meet him for lunch to discuss what he wants and when."

Jean looked from one to the other. "My instincts tell me that this may be our last chance."

They all nodded.

"As soon as you have the details, I want to be informed, and a plan will be put in place." She paused. "Each of you has done a wonderful job. Simply because we didn't get all we needed last night does not mean that any of you did less than what you were supposed to do. We'll get him. I know you all have to get to your jobs, so I won't hold you any longer. Before we leave, is there anything you want to discuss, any questions?"

"What will happen if we can't get him to incriminate himself this next time?" Mia asked.

"We'll deal with that when the time comes. We're going to operate on the premise that he will incriminate himself and we will shut the operation down."

Nods of agreement all around.

"Ladies, have a great day." Jean walked out.

"I've got to run. Richard has a ten-o'clock court case this morning and if I'm not there to hold his hand, no telling what will happen to his poor client," Savannah joked.

Savannah worked as a paralegal for a private law firm with a great but needy boss. Danielle and Mia had been hounding her for years to go back to school and finish her law degree. Then she could hire Richard, since she was smarter than he was anyway and pretty much ran the company.

"Me, too," Traci said. "I'm going to work on getting an advance copy of the guest list for the Poconos. If I do, I'll pass it along." She finished off her cup of tea, grabbed a blueberry muffin and headed out.

Jasmine caught up with her in the hallway.

"Traci…"

She stopped and turned.

Jasmine walked up to her. "It's good to have you back," she said quietly.

Traci smiled. "It's good to sort of be back. I'm just helping out."

"I didn't think I'd ever see you again…after everything went down with you and Jean."

Traci lowered her head. "It was a rough time. I didn't really have much of a choice. I had to leave, start over."

"So…are you part of the team again?" she asked, a hopeful hitch in her voice.

"We'll see. That's up to Jean."

"We could sure use you around here. We've had a few members from this region retire or move away."

Traci's chestnut-colored eyes crinkled at the corners as she grinned. "How's the pay these days?"

"The per-assignment fee is still the same, but we get incentive bonuses, which is new."

"Hmm. Something to think about. Once this assignment is over I'll be out of a job. And again, it's not really up to me about coming back. It's up to Jean." She looked at her watch. "Oh, wow, I've got to run." She stepped up and embraced Jasmine, so very proud of her protégée.

"Even if you don't come back to TLC, let's not lose touch again," Jasmine spoke into Traci's ear.

Traci stepped back and held her shoulders. "We won't. I promise."

Jasmine tightened her lips and nodded as Traci hurried down the stairs and out into the street.

Traci arrived at Avante Enterprises and assumed her role as Brenda Forde, executive assistant. She checked in with the front desk for messages, then went to the office of the entertainment director to see if they'd downloaded any of the news articles on the red-carpet event for Raven. There were separate departments for entertainment, corporate and small business management, each headed by a different director with a two- or three-person staff. All the directors reported to her, and she, in turn, reported to Michael.

She took the printouts of the news clippings and went to her office. She took off her kidskin suede jacket and hung it on the standing rack in the corner of her office. Just as she sat down behind her smoked-glass desk, her phone rang. Peeking at the flashing light, she saw that it was Michael.

Bracing herself, she picked up.

"Yes. Good morning."

"Great event last night," he began.

"It certainly was."

"I was hoping you had a few minutes this morning before things got busy. I wanted to go over a couple of things with you."

She sighed to herself. "Sure. Can you give me about five minutes?"

"No problem. Have you had breakfast? I can order something."

"No, thanks. I'm fine. I'll see you in five."

Traci flopped back into her chair and spun it toward the window. She wanted this thing to be over. She wanted to get her old life back. She wanted to get away from Michael and bury the memories and the hurt and humiliation. She pressed her fist to her mouth to keep from screaming. So many times she questioned what she'd done. This was the man she'd loved. But she'd betrayed him like Judas. And she couldn't help but ask herself if it was pure jealousy and a desire for revenge or because she truly believed that what he was doing was wrong.

She slowly stood up. Unfortunately, it was too late to turn back now. All the wheels were in motion and a part of her ached at what the days ahead would hold.

Michael's door was partially open when she arrived. She tapped and poked her head in.

He glanced up from his computer screen and quickly clicked off the page he was on. "Hey, come on in." He got up and walked over to the small island that held the coffee machine. "Coffee?"

"No, thanks." She sat down opposite his desk and noticed the screen saver on his computer.

He poured himself a cup and returned to his desk. "So, let me hear your thoughts about last night."

"I thought it went off without a hitch." She handed over the copies of the early reviews.

He briefly glanced at them, nodding and smiling before setting them aside. "I wanted to thank you for all of your help. Raven was a difficult client to handle, but you made it work."

"Thank you."

He was quiet for a moment. "I want to host a private gathering at my place in the Poconos for some of my clients in two weeks. It will be for the entire weekend."

"Okay. Do you know who you want to invite?"

"I'll put the list of names together and get it to you so you can begin contacting them." He took a sip of his coffee. "I want to use MT Management again."

She didn't respond.

"How do you feel about that?"

"Why should I feel one way or the other?" she said, a bit more harshly than she intended.

"Look, I'm sorry for how things turned out between us. I shouldn't have led you on all this time, let you think that it could be more than what it was. But you have to know that I do care about you, Brenda, at least as much as I'm capable of caring for anyone. You're an incredible woman. I never wanted to hurt you and I hope that what happened with us isn't going to inter- fere with us continuing to work together, especially since you've made it clear that…we can't have what we once did."

"What about Mia? Did you only care about her as much as you were capable of caring for anyone?"

He glanced away. "Maybe more than that. But she

left me, and with good reason." He sighed heavily.
"After that I haven't been able to commit myself to
anyone. So…this has nothing to do with you."

"I was just a replacement," she challenged.

He didn't respond.

"I guess that's my answer." She got up. "I need to
get some work started on the Pocono event. I'll work
with Mia to put it together." She turned to leave.

"Brenda…"

Her hand stilled on the knob of the door.

"I'm sorry."

She straightened her shoulders and walked out.

Within the hour Michael e-mailed her the list of ten
men he wanted to invite to the gathering. Even Traci
was impressed. She immediately e-mailed the list to
Mia. It was up to her now.

Mia was thinking about the information that Traci
had e-mailed to her earlier as she prepared dinner. The
guest list was staggering. If this final sting panned out,
it would rock the city. The list included Senator Max
Hopkinson, who was currently running for reelection;
CEO Carl Ruthers, founder of Ruthers Technology and
the man who had single-handedly revolutionized iden-
tity-scanning systems worldwide; and Breck Hamilton,
the chairman of Backstreet Records, among others. She
couldn't begin to imagine the fallout.

She put two handfuls of mixed greens into the col-
ander, rinsed them then tossed them into a teal-and-
white-colored ceramic mixing bowl that she'd picked
up on a business jaunt in Mexico a couple of years earlier and began adding her ingredients. She'd already

grilled a fresh piece of salmon, which she began to slice into slender pieces. She would add this as the final topping.

The wine was chilled. She had showered and applied body lotion in Steven's favorite scent. She'd slipped into a brand-new Victoria's Secret teddy in a shimmering hot pink that did wonderful things to her skin.

She put the salmon salad in the fridge to chill just a bit, cleaned her fingers—first with lemon juice, followed by warm water and soap, to get rid of the fish smell—then hurried into the living room to lower the lights and put on a CD of the Dells' greatest hits to be followed by her favorite, Luther. But she was pretty sure they'd never be sitting around long enough to actually hear it.

Several small aromatic candles burned in strategic places around the room, enveloping the space in the soft scent of lavender.

Mia took a look around, satisfied with her setup. She planned to give Steven the loving that he deserved and that she wanted. Being with him, being a part of him, seemed to help exorcise Michael from her system and keep at bay the double life that she led. When she was with Steven, she could just be Mia, the neurotic, quirky event planner who refused to wear her glasses. And that was okay.

She smiled at the thought. It had taken almost making a fatal mistake with Michael, having his true side and her own weakness revealed to her for her to realize what it was that she already had. Michael was a fantasy, a passion from her past. Steven was her here, her now and her tomorrow.

As she toweled off her hands, she heard the front

door open. She tossed the towel onto the counter, grabbed the wine from the bottom of the fridge, along with the two long-stemmed wineglasses, and met Steven just as he was putting down the briefcase that held his laptop. That's when he spotted the hot-pink beauty in the archway of the kitchen that opened onto the dining and living-room area. He also noticed the low lights, the heady scent of jasmine and the dark look in his woman's eyes.

The corner of his mouth rose ever so slightly. He shrugged out of his jacket and hung it on the coatrack near the closet door. He moved slowly in her direction, as she posed provocatively against the frame of the archway with the two glasses swinging from her hand.

"Hey, handsome," she said, her voice soft and inviting.

Steven walked up to her. "Hey, yourself." He took the bottle from her hand, leaned down and kissed her softly. He uncorked the bottle. She held out the glasses and he poured.

They touched glasses and took their first sip before they both turned to the sound of the Dells' "Stay in My Corner."

Steven tossed his head back and laughed, then looked down into Mia's teasing gaze. "You know that's the jam."

He took the glass from her hand, set his down, along with the bottle of wine, then slipped his arm around her silken waist, pulling her up against him. "Can I have this dance?"

"I'd love to," she whispered.

They moved to the center of the living room and fell into perfect step with each other, swaying to the serious old-school love song. Mia rested her head on Steven's chest as he held her, running his hand up and down along the soft fabric, intermittently cupping her rear to pull her tighter against him.

Mia was on a natural high: the music, the aromas, the man. They all contributed to her feeling of peace, mixed with a sensual heat that made her almost light-headed with the growing need that rushed through her insides, much like the hot flame of a match tossed on kindling.

"I fixed dinner," she murmured against his ear as the song was drawing to its hip-grinding last note, which made the standard a favorite among generations of slow dancers.

"We can bring it inside," he said, nibbling on her neck. He stroked her back, running his hand along the curve of her hip.

"We could. Why don't you get settled and I'll serve you dinner in bed."

"Loving the sound of that." He kissed her and headed off toward the back of the condo.

Moments later, Mia heard the sound of running water. She returned to the kitchen, took out the salad, got plates and silverware and placed them all on the large serving tray that they used when they ate in bed. She added linen napkins, two clean glasses and the bottle of wine. Balancing it all like a professional, she took it to their bedroom and set it all on the side table. She turned back the blanket, fluffed the pillows and dimmed the lights.

Looking around with her hands on her hips, she was satisfied with the ambience.

Michael stepped out of the adjoining bathroom, followed by a rush of steam. He had a towel wrapped around his waist and was drying off his hair and face with another one. When he pulled the towel away from his face, his eyes lit up.

"Woman, you sure know how to welcome a man home from a hard day's work."

Mia sat on the side of the bed, her long legs crossed at the knee. "I try." She patted the space next to her. Steven didn't need to be invited twice. He read her body language very well.

Once he was next to her, she lifted a forkful of the salmon salad to his lips. "Taste."

His eyes closed in what looked like ecstasy. "Hmm, delicious." He chewed slowly.

"Here, have a sip." She held up the glass of wine to his lips.

He took a long swallow, removed the glass from her fingers. He reached around her and filled a fork with the salad and fed her, then offered her a sip of wine.

The entire ritual of feeding each other, the submissiveness of allowing yourself to be fed, and the dominance of being the provider was an intoxicating, sensory turn-on for them both, as the positions of power and vulnerability shifted back and forth between them.

When the food and most of the wine was gone and their roles had blurred, all they wanted to feast on was each other.

Tonight Mia was feeling her feminine power, and as much as she loved Steven taking the lead, tonight was her night. She removed their plates and glasses, setting them back on the tray. She stood in front of him as he gazed up at her, trying to anticipate what she might do.

She reached down and loosened the towel around his waist, then instructed him to take it off and sit back down. When he was seated and she eyed his steadily growing erection, she took the first strap and then the other of her teddy and pushed them down her shoulders and shimmied out of it, allowing the fabric to float into a pink pool at her feet. She stepped over it, draped her legs on either side of Steven's hard thighs. She clasped the back of his head and pulled him flush against the softness of her stomach, allowing him to momentarily inhale the scent that he loved.

She took his hands and lifted them to her breasts, which demanded to be fondled.

Steven cupped them, their ripeness overflowing his palms. He allowed his thumbs to gently graze back and forth across her nipples, the way he knew she liked it.

Mia moaned. For a moment her eyes closed, as she gave in to the sensual delight that fired through her veins. As he caressed her, she slowly lowered herself onto his hardened shaft, which was pointing toward heaven. As she slid down on the hot thickness of him, her mind spun, her belly was on fire, her heart pumped as she felt her insides open up to welcome him.

She enveloped him to the hilt and, as always, it took a moment for her body to adjust to the solid rock hardness of him, which seemed to grow thicker with every beat of her heart, taking her breath away.

Steven grabbed a handful of her behind in each palm, his mouth replacing where his hands once were.

Mia cried out his name, wrapped her hands around his neck, planted the balls of her feet solidly on the floor and rode him like a seasoned rodeo rider, making Steven holler with pleasure.

* * *

Later, they rested in a tangle of sheets and limbs, talking softly to each other about their workday, when Steven sprang his surprise.

"This is the kind of time we need to spend together," he began.

"Hmm, umm," she mumbled against his chest. She ran a manicured finger down the center.

"I know we are both crazy busy with work, so I figured the only real alone time we're going to have is if we get away somewhere."

Her eyes opened slowly.

"That's why I went ahead and got us two tickets for a Bahamas weekend getaway, everything included. I knew if we kept talking about when we have some free time to do something, it would never happen. So I got us tickets for two weeks from now. We leave on Thursday and come back on Sunday. That will give us both some time to prepare staff, get anything important out of the way."

"Weekend after next?" She was paying attention now.

"Yep, all paid for."

Mia's stomach knotted. It was the same weekend as the Poconos. What the hell was she going to do?

Chapter 21

Mia barely slept. Her eyes were wide-open when the sun crested the horizon. All she could think about all night was her dilemma. How damn Twilight Zone was it that Steven had bought tickets to the Bahamas for the same freaking weekend as Michael's getaway weekend for his "special" friends. Her eyes felt as if someone had shoveled sand under her lids, but she couldn't lie in bed a minute longer.

While Steven was still sound asleep, she tiptoed into the kitchen with her cell phone pressed to her chest and, checking to make sure he hadn't awakened, she dialed the girls, leaving urgent messages on all their cell phones. They needed an emergency meeting ASAP.

Mia did all she could not to push Steven out the door. Today of all days he wanted to linger, talk, make love again…and again. Any other time, she would have been all for it, but she had cases to crack and people to see.

· Sometime during the night it had rained. The streets were still wet, with water pooling in the numerous indentations of New York City sidewalks and streets. By the time she reached her car, which she'd parked on the next block, she felt as if she'd completed the Olympic hurdles. Her condo had a parking facility attached to the building—and well it should, for all the money the tenants shelled out—but she'd never bothered to take advantage of it, especially during the spring and summer. Parking around the corner or down the block gave her a chance to get in her minimal amount of exercise. Steven had practically begged her to use the parking garage, especially because she had so many late nights, but she'd been adamant. The winter would be there soon enough, she'd explained, and she would be forced to park in the garage and take the elevator, and so that would bring an end to her meager attempt at fitness.

Once behind the wheel, she turned on the radio to keep her company and to keep her mind off her newest dilemma. The *Steve Harvey Morning Show* was on, and one of the hosts was tearing into some poor soul about discovering that her man had a whole other family on the other side of a very small town in North Carolina.

Mia just shook her head and chuckled. If only she could write to Steve about her ongoing drama. She'd pay good money to hear what he had to say about it. He'd probably tell her that she was lying about the whole mess.

What she really needed was Danielle and Savannah's input. They'd always given her sound advice and now that they knew the whole story, she was sure they'd be objective. She'd even invited Ashley, whose personality was a nice fit for their group. The fact that she, too, was a Cartel member only strengthened the bond.

Unfortunately, bad weather brought out the worst drivers. They suddenly became totally inept at moving from point A to point B with any degree of speed. The ultimate result was that Mia's fifteen-minute ride turned into a half hour of stop and go.

Finally, she reached The Shop and, shock of all shocks, Danielle, the queen of "Janie Come Lately," had actually arrived first and was holding down their favorite booth. She really must be off her game, Mia thought as she moved toward the table, especially if Danielle of all people was the first to arrive anywhere. Maybe the moon was in Aquarius or something.

"Hey, girl, what in the hell are you doing here so early?" She sat down and slid across the booth on her side until she reached the end. She placed her purse between her and the partition.

"I'm trying to turn over a new leaf," Danielle confessed. "Being early, less cussing, listening before speaking, being considerate of others." She took a sip of tea.

Mia sat there with her eyes wide with disbelief. "You're kidding me, right?"

Danielle made a face. "No. For real."

"Why?" Mia asked, totally perplexed. "We're already used to you being a tactless, late, pain in the neck, supersweet friend. If it ain't broke, don't fix it."

"I think that was some kind of compliment, but I'm not sure."

"Did Nick get on you about something?"

"No. Actually during a photo shoot, one of the product placement items was this book, *Twenty Days to a Better You.* During the break I checked it out and figured, why not?" She shrugged lightly.

"Hmm. How's it going so far?"

"Got me here early." She grinned. "But it's too soon to tell. Somebody piss me off and it's on."

They laughed just as Savannah and Ashley pushed through the door, both shaking out their umbrellas. A flash of lightning was followed by a roll of thunder.

"Damn, I thought this kind of weather was reserved for April," Savannah groused as she kissed cheeks, slid out of her raincoat and sat down.

"Hey, y'all," Ashley greeted them. She fluffed her fro and hung her jacket on the back of the booth chair. She turned to Mia. "So what's up and who's paying for breakfast?"

"Now that's what I'm talking about," Danielle said. "I knew I liked you for a reason. Straight, no chaser."

"Well, since I called the meeting, I guess I'll pay for breakfast," Mia said. She flitted her hand around the table, as if sprinkling fairy dust. "But everyone choose something different. That way I can charge it as a business expense." She grinned.

Danielle and Savannah shook their heads. Mia was notorious for finding creative ways to use her business account.

"So, sister girl, what's the story?" Savannah asked.

Mia drew in a long breath then leaned forward. "Well, you all know that Michael is planning a private party."

Nodding heads all around.

"Last night—"

"What can I get you ladies this morning?" the waitress asked, cutting Mia off.

They each placed their orders—everything from egg-white omelets to Belgian waffles. Once the waitress was gone, Mia continued.

"Steven and I...well, we had a fantastic night." She blushed and the girls humm-ummed her, knowing just what she meant. "So afterward we were lying there, and I'm thinking, 'Yes, this is where I want to be, where my heart is,' ya know, and he starts telling me that we really need more time like this together without a lot of distractions...blah, blah, blah. So I'm all for it. Sounding really good, right. Then BAM. He drops an atom bomb. He got us two round-trip tickets to the Bahamas."

"Whoa. You go, girl," Ashley said.

"That's what I'm talking about," Danielle added.

"I hear a *but* in there somewhere," said Savannah, always the astute one.

"A big one. The tickets are for the exact same weekend as the private party."

"Daayum," they chorused, turning the one word into two.

"Talk about bad timing," Ashley said.

"I have no idea what to do. I have to be up in the Poconos."

"You need to go with Steven," Savannah said emphatically.

"I agree," Danielle said.

"But how am I going to explain my absence to Michael?"

"You don't. I'll take your place," Savannah said.

"What?"

"We'll make it work. Danielle is already one of the ladies. I'm helping out because you're ill. I'll work it out with Traci. Ashley had to cover one of your other events." She shrugged her shoulders and held her palms facing the ceiling. "Simple."

Mia looked from one expectant face to the other. "Do you really think he'd go for it?"

"What choice does he have?" Danielle said. "You don't tell him jack until the last second. By then all the players are in place."

Mia nodded slowly. "I can't jeopardize what Steven and I have. I just can't. I cringe to think I was involved with a man who could do what he's doing." She gave a slight shiver.

"Let's be honest. Michael Burke is fine, charming, intelligent, well-off. What woman wouldn't fall for him?" Savannah said. "And, to be honest, I really believe he cared for you and still does. But that doesn't excuse what he's done and is still doing. Besides, if he would cheat on his wife, one of these days he'd do the same thing to you."

For a moment Mia looked crestfallen. Hearing the hard truth was definitely a reality check. "Let's work this plan, then," she finally conceded. "I'm sure this will be my last assignment once Jean finds out that I opted to pursue my love life instead of my job."

"Jean will get over it," Ashley said. "If she can take Traci back into the fold, she'll do the same for you."

"I sure hope so."

Danielle and her fiancé, Nick, decided to take in a movie instead of going home after the end of their day of shooting.

"I think things went pretty well today," Nick said as they stood in line waiting for tickets to Denzel's latest movie.

Danielle hooked her arm through Nick's. It had taken her a while to feel comfortable expressing her feelings for Nick in public. For one thing, they worked together. And then there was the whole race thing. Although both of them—in the animal kingdom—would be considered mutts for their mixed breeding, Danielle had always lived as a black girl in an "I'm not sure what she is" body. Nick, on the other hand, grew up as a white boy with white-boy privileges, even though his heart and soul were darker than hers.

But none of that mattered anymore. She'd made her peace with herself and, more important, with her family—her dad, in particular—and ever since then she had felt as if the weight of the world had been lifted from her shoulders.

"Fortunately, everything was in studio. I'm hoping tomorrow is better. We have the shots to take for the winter coat line for JCPenney."

"I know. We'll improvise."

Nick paid for their tickets and they walked inside, both heading straight for the popcorn. They turned to each other and grinned. Popcorn was the thing that had broken the employer/employee ice between them. Danielle was a fiend for popcorn. She could never turn it down. And one afternoon during a photo shoot on Long Island, Nick had whipped out a bag of popcorn and Danielle had begun to salivate. When Nick offered her some, she nearly screamed yes. As they shared the oversize bag, they started talking, finding that they had tons of things in common: music, movies, books, neighborhoods, musicians, architecture. It was amazing and the rest, as they say, is history—in the making.

"Make sure you ask for extra butter, 'cause I ain't sharing," Nick said.

Danielle rolled her eyes.

They placed their orders and walked into the darkened theater. They had about ten minutes before the feature presentation, so they settled down to watch the previews. It was Nick who changed the direction of their inconsequential conversation.

"So what's new with the Cartel?" he asked.

On her last case, Danielle had broken one of the cardinal rules of the Cartel; she'd told Nick some details after he discovered her kit. Not everything, but enough for him to know that she had "another life," one that she wouldn't always share with him. Actually, he'd had a hand in her last case, which had involved identity theft.

"It's Mia's case this time," she said, before shoving a handful of popcorn in her mouth.

"Anything you can talk about?"

"I wasn't supposed to say that," she said, with a hint of laughter in her voice.

"My bad."

"All I can say is that it's major. There's a party coming up soon. Very exclusive. Very highbrow guests."

"I can mingle," Nick said. "Something like that you need a bartender, right?" He grinned into the darkness. "I'm your man."

She munched on her popcorn. "I'll let you know. But don't count on it."

"Party pooper."

She poked him in the side with her elbow. Relaxing in her seat, she was amazed at how far they'd come.

Both of them had struggled with intimacy issues, trusting another person totally. But once she finally opened her heart and spirit to Nick, everything changed. She relished the fact that she could trust him with her darkest secrets, even being a member of the Cartel. That level of trust brought them closer. She glanced down at the diamond sparkling on the third finger of her left hand. Yes, things had definitely changed for the better. And, if need be, she would certainly take Nick up on his offer. Nothing like having two spies in the family.

Mia dreaded what she was about to do, but she had no choice. Throughout the night, she'd struggled with what she would say and how Jean would react. But truth be told, she'd rather jeopardize her standing with the Cartel than with Steven.

She parked her car across the street from the brownstone. For several moments she sat behind the wheel, rehearsing in her head what she was going to say. She watched the comings and goings of the men attending the Pause for Men Spa. One of these days she was going to pay the spa a visit just to see what all the hype was about.

Unable to stall any longer, she took off her glasses, tucked them in the glove compartment, grabbed her coat and got out.

Claudia answered the door.

"Good morning, sweetheart."

"Hi, Claudia."

"You don't sound happy."

"I'm not looking forward to my conversation with Jean."

Claudia patted her shoulder. "Whatever it is, I'm

sure it will work out. Jean really isn't as bad as everyone thinks."

"Thanks. I'll keep that in mind while she chews off
my head," she said, laughing derisively. "And we really
need to get together to talk about your wedding plans."

"I know. Time is flying by. But we'll make time to
talk once you're finished with your assignment."

"That might be sooner than you think." She took
a deep breath. "Wish me luck." She headed upstairs.

When she'd called earlier to tell Jean that she needed
to speak with her in person, she got a sense that Jean
already knew what she was coming to say. She walked
down the hall of fame until she reached Jean's office.
She knocked on the door.

"Come in."

Jean barely looked up when Mia came in.

"Have a seat."

Mia's throat was suddenly bone-dry. She thought
she might suffocate.

"You wanted to talk. I'm listening." She peered at
Mia through the lenses of her red-frame glasses.

Mia cleared her dry throat. "I'm not going to be able
to handle the event in the Poconos…"

She went on to explain, as best she could, her current circumstances. She laid out plan B, which had the
approval of Savannah and Danielle.

While Mia rambled on about the whys and where-
fores of her predicament, Jean didn't move, didn't seem
to blink, didn't appear to breathe. Mia was certain that
at any moment Jean was simply going to implode.

Stumbling toward the finish line, she wrapped up
her monologue and awaited Jean's verdict. She'd re-
signed herself to the notion that she would be kicked

to the curb. However, Jean's response was more devastating than she imagined.

Slowly, Jean removed her glasses and set them down in front of her on the desk. She zeroed in on Mia, making her squirm in her seat.

"The downfall of some of my best operatives has been over a relationship. If you intend to succeed, you must find a way to separate the two. I'm disappointed in you, Mia. But I know that Savannah and Danielle can handle it. They've proven themselves."

Mia felt physically stung by the barb.

"Do what you must." She put her glasses back on and returned to what she was doing before Mia came in.

Mia took that as her cue to leave. And as far as she was concerned, she couldn't get out of there fast enough.

She couldn't even face Claudia so she hurried out and practically sprinted to her car.

Hot tears of defeat and frustration filled her eyes. She'd failed before she'd gotten started. She lowered her head to the steering wheel and let the tears fall. She wasn't a quitter. Her entire life was built on organization and thinking outside the box. She was analytical by nature. And she'd somehow let what came easy to her get away from her. She'd allowed herself to get distracted and out of focus.

She had to return to what came natural to her. Planning.

Chapter 22

Mia took her time getting to her office. At this point, she felt her day could only go from bad to worse. Throughout the ride downtown, she played out a variety of scenarios to make the impossible possible—everything from going with Steven to the Bahamas, buying an extra ticket and flying back to New York then returning to the island. That, of course, was beyond ridiculous. How would she ever explain her absence to Steven for hours on end? She'd even considered telling Steven everything—except the part about her and Michael's past—and taking him with her to the Poconos then flying off to the Bahamas. But she was already on the blacklist with Jean. The last thing she needed to do was involve Steven.

She eventually dragged herself into her office, feeling as gloomy as the overcast day.

"Can't be that bad," Ashley said, upon seeing her distraught expression.

Mia shrugged out of her coat and draped it across her arm. "It is."

"What happened?"

"She told me I was a disappointment and that she was sure that Savannah and Danielle could handle the assignment. After all, *they'd* proven themselves."

Ashley grimaced. "Ouch. Sorry. Look she's probably disappointed, sure, but she'll get over it. The Cartel will be there with or without us, but we have to have a life, too. If I was in your shoes, I'd do the same thing… if that's any consolation."

Mia half smiled. "Thanks." She sighed heavily. "Any messages?"

"Not sure if you want to hear it, but Michael called to remind you about lunch."

Her day had just gotten worst.

Michael had made reservations for them at the Russian Tea Room—pretty swanky for a simple lunch. But she wasn't buying so no need to complain. Hopefully, the serene and upscale atmosphere, suffused with old-world charm, would have enough of an ambience to lift her dour mood and help her get through an hour or more in Michael's presence.

She arrived at one-thirty and was shown immediately to her table. He must come here often, Mia thought as she was ushered toward the back. The moment she said she was meeting Michael Burke for lunch, the hostess's bright blue eyes lit up. At this point, unfortunately, Mia couldn't tell if the recognition was due to Michael's standing in the business community or if this young girl was part of his stable of escorts.

As she approached their somewhat secluded booth, Michael spotted her. A slow smile—the one that creased the corners of his eyes and did something to her insides that she was never able to explain or understand—moved across his mouth, showing just a hint of teeth.

Her heart knocked hard in her chest, forcing the blood to rush to her head. For an instant she felt dizzy, as if she were about to swoon like the ladies sitting on a Charleston porch at the height of summer, sipping mint juleps.

He extended his hand to her and she found herself enveloped in its warmth. He slid his other lightly around her waist, then kissed her gently on the cheek before helping her into her chair as the heady scent of his cologne short-circuited her thoughts.

The moment she sat, she reached for the glass of water and took several swallows as Michael swung back into his seat opposite her.

At least the water had a cooling effect and she slowly began to clear her head. Michael always had that power over her, to be able to seduce her mind and body with no more effort than simply being in her space. His smile, his touch, the scent of him were all aphrodisiacs, and even after all these years that combination was still as potent as it had ever been.

That was what kept her on the fence. That was what made her so indecisive and hesitant. She wanted him to be the Michael she knew—an adulterer, certainly—but not a common pimp.

"Thanks for coming," he said, the familiar timbre

of his voice snapping her out of her musings. "I appreciate it."

"I try to accommodate my business clients as much as possible." She folded her hands in her lap.

The waitress appeared to take their drink and food orders.

Michael ordered wine and a Caesar salad, Mia a bottle of Pellegrino and grilled salmon salad. They returned the menus to the waitress.

"I must tell you again how impressed I was with the red-carpet event. The calls haven't stopped coming in about what a great time everyone had."

Mia nodded and smiled. "It's what I do."

"You were always good," he said, his voice lowering to a tone too intimate for a business lunch.

Mia adjusted herself in her seat and took out her notepad. "So, what did you want to talk to me about?" she asked, trying to stay focused.

The right corner of his mouth rose upward for a split second. "All work and no play…"

"Michael—"

"Okay, okay." He clasped his hands on top of the table and Mia couldn't help but notice the fresh manicure and the way his long fingers laced in and out of each other. "My house in the Poconos is fine for the party. There's plenty of space. I think it would still make sense for you to come up and take a look first."

Mia made a note then returned her gaze to Michael.

The waitress reappeared with their drinks order and food.

"However," he continued, "my guests will be…staying over for the weekend. They are going to need accommodations in the immediate area. So I will need ten suites reserved."

The light bulb went off. That was her opening! "I'll take care of it and ensure that your guests have only the best. I'll need a list of their preferences and any special requests."

"Of course. I'll make sure that Brenda gets that information to you as soon as possible, as well as the catering menu. We'll need some entertainment as well. I was thinking a small jazz band."

Mia's mind was racing. She just might be able to pull this off after all. "Of course. I know just the band. They'll be perfect."

Michael took a sip of his drink before focusing on his salad. He stabbed the fork into his food then stopped. "Tell me why you've been avoiding…us."

Her stomach rose and fell. "What are you talking about?"

"Us." He suddenly covered her hand with his. "Please don't pull away. Just hear me out. I know I made mistakes. I should never have cheated on my wife and had you living the kind of life that wasn't worthy of you." He paused. "I never saw you as the other woman—but as *my* woman, the one I wanted to be with. But by the time I got my act together, you were gone. I'd give it all up, everything, the business, the deals…other women if I could have you."

"Michael, too much time has passed."

"Enough to heal the hurts, the disappointments?"

She looked away.

"All I ask is that you give me a chance—one chance to prove to you that I've changed. Please."

"How are you going to do that?"

"You'll see. After the party, you'll see."

Mia stared at his bowed head as he ate his food. *What did he mean?*

She shouldn't even be entertaining Michael's thinly veiled proposition. He always had a way of making her see and believe what he wanted. That was his strength and her weakness. But there was no time for weakness, not now, she thought as she maneuvered her car around the late-afternoon traffic.

After he'd made his declaration, he'd steered clear of anything else on a personal level. They talked about politics, the upcoming election and what it could mean for the country. They talked about movies, music, all the things they had in common, and for a while she totally forgot that this could never be. For a while she was the old Mia Turner who was totally enamored of the dashing Michael Burke. That was then, she reminded herself, reliving the easy banter that had characterized their past relationship. No place for memories now, she reminded herself as she pulled into the last parking spot on the block.

Yet, his statement clung to her like a static-charged skirt against panty hose without a slip. And as much as she tried to disconnect the electricity that drew the skirt to the hose, she couldn't. It just kept on clinging, riding up and down her thigh, making her uncomfortable.

Mia turned off the ignition and got out. She glanced skyward. Dark clouds still hovered threateningly over the city. Even though it was only October, it felt like snow. Shivering slightly, she pulled her coat around her and hurried toward her office.

"Getting really cold out there," she said in a huff as she came inside.

"I was listening to the news. They're expecting the temperature to drop into the twenties tonight."

Mia grumbled.

"So how did it go?"

Mia's brows rose. "I think I may have found a way." She pulled up a chair near Ashley's desk and detailed her plan.

"Sounds like it just might work."

Mia got up. "I'm going to start making some calls."

Mia brought her electronic Rolodex up on her computer. Her business and reputation were built on who she knew, and Mia knew everyone who mattered. She pulled up her list of resorts, then began sorting them by location. There were three in the Pocono area. The first call didn't pan out. There were not enough rooms free. The second call was another bust. The manager was unavailable and the assistant sounded as if she was still in training. Mia tossed up a silent prayer and made her third call.

"Mt. Pocono Resort and Lodge," the young voice answered.

"Good afternoon. My name is Mia Turner of MT Management. I want to arrange a gathering for a party of ten."

"Hold on. Let me get you the booking manager."

Mia nervously tapped her foot as she waited. A few moments later a male voice came on the line.

"Mia?"

"Yes."

"Mia, it's Leon Winston."

Her eyes widened in surprise. "Leon! Oh, my goodness. When did you move out of the city?"

He chuckled. "Actually, I didn't. I stay up here during the week and come down to the city on weekends. How in the world are you?"

She'd worked with Leon several times over the years. He'd been a manager at the Hilton for ages. The last time they'd worked together was on a celebrity party.

"I'm doing well. Busy but good."

"So what can I do for you?"

"It's a bit complicated, but I need to book ten suites for three weeks from now."

"Wow, cutting it close. But we're just outside of the winter season…hmm, hang on."

Mia's heart pumped. This was her last shot.

Leon came back on the phone. "We can make it work."

She exhaled a major breath of relief. "You are a lifesaver."

"For you, anything."

"There's something else."

"Shoot."

"Should anyone call you and ask why the suites weren't booked for the weekend after next, just say that they were unavailable."

"Not a problem."

Mia shut her eyes in relief. "Great. Thanks so much. Shoot me an invoice and I'll get the payment out to you."

"Sure thing."

"And, Leon, thanks."

"That's what friends are for. I'll e-mail you a link

to the resort. You'll be able to take a virtual tour, get a sense of the space. Any questions, just call me."

"Will do. Take care, Leon."

"You, too. Thanks for the business."

She flopped back into her seat. Mission accomplished. She smiled in triumph. There was only one glitch. If anything was to go down, it had to take place at Michael's home. There was no way that she was going to involve her friend, Leon. She didn't want his business—or hers—connected to the sting.

She pushed up from her seat and went out to bring Ashley up-to-date.

Ashley shook her head in amazement, a big grin stretching across her mouth. "I knew you'd find a way."

"Let's just hope that it works. No more surprises."

Chapter 23

She knew he was going to be upset. Michael was accustomed to having his way—all the time. However, she was shocked by the explosion of his temper.

"Three weeks!" His voice boomed through the phone, rocking Mia back in her seat. "I didn't say three weeks, Mia. I specifically said two and for a damn good reason. This is unacceptable. You're going to have to change it. Now! And if you can't, I'll get someone else to handle this."

She gripped the phone to keep her hands from shaking. The last thing she needed was him flying off the handle and getting someone else to take over the assignment. She couldn't let that happen.

"Then get someone else," she said, combating his tirade with cool calm. "I'm sure you can find someone much more capable than me. And that someone else will tell you exactly what I just did—there is nothing available in your area for the week you wanted unless you want your very special guests to bunk together. So, since you will no longer be needing my services… have a good day, Michael."

She drew in a breath, threw up a silent prayer.

"Wait."

Her entire body trembled as she waited.

"Yes?"

"Look, I'm sorry. I'm sure you did everything you could."

Mia could almost see his face contorting as he apologized. "So what are you saying?"

She heard him mutter a curse through the phone.

"Three weeks."

She hoped he couldn't hear the thudding of her heart. "Fine. I'll get right on it."

He hung up without saying goodbye, which was fine with Mia. Less chance for the wrong thing to be said.

It was time for a meeting of the minds.

The Shop was cozy and warm when Mia arrived, accompanied by Ashley. By the time they were settled and had ordered a plate of buffalo wings as appetizers, Savannah came in, her short hairdo slightly windswept around her cupie-doll face.

"Hey, ladies," Savannah greeted them, shrugging out of her coat. "Is it just us?"

"Dani should be here shortly. She had a shoot to finish that was running late. And I invited Traci."

"Oh," they chorused.

As if on cue, Traci came through the door, spotted the trio and headed in their direction.

"Hey, everybody."

"Hi." She looked around hesitantly.

"Have a seat, girl," Savannah offered.

Traci took off her coat and slid in next to Ashley. She folded her hands on top of the table. "Thanks for inviting me. I know this is kinda y'all's thing."

"Always room for one more," Mia said and offered a smile.

Traci took a seat next to Savannah.

"Hope you like buffalo wings," Ashley said, digging in.

"Yep." She picked one up from the plate.

"I want to wait until Dani gets here so that I don't have to say everything twice."

Savannah picked up a wing and dipped it in the blue cheese dressing, just as Danielle blew in on a blast of chilly air.

"Now the party can get started," she said in greeting. She squeezed in next to Traci. "Nice to see you here."

"Thanks."

"Let's get all the business out of the way and then we can eat, drink and be merry," Mia said.

"Now that's what I'm talking about," Danielle chimed.

Mia told them what she'd been able to pull off for the Pocono weekend, the juggling of the weekend date and having Leon back her up, should he ever be questioned.

"Don't ever let anybody tell you that you don't know the people who count," Danielle teased.

Mia winked. "So now I can spend time with my man, put the screws to my ex and hang with my girls. Who could ask for more?"

They all laughed.

"Of course, Ashley, you are going to have to be on the outside. I need you to photograph everyone coming in and out of there."

"Got it."

"Dani, you'll be one of the girls."

"Oh, guess I should have mentioned that Michelle called me this afternoon to tell me that Michael wanted me to be there."

"Great. Savannah, you'll run point—eyes and ears—girl."

"Not a problem."

"Traci, you have your end covered. We'll be working together."

Traci nodded.

"We'll stay in touch and Traci will keep us up-to-date on any changes from inside." Mia sat back. "We're good?"

"Yep."

"So enough about business. Let's talk beaches and moonlit nights," Savannah urged.

Mia laughed. "I can't wait," she said, her expression lighting up. "I can't remember the last time I was away that didn't have something to do with my job or a client."

"Make the most of it," Danielle said. "The good times are few and far between."

"I wish Blake and I could get away," Savannah said, "but I can't bear to leave Mikayla. Going to work is bad enough."

"How old is she?" Traci asked.

"Six months." She dug in her purse and whipped out her wallet, bulging with photos.

"Oh, boy," her trio of friends groaned.

"Don't get her started on Mikayla," Danielle teased. "We'll be talking about Pampers, baby bottles and how brilliant her baby is for the rest of the night."

Savannah waved her hand in dismissal and proceeded to show Traci pictures of her bundle of joy.

The waitress came to take their orders and the ladies continued their conversation, talking about their love lives, jobs, the latest books they'd read and what movie star they'd love to meet.

Before they knew it, it was nearly nine o'clock.

"I really have got to go," Savannah said. "Blake will start blowing up my cell phone in a minute and I want to give Mikayla her last feeding." She got up and prepared to leave.

"Me, too," Danielle said. "This has been great, as usual."

Mia reached for the check.

"No. Let me get it," Traci said. "My way of saying thanks."

All the ladies turned questioning gazes on Traci.

"I really appreciate y'all including me. It's been a long time since I had real girlfriends." She looked at each of them.

"We're glad to have you," Savannah said. She squeezed her shoulder.

"Damn, girl, if I knew you were paying, I would have ordered drinks!" Danielle teased. "Welcome to the club," she said, her tone serious but welcoming.

"Thanks."

"Be sure to take plenty of pictures," Savannah said as she waved goodbye.

"I want audio," Ashley said.

Ashley stood. "Just have a good time, girl. This mess will be here waiting when you get back."

If she knew nothing else, that was definitely true. Mia got her coat and purse and followed her friends out into the night.

Chapter 24

Steven had spared no expense for this trip. He'd refused to tell her where they were staying. But the trip started off with them flying first class, being picked up by a driver at the airport and then taken to Sandals Resorts.

The driver opened Mia's door and she stepped out with her mouth open. She spun toward Steven and flew into his arms.

"Sandals," she squealed.

"Couples only," he said into her hair as he swung her around.

She wiggled up against him, reached up and kissed him tenderly on the lips. "Thank you," she whispered against his mouth.

"For what?" He brushed some hair away from her face.

"For doing this for us."

"Lady, you ain't seen nothing yet." He swept her up in his arms and carried her laughing and giggling into the hotel lobby.

Once they checked in and were escorted to their room, Mia was shocked once again. The room was magnificent, with a terrace that overlooked the ocean, a sprawling sunken living room, full kitchen, master bedroom and bath. The décor was pure island bliss. Sheer white drapery wafted in the windows, low-slung furniture in bamboo and white canvas dotted the gleaming wood floors. The scent of clear blue ocean water settled all around them.

Mia turned in a slow circle, taking in the space. "This is beautiful," she said softly, turning to face Steven, who watched her as if awestruck. "What is it?"

"You. You're the one that's beautiful." He crossed the short distance between them and took her hands. "I want us to have the best time. Anything you want, whatever you want to do for the next three days."

A devilish grin teased her mouth. "How 'bout we test out that king-size bed for starters?"

"You don't have to ask me twice."

After they'd christened the bed, they took a shower together then ordered room service and ate on the terrace under the stars, a traditional island meal of flying fish, plantains and seasoned callaloo, with mouthwatering mango sherbet for dessert.

Following dinner, which was accompanied by strains of calypso music in the distance, the crash of waves against the shore and the unmistakable sound of voices on the beach enjoying the glorious night, they decided to take a walk and get a feel for the island they'd heard so much about but had never had the chance to visit.

They strolled along the beach, holding hands, something they rarely had a chance or the time to do. The balmy air was intoxicating, and they felt light and carefree.

"I can't believe how good I feel after only being here for a few hours," Mia said, leaning against Steven as they walked along the sand.

"It is kinda magical. Must be the sea air and the sense of being worry free. I haven't seen anyone rushing, looking stressed or using a BlackBerry."

Mia laughed. "You're absolutely right. It's a completely different world." She stopped, pulled him to her. "And I love it. I love you."

He threaded his fingers through her loose hair, lowered his head and slowly took her mouth to his. His insides seemed to fill, his heart raced and an exquisite sense of peace flowed through him. He caressed her back, holding her close. This was paradise, he thought as his tongue played with hers. Paradise was being with the one woman who made waking up every day an adventure, filled with limitless possibility.

The following day Mia and Steven went into town and spent the entire day window-shopping, shopping for real and sampling all the island foods that their stomachs could hold. They stopped and listened to a steel drum band on a street corner. Open-air shops with tantalizing trinkets beckoned them.

By the time they returned to their hotel, they were weighted down with bags, having bought souvenirs for all their friends and loads of knickknacks for their condo.

"We're going to pay through the nose to get all this stuff back," Mia said as she unpacked their spoils. "We'll need another suitcase just for all the things we bought."

"I know. But it was worth it. I had a great time today. What about you?" He pulled his shirt over his head and tossed it on a lounge chair near the window.

Mia plopped spread-eagle on the bed. "I'm having a ball. We definitely must do this more often."

"All we have to do is make it happen. I have a surprise for you for tonight."

She sprung up. "What?"

He angled his head to the side and wagged his finger at her. "If I told you—"

"It wouldn't be a surprise," she finished for him and plopped back down, this time adding a pout.

"Making faces won't get me to talk."

She folded her arms defiantly. "Fine."

"Just wear something light and pretty. That's all you need to know."

Mia had purchased an entire new wardrobe for their minivacation. She stood in the doorway of the bedroom closet contemplating what to wear. She decided on a burnt-orange sundress made of a gauze material that was as light as air and kissed her ankles. She pulled her shoulder-length hair up into a loose knot on top of her head, added simple gold hoops in her ears and a dash of lipstick. Slipping into a pair of sandals, she was ready.

"Perfect," Steven said from behind her.

She turned. "You like?"

"Very much." He came up to her and ran his hand along the fabric of her dress, the heat of her skin coming right through the thin material. "It's going to be hard concentrating on dinner when I know that you have nothing on underneath this dress," he said, his voice growing thick.

"Try," she whispered. "It will make it more fun later."

He hooked his arm around her waist and nuzzled her neck until she moaned in delight. He gave her a quick kiss in that hot spot on her neck before releasing her.

When they reached the lobby, they were met by the concierge.

"Your car is right out front, Mr. Long."

"Thank you."

"Car? Where are we going?"

"Surprise, remember?" He took her hand and led her outside to the waiting car.

Mia got in beside him. "Do you even know how to drive on the wrong side of the street?" She buckled up.

Steve chuckled. "We'll see."

Mia held on and they took off.

Driving through the narrow, busy streets was a test of nerves and certainly skill. But Steven was cool, calm and collected as he wove his way around the dirt and cobblestone roads.

The evening was picture-perfect. The sky was absolutely clear, with sparkling stars dusting the sky, and the moon hung at a precarious angle, joining the constellations in brilliance. A gentle ocean breeze cooled the air and carried the intoxicating scents of island foods and fruits.

Soon, Mia realized that they were driving out of the town proper and little by little there were fewer people and buildings to see. Now all that was in view were scattered cottages and a few strollers walking along the beach.

Finally, Steven brought the car to a stop near a cove of trees tucked away from what was left of civilization.

"Where are we and how in the world did you find this place?" Mia asked as she unbuckled her seat belt and got out.

"I asked around," he teased. He went to the trunk of the car and opened it, pulling out a huge basket. He shut the trunk door, came around to Mia and took her hand. "Come on."

"Is that what I think it is?" she asked, excitement lighting her voice when she saw the oversize basket.

"We'll have to see, won't we?"

He led them to an even more secluded place along the beach, protected by what looked like a small cave and beautiful foliage. He set the basket down, opened the top and pulled out a blue-and-white blanket that he spread over the sand, followed by a bottle of wine, and dish after dish of island delicacies. To top it off he took out a small radio and tuned it to the local station that was playing sensual island beats.

Mia was awed. "I can't believe you did all this," she said as Steven handed her a glass of wine.

"It wasn't easy sneaking phone calls and making arrangements when we were together just about every minute. Why do you think I was taking so many showers?" he joked. "The hotel must have thought I was nuts. Every time I called there was the sound of rushing water in the background and I was always whispering."

Mia tossed her head back and laughed. "I can only imagine."

"To us," he said, raising his glass to hers.

She touched his glass with her own. "To us. And many more exquisite nights under the stars," she said on a breath, gazing heavenward.

They sampled each of the dishes that the hotel kitchen had specially prepared, talked of inconsequential things, childhood faux pas, the state of the world and when they planned to take another trip together.

After they finished eating, they decided to walk off their meal with a stroll along the beach. Leaving their shoes behind, they waded in and out of the water, darting among the waves as the sand slid from beneath their feet, threatening to take them along for a ride.

"When I was kid," Steven began, "I guess I was about eight, the closest I'd ever come to water outside of the bathtub was the community pool in Philadelphia, where I grew up. I remember one hot-ass summer day my dad took my brother and me to the pool. I couldn't swim, but my father was determined to make me learn." His expression grew pensive in the moonlight as the memories came rushing back.

"I just couldn't seem to get it right and my dad was getting more and more frustrated. I started crying because he was so angry. Then, out of the blue, he smacked me. Smacked me so hard he knocked me down."

Mia gasped and gripped his hand tighter.

"Everyone was staring. A woman tried to intercede, and I remember my dad dared her to try and she backed off, shaking her head and muttering under her breath. Then he turned on me. Told me what a weakling I was, a crybaby. How could I be *his* son? Real men don't whine and cry."

Mia felt his pain and humiliation as if it were her own.

"We finally left the pool and all I could think about was that I wanted to disappear. But when we got in the car, my dad wiped my nose, patted me on the head and told me he was sorry. I was so shocked and confused I didn't know what to say. He went on to tell me that he had to do what he did because I had to be tough, I had to be strong. Especially as a black man. You can't show emotion or become attached to anything or anyone—especially a woman."

He drew in a breath and slowly exhaled, as if trying to physically exorcise the ugly memories.

"He didn't elaborate on it that day, but he did as I got older. Never let a woman know that you care. Never show her emotion. They'll trap you, and once they trap your heart, you're done. And ain't no hurt like the kind of hurt a woman can put on a man."

"My God, how cynical. How could he try to put those kinds of thoughts in your head?"

Steven chuckled sadly. "The really sad part is I believed it. I lived it. But being around Blake and Savannah began to change me. I saw how they were with each other, how they truly cared for each other. I wanted that. I wanted more than just physical intimacy. I wanted to be touched inside." He swallowed back the sudden knot in his throat. "Damn, I sound like just the guy my father never wanted me to be."

Mia stopped walking. She turned him to face her.

"But that's the man I want. I never realized just how much until the night you told me 'something almost happened,' and I thought I was losing you. We all have our baggage—I know I do—but we can get through anything if we work at it. I never thought I could be this happy. And, yes, there have been times when I've had my doubts, but you've never given me a reason to doubt the kind of man you are or doubt that you truly care for me and about me." She stroked his cheek then cupped it in her palm. "You're a good man. A hard-working, honest, intelligent, fine, sexy, black man." Her eyes darkened. "I'm getting turned on just talking about you," she said in a throaty whisper.

He leaned down and kissed her slow and deep, the water lapping at their ankles, the moon silhouetting them against the night. "We can do something about that." He brushed his thumb across her nipples, which rose to hard peaks, making her shiver in delight.

"Here?" she asked against his probing mouth.

He looked around. "Nothing watching us but the stars."

Mia giggled. "Race you back to the blanket." She pulled her dress over her head and took off toward the blanket with Steven hot on her heels.

Chapter 25

The week leading up to the event in the Poconos was a constant flurry of activity—meetings and more meetings, phone calls, checks and double-checks. It was essential for all the players to be coordinated and in place. In addition to which, Mia was entrenched in the planning details from catering to décor and entertainment. But what made it all go down easy was that she was still floating on cloud nine from her long getaway weekend with Steven.

Since they'd been back, something was different between them. They seemed to have bonded on an entirely new level. And, oh, it was so very sweet. At times, instead of working, she found herself daydreaming about Steven and longing for the life she knew they could have together—and seemed to be working toward.

Finally, the night arrived. Michael had given Traci a set of keys so that she and Mia could drive up early to do a walk-through. This gave them the perfect opportunity to plant several listening devices throughout the house, as well as hiding two minicameras in the oversize vase of flowers that sat on a glass table facing the door.

Ashley, equipped with a telephoto lens, was stationed in a parked car just outside the property on the main road, with perfect access to the comings and goings of Michael's house. She'd already wired the ten suites at the resort, saying to Leon that she was doing a last-minute check on the accommodations. They weren't taking any chances that they would miss an incriminating conversation.

Savannah arrived under the pretext of being an additional member of Mia's team—which, of course, she really was.

Michael arrived just before six.

Mia's heart thundered in her chest. Tonight was the last opportunity she might have to bring this awful episode to a conclusion, and there was no room for error, sweet talk or tainted memories.

"Michael," she greeted him warmly. "We were just going over last-minute details. The caterer is here and the band is setting up in the back."

He took a look around, nodding his head. "Everything looks great."

"I'm sure your guests will be pleased. Oh, I wanted to introduce you to Savannah Fields." She turned to Savannah. "Savannah, this is our host, Michael Burke."

"Great to meet you," she said, shaking his hand. "I've read wonderful things about you."

"You look familiar."

Savannah smiled. "I was at the red-carpet event for Raven."

"Ahh, yes. I never forget a face."

"Savannah often helps out when I put together events. She's a whiz with details."

"Glad to have you here. I hope that you'll have some time to enjoy yourself tonight."

"I'm sure I will." She turned to Mia. "I'm going to check on the caterers and make sure they're ready as soon as the first guest walks in."

"Which should be soon," Michael said.

"Then I'd better get on it. Excuse me." She headed toward the kitchen, leaving Mia and Michael alone.

"I'm hoping that when all the dust settles with this shindig we can get together without business on the table between us. I made a promise to you and I intend to keep it."

She couldn't risk alienating him now. Not with so much at stake. "Fine. We'll talk."

He smiled, that old familiar smile, but it also held something more than familiarity. It seemed to radiate relief.

The doorbell rang, signaling the arrival of the first guest.

"Showtime," Mia said, thankful for a reason to get away.

One by one the guests arrived. Mia recognized a number of the women from the red-carpet event several weeks earlier. Danielle came in with Michelle and they quickly began to mingle with the guests.

Nick had convinced Danielle to let him help out, and

when she proposed the idea to Mia, Mia decided that he would be perfect to act as valet. In that capacity he was to put tracking devices on all the women's cars.

The evening wore on and the crowd grew livelier, filled with food and plenty of good liquor. The party atmosphere was in full swing. As they grew more relaxed, the couples began pairing off. Some went upstairs, while others headed for the suites at the resort.

Danielle, realizing that the clock was ticking, knew that she had to get out of there before she got squired away by one of the male guests. Fortunately, as in most cases, there were at least two women for every man. When she excused herself from a mind-numbing conversation with a Wall Street exec who was bending her ear about stocks and bonds, she slipped outside and made a beeline for her car, waving to Ashley as she steered out onto the road. She pulled the mini-mic loose from the clip on her dress and tucked it inside her purse.

It was nearly 2:00 a.m. by the time the last guest left the house. The caterers were packing up and Mia, Savannah and Traci subtly removed the cameras and recording devices as they went from room to room, putting everything back in order.

Michael was reclining on the couch, nursing the last of his drink with a very self-satisfied look on his face. "Fabulous event."

"Thank you," Mia said. "I had good help."

He pushed up from his chair, took a white envelope from the breast pocket of his suit and handed it to Mia. "The balance for tonight."

She lifted her chin and wondered how many other

women were being paid off tonight for their services. "Thanks." She tucked it in her purse. "Well," she breathed, "we need to get back." She turned for the door.

"I'll call you next week…to talk about what I mentioned."

"Sure." All she wanted to do right then was run as fast as she could into Steven's arms and put this night and all that had led up to it away for good.

The following morning, Mia contacted each of the team members to give them instructions on when and how to transfer all their information. The audio and videotapes were damning. There was no way that anyone involved would walk away scot-free. But until all the information was compiled and reviewed, it was still anyone's guess.

All the surveillance information was uploaded to Jasmine's computer at the brownstone, where she would sort and organize it before presenting it to Jean.

Their job was done, Mia thought as she sent her final transmission. Now the waiting began. But until then she could sure use the company of her girlfriends.

Everyone seemed to be talking at once. The drinks flowed and fingers were sticky with hot sauce from their favorite appetizer—buffalo wings.

Unexpected snow had begun to fall so Mia, Ashley, Danielle, Savannah and Traci enjoyed being able to huddle together.

"We did it, y'all," Danielle said, raising a wing to her lips. "I thought for sure I was gonna have to get physical with that guy who kept telling me he had someplace 'really nice' he wanted to take me."

"Oh, you mean, Congressman Stanley?" Traci asked with a smile.

"Yeah, him." She shivered, remembering.

"I got an early report from Jasmine on some of the women," Mia said.

Everyone leaned forward.

"Y'all will never guess in a zillion years who they are."

"Who?" they all asked at once, causing a few heads to turn.

Mia lowered her voice. "Housewives from Long Island. And the ringleader is the PTA president."

They all erupted in fits of laughter.

"Well, if it's not Wisteria Lane!" Ashley said.

"Yeah, some truly desperate housewives," Savannah added.

Danielle suddenly tapped her water glass with her fork. She made a big deal about clearing her throat. "I have an announcement to make."

All eyes were on her.

"Nick and I finally set the date!" Her face lit up and a big old Kool-Aid smile widened her lush mouth.

"Oh, my goodness."

"Hallelujah!"

"'Bout time that man finally made an honest woman out of you."

Danielle shook with laughter. "I'm trying to tell ya."

"So when is the big day?" ever-practical Mia asked.

"Second week in January."

Mia's eyes widened. "Hey, how about a double wedding? Claudia and Bernard were talking about De-

cember, but what if I did both of them in January?"
She looked from one face to the other. Before anyone
could react, Savannah had her mother on the phone,
telling her the plan.

"She loves it!" Savannah said after disconnecting
the call.

"Well, I will definitely have my work cut out for
me," Mia said. "But this is the kind of work I'm going
to love doing." She leaned over and hugged Danielle
tight. "I'm so happy for you, girl."

Uncharacteristic tears filled Danielle's eyes. "I'm
really happy, y'all. I'm really getting married."

"Now that deserves a toast," Ashley said.

They all raised their glasses.

"To Danielle and Nick."

"To finding true love."

"To great sex."

"To girlfriends."

They all touched glasses.

"Well, ladies, we done good," Savannah said as they
prepared to leave.

"I wonder what the next assignment will be," Danielle asked, slipping into her coat.

Ashley stood and stretched. "Knowing Jean, I'm
sure she'll find something to put us to the test."

They raised their empty glasses and toasted to that.

Chapter 26

Mia, always looking for a novel way to throw a party, had planned a dual bachelor and bachelorette party for Claudia and Bernard and Danielle and Nick. She didn't spare any expense when it came to food and decorations and had worked all day with the help of Ashley and Traci to ensure that everything was absolutely perfect when the guests arrived. She'd even hired a bartender and a waitress so that she and Steven could enjoy the festivities.

The party was to officially start at seven and by seven-fifteen their two-bedroom condo was packed like a nightclub. Savannah and Blake came first and brought Mikayla, to everyone's delight. Bernard had invited the ladies from the health spa along with each one's significant other—Ann Marie and Sterling, Stephanie and Tony, and Elizabeth and Ron—all of whom felt like part of the family from the moment they came through the door, loaded down with gifts.

Champagne flowed, laughter filled the air and the feeling of love and affection was contagious.

Over the sound of music and animated conversation, Mia darted into the kitchen to answer the phone.

"Turn on your television."

"Jean?"

"I think you'll like what you see."

She hung up the phone and returned to the living room. While everyone else was occupied, she turned on the television to CNN. Breaking News was the banner across the screen.

A reporter was standing in front of a house in Hempstead, Long Island. Police were bringing out a woman in handcuffs. Mia gasped. It was one of the women from the party.

Savannah sidled up beside her and her mouth dropped open as the reporter went on to explain that a major escort ring has just been broken, with many of the alleged escorts being wives and mothers in this small suburban community.

By this time everyone in the room was focused on the television screen.

"Turn up the volume," Claudia said.

The picture switched to a house that Mia immediately recognized as Michael's home on Sag Harbor. Her stomach seesawed.

"Initial reports indicate that many of the customers hold political office. Warrants have been issued, although the names of the accused have not been released to the media. According to the attorney general, this is the biggest sting operation in New York City history. We will keep you posted as more information becomes available."

Mia hid the tide of emotions that rolled in her stomach. This was the man she'd once loved, and had tossed aside all her convictions of right and wrong to be with him. But he was not the man that she thought she once loved. Michael was a man who lived for the next deal, the money, and didn't care who he used to get what he wanted. It had taken this case and finding out who he really was for her to once and for all put a period at the end of their relationship. She may never know what it was he wanted to tell her and it didn't matter. It was over and she was glad she'd been the one to bring it to an end.

A ripple of "wow" undulated through the room before they each shook off the effects of what they'd just seen and returned to party mode.

The girls, including Claudia, slipped into the kitchen unnoticed.

"To success, ladies," Mia said, looking from one to the other. "I couldn't have done it without each one of you." She raised an empty glass in mock salute.

"What are you ladies celebrating?"

"Just girl stuff," Mia said, sliding her arm around her man's waist.

"Well, I have something to celebrate, too."

"What?"

He took Mia by the hand. "Come on and I'll show you." He ushered her back into the living room, with all her friends trailing behind.

"Excuse me, ladies and gentlemen," Steven shouted over the music and laughter.

Blake crossed the room and lowered the music.

"Since this is a day of celebrations for two of my favorite couples—" he turned to Mia "—I want to celebrate the rest of my life with you."

A soft gasp of expectation filled the room.

"I want to come home to you, sleep and wake with you. Share my joys and sorrows with you." He reached into his pants pocket and took out a diamond ring set in platinum with tiny diamonds encrusted on the band.

Mia began to shake.

"You're my world."

"You go, boy!" Blake cheered.

Mia's eyes filled.

"Say you'll marry me and finally make me complete."

For a moment she couldn't breathe, she couldn't think. It all seemed so surreal. And when she looked into his eyes, saw the depth of his feelings for her hovering there, the dam finally broke.

"Yes, yes, yes, I'll marry you."

Whoops of joy exploded in the room.

Steven put the ring on her finger and gathered her up in his embrace. "I love you," he said for her ears only. "I love you," he repeated.

Her heart swelled to bursting and tears spilled from her eyes. This was joy, Mia thought. This was true happiness. One man devoted to one woman, wanting only each other and the best for each other. This was love. The real thing, and she was never going to let it go.

They kissed as if they were the only two people in the room. And to them they were.

* * * * *

LONGING AND LIES

Chapter 1

The month of April had definitely lived up to its reputation. For a solid week, it rained in every variety from
bad-hair-day mist to outright downpours complete with
thunder and lightning.

Ashley Temple sent up a prayer of thanks as she
pulled back her bedroom curtains to usher in the first
rays of sun in a week. She stretched catlike, raising her
face to the warm rays that beamed through the window.

The previous week had been difficult for more reasons than bad weather. She'd recently finished up an
assignment where she'd had to pose as a college coed to
break up a drug-trafficking operation on campus. She
developed friendships with some of the girls that she
ultimately had to turn in. She could still see their faces,
the looks of betrayal, the hurt and terror in their eyes.

She sighed heavily and turned away from the new

day. There were times when she wished that The Cartel was not part of her life. As a member of the secret organization, she could never have a real life, because part of who she was and what she did could never be revealed to anyone outside of The Cartel's inner circle. That fact alone limited forming any long-lasting intimate relationships. And as she crept past the age of thirty, the desire to find someone and something permanent was beginning to fill her thoughts more each day.

However, there were some wonderful benefits. She'd met some of the most incredible women through The Cartel and forged unbreakable friendships. Savannah, Mia, Danielle and more recently Traci, were the savviest sisters she'd ever met. Somehow they'd all managed to maintain the man in their lives, get married or engaged, have kids and still kick major butt when duty called. So there was definitely hope for her at the end of the "espionage rainbow."

She was closest to Mia, having worked as her assistant at MT Management—Mia's event-planning firm—for the past year and being a shadow on Mia's last assignment that involved an elite illegal escort service. That assignment had been harrowing at best, testing the ladies on many levels, but it had been nothing compared to MT Management's crème de la crème affair, the coordination of the triple wedding ceremony for three of The Cartel members: Claudia and Bernard, Mia and Steven and Danielle and Nick. Although they'd all returned back to work, they were still gooey-eyed and bubbly. If she didn't like them all so much, it might just turn her stomach.

Ashley turned away from the window, sat down

on the side of the bed and put on her sneakers. She wasn't expected at the office until ten, and she wanted to get in her morning run before the streets grew too crowded with the mad dashers en route to work in bustling Manhattan.

She loved the city, she thought, stepping outside and taking a deep breath of rain-washed air, particularly the eclectic atmosphere of lower Manhattan where she'd lived for the past five years. It was a mixture of young and old, exciting and sublime, from mom-and-pop stops to reservations-only restaurants. The aroma of foods from around the world wafted through the air, giving the city its own unique, and often mouth-watering scent.

Ashley did a few stretches on the front steps of her four-story apartment building before slowly taking off down Avenue A. She waved to Herbie as she jogged by his newsstand, making a mental note to pick up a paper on her way back and a lottery ticket. She was no more than three blocks from her apartment when the vibration went off on her hip. She glanced down at the illuminated screen of her BlackBerry. "Anonymous." She knew exactly who it was.

Ashley circled the block in her tan 2000 Honda Accord before finding a parking space on 126th Street, across the intersection from TLC's headquarters.

As she walked down the street, she was continually amazed at the gentrification that had taken place in Harlem over the last decade and even more so in the past two years. It was almost unrecognizable except for the tree-lined blocks that still embraced the stately brownstones, many of which had been restored to their former glory, when Harlem was in vogue and the salons were frequented by Langston Hughes, Adam Clayton Powell and the like discussing the "Negro condition."

Ashley reached her destination and spotted several well-toned guys entering a brownstone, which was actually the Pause for Men Day Spa, owned by four women. She'd had the opportunity to meet them and visit the spa on several occasions and was totally impressed with what they had accomplished. And with The Ladies Cartel headquarters tucked unobtrusively across the street, it was a testament to the power of women on this stretch of street in Harlem.

Ashley approached the brownstone. To the casual observer, TLC headquarters was simply another restored brownstone that ran the Tender Loving Care body products business, which would account for the traffic of women and the often large, all-female gatherings. However, it was anything but that.

She rang the bell and moments later Claudia answered the door. Claudia was Jean's right hand and long-time TLC operative. What was most intriguing was that she was Savannah's mother, and it had been Claudia who recruited her own daughter into the organization, and in turn Savannah brought in Mia and Danielle.

"Hello, sweetheart," Claudia greeted, clasping Ashley's shoulders and kissing her cheek. "You look stunning and stylish as always," she said, taking in Ashley's wild, spiral afro, knee-high brown suede boots over a pair of very tight jeans, layered T-shirts and a thick, brown leather belt hanging low on her slender hips.

Ashley grinned. "Thanks." She stepped in. "How's married life?"

Claudia beamed. "Wouldn't have it any other way."

"Don't wear Bernard out with your bad self," Ashley teased.

Claudia made a face. "Now where's the fun in that?"

They both laughed.

"Jean is waiting for you," she said as they approached the stairs. "You should be very proud of yourself."

Ashley looked at Claudia over her shoulder. Her brow creased. "Proud of myself? Why?"

"Jean rarely picks the same operative for assignments back-to-back." She smiled slowly. "She thinks very highly of you."

For an instant Ashley's stomach tensed. The corner of her mouth flickered. "I guess that's a good thing. Huh?"

Claudia merely smiled and turned away.

Ashley drew in a breath, turned and headed up the stairs to Jean's office on the second floor. As she went up she passed the Hall of Fame that held the pictures of many of the TLC operatives on the wall, hers included. She made a mental note to give them an updated photo. One of the most recent additions was Brenda's picture—the prodigal daughter—who'd returned to the fold during Mia's last assignment.

She went up the next flight and down the hall, tapped lightly on Jean's partially opened door.

"Come in."

Ashley stepped inside and was surprised to see Bernard sitting in the office, as well. Bernard Hassell, Claudia's husband, was Jean's connection to Homeland Security, the FBI and CIA. Bernard's influence ran so deep into that side of government that it was a little scary. None of the TLC members wanted to know what he really did. It was simply better not to. Other than that, he was a great guy and a dead ringer for Billie Dee Williams.

"Please have a seat," Jean instructed as she took off her signature red-frame glasses.

Jean Wallington-Armstrong—although she rarely used her married name—was at that magic point in her life where she could have been thirty or fifty. She was in excellent physical shape, known to jog four miles a day and workout in the gym three times a week. Her skin was still smooth with a light sprinkle of freckles across her nose. Her arresting green eyes didn't miss a trick and her lustrous red hair glowed with vitality. She could easily be mistaken for the actress that played Addison on *Grey's Anatomy* before moving on to star in *Private Practice*. But most of all it was the power that Jean exuded, from her commanding presence to her no-nonsense attitude that mesmerized everyone who met her, which was why it was so hard to believe that any man could have gotten away with hurting her emotionally—like her ex-husband did. At least that was the urban legend that circulated around The Cartel. No one spoke about it outright, but there were whisperings, especially when Brenda returned. But that was another story.

"Bernard, good to see you."

He nodded his head. "You, too. Congratulations on the high school case. Great job."

"Thanks," she murmured. She took a seat opposite Jean.

Jean opened a folder then looked across the wide oak desk at Ashley. "The reason I asked Bernard to join us is that he is going to be involved from the beginning."

Ashley rested her oversized purse on her lap, crossed her ankles and waited. That was an interesting twist, she thought. Bernard usually brought up the rear or came on board when things got a bit dicey. So to have him involved from day one put her on alert.

"There has been a rash of children that have gone missing. Babies, infants. Some of them from their homes or right from the hospital never to be seen again. The government is keenly aware of this." She flashed Bernard a look.

"But with a war on two fronts, the weak economy and a host of other national and world issues, they don't have the manpower to tackle this the way it needs to be tackled," Bernard said.

As they talked, explaining her assignment, Ashley fought down the nausea that brewed in her stomach. Her temples pounded and she felt the beads of perspiration lining her forehead and trickling down the center of her spine. She took in short breaths to steady her stomach as her heart thundered in her chest. Why her? Why did they pick her for this? Oh, God. Her throat clenched.

"We will need you to infiltrate several of these agencies," Jean was saying, cutting into Ashley's twisting emotions. "We think that is the best starting place. These agencies serve as the conduit from the places of abduction to the buyers. We're just hoping that these children have not been taken out of the country."

Ashley rubbed her damp palms along her thighs.

"Are you all right, Ashley?" Jean asked.

Ashley's gaze snapped toward Jean. She swallowed.

"Yes. I'm fine. Just thinking…how horrible it must be for the parents."

Jean looked at her for a moment before continuing. "We decided that the best cover for this assignment is for you to have a partner."

"A partner?" she echoed.

Bernard cleared his throat. He turned to Jean. "May I?" Jean nodded for him to go ahead. He leaned backward and folded his arms. "We need to ensure from the onset that your cover is tight. To do that we decided that it was best that you be part of a couple."

"A couple?" she repeated for lack of something concrete to say.

"Yes."

Jean opened a folder and adjusted her glasses on the bridge of her aquiline nose. "The FBI is part of this operation. I asked Bernard to go through the files and select the agent that would be best suited for this. His name is Elliot Morgan. He's just returned from an operation overseas."

"I've already briefed him on what needs to be done," Bernard added. "And he's agreed."

Ashley adjusted herself in her seat.

"He should be here shortly, but we wanted to speak with you first. So if you have any reservations, now is the time to let me know," Jean said.

Ashley cleared her throat. "I've just never worked with a male operative before," she said, looking from one to the other.

"Under normal circumstances we try to tailor all of our assignments for Cartel members only. But this is a highly sensitive case. In addition to which, the FBI wants to be involved."

Ashley nodded. The knot of tension tightened in her stomach. Did Jean know about that dark, painful part of her life? Is that why she was selected for this assignment?

There was a light knock on the door.

"Come in," Jean called out.

All heads turned in the direction of the opening door.

Chapter 2

Elliot Morgan's trained dark eyes took in the room and its occupants all at once. He was still tense and edgy from his undercover assignment in London where he was on the trail of a serial bomber. His senses remained on high alert, expecting the unexpected at any moment. In his shady world where no one was who they claimed to be, everyone was suspect. He'd seen more in his thirty-six years than most people had in a lifetime.

Ashley's breath stopped somewhere in her chest and wouldn't budge. The new arrival had virtually sucked up all the air in the room. Tall, dark, athletically muscular, he brought to mind the sleekness and danger of a predatory panther. His features were hard and chiseled with deep probing eyes and full lips. His closely shaven hair was more of a shadow than anything else. But it was more than his physical presence that was breathtaking. It was clear by the way he moved, the way he looked at each of them that he wouldn't hesitate to make them a distant memory without hesitation. His body and demeanor was as much a weapon as anything that could be put in his large hands.

"Elliot." Bernard stood. "Come on in."

Elliot closed the door behind him and came fully into the room. His expression was unreadable as he approached the trio.

"Elliot Morgan, Jean Wallington and Ashley Temple."

Jean extended her hand, which he shook. "Ashley is one of our most skilled Cartel members," she said.

He turned slightly to his right. His jaw clenched. He extended his hand. "Pleasure," he murmured taking her hand.

Ashley offered a tight-lipped smile and a short nod of her head.

Elliot pulled up an available seat.

"We were briefing Ashley on the situation and the plan that we've designed. I want you both to know that we understand perfectly that this assignment is out of the norm for you. I know you had your reservations, Elliot about working with someone."

"It's not what I do," he said tersely. He turned to Ashley. "No offense, but I work alone." His hard gaze dared her to refute him.

Ashley lifted her chin. "I feel the same way," she tossed back, ready to go toe-to-toe.

"But as you both know," Jean cut in, "in this business it's what's best for the operation and not our personal preferences." Her stern green gaze went from one tight face to the other.

"If we didn't think the two of you were the right ones for this assignment we could have easily gotten someone else," Bernard firmly stated. "Your expertise with uncovering information and taking on whatever persona necessary is going to be an asset," he said to Elliot. Then he turned to Ashley. "You have an excellent record of getting suspects to trust you. That was apparent on your last assignment. Those are some of the skills we need," he added, addressing them both.

"And we needed two operatives who didn't have any personal attachments that would hamper the assignments," Jean said.

"You mean, 'Who didn't have a life,'" Elliot said, his tone sarcastic as he tossed a meaningful look at Ashley.

Her eyes flashed. She pushed up from her seat. "Look, I'm sorry that you went to all of this trouble, but I'm not the one for this job." She snatched up her purse.

Bernard caught her wrist. "Wait. Please, sit down."

She drew in a long breath, cutting her eyes at Elliot before returning to her seat.

"Short temper is a hazard in the field," Elliot said in that low-key timbre, as he fingered the stud in his ear.

"Elliot," Bernard said, the one word more a warning than a salutation.

"I don't see how this is going to work," Ashley said, crossing her long legs. "It's clear that we won't be able to get along."

"You're going to have to find a way to work it out," Jean admonished. "This can't be about the two of you. This is about saving families from tragedy and young children from a life of misery or worse. So put your personal differences aside and keep your eyes on the prize—finding out who is behind the black-market baby operation in New York City. Are we clear?"

Silence enveloped the room.

"Well?"

"Fine," Elliot conceded.

Ashley smiled inwardly over the fact that he caved first. "Of course."

"You're both professionals. You'll work it out," Bernard said. "You're going to have to, especially since you will not only be working together, but living together as well."

"What!" they yelled in harmony, simultaneously leaping up out of their seats. Their choreography was so perfect, if the situation weren't so absurd it would be funny. They glared at each other.

"Sit down!" Jean slapped her palm against the desk. She snatched her glasses off and pinned them both with a withering gaze. "Enough. If the two of you thought this was some sort of democracy, you're wrong. It's not. You are a federal agent, Mr. Morgan. You don't get to pick and choose. Ashley on the other hand is not." She looked at Ashley. "So if you think you can't *handle* this assignment, leave now."

Ashley was so furious that her insides shook. He was an arrogant bastard! And it was clear from everything he'd said and the way he'd addressed her that he didn't think much of her or her abilities. How in the world were they going to live under the same roof? But she wouldn't let him get the best of her. And she certainly didn't want Jean to think that she couldn't handle the likes of Elliot Morgan. If she did, it would compromise anything she was assigned in the future.

"Two separate bedrooms," Ashley demanded more than stated.

"Fine with me," Elliot said, a twinkle in his dark eyes.

"Of course," Jean said. "Now, can we get back to the business at hand without any more outbursts?"

Ashley and Elliot settled back in their seats and listened to the plan.

More than an hour later the meeting ended. Ashley and Elliot each had a folder of information that they had to commit to memory, because once they opened the envelope the contents would evaporate from the page after more than an hour in the open air. It detailed their cover—who they were pretending to be until the case was solved—and several possible scenarios to gain access to the list of fertility clinics and adoption centers around the city.

Before they left they were told to stop in and see Jasmine, The Cartel's techno whiz. She would provide them with their new identification, and the dummy bank account they would share. Jean was making arrangements for the apartment that they would move into within the week. Everything was falling into step except Elliot and Ashley.

"After you," Elliot said as they left Jasmine's office.

Ashley looked up at him and caught the half grin on his lips. She brushed passed him. "Don't play the gentleman for my benefit," she snapped.

"Still testy," he murmured as he followed her up the stairs to the first-floor exit.

She stopped in her tracks and spun around, nearly colliding into his hard-muscled chest. The heady scent of his cologne clouded her thoughts. For a moment she forgot her retort then her good sense returned. "Look, the less we have to say to each other the better. Just do your job and I'll do mine. How's that?" She didn't wait for a response but turned and strutted out leaving the door swinging on its hinges.

Elliot stepped outside and watched her as she walked down the street with her head high, looking neither left nor right. He leaned against the fence, took out his pack of cigarettes and stuck one in his mouth. He lit the tip and watched a curl of smoke float into the air. He'd been in enemy territory before. Ashley Temple would be a walk in the park. He strode off in the opposite direction.

Ashley gripped the steering wheel so hard her palms began to sting. She couldn't get the smug image of Elliot Morgan out of her head. The way he looked at her. The way he moved. The way he…smelled. Her heart thudded and she frowned in annoyance.

But if she was honest with herself, it was more than Elliot that had her mind spinning. It was the assignment: missing children. Did Jean know the truth? The nightmare was still as fresh in her spirit today as it was more than two decades ago. Her throat clenched as those horrible days bloomed anew.

Chapter 3

Ashley found a parking space a block away from the office. She took the time walking to compose herself before Mia read the anxiety all over her face. Living with a man she didn't know! Even for The Cartel that was asking a bit much. What made them think that she and Mr. Arrogance could ever in this lifetime work together?

She was going to have to do some serious meditating in order to ready herself for the assignment. Even if it was the highest of compliments to be chosen by Jean for two assignments in a row, she wasn't sure that she was cut out for this one.

Ashley pushed open the door to MT Management, Mia Turner's event-planning business and was pleased to see Savannah and her baby daughter, Mikayla.

"Hey! This is a surprise." Ashley dropped her purse

on one of the desks and went straight to Mikayla and
scooped her up for a kiss. "How's my girl? Look at
you, looking all beautiful." She nuzzled her neck to
squeals of delight.

"Can't a sister get some love?" Savannah asked in
mock hurt.

Ashley waved her hand in dismissal. "Later." She
went on kissing and hugging the baby before finally
setting her back down in the stroller. "What brings
you here? Off today?" She kissed Savannah's cheek.

"Took an R&R day. My boss was working me to the
bone." She laughed good-naturedly. "Plus I needed to
spend some time with my pumpkin," she added, stroking her daughter's curly head. "Thought we could do
lunch. Danielle is on her way."

"Sounds like a plan."

"I hear you got another assignment."

"Word travels fast in this town." She plopped down
into the seat opposite Savannah and stretched her legs
out in front of her.

Savannah giggled. "What's a little espionage between friends."

"Yeah," she said halfheartedly.

Savannah tilted her head to the side. "Problem?"

Ashley blew out a breath of frustration. "Something
like that."

"Hey, Ash," Mia said breezing into the waiting area
from her back office. "How'd it go with Jean?"

"Since we're doing lunch today, why don't I wait
until we're all together."

As if on cue, Danielle came sailing in, fashionable
as always and dramatically swept off her sunglasses.

"Hey all." She looked from one face to another. "Gee, I feel like I walked into an intervention. What's up?"

"Ashley said she'd tell us over lunch," Mia offered.

Danielle arched a brow. "Sounds serious."

"Not that bad, but bad enough," Ashley said.

"So why are we all sitting around," Danielle said. "I want to hear this."

The stunning quartet gathered purses, keys, cell phones and stroller and headed out.

They arrived at their favorite eatery, The Shop. They'd been coming as a group for so long, they had their own booth and the waitstaff knew them by name.

The quartet settled down in their seats and flipped open their menus.

"Does this little gathering call for drinks?" Danielle asked.

"I could sure use one," Ashley said. "But it's still early. Oh, what the heck. Let's order a round."

"That serious, huh?" Savannah asked.

Ashley sighed and leaned back against the worn brown leather seat. "I'm probably making more out of this than necessary, but the whole thing just rubs me the wrong way."

Phyllis, the waitress, came to take their orders. It was a round of their favorite, grilled salmon salad with tahini dressing and mojitos. With that out of the way, all eyes were on Ashley.

She told them about her meeting with Jean and Bernard.

"So far so good," Mia said.

"Then in walks Elliot Morgan."

Three pairs of eyes widened as Ashley described

their meeting and the not-very-subtle animosity that flashed between them.

"He's pompous, arrogant and so full of himself," Ashley groaned. "And they want us to live together!" She folded her arms and pouted like a three-year-old.

The women broke out into laughter.

"Girl, your problem is you haven't had a man in your air space in so long you don't know how to handle it." Savannah chuckled.

"For real," Danielle concurred.

Ashley was visibly appalled at the lack of support from her girls. They were supposed to be on her side. Sure, she hadn't had a real relationship in longer than she cared to admit. She knew she had commitment issues, deep-seated fears of loss. Loss that she hadn't shared with anyone, not even her girls. There was a part of her that believed she didn't deserve someone to care about her and her about them. The guilt of all those years ago still haunted her.

They all nodded, biting back smirks. Even little Mikayla was laughing and kicking her feet in her stroller.

Mia leaned forward, schooling her expression. "Look, sis, no one knows better than me how weird it can be living with a man. When Steven and I got together it was tough at first."

"Yeah, but he's your *man*. Now your husband. That's something completely different. I don't know this jerk from a hole in the wall."

"You did say he looked like Idris Elba, didn't you?" Danielle said, egging her on.

Ashley rolled her eyes.

"Look, it's just an assignment. You'll have separate rooms and separate lives outside of the case," Savannah said, always the practical one. "Just worry about the job."

That was just it, Ashley thought. The job. But maybe Savannah was right. Focus on the assignment. It may well lead her to what she'd been searching for over the past twenty years—answers.

Elliot turned the key in the door of his third-floor walk-up on West Eighth Street in the Village. He'd found the place after a less-than-exhaustive search, but fell for it right away. His apartment was in a prewar building, with vaulted ceilings and enormous rooms. His one-bedroom apartment in any other neighborhood in Manhattan would go for three times the amount with the rooms cut down to bite-size pieces. The neighborhood was an eclectic blend of class, culture, language and age, from seedy to high end and everything in between. It was a mecca for the artsy and a paradise for lovers of music, avante-garde shops and cozy cafès. The perfect place to blend in, able to see and go unseen.

He locked the door behind him and began tugging his fitted T-shirt over his head as he strolled from the front hallway, through the mostly unfurnished living room to his bedroom located in the back, facing the park. He tossed his shirt on the bed and absently rubbed the raised, circular scar on his shoulder, the result of a gunshot wound from a man who wished he'd been a better shot. Elliot clenched his teeth. He'd been distracted that afternoon in the alley, by memories of the argument he'd had with Lynn the night before.

It's the first rule in his line of work; relationships are a distraction. Hit It and Quit It, was the slogan among the guys. He should have listened. Then what happened later would not have mattered as much, wouldn't have hurt him so much. It changed him. Now he was a poster child for the boys' club mantra.

Elliot pulled the envelope he'd gotten from Jean out of his back pocket. He unfolded it and tried to flatten it out on the bed by running his fist over it. It refused to succumb to his manipulations and curled back up.

"Figures," he groused, flopping spread-eagle across the bed. He tossed a thick, muscled arm across his eyes and a crystal clear image of Ashley popped behind his lids with such preciseness, the near-reality shot a jolt of denied longing to his groin. He felt his shaft throb and jump against the zipper of his jeans. "Down boy," he grumbled, and forced his mind to the issue at hand—a new, unwanted assignment. He was a field operative. His specialty search and dispose. As a former Navy Seal he'd been trained for combat, for dealing swiftly and with stealth against the unseen enemy before he joined the FBI and worked as a part-time handyman for the CIA in their even shadier operations. This assignment was a slap in the face. Missing babies! He didn't even like kids. They were a nuisance. Not to mention messy and noisy.

He ran through a laundry list of higher-ups that he may have pissed off to get saddled with this assignment and couldn't come up with anyone. He lurched forward and sat up, snatched the envelope and opened it.

It pretty much laid out what Jean and Bernard explained earlier. But in reading the documents, he got a sudden chill when he went over some of the pain-filled stories of the parents whose infants went missing. Included in the envelope was a list of adoption centers, fertility clinics and local hospitals.

A deep frown creased his brow. What kind of person would steal a baby from its parents? But he knew the answer. Money and greed were great motivators, and combined with persons of no conscience made for ugly scenarios. He released a heavy sigh as the ink began to fade on the pages.

These parents deserved some justice, he concluded. So he'd just suck it up and bring a clean and quick end to this madness. A half grin lifted the side of his full mouth. As a minor benefit he'd get to play hubby with the very sexy Ashley Temple, whether she liked it or not. He chuckled at the thought.

Chapter 4

"So are you feeling a little better about things?" Mia asked once she and Ashley had returned to the office.

Ashley gave a slight shrug of her shoulder. "I suppose." She turned to Mia, her hand planted on her slender hips. "I've never lived with a man. Let alone a perfect stranger." She frowned. "I like my independence."

Mia dropped her oversized purse on the desk and looked at her friend. "Is that all that's *really* bothering you?"

Ashley glanced away for an instant then looked at Mia. She almost smiled. "He is kinda fine in a pain-in-the-ass sort of way."

They both giggled.

Ashley dropped her tense shoulders. "I guess it will be all right. The main thing is finding out who is behind the stealing and selling of babies." A shiver ran through her.

"Exactly."

Ashley pushed a smile onto her face, highlighting her prominent cheekbones. "So," she said on a breath, "what's on the agenda for today?"

But even as Mia ran down the list of upcoming events they had to take care of, Ashley's mind was elsewhere. *Elliot Morgan. Babies. Twenty years. Maybe this is a blessing in disguise.*

Ashley walked through her small one-bedroom apartment, which she'd worked diligently on to transform from the drab place she'd originally rented into her cozy abode. Being an R&B music buff, she had one wall in her living room dedicated to some of her favorite artists: Smokey Robinson, Stevie, Luther, Gladys, Anita Baker, The Temps, James Brown, Michael Jackson, Jazmine Sullivan, Earth, Wind & Fire, Frankie Beverly and Maze, and Maxwell to name a few. Her collection was extensive, going back to some classic 45s and collector's items album covers.

The sparkling wood floors were dotted with oversized pillows, low tables and standing plants. Rather than curtains or blinds in the windows, they were covered with hanging philodendrons.

But her bedroom was truly her sanctuary. Her queen-size bed with its downy pillow-top mattress took up much of the small space. But it was truly fit for a queen. To conserve room, she had her flat screen television mounted on the wall. The one great amenity was the walk-in closet that housed her extensive wardrobe, another one of her addictions—clothes.

That brought to mind these new living arrangements. How was she going to get along without her music and all of her clothes and shoes? Sighing she tugged off her cropped sweater and put it in the bag for the cleaner.

She sat down on the foot of the bed and pulled off her ankle boots, just as her cell phone began to ring. She pulled it from the case on her hip and frowned at the unfamiliar number. She pressed the talk icon.

"Hello?"

"Hi. Ashley?"

The low timbre shimmied up her spine. "Who is this?"

"Sorry. It's E—uh, Elliot Morgan."

Her heart bumped against her chest. She cleared her throat. "Oh," was all she could sputter as she tried to get her brain to catch up with the fact that he was on the phone.

"Look, I know I was being a jerk earlier today. And we, uh, probably got off on the wrong foot."

Her brows rose in surprise. "Probably," she teased and could almost see a smile on his face. She crossed her legs.

"So I was thinking that before we do this live-in thing maybe we should try to get to know each other… first."

"Meaning?"

"Have you had dinner?"

"No, I haven't." She swallowed over the sudden knot in her throat.

"Can I interest you in dinner?"

What the hell! Was he asking her out on a date? Her pulsed pounded and her thoughts short-circuited.

"Hey, maybe that was a bad idea. Guess I'll see you on moving—"

"No. I'm sorry. You just caught me off guard. Dinner. Sure."

"I can pick you up in about an hour. Is that enough time?"

Her eyes widened even further. A real date. "Okay." She started to give him her address.

"I already have it. In the file," he added by way of explanation.

"If Jean is nothing else, she's thorough. I'll see you in an hour."

"Right." He hung up.

Ashley sat with the phone in her hand for a good two minutes mesmerized by what had transpired. Maybe the "real" Elliot Morgan would show up at dinner. She shook her head, her spiral curls and twists dancing on her head. Taking a quick look at her watch, she hopped up from her bed and began peeling off her clothes as she darted for the shower.

After numerous wardrobe changes, she'd finally settled on elegantly casual. She selected a pair of black straight-legged jeans, a pearl-gray blouse that shimmered in the right light, with a black silk button-up sweater. She was only five foot six in bare feet and Elliot was well over six foot, so she opted for her Ferragamo black ankle boots that oozed comfort even after long hours on your feet. She captured her hair carefree away from her face with a sparkling gray head band, pulling it into a halo around her face. Minimal makeup, a dab of African musk behind her ears and on her wrists and she was ready just as the doorbell rang.

Her stomach wobbled for a second and heat popped in her ears. She took a quick look in the mirror, left her bedroom and scanned the living room en route to the door, confident that everything was in its place. She went to the intercom, confirmed that it was Elliot and buzzed him in. Her heart pounded. Moments later her front doorbell rang. Straightening, she grasped the knob, turned it and opened the door.

The air stopped in her lungs. She wasn't sure what to expect, but seeing him again did something to her that she couldn't explain if you paid her. Everything about him was more intense, more magnified, bigger and brighter than when she'd seen him for the first time.

Was it the dark, searing eyes that seemed to peek into her soul from beneath half-lowered lids and silky lashes, or the cool chocolate of his complexion that blended seamlessly with his shirt, slacks and hip-length suede jacket? The combination was so enticing and perfectly matched that his attire was more second skin than a cover-up. Perhaps it was the half smile that moved like a lazy river across his full lips giving just a hint of beautiful teeth.

"Hey," he said, his low, almost gritty voice snapping her out of her momentary trance.

"Hi. Come on in. I need to get my jacket and purse." She turned and commanded her lungs to inhale and exhale as she crossed the space on shaky legs, knew he was watching the sway of her hips and prayed that not only did he like what he saw, but that she didn't trip.

Miraculously she made it to her bedroom. She drew in long, calming breaths of air. Blinking several times she focused on what she needed to do. She took her purse from the top of her dresser, checked for her cell phone, ID, house keys and wallet. She took her jacket from the back of the overstuffed armchair that sat like a Buddha near her window then went back out front.

She entered the room and watched him for an instant. He was turned halfway away from her, running his finger along the frame of a photograph that rested on a table in the short hall. His body was fluid almost as if it moved to some sultry beat in his head, so different from the tightly coiled man of earlier in the day. "All ready," she announced.

He only turned his head in her direction, let his eyes run over her for a hot flash of an instant. "Cool. Let's go."

Elliot opened the door for her and as she passed him she caught the faintest hint of something manly, a clean and seductive scent that was more him than off the shelf. She liked it. She locked the door behind them.

"Did you have someplace in mind?" she asked as they walked down the stairs to the outside door. She felt his heat as he walked inches from her on the wide staircase.

"Why don't I surprise you?"

She glanced up at him as he reached around her to open the door. His arm brushed her shoulder and she was certain she felt a jolt of heat race down to the pads of her fingers.

"I like surprises," she said. "Most of the time."

"We'll hope for the best."

They stepped outside into the cool spring night. He pointed to a midnight-blue Jaguar parked across the street.

"You're getting paid too much, or I'm in the wrong business," she teased him as he opened the door of the lush automobile, its interior still carrying the scent of brand-new leather.

"Every now and then you have to treat yourself, especially in this business," he said, as they settled in the car. "Unfortunately, I'm out of the country so much I rarely get a chance to drive it."

Ashley fastened her seat belt. "How often do you... travel?"

He put the car in gear and she felt the gentle hum of the motor vibrate beneath her. Or was it more than the car that had her vibrating?

His jaw tightened. "I'm usually out of the country eight to ten months a year." A hardness settled over his face, sending his prominent features into sharp relief.

"Hey, I'm sorry," she said. "It's obvious that's not something you want to talk about."

He turned his head in her direction as he pulled up to a red light. For a moment he took in her profile, the slight jut of her chin, the long lashes that shadowed her eyes, the pert nose and firm set of her glossy lips. Everything about the way she stared straight ahead to the line of her shoulders indicated that he'd done it again—went on the attack for no good reason. At least none that anyone other than himself would understand. It was complicated, too complicated to explain the kind of limbo life that he lived. His constant sense of disconnection, waking up day after day not knowing where he was or who he was pretending to be.

"Sorry," he offered. "Tough topic. Let's talk about something else." He gripped the steering wheel a bit tighter as her intoxicating scent wafted beneath his nose.

"Have you ever lived with a woman before?" she boldly asked.

Elliot tossed his head back and laughed from the pit of his gut. "You're definitely direct," he said, still chuckling.

A tiny smile teased the corners of her mouth. "So I've been told," she tossed back. She angled her gaze in his direction. "Well?"

He drew in a breath and relaxed against the smooth leather interior. "Actually, no. This will be a first for me." He turned to look at her and their gazes bumped against each other for what felt like a blissful eternity.

A car horn blared behind them. They both jerked away from the thing that held them in place. Elliot pressed down on the gas and took them across the intersection.

He cleared his throat. "So, uh, what about you?"

"No." She paused. "Guess it'll be the first time for the both of us."

His mind went racing off in a million directions at once, all of them forcing him to adjust his position in his seat. Was this the same uptight, headstrong woman he'd met earlier? He knew there was fire beneath her she-warrior armor, but this was the kind of fire that burned from the inside out. Then his years of dealing with adversaries and those pretending to be something that they weren't kicked in.

"The lounge is on the next block," he said, changing subjects to one in which he could control. "Hopefully I can find a parking space."

Ashley instantly noticed the shift in attitude and the sudden cool breeze in the car. She flicked a brow in dismissal and folded her arms. *Just like I said in the beginning*, she mused to herself, *a pain in the ass*. This was going to be a long night.

Chapter 5

They spent the next few minutes of the drive in an unspoken truce of silence. Ashley zeroed in on the passing traffic and pedestrians as if they were creations of the great Da Vinci and she had been commissioned to unlock the mysteries of the swaths of color and movement. In reality she didn't see a thing, blinded by flashes of red as her temper continued to boil. Her body curled into a tighter and tighter knot of tension as the minutes ticktocked in her head.

Why was it so easy for him to irritate her to the point of distraction? She'd had her share of relationships. She knew how to handle men—both casual and serious. Elliot Morgan was a new breed, however. Her lips tightened into a line so thin as to be almost invisible.

She was so intent on her ire that she didn't realize they'd come to a stop until her door was pulled open and Elliot's large hand was extended for her to take. She blinked and looked up into his face. Whatever it was that had her coiled tight enough to snap, slowly began to unwind, and she felt the slow thud of her heart against her chest. The veil of red that had descended in front of her eyes was lifted, and even in the twilight of evening she could see sunshine.

She made herself breathe as she placed her hand in his and felt the strength of his grasp pull her to her feet. He didn't bother to step back. When she stood there was a mere breath that separated them. For a moment they faced each other and she sank into the depth of his dark eyes and traveled to exotic places along the planes of his face.

"It's right up the street," he said, his voice low, stroking her below her waist as surely as if he actually touched her there.

She bobbed her head and muttered, "Okay."

He moved back to give her room and she felt as if a chasm had opened in front of her and she longed for the security of his warmth and closeness. Somehow he managed to reach around her to close the car door, having her momentarily encircled in his warmth. He gave her a half smile and extended his hand in the direction of the club. Ashley fell in step beside him doubling her pace to keep up with his long stride.

The half-block-long line signaled that they had arrived.

"Wow, it must be packed," Ashley said. "We'll never get in." She peered around the line of bodies.

"Not a problem." He took her hand and walked her past the crowd, right up to the front door. "Hey, Lou," he greeted the muscled man at the door. When Lou's

tight gaze and even tighter expression landed on Elliot, he actually smiled.

"Oh, man! Good to see you, brother. You have a
lovely guest, I see." He stepped aside to let them pass.

Ashley smiled.

"Be sure to see Gina," Lou continued. "She'll hook
you up with some good seats."

Elliot clapped Lou on the back. "Thanks, man."

"For you…anytime. Don't be a stranger."

Elliot had yet to let go of Ashley's hand, and the
longer he held it the more she liked it.

"I take it you've been here before," she teased.

Elliot chuckled. "Yeah, the owners are friends of
mine. Nick Hunter and Sam Blackstone. If they're
around I'll be sure to introduce you…in case you and
your friends want to stop by sometime." He guided her
to the hostess podium. "Gina," he cooed at the mode-
lesque woman, who was at least six feet tall with sharp
Ethiopian features—voluminous dark eyes, sweeping
forehead and high cheekbones. Her long, slender neck
gave her an even more regal appearance. Her ruby-red
lips spread into a slow smile as her long lashes lowered
over her eyes. She leaned forward taking Elliot's face
in her hands and kissing each cheek.

"You bad boy," she scolded. "Where have you been?
It's been much too long." Her accent was unrecognizable, a combination of nations that melded into something unique.

Elliot chuckled from deep in his chest. He looked
deep into her eyes, lowered his voice. "Now, Gina, you
know if I told you, I'd have to make you disappear."

Gina tossed her head back on her long stem of a
neck and laughed an almost musical melody. "You and

your secret games." She finally turned her attention to Ashley. "Welcome to Rhythms. Do not let this man charm you into doing anything naughty. He can be very persuasive."

"I'll keep that in mind," Ashley said, not sure if the quickening in her stomach was from being let in on some private joke or the fact that Gina may have been a willing recipient of Elliot's charms.

"I'll show you to your table." She took two menus from the stand and led them to the center of the club with a table in front of the stage.

Elliot helped Ashley into her seat.

"Nick is playing tonight," Gina said, placing the menus in front of them. "You're in luck. Maybe you can sit in on a set."

Elliot chuckled and shook his head. "I'm too rusty to get up there with the boys. It's been a while." He leaned casually back in his chair, his thighs spread and his arm draped across the top of the seat.

"Your server will be along to get your drink order." She focused on Ashley. "You should convince him to play tonight." Gina squeezed his shoulder and gave him a quick wink before walking away.

Elliot lowered his head for a moment and shook it as he chuckled softly.

Ashley rested her forearms on the table and leaned forward. "So what is it that I should be convincing you to play?"

"Naw. Don't even go there." He waved off her question and almost looked embarrassed, his usual swagger momentarily gone.

"Why? Got something to hide?"

His gaze connected with hers. "No."

"Do you play some kind of weird instrument?"

"No."

"Tuba?"

"No," he sputtered.

"Harp?"

"Very funny."

"Banjo!"

He cracked a smile.

"I got it. The recorder!" Her eyes widened in delight.

Elliot laughed. "Not since I was about six," he confessed.

"I knew it," she teased and sat back, waiting expectantly.

"Trumpet," he finally admitted.

She tipped her head to the side in appreciation. "Really? Wow. That's Miles Davis's instrument of choice."

"So you know a little something about music. I should have figured as much with that collection you have at your place."

She grinned. "One of my passions." She paused. "So, how long has it been since you've played?"

He thought about the last time he performed. It was before his last assignment in Europe, which lasted nearly ten months, before everything got so dark and ugly and he couldn't tell the good guys from the bad, right from wrong. He glanced away. "A while," he said, his voice distant and detached, almost wistful, Ashley thought.

She watched his profile in the light and shadows of the club and the parade of emotions that loosened and tightened his jaw. "I hear it's like bike riding. You never forget, you just have to get back on."

He ran his tongue across his lips. His eyes settled on

her mouth for a moment and Ashley felt a sudden pulse beat between her legs. She adjusted herself in the seat.

"That's what you heard, huh? Just get back on?" His gaze bore into hers.

A warm flush rose up from the pit of her stomach and settled in the center of her chest. She drew in a breath, her taunting challenges of only moments ago having dissipated under his smoldering gaze and innuendo.

The waitress appeared to take their drink orders and the momentary spell was broken.

Elliot lifted his chin toward Ashley. "What would you like?"

You! Her body shouted, even as her mind remained in disagreement. *I want to find out if everything is as hard as those biceps and thighs.* She cleared her throat. "Hmm, apple martini, please. Frozen."

The waitress nodded. "And you, sir?"

"Courvoisier on the rocks."

"I'll be right back with your drinks."

The momentary reprieve gave Ashley the opportunity to pull herself together, take her eyes, mind and body off of Elliot and take in the surroundings.

The club gave off a feeling of back-in-the-day night spots of Harlem: dark, cozy, low music playing in the background, the smell of food wafting in the air.

"This place seems really nice," she said. "I don't know how I missed it."

"Nick had been negotiating to get it opened for a while. The building was abandoned and in pretty bad shape from what he told me. And not in the choicest of neighborhoods at the time."

"The neighborhood has definitely changed. There

was a time when most folks wouldn't come over here at night."

Elliot nodded his agreement. "It's like that all over the city, Harlem in particular."

The waitress returned with their drinks and set them on the table. "Are you ready to order or do you need a few minutes?" She looked from one to the other.

"Any suggestions?" Ashley asked.

"The seared salmon is excellent," she said. "Or if you prefer we have stuffed chicken breast, hot wings, crab cakes, salads …"

Ashley turned her attention to Elliot and lifted her brows in question.

"You can't go wrong with the crab cakes," he said.

Ashley nodded with a smile. "I'll have the crab cakes and wild rice with a small side salad."

"Make that two," Elliot said.

"Great." She collected the menus and walked off.

Just as they turned their attention toward each other, the contact was broken once again.

"E!"

A tall, dark and extremely handsome man came up and clapped Elliot on the back. Elliot looked up and his expression beamed with pleasure. He pushed back from his seat and stood and the two Adonises—one more gorgeous than the other—did that hearty man-hug thing.

"Wow, my brother, when did you get back in town and why didn't you call me?"

Elliot chuckled deep in his gut. "Look, man I just got back day before yesterday. Getting my legs back under me."

"Yeah, yeah," he teased, throwing his arm around

Elliot's broad shoulder, and turned to Ashley. "And who is this beautiful lady?"

Elliot extended his hand toward Ashley. "Ashley Temple, this is Nick Hunter, the coowner of this joint."

Nick cut him a look, then shot Ashley with a smile that could melt a glacier. "My pleasure." He came around to Ashley's side of the table and shook her hand. "Welcome to Rhythms."

"Thank you. You have a great place."

Nick straightened and tugged in a deep breath. "It took some work," he said with obvious pleasure, "but we did it." He turned back to Elliot. "You guys have everything you need?"

"Yeah, yeah," Elliot said.

"Tonight is on the house. A welcome-back gift," he said to Elliot, "and a welcome, too," he said to Ashley. He started backing up. "Gotta get ready for my set. You know you're playing tonight so get your lips together."

"Man, come on," Elliot said.

"Forget it. Not taking no for an answer." He walked off, grinning.

Elliot flopped back against the cushion of the chair. Ashley giggled.

"The only way out is to leave now. And I have no intention on missing out on those crab cakes." She folded her arms beneath her breasts and challenged him with her steady gaze.

A slow smile crept across his mouth. "Must be some kind of conspiracy," he groused good-naturedly, hiding his soul by lowering his lids over his dark eyes.

"How long have you been playing trumpet?"

"Since high school. Played in the school band."

"You!" she said, delight shining in her eyes and lifting her voice.

He chuckled. "Yeah, go figure. My folks thought it would keep me out of trouble."

"Did it?"

He shrugged. "Not according to them."

"I can imagine you must have been a handful."

His voice lowered, his eyes lifted and settled on her face. "Can you?"

Something hot and sweet moved around in the center of her chest. Slowly she ran her tongue across her mouth, tried to swallow and couldn't. She reached for her drink and took a short sip.

"Well?"

Her brows rose. "Well, what?"

"You said you can imagine me being a handful. I asked you if you could."

"Oh—" she glanced at the table "—You give the impression that you would do all the things that little boys do."

He eased closer across the table. "And what do you imagine us little boys doing?"

Her eyes crinkled with laughter. "Chasing dogs, tugging little girls' ponytails."

He slowly spun his glass on the table. "When little boys grow up they stop tugging ponytails and chasing puppies. They'd rather—"

Before he could finish, their food arrived and the lights dimmed on the stage as the band took their places.

"Welcome to Rhythms!" Nick said, taking the microphone. The room erupted into applause. "We have a full night of entertainment for you, and I want you to put your hands together for my man Elliot Morgan who will be joining us tonight on trumpet."

Ashley applauded with all the others, her hands clapping high above her head. "Whoo-hooo," she shouted, laughing heartily.

He wagged a warning finger at her that only made her laugh harder.

The band began with an original composition then segued to several standards, which all had the rapt audience bobbing their head and popping their fingers. From her perfect position at the table, Ashley could watch Elliot's every move, catch every nuance and expression. What she saw was a man who was comfortable in his own skin, who could easily transition from gentleman to lethal weapon in the blink of an eye, thoughtful, funny, talented and heartbreakingly sexy all rolled up into one fine package. It could be so easy for her to succumb to his obvious charms, but the reality was they were partners in the investigation of a serious crime. Taking it beyond business was inappropriate, not to mention that he simply rubbed her the wrong way.

Her musings were interrupted when Nick took the mic and announced to the crowd that Elliot would be joining them for the rest of their set. Whoops and hollers of approval, along with the house spotlight followed Elliot's reluctant progression from his seat to his place on the stage, where Sammy handed him his instrument of choice. "We've been keeping it warm for ya," Sammy whispered, as Elliot removed his trumpet from the case.

For a moment he looked at it with a mixture of awe and reverence. He'd left it in Nick's care when he took off months ago for Europe. A smile moved slowly across his mouth as the gold valves glistened against the muted light almost like a beacon.

Elliot lifted the trumpet out of the case, reached for a reed and fixed it to the lip of the instrument. Slowly he brought it to his mouth, shut his eyes and blew out several notes to test the quality, range and his rusty skills. Satisfied, he turned to Nick and gave him a short nod of his head.

Nick eased into Miles Davis's "The Man with the Horn," and Elliot picked up on the melody as if he'd never been away from his trumpet.

Ashley was mesmerized by this *new* Elliot that was on the stage. He was a chameleon, ever changing. The moment she thought she had him pegged, he'd switch up on her, leaving her to question her instincts.

He finished out the set with the band to jubilant applause before hopping down off stage and returning to his table. Ashley was still applauding, a smile beaming across her face.

"You were fantastic!" she enthused, grabbing his hand before she could stop herself.

The spontaneous moment stunned them both. Elliot's gaze fell to the hand that covered his. Embarrassed, she pulled her hand away but not before Elliot caught it. He looked into her eyes as his fingers grazed hers.

"So you liked it?" he said, his voice low and intimate. He ran his thumb across her knuckles.

Ashley's pulse throbbed. "I don't know why you doubted yourself," she managed to say. "You were right at home up there."

"Didn't want to make a total fool of myself," he half joked, "especially with you watching."

"Can I get you anything else from the bar?" the waitress said, snapping the line of tension between them. She picked up the empty plates and looked from one to the other.

Ashley took the reprieve to ease her hand out of Elliot's warm grasp. "I'm fine, thanks."

Elliot lifted his half-empty glass. "I'll have another."

"Right away."

Elliot leaned back in his chair and appraised Ashley from beneath lowered lashes.

"What?" she finally said, after his stare began to make her uncomfortable.

He gave a slow, short shake of his head. "Can't quite figure you out."

"What's that supposed to mean?"

"Don't get twisted out of shape. I'm just saying I can't figure you out."

"Funny, I thought the same thing about you."

The corner of his mouth jerked up into a grin. "Really?"

"It wasn't a compliment," she lightly teased.

He leaned forward. "It's late. I should get you home."

His sudden change in demeanor caught her off guard. Barely seconds ago he was practically in her lap and now he was ready to dismiss her like the final class of the day. She flicked a brow, and picked up her purse from the table.

"Ready when you are." She stood.

Elliot got up and took her jacket from the back of her chair. "I don't think so," he whispered and helped her put it on.

Ashley glanced at him over her shoulder, but his expression was unreadable. She adjusted her jacket and tucked her purse under her arm. The warmth of his hand at the small of her back seeped through the fabric. She walked just far enough ahead of him that he had no choice but to let go. For a moment she was smugly satisfied. She knew it was a childish little triumph, but she didn't care. How dare he turn off and on like a light and expect her to do the same? Who did he think he was anyway?

She pushed through the door and out into the cool evening. With every step they took in the direction of the car, she grew more annoyed. She stopped in midstep and swung toward him just as his arm snaked around her waist and pulled her flush up against him. His dark eyes burned into hers and she could feel her heart banging against her chest.

"I'm not the one to play with," he said, barely moving his lips.

Her eyes widened in a mixture of alarm and sexual excitement. She could feel the hard lines of his body, the heat that rose from his skin, the danger that radiated from his eyes.

"I would give you the same warning," she said on a husky breath, "but I know you don't take advice very well." She pulled away from him and challenged him with a hard gaze of her own.

His mouth moved into a lazy grin and his soft chuckles taunted her. "Come on. I'm tired." He continued toward the car and she fell into silent step beside him.

Seething as she jammed the seat belt into place, she prayed for a quick end to this torturous assignment.

Chapter 6

Ashley awoke the following morning totally exhausted. For the few moments of sleep that she'd been able to catch, she'd been tormented by images of Elliot. He'd chased her throughout the night, turning up around corners, behind doors, at the end of every path she took. Each and every time he had that self-satisfied look on his face. But she'd always been able to slip out of his grasp. Just as he would reach out for her she would dart away. Until the last time. She'd struggled so hard to get out of his hold that she'd nearly fallen out of the bed.

So here she sat bone weary and bleary-eyed. At least it was Saturday and she didn't have to worry about going into the office. Groaning, she eased out of bed and shuffled to the bathroom for her morning rituals.

Feeling moderately better after a hot shower and

pampering her skin in shea butter lotion, Ashley went to the kitchen to put on some coffee when the doorbell rang. Frowning, she tightened the belt on her robe and walked barefoot to her intercom.

"Who?"

"Ashley, it's me Bernard. Can I come up?"

Bernard! That was a twist. She buzzed him in. Moments later there was a light knock at the door.

"Is something wrong?" she asked as she stepped aside to let him in.

"No. I should have called first," he said, turning toward her. "It was kind of a spur-of-the-moment decision."

Slowly she shut the door then led the way to the living area. "Make yourself comfortable. I was making coffee. Want some?"

"Thanks. That would be great." He sat down on the edge of the love seat after taking off his jacket. He draped it across his lap.

Ashley stood in front of her coffee maker watching the hot liquid percolate and wondering what in the hell Bernard was doing sitting in her living room at ten on a Saturday morning. She took mugs from the cabinet and filled them to just below the rim. She brought his mug and set it down on the coffee table. "I only have soy milk and Sweet'n Low."

He waved away the offer. "Black is fine." She nodded and returned to the kitchen to finish fixing her coffee. Bernard was just getting off his cell phone when she took a seat opposite him on the couch. "So…what's up?" She took a sip from her mug and waited.

"I know that you as well as all the other Cartel members are used to working alone or at the very least, working with each other—"

"Listen, if you came all the way over here to lay down the law—"

He held up his hand. "Whoa, whoa, hear me out."

She drew in a breath and slowly let it go. "Sorry," she muttered.

"As I was saying, I know this goes against protocol. And I know that you and Elliot didn't hit it off…"

The mere mention of Elliot's name set off all of her bells and whistles. Coffee sloshed over the top of her mug and dribbled onto her lap. She grabbed a napkin from the table and dabbed at the spot, muttering under her breath.

"…but Elliot is the best at what he does. He always has been. I know he can be rough around the edges. He's been through a great deal. Especially over the past two years."

Ashley sat up a bit straighter as she listened.

"Before he got sent out on his last assignment overseas, he'd lost his mother to cancer and months later, his younger brother to a drive-by. He internalizes. He blames himself."

"Why?" she dared to ask.

"He felt that he should have been there for his mother, found her the best doctor, the cure," he added, throwing up his hands and shaking his head in frustration. "And his brother…he was always in trouble. He'd been trying to get his mother to move out of the neighborhood for years, but she'd refused." Bernard caught Ashley's focused gaze. "He nearly quit after the double whammy. It took more than a year for him to get back in the saddle. And this last year overseas

was hard. Lives were lost. But the case was solved.
I brought Elliot onto this case not only because he's
good, but because he needs to decompress and wind
down from a helluva rough two years."

Ashley swallowed the last of her coffee and slowly
set down her cup. She didn't want to feel anything
but animosity toward Elliot, but that silent pact she'd
made with herself went out the window after listening to Bernard.

"He'd have a fit if he knew I said anything to you,
but I thought that if you had a little insight into Elliot,
it would help the two of you work together better to
solve this case."

"I appreciate you telling me this. And I promise I'll
never say a word to Elliot."

Bernard lowered his head and nodded then looked
across at Ashley. "You two find the bastards that're
stealing these kids." His jaw clenched as he pushed up
from his seat. "Thanks for the coffee." He walked toward the door. With his hand on the knob he turned to
Ashley. "You'll probably be hearing from Jean. She has
the apartment and she'll want the two of you to take a
look." He dug in his pocket and placed a gold band in
her palm. "You'll be needing that."

She looked down and the gold sparkled back at her.
Her heart thumped. "Thanks," she mumbled and closed
the door behind him. *Wow, it wasn't even noon and her
day was off to a flying start.* Her fingers closed around
the ring and squeezed.

Of course, Ashley heard from Jean sooner rather
than later and was informed that she was expected

at the apartment at 3:00 p.m. and that she was *Mrs. Morgan.*

At five minutes to three, Ashley eased her Honda into an available parking spot on West 121st Street, walking distance from the Cartel headquarters and the day spa, Pause for Men. She checked her Black-Berry for the address—811. She turned off the car and stepped out, adjusting her purse on her shoulder. She verified the address then headed off toward her right. She stopped in front of a newly renovated, six-story apartment building and checked her watch. Three on the dot. A young woman came out of the front door carrying her Yorkie in her purse and hurried off down the street. Ashley sat down on one of the benches that braced either side of the glass-and-wood front door and waited.

Before she could get herself settled, she glanced down the street and saw Elliot and Jean coming her way. For some inexplicable reason the sight of Elliot caused a tingle of excitement to shimmy up the inside of her legs and settle into a fluttering pool in her center. Slowly she stood.

"Sorry if we kept you waiting," Jean said by way of a greeting, but offered no further explanation as she breezed by her. She took a key from her purse and opened the front door.

"Rest well?" Elliot said for only Ashley's ears as he held the door open for her.

She glanced quickly over her shoulder and her gaze landed on the pulsing cords of his neck then slowly rose up to his lips that were set in a mocking grin. She almost rolled her eyes but didn't bother. "Fine," she said and caught up with Jean who stood in front of the elevator.

"The apartment is on the fourth floor. Although the building is six stories, there are only six apartments. Each of them take up the entire floor from front to back. Plenty of room. No reason for either of you to get in the other's way."

Neither Elliot nor Ashley missed the barb.

The elevator doors slid open and the trio stepped in. Like sentinels they took up positions on either side of Jean and stared straight ahead. The door slid open on the fourth floor and Jean led them down the hallway to the front door.

"I'm sure you'll both be very comfortable," she said opening the door and stepping aside.

The loftlike apartment was straight out of *Architectural Digest*—low glass-and-chrome tables, russet leather furnishings drew the eye to the center space. Beyond wooden arches was the dining room with a table that easily sat six. The open entryway veered left and right, set on gleaming hardwood floors with rafters to match in a deep, chocolate brown with a hint of red. Light beamed in from insanely high windows.

"There are bedrooms on either side, with a private bath in each. The kitchen is around this corner." Jean led the way to a state-of-the-art, stainless-steel heaven for even the most reluctant cook. The island in the center of the kitchen had four jets, a sink and built-in wok. The oven and double-door fridge stood on either side of the deep sink. Counters and cabinets of the same rich wood as the front room ran around the perimeter of the kitchen. "The cabinets and fridge are fully stocked. We tried to anticipate your needs. There's also a laundry room for your use." Jean pulled open a door that exposed a room nearly the size of a small bedroom that housed a washer and dryer, shelving and racks to hang clothes. Jean swept out of the room and returned to the front. She reached inside her purse, pulled out a thick folder and dropped it on the kitchen counter. "I suggest you stop by your respective apartments, pick up your essentials then get settled down to married life and this case," she said, lifting her chin toward the folder. "I'll be in touch." Jean moved toward the front door and walked out.

"I get to keep the crib in the divorce settlement," Elliot teased.

Ashley turned toward him and couldn't fight back the smile moving across her mouth. "Don't make me do a Madea on you and saw everything in half," Ashley tossed back referring to Tyler Perry's *Diary of a Mad Black Woman*.

Elliot tossed his head back and laughed, a deep soul-stirring laugh that warmed Ashley from the inside out, and for a hot minute she imagined what it would be like to hear his robust laughter each day. "Oh, you are dangerous," he said, wagging a finger at her. "You want me to drop you by your place to pick your stuff up?"

"Thanks for the offer. But I have my car."

He nodded slowly, his dark gaze rolling over her. "The only place she didn't show us is the bedrooms."

Her heart knocked in her chest. She looked away from him and walked over to the fridge. She pulled open one of the double doors. "She was right, fully stocked." She took out an apple from a bowl on the bottom shelf. When she stood and closed the door,

Elliot was right there. Her breath caught and stuck in her throat.

"Any more apples?" he said, but she would swear in a court of law that wasn't what he was really asking.

She swallowed and handed him hers. The hint of a grin lifted the corner of his mouth before he took a deep bite. She was mesmerized by the way his lips played with the fruit, the movement of his jaw as he chewed. She could almost taste the succulent juice that exploded in his mouth. Her nostrils flared and she tugged the door open to separate them, gave herself some room to breathe. She took another apple, slammed the door shut and walked out.

Elliot strolled out behind her, his eyes glued on the sway of her hips encased in the form-fitting jeans. Well at least they had what could serve as a small football field to separate their respective bedrooms, he mused. Besides, Ashley Temple came off as a woman who would have a padlock on more than her bedroom door. And his momentary flights of fancy of being locked between those beautiful thighs of hers, and thawing that chilly heart, was a waste of his brain cells. The last thing he was ready for was a tryst with his partner in the middle of a case.

"Plan on wearing your wedding band, Mrs. Morgan?" he asked coming into the living room. "Or are you one of those modern women who doesn't need the shackle of a ring?"

She glanced at him over her shoulder and was two seconds away from rolling her eyes, when she saw what he held in front of his face. His hand was covering those dangerous eyes, palm facing inward. The sparkle of gold from the third finger of his left hand completely caught her off guard. Seeing him with a wedding band on his finger—even if it was fake—unsettled her in a way that she couldn't find the words to explain. She dug in her jacket pocket and pulled out the band that Bernard had given her earlier. For drama's sake she took her time sliding it on her finger. She held up her hand for inspection. "Looks like we're stuck with each other."

There was nothing he loved more than a challenge. A slow grin moved across his mouth. He watched Ashley walk away. Touché, Ms. Temple. Touché. Let's see if you're up for the ride.

Chapter 7

Ashley returned to her apartment. She wasn't sure
how she felt about the past few hours of her life. The
reality that she would be living under the same roof
as Elliot Morgan, for an indefinite period of time, was
slowly beginning to solidify.

She tossed her purse on the couch, the wedding band
that she'd sarcastically flashed at Elliot, picked up the
light. She held up her hand. It suddenly felt heavy, as
if the enormity of what she was about to embark upon
was wrapped round her finger and had real meaning.
Don't be silly, she chastised herself. It may be real gold
but the union is a sham.

Her cell phone chirped inside her purse. She reached
for it, dug around inside and pulled out her phone.
"Hello?"

"Hey, it's Elliot."

She took in a sharp breath. "Yes. Is something wrong?"

"Not at all. I know you said back at the apartment that you didn't need any help, but I was planning on renting a small U-Haul to take my stuff and I figured you may as well put your things in there, too. Make the most of the space. Know what I mean? Pretty sure you'll want to take your music. Beats a dozen trips by car."

Why was he being so nice to her? His hot/cold personality was driving her crazy.

"Hello?"

"Oh…" She snapped to attention. "Uh, sure…I guess. When were you planning on the great escape?"

He chuckled at her quip. "How long will you need to get your things together?"

"I'll need at least a day…and I don't mean *to*-day. More like all day tomorrow."

"No problem. I'll get it set up for Saturday. Say around eleven."

Even though he was being the apparent perfect gentleman, his last comment, though couched in a question, was a final statement. Somehow, he'd played the whole scenario out in his head and like a chess master he'd anticipated her response.

Feeling that she'd probably been had, she was of the mind to tell him just what he could do with his U-Haul. But as her grandmother always told her, don't chop off your nose to spite your face.

"How 'bout nine?" she counter-offered, needing some infantile mental leverage.

"Oh, early riser. Nine is fine with me. See you then."

Before she could think of something snarky to say,

he'd hung up. Annoyed at herself for being so dim-witted around him she promised herself that she'd be on her game the next time they went head-to-head. She tossed her purse on the couch and stomped off to her bedroom.

Mia, Savannah, Danielle and Ashley sat in their favorite booth at The Shop sipping on mimosas. It was the end of a long day for all of them. Mia had client meetings and site visits all afternoon. Savannah was brain dead from studying for her bar exam, finally taking on the challenge after too much goading from her husband and friends. Danielle had spent the afternoon shooting a bevy of temperamental models for a Victoria's Secret ad. And Ashley had spent her day sorting through her belongings and deciding what to take to her new abode. The girls had agreed to help her pack once they'd had some food and a drink under their belts.

"To a relaxing weekend," Savannah said on an exhausted breath, raising her glass in a toast. Her sister friends did likewise.

"Since Ashley is so embroiled in her 'arranged marriage,'" Danielle quipped, winking at Ashley, "I took the liberty of looking up this Elliot Morgan who has our girl's panties all in a knot."

"He does not!" Ashley weakly protested.

"Anyway," Danielle continued drolly, before ceremoniously pulling out her iPhone. She moved her finger around on the touch screen until she found what she was looking for. She turned the phone to face her friends. "Behold, Mr. Elliot Morgan."

A series of wide-eyed oohs and ahhhs hopped around the table.

"Whoa, now that's what I'm talking about," Mia said squinting at the full-color head-and-shoulder shot.

Savannah nudged her. "Put your glasses on. He'll look even better."

"Very funny," Mia snapped, notorious for refusing to wear her glasses in public, which had become the standing joke between her friends.

"Hey, ladies. I heard the best of the best were going to be here," Traci said in greeting, stealing the line from *Top Gun.*

"Hey, T," they chorused, welcoming the newest member to the table and their sisterhood. Traci Bennett, originally known as Brenda Forde to the girls, had been an agent of Jean's years earlier. She'd managed to leave The Cartel and started a new life, and had Mia not been assigned to uncover an elite escort service run by her former boss and lover Michael Burke, Traci's identity may have remained secret forever. She'd been Michael's personal assistant at Avante Management and it was with her help that Mia was able to crack the case.

"What did I miss?" Traci asked as she slid into the booth.

"Mimosas and a picture of Ashley's new man," Danielle teased, which earned her a poke from Ashley.

Danielle giggled and passed the iPhone to Traci.

"Wow. You lucked out, my sister."

"Yes, but as the saying goes, you don't have to live with him."

Savannah leaned forward. "Come on. How bad could it be?"

Ashley sighed. "I don't know," she admitted. "I'm sure my imagination is making it out to be worse than it could ever possibly be. I…just…" She hesitated, hunting for the right words to describe her confusion. "He's…forget it." She looked from one to the other. "Let's eat. *We* have packing to do."

They ordered, talked, caught up with ongoing Cartel cases and one another's lives then headed over to Ashley's apartment.

"The apartment is unbelievable," Ashley was saying as she went through her closet.

"I'll have to start working on your housewarming party," Mia said as she folded and placed clothes in Ashley's suitcase.

Ashley stopped what she was doing and turned to Mia. "This case bothers me," she said, her voice low and intimate.

Mia sat on the edge of the bed. "You want to talk about it?"

"It's…I just wonder why Jean picked me. You know she always has a rhyme or a reason for everything she does. Nothing is random or coincidental."

"She assigns people to cases to either force them to prove themselves, test their loyalty or help them to discover their strength," Mia said.

Exactly, she thought. What is it for me? Her honey-brown eyes were almost pleading for an answer that she knew Mia couldn't give. What is it that Jean knows about me?

The girls did their inventory of Ashley's belongings and a thorough inspection of Elliot as he lifted boxes and bags onto the back of the U-Haul rig. They all but fell over each other, helping him and trying to make small talk, which meant uncovering his entire life in twenty minutes or less.

Elliot remained cordial and mildly amused at Ashley's protectors. But he admired their loyalty and concern for their friend, which elevated Ashley in his eyes. She was obviously a woman worth caring about. Even though he didn't have the time nor the inclination to get involved and deeply care about anyone other than himself and whatever he needed to get done.

He shut the door to the truck and turned to face five sets of evaluating eyes. They were all fabulous-looking women—from Traci with her smooth sophistication to Savannah with her petite sexiness. Danielle's avant garde allure to Mia's earthy sensuality. But Ashley was the one who gave him pause. She was wild and tame, spicy and sweet, mysterious and open all rolled into one delicious package.

"That's about it. Thanks for all your help, ladies." He leaned against the van, letting his gaze bounce from one to the other.

Ashley stepped away from her crew and walked toward Elliot. "Thanks," she softly.

He looked down into her eyes and he'd swear something jumped in his gut. He ran his tongue across his bottom lip. "Not a problem. I guess you'll drive your car?"

She nodded her head. "I'll follow you."

He lifted his chin in the direction of the quartet. "Will your friends be joining us?"

Ashley glanced over her shoulder and bit back a laugh as she peeked at the expectant faces of her friends. She turned back to Elliot. "Maybe next time."

Their gazes connected, then darted away. Elliot

walked to the front of the van then got in his car that was hitched to the front.

"I'll see you all later," Ashley called out, blowing kisses and waving as she opened her car door and got in. "Thanks for all your help." She pulled out behind Elliot. A tingle of anticipation and something akin to fear warmed her insides.

Chapter 8

It took them countless "excuse mes," "thanks," "no problems," and several hours to unpack and get relatively settled. They found themselves face-to-face in the center of the living room.

"All done?" Ashley asked on a breath, her hands hugging her hips.

"Yeah, how 'bout you?"

"Almost like home," she said in jest.

Elliot gave a half smile. "I was going to check out the fully stocked fridge. Hungry?"

Her stomach rumbled in response. "Starved."

He led the way to the kitchen and they checked the refrigerator and cabinets.

"I make a mean steak," Elliot said, pulling a package of sirloin from the freezer.

"Sounds like a plan."

They worked together in a comfortable silence, only interrupted by the click of cutlery, running water and Elliot's humming. Every now and again Ashley picked up on a tune he was humming and smiled, humming along with him. The vibe between them and the space they shared seemed as if this was the way it always had been between them.

Unconsciously Ashley squished the tomato that she'd held between her fingers when that singular revelation hit her. This was a job, not some reality TV show, she reminded herself, looking down at the minor mess she'd made on the counter. She stole a glance at Elliot who was putting the steaks in the oven. She drew in a long breath. Get it together, girl. She returned her concentration on finishing the salad that would round out their steak and potato dinner.

"There's wine in that cabinet by the window," Ashley said as they sat down to eat.

"I pass. I'll have a beer. Wine messes with my head."

Ashley grinned. "You're kidding, big strong guy like you."

He shrugged helplessly as he got up. "My Achilles' heel, what can I tell ya." He opened the fridge and held up a Coors, pointing the top in her direction.

"Sure, why not?"

He took out another bottle and returned to the table.

"The truth is," Ashley admitted, twisting off the top, "wine gives me a headache."

Elliot tapped his bottle to hers in a toast.

"So how long have you been working with Jean?" Elliot asked, cutting into his steak.

Ashley's finely arched brows rose for an instant as

she thought about it. "Hmmm. It will be three years next January."

"How were you recruited?"

"I was working for a marketing consortium as a consultant and one of my coworkers, Mae Lin, took me aside one day and told me bits and pieces about the organization and what she did. She told me I'd be great at it because I was always looking for the next challenge." Ashley grinned. "I was intrigued. She said it was like being in a secret sorority with cool gadgets to play with. But that the work was serious and when government agencies didn't have the manpower, the interest or the time, The Cartel steps in. She introduced me to Jean and—" she shrugged her right shoulder "—the rest is history."

Elliot leaned back and took a long swallow of beer. "Where is Mae Lin, now?"

Ashley smiled. "She's a news correspondent on *CBS News*."

Elliot's eyes widened in surprised amusement. "Say what? That Mae Lin?"

Ashley bobbed her head. "Yep. Cartel members are everywhere, doing everyday jobs and no one is the wiser. That's the beauty of the organization. Some of us know each other, but most of us don't, unless we meet during an assignment."

"Jean definitely runs a tight operation. The honchos at The Bureau and CIA headquarters think very highly of her."

"What is your story?" Ashley said.

His expression sobered. "Went to the navy after high school. Figured it was the only way I could afford a college education and get off the streets. I grew up in

Baltimore, around where they used to film *The Wire*."
He drew in a long breath and gazed off into the distance. "The things I saw in combat couldn't compare to life on the streets of Baltimore, especially back then." His hand tightened around the bottle neck. "I signed up for Special Ops. Stayed there for five years before I signed up with the FBI, which is where I met Bernard."

"I didn't know that the FBI handled cases outside of the U.S."

Elliot's dark eyes flashed at her. His body coiled as if ready to strike, making her heart lurch. In that instant she again witnessed how volatile Elliot could be with just a flip of the switch. "Jean and Bernard told me you were returning from an assignment in Europe…" she quickly added, hoping to snuff out whatever fire she'd lit.

By degrees she watched him physically relax, but his eyes remained wary.

"Let's say that I'm freelance and leave it at that. Okay?" He finished off his beer, pushed back from the table and took his dishes to the sink, rinsed, and then put them in the dishwasher. He turned to Ashley. "I'm going out for a while." He left without another word or a backward glance.

"Well, damn," she muttered in concert with the closing front door.

Elliot got in his car with no real destination in mind. All he was sure of was that he needed some space, some air between him and Ashley. He could feel the powder key of his emotions getting ready to explode and Ashley didn't deserve to be on the receiving end of that.

He glanced at the digital clock on the dash. It was still early. He hit speed dial on his cell phone. After three rings, Carmen Santiago's throaty voice filtered through the lines.

"Hello Carmen, it's E. You busy?"

"No. You in the vicinity?"

"I can be in about thirty minutes."

"I'm here."

"See you in a few."

He made a turn onto the West Side Highway and headed to Brooklyn.

After cruising around for about ten minutes, Elliot found a parking space and then walked back the half block. He jogged up the steps to the parlor floor apartment of the three-story brownstone and rang the bell. Moments later the glass-and-mahogany-wood door opened and Carmen stood in the doorway. He felt suddenly lighter.

"Come on in, babe." She welcomed him on tip toe and embraced him in a warm hug.

Elliot kissed her cheek and gave her a squeeze. "Girls asleep?"

"They're at a sleepover down the block. Friends from school."

"Wow. Sorry I missed them."

"Next time. Can I get you anything? I have some Coors in the fridge."

"Perfect."

"Be right back." She sauntered off barefoot to the kitchen in her oversized army T-shirt that hit her at mid-thigh.

Carmen was all of five foot two; compact, gorgeous and dangerous. She could easily take down a man twice her size in hand-to-hand combat. They'd met years earlier while they were stationed in Taiwan on assignment. Against all odds they actually became friends, confidantes. But the stress of her job was putting a strain on her marriage and after six years in Special Ops, she quit to be a full-time wife and mother. It took a while for Phil to accept and believe that there was nothing going on between Elliot and his wife.

There is a bond that forms between people when their lives are in danger and they depend on each other for survival. But the only thing Carmen was more devoted to than her job was her husband and their two daughters. When she lost Phil during 9/11, Elliot was there for her every step of the way and became a surrogate father to Jasmine and Petra.

"Here ya go," she said bouncing back into the room. She handed him the Coors, then plopped down on the love seat and tucked her legs beneath her. She pushed several curly ringlets of inky black hair behind her ears, revealing tiny gold studs. "So what's going on? How are you?" she quizzed, her dark eyes sparkling and deep dimples flashing. Behind the sexy, pixie image Carmen could run a mile flat-out in under five, was as accurate with a long-range rifle as she was with a .45 with a silencer. It was what made her so effective and efficient at her job. She took every enemy by surprise.

Elliot brought the bottle to his lips and drank slowly. "Still trying to get my legs under me from the last assignment. But they have me right back in the saddle."

"Are you okay with it?" she asked softly.

He looked into the gentle sincerity of her eyes. "The assignment, yeah."

"So what's the problem? I know you didn't drive your fine self all the way over here on a big Saturday night to tell me that all is well in Elliot Morgan's world."

He tossed his head back and laughed then leaned forward, resting his arms on his muscled thighs. "I have a partner. A woman. A beautiful, intelligent, funny woman." He took a sip of his beer. "She reminds me of Lynn."

"Oh…" Carmen expelled on a soft breath. She hated that witch. Not because she was beautiful and smart and funny and crazy in love with E. No, it was because of what his losing her did to him.

Lynn McKnight was like morning mist, you couldn't really see how it got there but it was all over everything, clinging, and then it was gone. She'd seeped into Elliot's pores, massaged his heart and stole a piece of his soul. He was ready to give everything up for her and live a regular life. Then the most unimaginable tragedy occurred while they were both stationed overseas. Elliot was devastated.

Losing Lynn turned Elliot into a different man; one who lived on the edge, was hard and indifferent, who limited his contact with others and had a woman only to satisfy his physical needs. So if he was in her living room talking about a woman, maybe her prayers were finally answered and he had returned to the land of the living.

"There is only one Lynn McKnight," Carmen said, not falling into the melancholy trap. "So why does she remind you of Lynn?"

Elliot eased back into the couch, contemplating the question, trying to find the words to express his emotions, which was almost foreign to his nature. He looked at Carmen who waited expectantly.

"It's not something that's tangible. It's not physical similarities or even personality," he said, growing frustrated. "It's how…she…" He ran his hand across his close-cut hair then shook his head slowly. "I don't know what it is," he grumbled.

Carmen smiled softly and threaded her fingers together on her lap. "Could simply be that she makes you feel something, E. Something beyond the next drama of our crazy lives."

Elliot chuckled. "You're probably right. I've been alone inside and out for a long time, Carm. The idea of feeling anything for anybody kinda blindsided me."

"That's usually the way it happens," she said with a grin. "It may be something and it may turn out to be nothing more than a momentary thrill." She studied his expression for a moment, the hard lines of his face, the taut physique, soulful eyes and that indescribable aura that floated around him. She knew all too well what the job could do to you. It made you cautious, leery of friendships. As operatives you lived with the never-ending suspicion that no one is who they claim to be. So when you do open that door and take a chance on letting someone in and they hurt or betray you, it only reconfirms what you have been trained to believe. "So tell me about the assignment."

Elliot drew in breath that easily helped him slip into his tactician persona, doling out facts, analyzing the information and not missing a beat.

They talked long into the night, bringing each other up to speed on their lives, their concerns about what was happening in the White House, the kids, mutual acquaintances and everything in between. They ordered pizza from Papa John's and as night drew closer to daybreak, Elliot knew he'd had one beer too many to make the trip safely back to Manhattan and crashed on Carmen's couch, just like in the old days.

He awoke the following morning to the scent of fresh brewed coffee and biscuits, and two pairs of sparkling brown eyes.

"Sssh, see I told you not wake him," Jasmine whispered, nudging her younger sister in the side.

"Ouch! I'm telling. Uncle E, she hit me," Petra whined, pointing an accusing finger at her sister.

Before either of them could react, he leaped from the couch, scooped them up into his arms and spun them around until they were delirious with laughter then unceremoniously dumped them on the couch, much to their delight.

"What is going on in here?" Carmen demanded with a faux frown on her face. She balanced coffee and warm biscuits on a tray. She set it down on the table.

Both girls looked at their mother with wide-eye innocence.

"Never mind," she conceded. She turned to Elliot. "Sleep okay?"

He stretched. "Nothing that a hot shower won't cure," he joked. "And some hugs and kisses from my favorite girls," he said, diving toward them and tickling their ribs. The room filled with squealing laughter.

Carmen shook her head. "There's everything you need in the bathroom."

"Yes, ma'am." He filled his mug with coffee then tossed a warning look at Jasmine and Petra. "I'm coming back to get both of you," he said, wagging a finger, which only sent them into another fit of girlish giggles. He snatched up a biscuit from the tray and headed to the bathroom.

"Let's go, ladies, breakfast is on the table." She hustled the girls off to the kitchen and for a moment lost herself in the sensation of having a man around again, which gave her all the more incentive to check out this woman who'd gotten Elliot's attention. She still had friends in all the right places that would be willing to do her a favor for old times' sake.

Several hours later, after swearing on the girls' SpongeBob blanket that he would come and see them soon, Elliot said his goodbyes and began the return trip to Brooklyn and his new home. Spending time with Carmen and the girls had done his mind and spirit a world of good, he thought as he cruised through the early Sunday-afternoon traffic of churchgoers. He wondered if Ashley went to church, what she believed in, if anything. He pushed those kinds of thoughts out of his consciousness. As Carmen had said while they talked last night, the main thing to remember is that this is about the job. *Sure, get to know her*, she'd advised, *but at the same time you can't let it cloud what you were assigned to do. And if there is any real vibe going on between you two, there's always time afterward to pursue it.*

She was right, of course, as she was about most things that had anything to do with dealing with people on a real level. At least through it all she'd maintained that part of her humanity. She had her children, which compelled her to feel, to care about someone other than herself. He didn't have that. And when his human side dared to make an appearance, he did all he could to stomp it back in place. It was a lonely life, but one that he'd grown accustomed to. It was simply easier that way. It was a lesson he'd learned the hard way. And if there was one thing you could count on when you dealt with Elliot Morgan, you never had to worry about him falling for the same thing twice.

Chapter 9

Ashley didn't know whether she should feel pissed off, disinterested or totally dissed by Elliot. They hadn't spent a full day together as "man and wife" and already he was spending the night out. What did that say about her appeal? she wondered morosely. She would laugh at the absurdity of it all, but the truth of the matter was she was actually annoyed. She realized much of it had to do with her lack of sleep. For the better part of the night she kept listening for Elliot's key in the door. That fact added to her annoyance on top of the *other* fact that she was up listening for him in the first place! Even in his absence, he was a thorn in her side. Well, her plan was to pluck the thorn and get on about the business of the case. She didn't care if Elliot Morgan spent every night out. That meant more room for her in the fabulous apartment. *Was he with another woman? Don't even go there*, she warned herself. It didn't matter if he was. *Did it?*

Shaking her head to dispel her roving thoughts, she went into her bedroom, retrieved her laptop and set up in the living room. Hunting through her pared-down collection of CDs, she selected Blue Magic's *Greatest Hits, Marvin Gaye Live*, Jill Scott, Kem and her new favorite, Chrisette Michele's *Epiphany.*

Settling down, she booted up her computer and opened up the information from her flash drive. Within seconds the list of adoption agencies and fertility clinics appeared on the screen. She began sorting them by geographic area and plugging them into her Google map, which she would sync to her PDA later. There were more than seventy locations to check out and no real way to determine which was more important than the other. Just as she opened another file to get the backgrounds on the parents, she heard the lock being jiggled in the front door. Her pulse began to race and her stomach knotted.

The front door opened and she heard heavy footsteps walking down the hallway in her direction. She looked a mess, she realized in alarm. She had on a baggy T-shirt and an old pair of sweat pants. She made a move to dart off to her room, but it was too late.

"Hello," he greeted without enthusiasm. His gaze settled on her for a minute and moved away.

Ashley pretended not to notice him. She studied the files in front of her, but couldn't make out anything that they said.

Elliot moved farther into the room. He stopped in front of her and looked down at the papers spread out across the table. "Are those the case files?"

"Yes, I thought it best that I get started," she said a bit more sharply than she intended.

He came around the table and sat down next to her. The manly scent of him rushed to her senses. She tried to ignore him, but she could feel the heat from his body press against her own. He reached across the table for the file, and his hand brushed against her arm. It was like an electric shock and she jumped as if she'd been struck.

"Something wrong?" he asked.

"No I'm fine," she snapped. "Why, is something wrong with you?"

He looked at her from the corner of his eyes. "We're a little testy today, aren't we?"

Ashley jumped up from her seat. She spun toward him, her hands on her hips. "We're supposed to be working on this assignment, and you decide to spend the entire night out!" She knew she sounded like a nagging wife, but she couldn't seem to help herself. She had no right to be upset. He was entitled to live his life anyway that he saw fit. She couldn't seem to control the emotions that tumbled within her.

"Look, I'm sorry about last night. I just needed to get out and clear my head. Went to see a friend."

Her heart pounded in her chest. *A friend?* She wouldn't dare ask him who it was. She didn't need to know. "Fine. You can do whatever you want. But we have a job to do."

"Then let's do it." His gaze held her in place for a moment.

She pushed out a breath of exasperation and slowly returned to her place on the couch. "I've broken down the list according to geographic areas. I thought it would be a good way to get started. That way we can visit specific areas at one time."

Elliot nodded as he looked at her notes. He had to admit, had it been him he would've gone about it the same way. He admired her forward thinking. "That makes plenty of sense to me. What we need to do now is get the names of the heads of all of these organizations. That way we'll know who we're going to be asking for when we show up for our appointment as Mr. and Mrs. Morgan."

Her skin warmed at the mention of "Mr. and Mrs. Morgan." She pretended that she didn't hear him and proceeded to explain that she had the list of names already.

"You have been a busy bee today, haven't you?" A small smile moved around the corners of his mouth.

Ashley dared to look at him and she'd swear she saw admiration in his eyes. "It's what I do," she said, turning back to the task at hand.

"I'm thinking we should start with the fertility clinics," Elliot said.

"I was thinking the same thing," she said.

"So, starting tomorrow morning we'll begin with the fertility clinics until we exhaust the entire list."

"I had no idea there were so many fertility clinics in New York."

"Guess there are a lot of people wanting babies," he said, his voice dropping an octave.

Ashley stared at the screen and thought about her parents and their twenty years of heartache. Yes, she fully understood how desperately parents can want a child, especially a child who had been stolen from them. The desire never leaves. The hole in your heart never gets filled. It's a never-ending ache, and you wake up every day and pray that this will be a better day, a different day, and that all the days before never happened. But then you realize that it has happened. And you are powerless to change anything.

Elliot gently touched her shoulder and felt her stiffen beneath his fingertips. "Are you okay?" he asked softly.

She swallowed over the sudden knot in her throat. She nodded her head. "Yes, I'm fine." Gentleness was the last thing she needed from him, the last thing she wanted. She couldn't handle it, not now. "Let's get back to this list," she said, trying to regain her composure, which was extremely difficult with him being so close, touching her.

Elliot slowly removed his hand from her shoulder. "Yeah, let's. We'll start with the Upper East Side clinics and work our way across town."

For the next hour they worked on developing their list. They knew they'd probably have to make appointments with all of these clinics. But their hope was that they could at least do a walk-in and get some brochures, talk to a couple of the employees and take a look around. One of their goals was to gain access to the clinics' databases. In order to do that, one of them would have to distract the receptionist or whoever was behind the computers. If that failed, they would have to try to plant a microcamera that was focused on the computer screen and on the keyboard. That way the camera could record the keystrokes and possibly access any passwords that were needed to get into the files. Once that was done, they would be able to pass that information along to Jasmine over at Cartel headquarters. She would then be able to download the files they needed. What they were looking for were client lists, the names and addresses of all the couples who had come to the clinics. It would all take luck and timing. And most important, their ability to work together.

Elliot leaned back from his slumped-over position and rotated his stiff neck. "I think that's about all we can do with what we have so far."

"You're right. My eyes are beginning to cross anyway." She saved all of the information they had compiled and closed down the computer.

Elliot stood, and the first thought that came to her mind was that he was getting ready to leave again. And it annoyed her that she cared one way or the other.

"I think we deserve a treat," he said, "for all the work that we've accomplished."

"A treat?"

"Yeah." He checked his watch. "It's still pretty early. Wanna go explore the neighborhood?"

"You call that a treat?" she asked in a teasing tone.

Elliot chuckled. "What if I bought you some ice cream to go along with the tour? Would that make you feel better?"

She smiled. "Butter pecan can do wonders."

"You're on."

Ashley got up and stretched tight limbs. "Then let me at least change and put on something halfway decent."

"I don't think you need to."

Their gazes connected and that hot sensation exploded in the center of her chest. "Even if you think so, I'm still going to change my clothes."

Elliot shrugged. "Your call. I think you look fine,

but I guess it's not for me to say." He turned and walked away.

Ashley stood there for moment vacillating between feeling utterly ridiculous and aggravated once again. It was totally exhausting trying to figure out Elliot Morgan. She headed off toward her room in search of something to put on.

Nearly a half hour later, Ashley emerged in a new outfit. She'd selected a long-sleeved white oxford blouse and a pair of tight-fitting black jeans belted at the waist with a black-and-silver scarf that was knotted and hung down to her knees running along her left side. Since he said they'd be walking she decided to put on her sneakers instead of her boots. She wasn't one to generally use makeup, but she did decide to brighten her eyes with a brush of mascara and bring out her full lips with a touch of gloss. She'd run her fingers through her hair to get the wild and carefree look that she liked. A double-stranded silver chain hung from her slender neck.

"Ready," she announced. Elliot turned from his perusal of the CDs that were stacked up on the entertainment unit. For an instant his eyes widened when he saw her.

She waited for him to comment on her appearance. But he didn't utter a word.

"You need a jacket," he said offhandedly and headed toward the door.

Ashley rolled her eyes, snatched up her jacket from the hall closet and followed him out.

"If I remember the neighborhood," Elliot said, once they'd stepped outside, "there's a Baskin-Robbins about three blocks away."

"I can wait," she said, falling into step next to him.

"I just don't want you to think I'm not a man of my word."

"You haven't given me a reason to think that—at least not yet."

"And I don't plan to." He took her hand and his large fingers wrapped around hers. Her heart felt as if it had short-circuited in her chest. For an instant her knees wobbled. She tried to pretend that holding Elliot's hand was something that she always did.

"We might as well look like the happy married couple. Shouldn't we?" He stole a look at her.

"Of course," she said, her voice sounding almost unrecognizable to her ears. "We have to keep up appearances."

"Exactly," he said, tightening his grasp around her hand.

As they walked, the tension that had taken hold of Ashley's body slowly began to loosen. She felt herself begin to relax and enjoy the closeness of Elliot next to her.

"This is an amazing city," he said. "There's always something to do, stores open twenty-four hours a day, night clubs, restaurants, anything that you could possibly want is contained on this tiny little island of Manhattan."

"Yep, the city that never sleeps."

"Do you get to go out much?" he asked.

"Not as much as I would like. What about you?"

"I've been away so long I feel like a tourist." He paused a moment. "About last night..."

"Listen, you're a big boy. You don't have to explain anything to me."

"I know I don't, but I want to."

Ashley glanced up at him. He looked straight ahead.

"This is all new to me. This whole thing about working with a partner. Moving in with somebody. It's not something that I'm used to or what I expected—started to rub me the wrong way, and I didn't want to take it out on you. I needed a little space and some breathing room. So I went uptown to see a friend of mine from back in my Special Op days. Maybe you'll get to meet her one day."

So it *was* a woman, she thought. "As long as you're feeling better, that's what's important." She pulled her hand away from his and made busywork of looking in her purse—for what, she didn't know. The only thing she was sure of at the moment was that she didn't want him to touch her. She found a pack of gum at the bottom of her purse and pulled it out. "What one?" she asked, offering him a stick.

"Sure. Thanks."

Ashley put a piece of gum in her mouth to keep her from saying something utterly ridiculous.

"It should be up on this next block," he said, tossing the foil wrapper in the corner trash basket.

They reached Baskin-Robbins and Elliot placed their orders for two butter pecan cones then they continued on their walk.

"If I remember correctly from the notes," Ashley said. "I think one of those adoption agencies is about two blocks away." She took her PDA out of her purse, turned it on and pulled up the data that she'd recently updated. She scrolled down the list of adoption agencies. "Here it is. Happy Homes Adoption Agency. It's two blocks away on 119th Street and Amsterdam Avenue."

"Let's take a look," Elliot said.

"It's probably closed."

"No harm in trying. We might get lucky."

They picked up their pace and quickly covered the distance to the agency. When they arrived they were surprised to see it was open. A young couple was walking out just as they approached.

Ashley and Elliot gave each other a questioning look.

"I'm game, if you are," Ashley said.

Elliot held up his ring finger and the gold band sparkled in the light.

Ashley pinched her lips together and dug in her purse for her wallet. She took her ring out and slipped it on. *Damn, it fit perfectly.* "I was a Girl Scout," she quipped. "Always prepared."

The right corner of his mouth curved upward. "Then you do the talking. I'll follow your lead," he said, surprising himself with his impromptu willingness to give up control.

Ashley gave a short nod of her head, tried to visualize what she would encounter on the other side of the revolving doors. They hadn't had time to run through what their cover story was going to be or practice their conversation strategy. But now she'd see if Elliot was as good as he claimed to be. "Ready?" she asked, looking up at him and not expecting the jolt that danced in her veins.

He took her hand. "Let's pretend we like each other," he said before moving toward the front door.

Ashley started to snap back a tart retort but he was

holding the door open and smiling as if he treated her with kid gloves every day.

She crossed the threshold and felt Elliot's heat right behind her.

"Reception, twelve o'clock," he whispered into her hair.

She turned and spoke to him through clenched teeth. "Don't start talking like that. It's ridiculous," she said before she noticed the barely controlled merriment on his face. He was determined to make her crazy. That's all there was to it.

Elliot put his arm possessively around her waist and drew her close so that their hips bumped when they walked.

"It's okay, baby, we're just going to ask some questions," he said, catching her off guard but loud enough to catch the attention of the young woman behind the desk, which was apparently his intention. What happened to her taking the lead?

"Good afternoon. How can I help you?" the young blonde asked from behind the security of the horseshoe-shape desk.

The front reception area was warm and inviting. The off-white walls were dotted with framed photographs of loving-looking couples with chubby-cheeked babies. The desk was adorned with small racks of brochures featuring information on adoption, options and referral services.

Elliot tightened his hold around Ashley's waist. "My wife and I—" he gazed lovingly at Ashley "—wanted to get some information," he said, playing the uncertain-but-doting husband to perfection.

"Of course." She stood up and plucked several brochures from the racks on her desk and handed them to Ashley. "I'm sure you would want to speak with one of our counselors who could explain what we do here and everything that's involved."

"Can we do that today, or do we need an appointment?"

"Yes, you would have to make an appointment. I can do that for you now if you want."

Ashley and Elliot looked at each other for marital confirmation.

"Yes," Ashley said, "we'd like to make an appointment."

"Certainly." She settled back in her seat and stroked a few keys on the computer keyboard. She asked them the basic questions: name, address, insurance information and the reason for the visit. She entered the information into the computer, then looked up at them. "We have Tuesday open. There is a morning at ten, and an evening at six-thirty available with our counselor, Ms. Hastings."

"Evening?" Elliot asked, looking at Ashley for confirmation.

"Evening is fine," she agreed.

The receptionist filled out an appointment card and handed it to Ashley.

"You're all set. Tuesday at six-thirty. Oh, the first visit is consultation. We accept all major credit cards and cash of course, but no personal checks. The consultation is a minimum of one hour, sometimes longer. It's two-hundred and fifty dollars. You'll need to pay that before you see the counselor. So I always suggest that first-timers come at least fifteen minutes early to get any paperwork out of the way." She smiled brightly. "Any questions?"

"No. We're good. Thanks," Elliot said.

"Great then we'll see you on Tuesday."

"Would it be okay if we took a look around?" Ashley asked.

"Not much to see. A few offices, the lab, video room, record room." She shrugged. "That's pretty much it. But if you want to look around feel free. Most of the offices are locked. We only have one doctor on call today."

"I just want to feel comfortable," Ashley said, offering an explanation.

"I can't go with you. I need to cover the front. But you can walk around."

"Thanks." They strolled down the hall.

"Good move asking for a tour," Elliot said.

"Thanks. I figured it was a good opportunity for us to get a sense of the place without all of the foot traffic."

"Do you have your kit with you?" he asked.

"I don't leave home without it," she said referring to her jewels of the trade that included a micro listening device, computer disk, a video camera the size of a pot of lip gloss and of course the standard burglary tools.

Elliot took a few quick pictures of the layout with his cell phone and e-mailed them to himself to upload later.

"Pretty simple space," Ashley said as they retraced their steps to the front desk.

"Thanks a lot," Elliot said when they'd returned.

"Sure," the receptionist said. "If you have any questions, we need to reschedule your appointment. Give us a call. My name is Bernice, by the way. I'll probably see you on Tuesday. It's my late night."

"Thanks for everything, Bernice," Ashley said. "See you Tuesday."

Elliot and Ashley walked out.

"One down," Elliot murmured when they stepped outside.

"We've barely scratched the surface," Ashley said, thinking about the long list of possibilities.

"Don't remind me. What's going to help us put a major dent in this is gaining access to the files."

"I know," she agreed. "It'll be tricky."

"You were really good in there," he said, catching her attention.

She glanced at him briefly as they continued down the street and back to the apartment.

"We make a good team."

Elliot hesitated for a moment. "Yeah, we do."

They returned to the apartment, both feeling very proud of themselves.

"At least we have an idea of the setup," Elliot said as he tossed his jacket across the back of the couch.

Ashley unconsciously picked up the jacket and hung it in the hall closet. "It will definitely make things a little easier." She shut the closet door.

Elliot reserved comment but made a mental note to not leave his clothes laying around in plain sight. It was obviously a pet peeve of hers.

"We should talk about this living arrangement before we get too far into it and really get on each other's nerves," Ashley said.

"Now?"

She raised and lowered her shoulder. "Unless you

have plans," she said, chuckling to keep the sarcasm out of her voice.

"So talk." He dropped down into a side chair and zeroed in on her, giving her his full attention.

"Well...I like my privacy," she began, suddenly unsure what she wanted to say, especially with him staring at her like that.

"No problem. So do I."

"I like order." She folded her arms to ward off the shiver of delight that ran along her limbs when she looked at the fullness of his mouth.

"Uh-huh, what else?"

"I like to play my music. It relaxes me."

"Cool. I like music."

She stiffened. He was patronizing her, and she realized the more she spoke, the more ridiculous she sounded. "Forget it." She spun away in the direction of her room. Before she took a step, the strength and seductive touch of his large hand held her shoulder.

"Wait." Her heart thundered in her chest. She dared to glanced at him over her shoulder. For an instant she saw something soft in his eyes, but just as quickly it was gone.

"I don't like this scenario any more than you do," he said. "But for the time being, we're stuck with each other. The quicker we can get this case resolved, the sooner we can go back to our lives. This place is big enough for us to stay out of each other's way."

Ashley swallowed over the sudden knot in her throat. She lifted her chin. "Fine. My sentiments exactly." She pulled away from him and walked into her room. She plopped down across her bed. She was trembling all over. The heat of his touch still burned her shoulder. What was wrong with her? One minute she couldn't stand the thought of him. The next, she wanted him to kiss or touch her in all the places that had gone unexplored in for far too long.

She pulled herself upright. She knew that part of her frustration and trepidation went beyond Elliot. It was the case itself. It brought to bear the pain that she hadn't shared with anyone. Her family didn't talk about it anymore, but the haunted look still remained in their eyes. The same look was reflected in the eyes of the victimized parents the Cartel was now working for. She wanted to tell him that this was no ordinary case—at least not for her. It was personal. Yet she knew that above all, she could not let her own issues overshadow what she was assigned to do.

She got up and went to the dresser, dove beneath her lingerie and pulled out the twenty-three-year-old photograph.

It was one of those hospital photos. The ones they take of the infants. It was only one of two pictures of Layla. Her parents had one and she had the other.

She ran the tip of her finger over the tiny face. Her chest tightened. Where was she? Was she among the stolen children? Was she happy? Was she still alive? Where was her baby sister?

Chapter 10

Elliot sat on the couch, his long legs splayed out in front of him. He leaned his head back and closed his eyes. Instantly Ashley's face came to life behind his closed lids. The soft angles of her face, the wild cotton of her hair, her lips, the scent of her. It was all making him crazy, throwing him off his stride. After Lynn, he'd vowed that he would never again allow himself to become emotional about any woman. It had been eight long years. He stuck by his mantra. Then out of the blue, Ashley Temple gets thrown into his life and suddenly all bets are off.

From the moment he met her all the warning bells started to ring. Since they'd first met he hadn't been able to sleep without thoughts and images of Ashley invading his dreams.

They were powerful, potent, waking him from his

sleep with an erection hard enough to break wood. It took everything in him to keep from acting upon all the things that ran through his head. Thankfully prudence always won out. It was dangerous to mix business with pleasure. As a result he did everything in his power to turn his feelings off and push her away.

So far it had been working until a few minutes ago when he'd touched her just as she turned to look at him. The overwhelming desire to take her in his arms was nearly his undoing. Instead, he resorted to what he knew best, cold indifference. But it wasn't working. The throb between his thighs and the unyielding longing were testaments to that.

His jaw clenched. He pushed himself up from the couch with the intention of taking a cold shower, when what he believed sounded like soft sobs caught his attention. He stopped. Listened. It *was* crying.

Slowly, he walked toward Ashley's room. There it was again. Had he been that much of a bastard that he caused her to cry? His stomach tightened. He stood there for a moment, uncertain of what to do.

Gently, he knocked on the partially opened door. He heard some rustling and sniffling. "Ashley…is it okay if I come in?"

A moment of silence hung between them.

"Come in," she said softly.

Elliot eased open the door. Ashley's back was slightly turned from him as she swiped at her eyes with the back of her hand.

"What is it?"

He took a tentative step farther into the room and it was as if an alarm went off. Her body jerked in his direction.

Tears still hung in her eyes. Her cinnamon skin was flushed. The depths of her pain rose up from her center, crossed the space between them and grabbed at his heart.

Whatever reservations he may have had dissolved, replaced by his innate instinct to protect. He didn't think about it. His feet moved on their own. He was at her side. His arms were around her. Her heart thumped against his chest. Her sobs wracked her body, and he held her tighter. She seemed to mold herself to him, allowing his strength to become hers.

The walls that they'd erected between them began to crumble, brick by brick until they were exposed, breathing the same air, to the same rhythm of their hearts, wanting the same thing, each other.

Tenderly, Elliot stroked her hair, the strength of her slender neck, the gentle curve of her spine. She sighed at his touch. The trembling slowed and turned into something else. Her fingers pressed into the muscles of his thighs as he held and stroked her.

Neither dared to say a word for fear of breaking whatever magic spell had been cast upon them.

Elliot leaned back, just far enough to look down into her upturned face. Her eyes held hundreds of questions that his lips wanted to answer. By degrees he lowered his head until he could feel the moisture of her parted lips. And then he touched them with his own and an explosion went off deep in his belly and shot through his veins straight to his head.

He groaned as he took her mouth gently at first, still uncertain of her intentions until he felt her return his kiss, melting into his mouth.

The sweet sounds of her sighs echoed in the room.

Her arms rose upward, her hands clasped behind his head, pulling him deeper.

His tongue teased her lips then dipped into the honey sweetness of her mouth.

His hands began to roll along her body, familiarizing himself with the gentle curves he'd only imagined.

The thought of having her consumed him, clouding his good judgment. A battle of right and wrong ensued. Right won.

Against every carnal instinct that beat inside him he broke the kiss, but he still couldn't let her go.

Her wide, luminous eyes opened and settled on his face, questioning, waiting. He stroked her cheek as his gaze danced across her face.

She lifted the hem of her shirt and pulled it over her head. Her steady gaze dared him to look away and he knew he couldn't.

Her breasts rose in perfect crests above the cup of her bra, beckoning him to touch them. And he did.

His thumbs brushed across the soft flesh, and she whimpered, her lids fluttering like butterfly wings. He leaned down and kissed her there. One then the other.

She clasped the back of his head and pressed him deep against her. Her heart raced so rapidly she became lightheaded with desire.

"Ashley," he moaned against the rise and fall of her breasts.

She scooted back on the bed, pulling him with her until they were stretched out together, she pinned firmly beneath him. She felt the heartbeat of his need throbbing between her parted thighs.

He ground his hips against her and she gasped in delight. He flipped onto his side and unfastened her pants. She wiggled them down over her hips and kicked them away. His eyes steaming with longing, raked over her exposed flesh searing her skin like a hot iron. His fingers trailed along the band of her panties. She trembled as his fingers dipped in and touched her there, the center of her, the hard kernel of her desire. And she was sure she would explode.

She was wet, ready for him and that knowledge nearly sent him over the edge. He tried to think of anything that would keep his mind from what he truly wanted, lest he explode.

Ashley didn't give him that option. She unzipped him and, before he could take a breath, her butter-soft fingers enveloped his shaft. She stroked him in bold firm up-and-down motions until he couldn't stand it any longer.

He pulled away from her and stood up. He looked at her one last time before he turned and walked out of the door.

Stunned and shaking all over Ashley curled up into a knot, her humiliation complete.

What was she thinking? What had she done? She'd never be able to face him again. She buried her face against her knees. *Oh God*, she inwardly moaned.

She felt more than heard his return. She opened her eyes and Elliot was standing above her.

"I never made it past Cub Scout," he said sheepishly, holding up a foil packet in his hand. "Not always prepared."

She tugged on her bottom lip with her teeth to hold back a smile of relief.

Elliot eased down beside her. His eyes slowly moved over her expectant face. "Are you sure?"

She nodded her head.

Elliot leaned toward her and softly kissed her mouth. "So am I," he murmured. He reached behind her and unsnapped her bra. The lush, heaviness of her breasts rose to meet him. He took one taut nipple into his mouth, running his tongue in teasing laps across its surface.

Shivers of delight coursed along her spine. Her neck arched back, thrusting her chest forward.

Elliot pushed her back against the pillows, raised her hips and freed her of her thong. He played with her, taunted her, dipped his fingers in and out of her wet heat until she begged him to stop, to finish, to start. And he obeyed her every command.

He took the condom package, opened it and rolled the thin sheath down along his length. He turned to her. The pulse in her neck throbbed. Her eyes were dark with desire. He moved gently on top of her, her knees raised, bracing his sides. He lifted up on his knees and cupped her behind in his palms.

When the tip of him pressed against her wet opening, she let out a soft cry. He pushed past the tight ring, and slid deep inside of her.

They both moaned in unison at the sublime sensations that defied words.

Jolts of electricity bounced back and forth between them as Elliot moved smoothly in and out of her.

She raised her legs and wrapped them around his waist, and he was certain that he'd been dropped into heaven.

They moved together as if they'd made love hundreds of times before, understanding instinctively the needs and desires of the other. Yet, the familiar was so new and thrilling, taking them on a journey they'd never before traversed. To heights they'd never reached, to a climax that was beyond surreal, rocking them to their souls.

The experience was so potent, so powerful, that once, not even twice was enough. They loved, and loved until they were weak and satiated.

Chapter 11

Ashley rested her head on Elliot's chest. The steady beat of his heart kept time with hers. She drew in a long breath. The past couple of hours were straight out of a romance novel. The crying damsel in distress succumbs to the charms of the tall, dark and handsome hero. If anyone would have told her this scenario, she would have told them how ridiculous and cliché it all was. But it wasn't. It had happened to her.

Elliot caressed her back and drew her closer to him. He stared up at the ceiling. He'd broken all the rules, both personal and professional. The lines that were once clear were blurry. And he didn't care. That probably disturbed him more than anything else. That and the fact that he'd made love to a woman who was vulnerable. She didn't come to him out of any deep feelings or need, but simply because she was hurt, and it was more than likely his fault. He'd taken advantage of the situation. He never really tried to find out what was wrong. Rather, he let his own needs outweigh good judgment over just being a decent human being.

He squeezed his eyes shut. Nothing good could come of this. They both enjoyed a crazy, sexy romp, but that was it. It couldn't go any further. Besides, when this case was over, there was no telling how far they would send him on his next assignment or for how long. He couldn't become entangled with anyone, Ashley Temple in particular. It would be much too easy to fall for her, and falling for anyone was not his M.O.

"What made you come to my room?" Ashley whispered softly into the darkness that covered them.

Her question momentarily caught him off guard. It was as if she was reading his mind. "I thought I heard you crying." When he didn't get a response, he turned slightly toward her. "Were you?" He could feel her nod her head against his chest. "Do you want to talk about it?"

She inhaled deeply and expelled a shaky breath. "It goes back a long time," she finally said.

"What does?"

"The reason why I was crying." She hesitated, uncertain how much she should say. "It's a long story."

"We have all night."

"It's about the case. I've never told anyone, not even the girls. But this is very personal. I think it's the opportunity I've been praying for. And I can't let The Cartel know that I have my own agenda."

He turned fully toward her, gathered her close against him. "Tell me. I'm listening."

"It happened a long time ago, but it still feels like

yesterday. I was just a kid, an only child. I thought I would be the only child all my life. My mother and father gave me everything and then my mother got pregnant and everything changed. My parents were ecstatic. They never thought they could have any more children, and suddenly I wasn't at the center of their universe anymore. This new baby was. It was all that they talked about."

She paused as those days and months ran like a bad movie in her head. "I wanted to be happy, too. But I wasn't. There was a part of me that wished the baby away. I just knew that when it arrived my life would never be the same. I didn't want to share my parents' love with anyone."

Her chest heaved. Elliot stroked her hair. "It's normal to feel that way. Sibling rivalry. I hated my younger brother for years until he got old enough to hang out with."

"I wished her away," she said, her voice laced with an anguish that Elliot couldn't understand. But instinct told him that her story was going to take an ugly turn. This was something more than sibling rivalry.

"When she was born, my dad took me to the hospital to see her. My mom was so happy. I'd never seen her so happy. And I wished her away," she said again. "I wished so hard that it ached inside." Her voice cracked. "And my wish came true."

Elliot frowned in confusion. "What do you mean? What happened?"

"The day she was to come home, the nurse went to bring her to my mother and the baby was gone."

"Gone? What happened?"

"She wasn't in the nursery. She wasn't in any of the

bassinets. She was nowhere in the hospital. Someone had taken her."

"Oh, Ashley…" His voice dropped off into emptiness.

"To this day no one really knows what happened. My mother…had a breakdown. My father turned into a ghost. The police looked for her for two years. Nothing. No trace. No clue. Layla was never seen again."

He squeezed her tight. Felt the wetness of her tears against his chest. "You can't possibly blame yourself. You know better than that."

"The rational part of me knows it. But my heart reminds me of how desperately I didn't want her to be a part of the family. And then she wasn't. I've lived with the ugliness of those feelings for years. And then this case comes up, and the memories get dredged up again."

For several moments, Elliot was at a loss for words. The guilt that Ashley carried, whether real or imagined, was an enormous weight that had chained itself to her like an anchor. "Did the police exhaust every avenue?" he finally asked.

"So they said. There was a blip in the media for a couple of weeks and then that disappeared, too, just like Layla."

"What about videotape, sign-in logs?"

"Twenty-two years ago security was almost non-existent in hospital nurseries. Most casualties were baby mix-ups. A lot has changed since then, but not soon enough."

"Did your family try a private investigator?"

"They tried everything. But between my mother's breakdown, paying a detective, attorney fees and trying to live, my dad pretty much exhausted all of his finances. It wasn't until five years after the fact that the hospital accepted responsibility and agreed to a settlement. Believe me. My folks tried everything."

"You didn't have me," he said, surprising himself with his pronouncement.

"What?" She pushed herself into a sitting position.

"I'm saying I'm going to help you. This case, the information, it's everything you didn't have twenty years ago. And you have my help now."

"Why?" she asked, the disbelief rippling through the single word.

"I want to." He drew in a long breath and released it slowly. "Every case that I have been on throughout my career has always been for the 'good of the government.' It was a job that never touched me beyond the surface. I did what was necessary and moved on." He paused for a moment needing to make sure that he said the right words. "When I got this assignment I felt the same way. Just another job. Get in, get out. Everything looks different now."

"Different?"

"Yeah." He kissed her cool forehead. "Let's get some sleep. We'll talk more in the morning. We have a busy day ahead of us tomorrow."

Ashley sighed in contentment and nestled against the warmth of Elliot's body. It had been a long time since she'd been so open and vulnerable with anyone, letting them in on her darkest secret, her hopes and fears. She closed her eyes and tried to sleep, silently praying that she hadn't made the biggest mistake of her personal and professional life.

Chapter 12

Everything seemed different in the light of day, Elliot thought, as he stood under the pulse of the hot shower. Last night with the scent and sensations of Ashley deep in his pores he was liable to say anything. And he did. Truth be told, he was no knight in shining armor. He never had been and had no desire to be one now. But if he was nothing else, he was a man of his word. He wouldn't back down from what he promised to do.

He held his face up to the steamy spray. He'd been a fool to get caught up in her tears. Drawn in by her need. Now he was sure she believed that there was something more to what happened last night than what it really was—just two adults satisfying their basic needs.

He turned off the water. That's the way it had to be, he determined. When this case was over, they would go their separate ways and pick up their lives where they'd left off. Simple.

Elliot wrapped the towel around his waist. If it was so simple, why did it feel so complicated?

Ashley poured her second cup of coffee into her mug and sat down at the kitchen table. She heard the water in the shower stop, and instantly a vision of Elliot's naked body emerged in front of her, rippled and dripping wet. She squirmed in her chair.

There was no question that the sex between them was exquisite. As close to perfection as she'd ever experienced, but that didn't excuse the stupidity of it. She knew better. She'd felt raw inside. She'd needed comfort and he'd been there. They'd taken it further than they should have, and it was her fault. She acted like a cat in heat, disrobing for him, almost daring him to make love to her.

She took a sip of her coffee. But he should have seen how vulnerable she was. He should have walked away.

The more she thought about it, the angrier she grew at herself and at him. She regretted telling him anything about her sister. He'd probably try to use that against her as well. Dammit, she could kick herself.

"Morning."

She jumped, sloshing coffee on the table.

"Sorry. Didn't mean to scare you." He snatched a piece of paper towel from the rack above the sink and wiped up the spill. "Any more coffee?"

"Help yourself." She kept her attention riveted on the designs on the mug. Last night they had so much to say to each other. This morning was a series of awkward silences.

"I thought we'd go over the list this morning and start making the rounds," he said with his back to her.

"Fine." She pushed back from the table and padded off barefoot to her room.

Elliot felt the air leave his body. He leaned against the sink. This is going to be bad, he thought.

Ashley returned to her bedroom to retrieve the files and her laptop then went to the living room. She was in the middle of reviewing one of the clinics on the list, when Elliot appeared in the archway. She kept her attention on the computer screen.

"Since we decided on the upper East side as a starting point, I made a list of the three that we could check out today. I uploaded the information to your PDA."

She'd said all of this without casting even a glance in his direction, which was fine with him, he thought, although he was a bit stunned by her obvious indifference. It was usually the other way around. But as he took a seat on the end chair, he realized that there was nothing usual about Ashley Temple.

Their alibi was to be that they'd been married for six years and had tried unsuccessfully to have a child. They'd recently moved to New York from Columbus, Mississippi, because some of the best doctors and clinics were in New York. They were still torn between in vitro or adoption.

"I figured we can take my Navigator," Elliot said, sliding his arms through his brown leather jacket.

"Sure." She hunted around in her purse to make sure she had everything that she needed. In the event the opportunity presented itself, she would plant some listening and video devices. Satisfied, she zipped her purse, glanced up and was jolted to see Elliot staring intently at her.

"Something wrong?"

"No. Nothing." He gave a short shake of his head. "Ready?"

She nodded. She draped the strap of her oversized burgundy, leather purse over her shoulder. It was a perfect match to her ankle boots.

Elliot couldn't help but notice the perfect picture she made. Her cream-colored cable-knit sweater that topped an open-collared white blouse, paired with fitted black jeans, expertly defined Ashley's attributes. He may very well notice her, he thought as he pulled the door shut behind him, but she didn't seem interested in giving him the time of day.

Ashley made rocket science out of adjusting her seat and fastening her belt, whatever it took to keep her eyes and mind off of Elliot. This was as close as they'd gotten since he'd left her bed before sunrise. She felt empty and stupid and couldn't stop chastising herself for her actions. She never lost control like that before. What was wrong with her? She had acted like a…

"You want to talk…about anything?" Elliot asked breaking into her dark train of thought.

She stole a quick glance at him. He was staring straight ahead, and the strong line of his jaw was clearly outlined.

"Not really." She pushed her bag down on her lap and folded her arms on top of it. "I think we covered everything," she added.

The layer of sarcasm wasn't lost on Elliot. "Guess

we did," he volleyed back with the same level of feigned indifference.

They spent the balance of the drive in silence, with each of them asking themselves "What went wrong?"

It was just after ten when they pulled up in front of the first location, which was discreetly tucked away on the fifteenth floor of an office building. They went through the drill: answering questions, filling out forms and pretending to be the loving but desperate couple who wanted a baby.

"We'd love a newborn," Ashley had repeated at each stop before looking adoringly into Elliot's dark eyes. He'd squeeze her close then kiss the top of her head and look deep into the counselor's eyes. "Whatever my love wants. Money is no object," he'd emphasize.

By the time they'd reached the last stop for the day, no outsider would doubt that they weren't who they claimed to be.

While Elliot had charmed all of the women with his banter, good looks and make-you-wet smile, Ashley had been able to plant listening devices at all the locations: on the desks of the counselors and at the reception desks. She'd only been able to set up one micro camera, and had almost gotten caught when a young, female clerk walked in on her in the record room.

"I totally got turned around," Ashley sputtered, faking embarrassment. "I thought I was heading for the ladies' room." She laughed nervously.

"The restroom is around the next corridor," the clerk said, looking more frightened than Ashley. "You've really got to get out of here," she urged in a harsh whisper. "It's my fault for leaving the door unlocked. If my boss finds out, I'll lose my job."

Ashley lowered her voice and put a comforting hand on the young woman's shoulder. "Listen, I didn't see you. You didn't see me. It's just between us. I would never want to be one that caused someone to lose their job. Let me know when the corridor is clear and I'll slip out."

The girl went to the door and cracked it open. She looked up and down the hallway and frantically waved for Ashley to leave.

"Thanks," Ashley whispered on her way out.

The young woman bobbed her head and quickly shut the door. For an instant Ashley squeezed her eyes closed, inhaling deeply. She certainly couldn't afford any more close calls like that, she thought, as Elliot braked at the red light. She'd decided to keep that little mishap to herself.

"I don't know about you, but I'm starved," Elliot said. "Want to stop and pick up something or do you have other plans?"

"That sounds fine."

"Chinese, Italian, Thai, West Indian?"

"Hmm, some jerk chicken would sure taste good right about now," she said, imagining the hot spices bursting in her mouth.

"I knew I detected an accent," he said, his tone teasing. He snatched a look in her direction.

"Accent? Me no have no accent, mon," she mimicked, reaching way back in her family tree for her Jamaican roots.

Elliot chuckled. "That was really bad, you know."

Ashley pressed her palm to her chest. "I'm wounded."

"I'll try to make it up to you," he said, his tone suddenly soft and intimate.

Her pulse quickened for an instant. She ran her tongue across her lips. She wasn't going to let him get into her head again. "There's a great West Indian restaurant up on Amsterdam and One-nineteen."

"That's a nice little hop. Nothing closer?"

"I've been going there for years. It's worth the trip. It's really not far from the apartment, just far from here. And I'm pretty sure we won't find an authentic West Indian restaurant in this neck of the woods."

"Yeah, you're right. Guess I can keep my appetite under control for the drive across town."

Ashley lowered her head and grinned.

"We accomplished a lot for our first day out," Elliot said after a few moments of the returned silence.

"Once we activate all of the devices, hopefully, we'll get a hit."

"The real key will be the Trojan that will upload once we connect with them through e-mail. We'll be able to monitor all of their electronic communications."

If they kept the conversation on work, being in the same space would be bearable, Ashley thought as the Navigator picked up speed along the FDR Drive.

"I want to study each of the agencies," Elliot said when they pulled to a stoplight. "I want to go back at least twenty years, if not earlier, on all of them."

Ashley turned questioning eyes on him.

"I have a gut feeling that if an adoption agency was involved in your sister's abduction, it was right here in New York. We already have a buzz on the one on our list from the FBI. They are all highly trafficked. Almost too much. We need to find the source of their babies."

Her heart pounded as she listened to him, amazed and deeply touched. From the moment she'd opened her eyes that morning and throughout the course of the day, she'd convinced herself that all the pillow talk was just that—talk. She'd decided that Elliot wasn't going to ride in on his white horse and save the day. He'd gotten what he wanted, and so had she. This announcement, however, cast Elliot Morgan in an entirely different light. Maybe she was wrong about him.

"You're still willing to help me?" Uncertainty tightened her voice.

He glanced at her for a moment, caught the glint of hope in her eyes. "I may be a lot of lousy things, but I am a man of my word. If I say I'll do something, I do it."

"Thank you," she muttered, clearly chastised. There were few things worse than questioning a man's integrity.

Elliot gripped the wheel with more force than he intended until the pads of his hands began to burn and the crease in his forehead was so tight he was giving himself a headache. Had he totally been that much of an S.O.B. to make her think that he would back out on his word? If a man had nothing else, it had to be his word. It was his bond. Apparently, Ashley didn't think so.

He inhaled a tight, hot breath. Who was he kidding? He *was* an S.O.B. But he wasn't a liar. He switched on the radio to drown out the silence.

Ashley nearly leaped out of the SUV before it came to a complete stop. The tension had been so stifling that it had sucked up all the air. Her lungs burned as if she'd been running a marathon, and she realized that for long stretches of the ride she was holding her breath—waiting—for what she didn't know.

She pushed through the glass-and-chrome doors and was greeted by the mouth-watering aroma of peas and rice, plantains, stewed chicken, curried and jerk chicken, steamed vegetables and plenty of fast-talking island lingo. Feeling embraced by the familiar, she exhaled the breath that she'd been holding and felt her body begin to relax. She stepped up behind a young man with dreadlocks down to his waist and a red, black and green knit skull cap propped on top of his head.

She smiled as images of her summer trips to her grandparents homeland of Kingston, Jamaica, invaded her mind. Poverty and crime intermingled with beautiful weather, crystal-blue water and white sandy beaches. The trips stopped when Layla disappeared.

"What do you recommend," came the deep whispered baritone from behind her.

A sprinkle of goose bumps spread across her neck where she could feel the warmth of his breath touch her there. For a hot minute her mind went totally blank.

"Next!" the girl behind the counter called out, snapping Ashley out of her momentary black out.

Ashley stepped up to the counter and Elliot stood by her side. And then he did the damndest thing. He slid his arm possessively around her waist and pulled her securely against his side, looked down into her astonished eyes and said, "What are you having, baby?" in a voice that was so quiet, so personal, so incredibly intimate that the only thing she could envision was her legs wrapped around his back and the length of him deep inside her; and him looking at her like he was right now, as if she was the most important person in his universe.

She lightly ran her tongue along her bottom lip. He smiled as if that was some sort of invitation and she was jolted back to her senses. She turned away from him. "I'll have the jerk chicken with peas and rice."

"Vegetables or salad?"

"Vegetables."

"Make that two," Elliot piped in, full of cheer.

Ashley pressed her lips tightly together to keep from saying something she might regret.

Elliot paid the tab and carried their purchases back out to the Navigator and Ashley was just as hot as the jerk sauce on her chicken.

"What the hell was that back there?" she blasted him the instant the car doors were closed.

"What was *what* back there?" He stuck the key into the ignition and the eight-cylinder engine purred to life.

"You know exactly *what!* All the huggy, kissy, what are you having, baby. That's what."

She could hear how she sounded—like a nagging wife, the girlfriend that's called a "B" to her face and doesn't care—but she couldn't help herself. Elliot brought out the worst in her.

Elliot eased the SUV into traffic. His jaw tightened. This whole operation was wearing thin, really quick and they'd just gotten started. They'd been at odds since day one and now that they'd slept together it only made a bad situation horrific. "I guess I was still caught up in the charade." He cut a look in her direction. "Show's over. Happy?"

Ashley could almost see the steam rising off the top

of Elliot's head. He had every right to be angry. What had he done that was so awful? Touch her? Call her baby? The fault wasn't with him, but how his kindness made her feel when she knew it wasn't and could never be real.

The walls went back up.

When they returned to the apartment Elliot tossed his jacket on the couch, no longer giving a damn whether it pissed her off or not. He took the bag of food and brought it to the kitchen. Setting it on the counter he removed one of the foam containers then grabbed a beer from the fridge. He took everything into the living room and set up camp on the couch. He pointed the remote at the forty-two-inch screen and surfed for something to drown out the past half hour. He settled on an ESPN special "The Championship Knicks."

Ashley didn't say a word. Quietly she retrieved her meal from the bag on the counter and took it to her room. The more distance they put between them at the moment the better, she thought as she closed her room door.

She stared at the food that she'd been salivating over and couldn't take one bite. Instead she sprawled out on her bed and stared up at the ceiling.

When she emerged more than an hour later with the intention of putting away the uneaten food, she realized that the apartment was totally quiet. The living room was empty. She listened for any sounds. Silence. She eased down the hallway toward Elliot's bedroom. His door was open. That room was empty, too.

She dared to step inside. The room was surprisingly neat. The bed was made. All of his clothes were put away. A robe dressed the bottom of the bed and his laptop sat opened on the desk by the window. She walked to his closet and opened the door, ran her hands along his shirts and sweaters. The air held the intoxicating scent of him and for a moment she closed her eyes and inhaled deeply. Wrapping her arms around her waist, she slowly opened her eyes, closed the closet before taking a final look around and walked out.

Elliot contemplated what he was about to do during the entire drive. He didn't see any alternative. He parked the SUV and cut the engine. Before he could convince himself to change his mind, he got out of the vehicle and walked down the quiet tree-lined street. He stood in front of the house for a moment then walked to the door and rang the bell.

Moments later, a surprised Claudia answered the door.

"Elliot!" She pulled the door open. "Is everything all right?"

As always Claudia was impeccably dressed. Her oyster-colored long-sleeved silk sweater over tan slacks, with a thin gold chain at her unlined neck could easily take her from morning to night without missing a beat. Recently wed to Bernard Hassell, Claudia still had the glow of a happy bride.

He leaned down and kissed her cheek. "Everything's fine. I'm sorry. I should have called."

She waved off his apology. "Come in. Come in. I was just surprised to see you. I assume you came to see Bernard?"

"Is he here?"

"Yes, banished to the yard where he's smoking

those awful cigars." She wrinkled her nose. "Go on out back."

Elliot grinned. "Thanks." He walked through the sprawling ground floor of the three-story brownstone. The gleaming wood floors reflected the perfectly placed antique furniture and the off-white walls showcased the expensive art that went from Basquiat to Synthia Saint James. He passed through the dining room to the kitchen and walked out the back door.

Bernard was reclining on a blue-and-white-striped lounge chair, sipping on what looked like brandy and puffing happily on his cigar. He looked up when he heard the door squeak and his eyes widened for a moment before a slow smile moved across his mouth.

"Well, well. What brings you to the mountain," he joked, emitting a soft chuckle.

"I need to talk."

Bernard's smile slowly faded. His brows drew close. The sober expression on Elliot's face was a clear signal that this was no ordinary social call. "Sure. Have a seat." He extended his hand in the direction of the second lounger.

Elliot sat on its edge. He folded his hands on his thighs and leaned forward. "I need you to get me off of this assignment."

"I see." He adjusted the collar of his thick zip-up sweater to ward off a sudden gust of chilly wind that had started to pick up as the sun began its descent. "You want to tell me why?"

Elliot lowered his head and blew out a breath through puffed cheeks. He looked across at Bernard who regarded him with the patience born of a man who'd grown accustomed to long stories.

"I'm not the one for this job."

Bernard made a noise in his throat. "Of course you are or you wouldn't have been selected. You'll have to do a much better job of convincing me."

Elliot stood, jammed his hands into his jeans pockets and began to pace in front of the George Foreman grill. "You know I don't work well with a partner. Haven't for years."

Bernard didn't respond.

Elliot tried again. "We don't get along. It's a bad mix."

"It's getting a little chilly. Let's go inside." Bernard slowly pulled himself up, his marquee—good looks defying his nearly sixty years of age. He stamped out his cigar in the ashtray, took what was left of his drink, pushed open the door and led Elliot to his study. Bernard walked toward the window that looked out onto the dimming street. The lights had come on, giving the historic Sugar Hill neighborhood an old-world charm.

Bernard turned and leaned against the sill. He crossed his long legs at the ankles. "I'm still waiting to hear what you could possibly tell me to make me pull you from this case." He folded his arms across his chest. "This isn't high school where you get to pick and choose who you sit next to in class." His voice grew harsh. "Kids are disappearing. Families are being torn apart and you're talking to me about not getting along? You wanna tell me what the hell is really going on? 'Cause what you're telling me ain't cutting it."

"I slept with her," he shouted. "I crossed the damned line." He walked back and forth, ran his hand across his face. His jaw clenched.

"Have a seat," Bernard ordered after watching Elliot weave a trail across the imported Aztec area rug.

Elliot's tortured dark gaze snapped in Bernard's direction. Reluctantly he dropped down into a side chair, leaned on his elbows and pressed his forehead into his palms.

"If you're intention is to shock me, you haven't. Although I must admit I'm a little disappointed that you would be so reckless." He moved away from the window and sat down opposite Elliot. "You want to tell me what happened?"

"Not really. Just that it happened. Compromises everything."

"What does Ashley have to say?"

"We haven't spoken...not about that."

"Well, you're going to speak to me. Starting now."

"I know it was a mistake. All right. Maybe it was to keep us from killing each other." A flash of Ashley moaning beneath him filled his head and clouded his vision. The way she whispered his name, filled his ears. The way she felt, made him numb to everything else. The way she made him feel, had brought him to Bernard's door.

"Jean doesn't make mistakes," Bernard stated matter-of-factly.

Elliot's head jerked up. "What?"

"She doesn't make mistakes."

"I heard you the first time. I wanna know what you're talking about."

"Simple. When Jean sets up an operation she examines every eventuality. She's like a master chess player, always three steps ahead, anticipating the next move."

"So I'm being played like some kind of puppet?" he said, his voice rising in disbelief and outrage.

"I wouldn't go that far. You and Ashley were selected specifically for this job, because of your skills and because of who you both are." He gave Elliot a long, hard look, hoping to convey his message. "She's never been wrong. That's why she's so good at what she does. Just do your job, E." He paused. "Look, I know losing Lynn the way you did…I know it was hard. She was more than just your partner. But it wasn't your fault. No one could have known about the bomb. Not even you."

The horror of that day would live with him forever. They'd been stationed in Iraq, on a mission to uncover subversives. This was to be their last job. They'd decided to live a "regular" life. They were happy and eager to get the job done so they could return to the States. They'd gone into town the next morning, to the market. The streets were teeming with people, eager for fresh fruits and vegetables. Lynn had left his side to negotiate with the fish monger and then the explosion. The screams. The smoke. The flames. The sirens.

His throat tightened. He'd vowed never again to allow himself to become that attached to anyone, to feel like that about anyone. Since that day, years earlier, he'd worked totally alone. Until now.

Elliot jerked out of his seat. He stared hard at Bernard. "I don't like being manipulated. You can tell Jean I said so. When this thing is over…lose my number." He turned and stormed out, barely saying goodbye to Claudia.

Through the window Bernard watched Elliot drive off and wondered if this would be the first time that Jean was wrong.

Chapter 13

When Elliot returned to the apartment, the achingly soulful sound of Billie Holiday's "God Bless the Child," greeted him. The tightness in his chest began to loosen as the music glided through his veins. He went through the foyer. The lights in the living room were muted, but he could make out Ashley curled up on the couch, a glass of wine at her feet.

He walked all the way in. She didn't move and when he looked closer he realized that she was asleep. He slowly sat down on the footstool and watched the even rise and fall of her chest, the way her long lashes fluttered ever so slightly when she breathed. She looked perfectly angelic, a halo of wild, cottony hair framing her heart-shape face. As if drawn by some unseen force, he reached out and gently pushed aside a curl that hung by her eye.

She stirred. Her eyes flickered then opened fully. When they focused on him, she scrambled to sit up.

"Sorry." He held up his hands. "I didn't mean to wake you."

Ashley ran her hand across her face. "I need to get up anyway." She made a move to stand.

"No." He pressed her thigh with his hand, holding her momentarily in place. "Don't leave."

Her heart banged in her chest. The thigh he just touched felt hot.

"I'm…look, I'm sorry for earlier. I was trying to piss you off."

"Oh really. I hadn't noticed."

Elliot gave a short laugh.

They looked at each other and their tense expressions slowly began to soften.

"I have my ways," Elliot began. "It's not personal."

The comment, though made as an appeasement, stung Ashley. She'd been holding on to the false hope that maybe, buried beneath the thick skin, that Elliot had felt something when they'd made love. But they hadn't made love, she corrected herself. They'd had sex. Plain and simple. And she needed to stop being such a "girl" about it and move on.

Ashley straightened up and forced a smile. "No worries. I finally realized that you were simply being your obnoxious self," she said, nonchalant.

The corner of his mouth lifted. "Touché." He got up, stood over her. "Think I'll take a shower. Long day. Then I'm going to go check the surveillance, see if we picked up anything." He walked out.

Ashley remained where she sat, fighting the urge to throw something. This man had her totally off her game. She needed to get on track and focus. She got up, took her glass from the floor and walked off to the kitchen.

She stood over the sink and washed out her glass. If she was going to focus on the case and possibly uncover information about her sister's abduction, there was no better time than the present. She put the glass in the drain, flipped off the light and began to retrace her steps.

Elliot was coming from his room. The scent of his freshly scrubbed body preceded him.

They met in the center of the apartment, the couch and tables separating them. The hallway light cast them both in shadow.

"Still up?" He tightened the towel around his waist, crossed the open space and walked toward the kitchen. "I have a taste for something," he said opening the fridge and looking deep inside, "just can't figure out what it is." He stood, turned his head and looked at her from above the open door.

Ashley's heart was inexplicably pounding in her chest. He closed the door and she would've sworn that his towel was missing, even though she knew it was just her imagination working overtime.

He stared at her for a long minute. His stomach tightened. *God, you're beautiful.*

"Thank you," she whispered into the security of the semi-darkened room.

Damn! Had he actually spoken his thoughts out loud? Yeah, he was losing it, and quick. He rocked his jaw back and forth trying to think of a wisecrack comeback. He couldn't. He ran his hand across the top of his close-cropped head. Now what?

"Do you mean that?"

Elliot focused on her, thought about his conversation with Carmen and earlier with Bernard. There must be something incredibly special about Ashley Temple that had dragged him out of his self-imposed prison and stripped him of the prickly armor he'd worn for the past six years to keep any and everyone at bay.

"Like I told you earlier, I'm a man of my word."

Ashley's gaze faltered for a moment. "I believe that," she admitted. "And I swear I'm really not the wicked, short-tempered bitch that has taken over my mind. Ask my friends, I'm really likeable," she cried, playfully.

Elliot chuckled. "You definitely need to carry around your references." He waited a beat, enjoying the look of happiness in her eyes. "My friends call me E."

A soft smile lifted her full lips. "Hello, E. My friends call me Ms. Temple," she said with a mischievous light in her eyes.

"Oooh, do they?" he chuckled. He stretched out his hand.

Tentatively, Ashley moved toward him, walking around the table, past the chairs until she stood right in front of him. She looked into his eyes, then down at his hand. She placed her hand in his and his warm fingers closed securely around hers.

"Pleasure to meet you, Ms. Temple."

"Nice to meet you, E."

The thermometer rose from room temperature to sizzle in zero point ten seconds.

Inadvertently her lips parted ever so slightly as she stared into his eyes, seeing the same longing, the same desire that she knew he saw in hers.

Elliot stepped closer, still holding her hand. "This is crazy." Uncertainty mixed with possibility in his voice.

"I know," she whispered, captured by the caress of his smile. "We're supposed to hate each other."

He stroked her cheek with his fingertip, setting off ripples of delight that shimmied through her body. Her eyes fluttered as she let the sensation have its way with her.

"Hating people doesn't ever feel this good, I can assure you," he uttered, a moment before his warm lips brushed hers.

Her soft moan of pleasure was like finding the key to eternal happiness. Elliot's soul opened to welcome that little piece of joy. This was what he'd been afraid of—this feeling—and then have it taken away. That he knew he couldn't do ever again, but maybe for the moment he could pretend that this feeling was for always.

Elliot pulled her flush against him, his need for her pulsing against the towel that separated them. Her mouth was just as sweet and welcoming, taking him in like one who'd lost their way and had finally found the road home.

Ashley wrapped her arms around his neck, her mouth, her tongue eager to meld and dance with his. For now, nothing else mattered except the inexplicable need that she had for this man that drove her crazy. She didn't understand it, and probably never would. All she knew was what she felt: desire. She knew what she wanted, Elliot.

She gasped in surprise when Elliot suddenly scooped her up into his arms.

"Your room or mine?" he asked, his voice thick and heavy.

"Let's try your bed this time," she answered him in a sultry whisper.

"Say no more." He kissed the tip of her nose, her cheeks, her eyelids as he carried her down the hallway with ease. He pushed open his bedroom door with his foot and crossed the room to his bed in long-legged strides and eased them both down on his king-size bed.

"We'll hate each other in the morning," she said softly, her eyes wide and playful.

"You're probably right," he answered. "But let's not talk about it," he said before taking her lips to his own in a long, deep kiss. Finally he eased back. "Why worry about tomorrow when we have this whole night to concentrate on?" He kissed her again, softly, almost tentative this time as if it was the first.

The gentle exploration was more arousing than when their eager tongues were entwined. Ashley felt herself bloom like a flower awakened by the warmth of the morning sun. Her body grew full as her veins filled with desire and it flowed through her with growing urgency. Every tight muscle loosened. Her thighs eased apart as Elliot's strong and sure hands roamed her lines and curves.

He lifted up and pulled the towel away from his waist. Staring into Ashley's eyes he took her hand and placed it on his hardened shaft. They both moaned at the contact.

"That's how much I want you," he groaned, squeezed his eyes shut when she tightened her hand around him.

The feel of him in her hand was an erotic rush that defied explanation. It gave her a sense of power to know that she could make him feel this way—about her. Slowly she stroked him, feeling the veins and muscles tense and ripple beneath her fingertips.

Elliot groaned deep in his throat, grabbed her hand, squeezed it once, then pulled her hand away from its hold. He eased her back onto the bed, unfastened her pants and pulled them off her, tossing them to the floor. He took off her sweater and it joined her jeans.

He moved up on the bed and turned on the night light. "I want to see you," he said, his gaze searing a trail along her exposed flesh. He removed her panties, inching them down her thighs and across her legs like some sexy cabaret routine. He let his fingers caress her, moving across her stomach until it quivered, her inner thighs until they trembled, and ever so lightly across the perfectly tapered curly triangle that shielded the epicenter of her need.

Ashley moaned and gripped the sheet into her clenched hands when Elliot's thumb pressed her swollen clit. He massaged it until it was rock hard and fully exposed from its protective sheath. She writhed against his ministrations, her hips rising and falling to capture the pleasure that he was putting on her.

And then she was hot, wet, suckled and she cried out in blinding delight as his mouth and tongue intensified what his fingers had done. Her head spun and white light flashed behind her closed lids. Wave after shock wave of pleasure jettisoned through her. She tried to scoot away when the pleasure became so intense that it was almost unbearable. But Elliot had no intention of letting her get away. He gripped her hips, raising them higher, leaving her completely open to him and his hunger, to quench his thirst for her.

Her head thrashed back and forth as his tongue

flicked, laved and teased. Reason left her and all that remained was the driving need for release, which Elliot seemed intent on giving her.

Elliot inserted one finger then another. Ashley groaned but he didn't stop. He spread his fingers inside of her and gently slid them in and out, bringing tears of pleasure to her eyes. Her strangled moans spurred him on, and when her body began to tense, her thighs spread wider and her body open fully to him, he knew that she was on the brink of coming and he wanted to experience it with her.

"Ohhhh," she cried. "Ahhhh…E…yesss."

"In the drawer," he urged in a voice that was raw and gravelly. "Open it," he ordered as he continued to finger her toward ecstasy.

Barely able to focus, Ashley reached out to the drawer of the nightstand and pulled it open. She felt around inside and found a condom package.

"Put it on me." He pressed his thumb against her clit and her hips rose and bucked against his hand. "Do it." He could already feel the moisture forming on the tip of his penis and he knew it was only sheer will that kept him from climaxing.

Ashley fumbled with the condom pack and finally got it open. Another wave of electricity shot through her. Her eyes rolled.

Elliot came up on his knees and moved between her parted thighs, keeping his fingers in place. He was rock hard and at full attention.

Ashley rolled the condom over the head and down as far as it would go, which was only halfway.

With his free hand, Elliot pulled her bra down beneath her breasts forcing them higher. Her nipples were hard and full, calling for his attention. He lowered his head and drew the dark grape into his eager mouth and he pushed deep and hard inside her in one swift move.

A whoosh of air expelled from her lungs as her insides instinctively gripped him, the muscles opening and closing around him.

"Ahhhh," he groaned, moving in long, slow strokes willing himself to extend the incredible feeling that rocked them both. He draped her legs over his arms and pushed them back and as far as her body would allow and sunk into the depths of her essence, tapped the spot, once, twice, three times and then heaven and earth collided.

Ashley's entire body undulated in wave after wave of unspeakable explosions, as Elliot rode out his own fantasy, his longings, his wants and needs and finally they merged into one long jet stream of release that erupted within her.

For several joyous moments they bathed in the afterglow, entwined, joined. The rush of their breathing, the pounding of their hearts were the only sounds in the room. By degrees their breathing and racing hearts slowed to normal.

Elliot kissed her along the ridge of her collarbone, making her squirm. "Hate me yet?" he asked, thrusting gently into her as he felt himself growing hard again.

"Not quite," she said, feeling his swelling begin to fill her. She rolled her hips. "Maybe we…need to…finish working out…our aggressions," she said, halting between her words with each of his thrusts.

Elliot suddenly turned onto his back and took her with him, his thoroughly engorged penis binding them together. "Why don't you show me how aggressive you can be," he challenged. He reached up and cupped her breasts in his hands and gently massaged them, teasing the sensitized nipples between the tips of his fingers.

Ashley arched her back and braced her hands behind her on his muscled thighs. She milked him in a mind-blowing climax with quick up and down thrusts of her hips and the deep squeeze of her inner muscles that had them both seeing stars.

Later they lay side by side, the cool sheet covering their damp bodies to the waist. Ashley's insides still quivered and periodically Elliot's shaft jumped. But they both knew that enough was enough for one night.

"Since this is your room, I don't expect that you'll be getting up and leaving in the middle of the night," Ashley said, half in jest.

"I don't plan to." He paused a moment. "And I'm asking you to stay. If you want to."

She turned halfway toward him. "You mean that."

"Yeah," he said after several beats. "I mean it."

"I want to," she whispered.

They were quiet for a while, absorbing the reality behind what had just been said between them.

Ashley tilted her head to press against Elliot's shoulder. Elliot slid his arm beneath her and drew her close to him and he felt warm inside, something he hadn't felt in longer than he cared to remember. It was a comforting sensation, like everything was going to be okay.

"This isn't going to be easy," she said softly, thinking about the enormity of stepping out in the ocean of a relationship with Elliot Morgan.

Elliot exhaled slowly. "It never is."

She angled her head toward him. "You sound like

you have experience," she said, trying to sound light against his suddenly somber tone.

Several moments passed and with each ticking second, Ashley felt the panic rise as if waiting for an impending explosion any minute. And it did.

"Her name was Lynn," he said quietly.

Ashley's heart thumped. She didn't move.

"We met about eight years ago during training." Slowly he told her bits and pieces about his and Lynn's relationship, how they'd gotten together and how he'd lost her.

Listening to him tell her about another woman was difficult to hear, but it explained so much about who Elliot Morgan was and why he lived his life the way he did. This compounded with Bernard's revelations told Elliot's painful story. She understood all too well about loss and the devastating aftereffects it could have. She snuggled closer to him, listened to his heart. Maybe they weren't so completely different after all.

Chapter 14

The following morning they sat down at the kitchen table together after having prepared a breakfast fit for a crew of construction workers.

They'd awakened in a tangle of limbs and twisted sheets. Ashley's leg was draped across Elliot's hip, his large hand was clamped securely around her plump bottom. They made slow and easy love, taking their time as if waking in each other's arms was an everyday occurrence. The comfort and familiarity made the experience that much more enjoyable.

After a long, hot, sudsy shower, they both agreed that they were starving and pretty much fixed everything available from omelets to pancakes, turkey sausage, grits with cheese, wheat toast and fruit.

Elliot finished off his second plate and pushed it to the side. "Can't take another bite." He rubbed his stomach.

Ashley grinned. "I was beginning to think you had a bottomless pit down there instead of a stomach."

"Trust me, that's what it felt like." He looked across the table at her and his eyes darkened. "You drained me of all my essence, woman. I had to replenish, build my stamina back up."

"Oh, sure, blame it on the new girl," she joked while she collected the dishes, scraped them and loaded them into the dishwasher.

"I never did get around to checking the surveillance. Seems like the new girl got all of my attention."

"If you ask me, you get distracted much too easy," she said, sashaying past him.

He reached out, grabbed her around her waist and deposited her on his lap amidst a fit of giggles.

"A man is entitled to his distractions," he said cupping her chin and stealing a kiss. "As a matter of fact I feel a distraction coming on now."

Ashley pressed her palms against his chest. "We have a busy day. You have surveillance to check and I have to go to work. I do have a job you know," she added, teasing his lips with flirty kisses.

"It won't take long," he said into the soft hollow of her neck.

Ashley arched her head back to look at him. Her skin began to tingle.

Elliot tugged on his bottom lip with his teeth as he watched indecision transform into action. Ashley reached between them and tugged on the loose knot of the belt on her robe. The soft sea-foam-colored terry robe fell open allowing him to feast on her beauty.

He groaned softly and pressed his face between the

swell of her breasts, inhaled the sweet fragrance of her skin until he was dizzy with needing her again.

She stood and the robe dropped from her shoulders. She reached down and freed him from his boxers before slowly lowering herself onto him.

"From now on we have to be fully dressed at the kitchen table," Ashley shouted as she hurried down the hallway to the front door. She snatched her coat from the closet and when she turned, Elliot was right in front of her.

He threaded his fingers through the back of her thick hair and pulled her close up against him. He kissed her until her knees wobbled.

"It never stopped us before," he said against her mouth, while his free hand snaked beneath her blouse to caress her breasts.

She whimpered a weak protest, feeling herself dampening with desire. She grabbed his hand. "E, I have to go."

He ran his tongue along her neck. "I know."

"Then stop," she said, her voice hitching when he tweaked her nipple.

"I can't…" He turned her back to the wall and pulled her skirt up around her waist.

"E…" she moaned, knowing that her body was betraying her best intentions.

"Ssssh, baby," he hummed in her ear as his hand slid down around the band of her thong and stockings, to find her wet and wanting. "Just what I was looking for," he said, staring deep into her eyes as his fingers dipped in and out of the honey that was her essence.

Ashley stepped out of her heels and it was the last

signal that Elliot needed. He took a handful of her stocking and ripped them open from the crotch. Her red thong was about as much of a roadblock as dental floss. He grabbed her and lifted her up, pressed her securely against the wall as she wrapped her legs around him.

On still-shaky legs, Ashley finally arrived at MT Management. She'd called Mia from the car to let her know that she'd be late after taking yet another shower—alone—and changing her clothes. They had a meeting with a potential client at eleven and she walked in the door with barely fifteen minutes to spare. She put her purse in her desk, greeting Melody, the new intern, then walked to Mia's office in the back of the ground-floor space. She knocked on the door.

"Come in," Mia called out.

Ashley opened the door and stuck her head in. When Mia looked up and saw her, Ashley would have sworn that there was a big old scarlet letter posted on her forehead for all the world to see. But of course that was ridiculous.

"Hey. 'Morning. Everything, okay? You're never late." She went back to reviewing her file.

Ashley swallowed. "Yeah, I'm fine. Just some things came…up this morning."

"Not a problem, the client called just before you got here and needs to push the meeting back until later this afternoon."

"Oh, great," she said, breathing a sigh of relief. "It will give us some time to go over our notes."

MT Management was Mia's dream come true. It was the perfect complement to her personality. She was an obsessive organizer and her attention to detail and planning the perfect event from your basic baby shower to mega corporate getaways was legendary. She knew everyone who was anyone worth knowing to get a job done. Mia Turner's contact list could go on the market for millions, which was why MT Management was the most highly paid, sought after event planning business in New York.

Mia swept her glasses off the bridge of her pert nose and closed the folder in front of her. She waved off Ashley's comment. "We have time to discuss business. You've been off the radar the past couple of days. What's happening with the case and the man you love to hate?"

Ashley tugged at the collar of her blouse.

Mia squinted. "Is something wrong?"

Ashley flashed an awkward smile. "I wouldn't say wrong exactly."

Mia's brows rose. She got up from her desk and went to close the door. She sat back down and buzzed Melody on the intercom. "Mel, hold all my calls for a few minutes, okay."

"Sure thing, Ms. Turner."

Mia turned her attention fully on Ashley. "If you want to talk I'm all ears and I have all day." She waited a beat. "You were there for me through the whole Michael debacle." Her voice softened. "You were the only one I trusted to listen without question or judgment. Not even Savannah or Danielle. I'm willing to do the same, whatever it is."

Ashley drew in a long breath and let it out slowly. "How 'bout if I tell this tale just once?"

Mia's somber expression brightened. "Then, girl, it must be juicy!" She pressed the intercom again. "Mel, do me a favor and call Mr. Archer. Tell him I deeply apologize but we'll have to reschedule at his convenience." She hung up and before Ashley could say a word, Mia had contacted Savannah, Danielle and Traci who all agreed to drop everything and meet her and Ashley at The Shop in an hour.

Ashley simply shook her head and went along for the ride. Once Mia was revved up and had an agenda there was no stopping her. Besides, who better to air her dirty laundry than with her girls.

Danielle and Traci were already at their booth when Ashley and Mia walked in.

"Hello ladies," they all greeted in unison, buzzing one anothers' cheeks.

"Where's Savannah?" Mia asked, sliding in next to Traci.

"She texted me a few minutes ago, said she was stuck in traffic, but was on her way."

"Guess we can order in the meantime," Mia said.

They flipped open their menus and gave their orders to the waitress, just as Savannah breezed in.

"Sorry I'm late," Savannah said, a bit breathless. She squeezed in next to Mia and blew kisses to everyone. "So what's so pressing to get us all up in The Shop on a Tuesday?" she asked with a big grin.

"I think sista girl here has some things she needs to get off her chest," Danielle quipped, looking at Ashley.

All eyes turned to Ashley.

She looked from one expectant face to the next. "All right, all right, you beat it out of me. I slept with him."

Four mouths dropped open at the same time but nothing came out.

Traci was the first to recover. "Are we talking about the same man that less than a week ago, you couldn't stand the sight of?"

"You don't have to put it quite like that," Ashley said meekly.

"Okay, so how would you put it?" Dani asked.

Ashley swallowed. "It's not that simple."

"It never is, sweetie," Savannah said. She reached out and covered Ashley's hand. "Tell us what you want to, and keep what you don't to yourself," she said gently, always the diplomat.

Ashley pressed her lips together. Slowly she shook her head. "I don't know...one minute we at each other's throats and the next we were rolling around in bed... in the shower...in the chair...in the hall..." Her voice drifted off as the images of the two of them played in full color in her head making her toes curl right inside her Jimmy Choos.

The quartet's brows were raised so high they all but disappeared into their hairlines.

"Forget about keeping anything to yourself," Danielle finally said. "I want details." Her voice rose two octaves. "In the hall?"

Mia threw Danielle a look.

"What, what did I say?" Danielle asked, looking innocent.

Mia just shook her head.

The waitress arrived with their food.

"You can share my plate," Traci said to Savannah who'd never gotten around to ordering. She pushed the plate between them.

"Can we have a round of mimosas?" Mia asked the waitress before she left the table.

"Make mine a double," Ashley muttered.

Over drinks, good food and friendship, Ashley tried to unravel the story that had suddenly become her life. She told them of the tension that simmered between her and Elliot like a pot of stew ready to boil over. How they'd finally talked, about themselves, life, the world. She told them about Lynn and how it had devastated him, leaving him unwilling and pretty much unable to care about anyone, especially someone that he worked with. And then she told them about the weight that she'd carried in her heart for the past twenty-three years.

"Oh my God, Ashley," Savannah cried, the only one so far out of their group who had a child and could completely understand a parent's worst nightmare.

"Why didn't you ever say anything to us, to me?" Mia asked.

"It's hard. It's still hard to talk about. Guilt is a terrible thing." She sniffed, fighting back tears. "When I got this case I thought that maybe this was the chance that had eluded me and my family for years. I finally had the means and resources of doing what the police couldn't do years ago."

"Do you think that's why Jean selected you, because she knows?" Savannah asked, understanding all too well the reach and wealth of knowledge that Jean possessed.

Four pairs of eyes settled on Ashley.

"The thought did occur to me. It wouldn't surprise

me one bit. But I didn't want to mention it to her if she didn't know."

"That's probably best," Traci said.

They sipped their drinks.

"So, other than mind-altering sex, how do you feel about Elliot?" Mia asked, breaking the silence.

Ashley offered a shadow of a smile. "I like him. I really do. Beneath the tough exterior and all the bluster, there's a decent, caring man. Someone that I want to get to know better." She paused for a moment and looked from one supportive face to another. "I want it to be more than great sex."

Mia squeezed her hand. "I don't want you to get your hopes up, Ash. From everything you've told us about Elliot he's not one to settle down. His job and the challenge of it have become his life. This may just be another assignment for him. You have to prepare yourself for that."

Ashley bobbed her head. "I know. But I'm willing to see how far it will go before it's over. And I intend to make the most of every minute."

After the two-hour lunch they all decided to call it a day and promised to touch base with each other during the week. Ashley returned to the apartment and found it empty. She walked through the sprawling space touching the things they'd touched, breathing the air they'd breathed. She walked down the hall to her bedroom. She pushed open the door and her breath caught in her chest. On the nightstand was a crystal vase filled to overflowing with a burst of orange and peach colored roses. Propped up in front of the vase was a plain white envelope.

She crossed the room and lifted the envelope, turned it over and opened it. There was a card inside. The handwriting was even and strong.

"It was real. Don't doubt it. See you later. E."

She pressed the note to her chest, leaned down and inhaled the heady scent of the roses. She read the note again. Maybe her life had morphed into one of those sexy romance novels, where the inexplicable is commonplace. But every romance novel has a happily-ever-after ending. She placed the card on the table. She only wished she could flip the pages of this chapter of her life to the epilogue.

Chapter 15

At precisely six-thirty, Ashley and Elliot were seated in the front office of Happy Homes Adoption Agency. Elliot held Ashley's hand and the warmth and comfort of it was no pretense. She locked her fingers around his and easily slipped into her role as his loving wife.

"We at Happy Homes are very proud of our success record of pairing eligible parents with the perfect child," Gail Hastings, the case worker said. She looked over their application, nodding her head as she reviewed the information. She looked up at them. "Of course we'll have to verify everything and make several house visits. It's all part of our procedure."

"We totally understand," Elliot said. "All we want is the chance to be the great parents that I know we can be."

Ashley leaned forward, zeroed in on Gail. Her voice

wobbled. "We've tried everything," she said. "In vitro didn't work and we began running out of money. We're down to our last hundred thousand dollars." She turned sad eyes on Elliot. "We can't risk going through the heartache and disappointment again. Adoption is our last chance." She lowered her head and covered her face with her hands.

Elliot put his arm around her shoulders and pulled her close. He mouthed, "I'm sorry," to Gail. She nodded her head in understanding.

"We'll certainly do everything we can, Mr. and Mrs. Morgan." She handed Ashley a tissue.

Ashley sniffed and wiped her eyes. "Thank you," she murmured.

"We have all of your information. We'll be in touch." She stood. The interview was over.

Elliot helped Ashley to her feet. He extended his hand to Gail. "Thank you for your time."

"Of course."

They turned to leave. Once they were outside, Elliot spun her around and kissed her fully on the lips. "You were damned good in there and the tears were a nice touch."

Ashley grinned. "I was kinda good, wasn't I?"

"Very. Let's go home and celebrate."

Curled up together on the couch, Ashley sipped on a glass of wine and Elliot worked on a bottle of beer as they watched video images from several windows on their computer. The images were from five of the locations they'd visited.

"Nothing out of the ordinary," Elliot said.

"What about audio?"

"I played the tapes earlier today. Nothing."

"Hopefully by tomorrow, we'll get a hit from the e-mail account."

She draped her legs across his lap. "This is like looking for a needle in a haystack. There are hundreds of agencies and who's to say that the ones on our list are even involved?" She tossed her head back against the cushion of the couch and closed her eyes.

"We're just getting started," he said. "We'll keep digging until we find what we're looking for." He leaned over and kissed her forehead. "We have two more to visit tomorrow." He took a last look at the recorded video then shut down the computer. "Patience," he added.

She opened her eyes and looked at him. "I've been patient for twenty-three years," she said softly. "I'm about out of patience."

Elliot stroked her cheek. She captured his hand and held it against her face. "Ready to turn in? It's after midnight."

"Your room or mine?" she asked.

"Let's do something wild and crazy." He rubbed her thigh.

She sat up. "Something more wild and crazy than what's been going on since we met?"

"Yeah, my room, two nights in a row!"

She laughed. "You're on."

"Last one in fixes breakfast," he said, leaping up from the couch and making a move for the hallway.

Ashley grabbed the tail of his shirt, throwing him off his stride and pushed past him. She took off down the hall with Elliot hot on her heels. She yelped and giggled as she burst through his door.

He grabbed her and tossed her on the bed, landing solidly down next to her. He rolled on top of her, smothering her laughter. "You cheated," he said, nibbling her neck.

"You got a head start."

"You know what they do to cheaters?"

"What?"

"They get exposed…for who they really are," he said, as he began unbuttoning her blouse.

"I plead guilty," she murmured against his mouth. "Guilty as charged."

Over the course of the next three weeks, they worked tirelessly, going on interviews, filling out forms and watching videos. The Trojan that was planted on the computers at the agencies through e-mail transmission turned up nothing out of the ordinary. From everything they'd discovered so far, the agencies on the list were all above board.

In between being frustrated by their lack of progress, they explored the city together, sat up long into the night sharing stories of their youth, high school, college, movies and music that they loved and hated. They found out that their favorite movie of all time was *When a Stranger Calls*.

"I think I woke up the whole neighborhood with my screaming," Ashley admitted over her laughter. "When the babysitter found out that the murderer had been making calls from the attic right in her house, oh my goodness, I lost it."

"That part had everyone going. But the sequel got me," Elliot admitted. "When that nut painted himself as part of the wall and stepped out behind her…"

"Yes," she squealed, giving a little shiver. "That was over the top."

Elliot talked about the rough life he'd lived growing up in Baltimore, the losses he'd seen, the destruction. "I guess that's why I chose the life that I did. Danger was part of my makeup. Survival. You know."

"But do you ever get tired of it? I mean the never knowing."

He breathed heavily as he twirled a strand of her hair around his finger. "Most of the time I don't think about it. At least I try not to. It's a job, a job that keeps my mind from focusing on me. But sometimes I wake up in some strange hotel, in some strange city and I have to ask myself what the hell I'm doing."

She listened to the steady beat of his heart. "What answer do you come up with?"

"I'm still trying to find out," he said, his voice taking on a wistful tone. "Maybe one day I will."

As Ashley lay curled next to him, she wondered if she would be a part of his *maybe*.

"It's been more than a month," Ashley said as they drove to the 40/40 Club for dinner.

The famed eatery owned by Jay-Z—rapper, producer, entrepreneur—was noted for the good food, friendly service and being a frequent haunt of celebrities. Somehow, through Elliot's vast array of connections, he'd secured VIP passes to see a one-night-only private show by Mariah Carey. Since her return to the spotlight after nearly a ten-year hiatus she was the hottest ticket in town.

"I know. I was sure we would have found something by now. Even I'm beginning to get impatient."

"Maybe we've been looking in the wrong places?"

"Any ideas?"

"What about the hospitals? That's where they snatched my sister. Everyone knows that even with precautions, hospital security sucks, especially in urban and low-income areas."

"If we took on the hospitals, that would expand our search exponentially. We're talking hundreds of metropolitan hospitals and thousands of employees, not to mention patients and their guests."

"True." She blew out a long sigh, her small bubble of hope bursting in her ears.

Elliot stole a glance at Ashley and saw the disappointment that pinched the corners of the mouth he loved to kiss. He reached across the gearshift and grabbed her hand. "We'll map out a plan, starting with the most likely hospitals and work our way through them."

She turned to him.

"Your sister is out there somewhere. If we can find the source of the abductions, I believe it will lead us to your sister. Don't ask me how I know." His eyes creased in concentration. "It's just a gut feeling."

Ashley swallowed over the sudden knot in her throat. "Thank you," she whispered.

"Don't thank me yet. And don't go getting all teary on me, we have some partying to do tonight."

She sniffed and her expression brightened. "That we do."

When they arrived at the 40/40 Club they were met at the door by a tuxedoed security guard who checked their names off on the VIP list before hand-ing them over to the hostess to seat them. The setting was straight out of *E! Hollywood*. A red carpet ran from the door to the center of the space. Multileveled seating gave the invited guests a good view from any location. The stage was set up on a center platform and Mariah's band was in place, warming up with mini-renditions of some of her hits. Just a quick look around attested to the who's who that had come out to support "The Voice."

"I'm totally impressed," Ashley said, as Elliot helped her into her seat.

He kissed the back of her neck. "That was my secret plan all along."

Within moments a waitress came to take their drink and dinner orders. The show was scheduled to start in less than an hour and the feel of anticipation electrified the air. Even the *celebrati* were awed by the chance to see her up close and personal after such a long absence. What made it extra special was that it was not televised, there was no media, just friends and devoted fans.

Their drinks arrived first and just as Ashley was taking her first sip of her apple martini, she squinted into the muted lighting and swore she spotted Gail Hastings sitting on the far side of the room.

"Is that Gail, the case worker from Happy Homes?" she asked, trying not to point, but steering him in her direction with a lift of her chin. "Over there on the second tier."

Elliot turned halfway in his seat.

"She has on the mint-green dress."

Elliot stared a bit harder. "You're right, it is her."

"Guess she has friends in high places, too," she said half in jest, partly in curiosity.

"Hmm," Elliot murmured. The hair on the back of his neck began to tingle the way it did when he was within inches of his target.

They didn't have time to focus on it any longer. The lights dimmed, the MC came to the mic and introduced one of the greatest voices of her generation.

For the next hour the audience was mesmerized and transported as the diva took them from her early work, to everything in between, up to her latest album. Intermittently she would share a little anecdote about how she'd come to sing a song or the first time she sang it. And before anyone was ready to let her go, the show ended to a thunderous standing ovation.

"Oh my God, that was incredible," Ashley gushed. "I can't begin to thank you for this."

He winked at her. "I can think of a few things."

She swiped his arm. "Naughty boy."

"You spoil me." He took her hand and kissed the back of it.

"Hey, there she is."

Elliot still held her hand but turned in his seat. He pulled her up to her feet. "Get your purse."

She took her purse and let Elliot lead her over to the bar.

"Gail?" she said, dipping her head to the side.

Gail turned from the bar and the surprise on her face was camera-ready. "Oh…Mr. and Mrs. Morgan." She pressed her hand to her chest and looked around as if the answer to their sudden appearance was somewhere behind them. "What a pleasant surprise. Did you see the entire show?"

"Yes, we did. Pretty hard to get tickets," Elliot said. "You're one of the lucky ones."

A tall, silver-haired gentleman came to stand by Gail's side. He stuck out his hand. "Dr. Ettinger."

"Most people don't know we're married," Gail said softly, allowing Elliot and Ashley in on their secret. "It just makes things messy at work. You understand."

The bulb went off in Ashley's head. This was *the* Dr. Ettinger who actually owned and operated the agency. She'd run across his name and picture in the files.

"Of course," Elliot said and flashed a grin. "Your secret is safe with us."

"So you two are in the market for adoption," Ettinger said, looking from one to the other.

Ashley linked her arm through Elliot's. "Yes, Doctor, we certainly are. Talking with your wife…Gail really gave us a lot of hope."

"I know you two are eager," Gail said, "but I'm confident we'll find a baby for you."

"Yes, I'm sure we'll be able to help you," Dr. Ettinger added.

"Thank you, Doctor," Ashley said.

"Have they had their home visit yet, dear?" the doctor asked.

"No, they haven't."

"Well, why don't we at least get that ball rolling while we finish up the background check."

"Of course." Ashley turned to Elliot with excitement in her eyes. "We'd welcome a visit. It brings us closer to our dream."

"Good. You should be hearing from us this week," Gail said.

"Thank you so much," Ashley gushed.

"Of course. Our job is to bring good people together with beautiful children who need a home. Unfortunately, it often takes some time to find a good match," Dr. Ettinger said.

"We, uh, totally understand that this whole process can be…costly," Elliot said, "but we're willing to pay whatever is necessary to bring a healthy baby into our lives and make a home for him or her." He spoke directly to Dr. Ettinger.

He clasped Elliot's shoulder and patted him. "We won't even concern ourselves with that right now. Let's just get you two through the maze of paperwork and take it from there."

Elliot bobbed his head.

"We better get going, sweetheart," Gail said, "Jackson and Phyllis will be wondering what happened to us."

"We're meeting friends for a late drink," Dr. Ettinger offered by way of explanation.

"Sure. Good night. Thanks for talking with us. We don't want to hold you up." Elliot stuck out his hand and shook the doctor's and then Gail's hand.

"You should get a call this week about scheduling a home visit," Gail said as she turned to leave.

Elliot and Ashley watched them as they walked out, and neither could deny the unsettling feeling that Dr. and Mrs. Ettinger had left behind.

Chapter 16

"Jazz, I need you to do a full background search on a Dr. Thomas Ettinger," Elliot was saying into the phone as he looked over the brochure from Happy Homes Adoption Agency.

It was Jazz who'd designed the kits that the ladies used, that came complete with micro cameras disguised as lapel pins or magnetic disks, bubble bath that could knock out a horse, dusting power that was actually to lift fingerprints and a host of other necessary gadgets. In addition to which she was a master researcher and software developer. If there was any dirt under the fingernail of a subject, Jasmine could find it.

"Not a problem," she said, "I'll get on it. As soon as I have something I'll let you know."

"Oh, and Jazz, look, this is just between us, but I need you to take a look at a cold case…"

* * *

"So how is everything going between you and Elliot?" Mia asked as they prepared a PowerPoint presentation for a client.

Ashley smiled. "I wish I could complain but I can't."

"You actually sound happy."

She turned to Mia. "You know what...I am. For the first time in a very long while, I feel happy inside, Mia. I look forward to the end of the day, the nights, the mornings. We enjoy each other, in and out of the bed," she quickly added. "And as much as I hated to admit it, he's damned good at what he does and we work well together."

Mia nodded as she listened to her friend gush about her blossoming relationship, and dared to ask the question that sat in the room like a third person. "Are you falling in love with him, Ash?"

"I know it sounds silly and so romance novel cliché but I'm already in love with him. I've never felt this way about anyone before."

"And what about Elliot? Do you think he feels the same way?"

Ashley blew out a slow breath then looked at Mia. "I don't know."

Mia leaned forward on the desk and linked her fingers together. "Ash, I know you're a big girl and you can take care of yourself in a street fight, but this is different. There are feelings involved. What are you going to do when this case is over and they send him off to who the hell knows where for months at a time? Are you prepared to deal with that?"

Ashley pushed back from the table and stood. She turned her back to Mia and slowly paced the floor. For a moment she glanced up at the ceiling as if the answer may be somewhere in the heavens. "It keeps me awake at night," she said, her voice distant and thin. "Sometimes I wake up in the morning with this paralyzing feeling that he's gone. And I can't move until I check every sound in the apartment, and hear his footsteps, or his off-beat humming, or the shower." She swallowed. "Just something to let me know that he hasn't left me, at least not yet." She turned and faced Mia. "But whatever happens I'll deal with."

"I know you will, sis." She waited a beat. "On another note, how is the case going—any leads?"

"We're not really sure but of all people to run into the other night…" She told Mia about their encounter with Gail and her husband Dr. Ettinger.

"It could be something or nothing at all. This is New York and you're liable to run into anyone. She could have been nervous for the reason that she said, most people don't know that they're married." She shrugged. "What's your gut telling you?"

"I can't put my finger on it. But their demeanor changed somehow during the course of the conversation."

"What do you mean?"

"They just all of a sudden wanted to bend over backward to accommodate us." She focused on Mia, trying to convey the sense of something awry to her.

"Could be that it eased an awkward situation or that they want you to help them keep their little secret if they help you."

"I suppose. One good thing came out of it all."

"What's that?"

"We got our appointment for a home visit. Tomorrow, 10:00 a.m."

Elliot and Ashley finished taking a last look around the apartment. Even though Ashley spent most nights in Elliot's bed, for the purposes of the visit they'd moved all of Ashley's belongings into Elliot's room leaving her room as the guest room or potential nursery.

The doorbell rang at precisely 10:00 a.m. Ashley looked to Elliot. "Ready?"

"Yes, dear," he teased, giving her rear a gentle love tap.

"Not in front of company," she said, leaning up to him and kissing him full on the lips. She used her thumb to wipe away the residue of her lip gloss.

Ashley buzzed the front door and watched on the lobby camera as a young man and woman approached the elevator.

"They're on their way up."

Moments later their front doorbell rang. Ashley and Elliot answered it together. The team introduced themselves as Wendy and Glen. They showed their identification along with a printout on Happy Homes letterhead indicating the appointment time and place.

They were young—in their late twenties to early thirties, very social-service-looking—serious about their work. They came complete with a checklist of questions, forms and a digital camera. While Elliot and Ashley filled out forms, Glen took photographs of the apartment.

"Is this where you plan to live?" Wendy asked, but it almost sounded like an accusation.

"Yes. Is that a problem?" Elliot asked.

"No." She made some notes. "Are you planning to work, Mrs. Morgan, once you get the child?"

"No. My plan is to stay home and raise my baby." She looked to Elliot for confirmation and he nodded in agreement.

"I see," Wendy said, but clearly she didn't, as she sounded, once again, disturbed by their answers.

Glen returned to the living room. "All done," he announced. "You have a beautiful place."

"Thank you," Ashley said.

Wendy shot Glen a look of reproach. His pock-marked face reddened.

Wendy closed her leather folder with a snap and stood. "I think that covers everything." She reached into her wallet and took out a business card. "If you have questions, you can call. Thank you for your time."

"How long will the process be now that we've had a home visit?"

"Every case is different," she said noncommittally. "Good luck." She turned and walked toward the door with Glen trailing behind.

Elliot walked with them to the front door and let them out. "Thanks again," he said, shutting the door behind them. "Feel a little chilly in here to you?" he asked, tongue in cheek.

"That is one cold sister," Ashley said. "Not a smile, not a kind word."

"No personality." He flopped down on the couch. "Can you imagine parents who are really looking to adopt and have to deal with her?"

Ashley shook her head. "After all we've been dealing with this past month and a half I almost feel like I am trying to adopt."

Elliot made a sound in his throat. "I know. Weird. I feel the same way."

Ashley curled her legs beneath her and adjusted her body in his direction. "You ever think you'll have kids of your own?" she asked and the instant the question was out of her mouth she wanted to snatch it back.

He clasped his hands behind his head and leaned back against the couch cushions. "The kind of life I lead, there's never been room in my life for kids, family, settling down. It just wouldn't be fair."

Yet he'd been willing to settle down once before, with Lynn, Ashley thought. But apparently not with her.

"Hey." She popped up from her seated position. "Wanna check out a movie tonight, if you don't have plans?" she asked to change the direction of the conversation. She didn't need him to see how his answer had affected her.

"Hmm, sure, why not. Doesn't that new Jamie Foxx movie start tonight?"

"Yeah, I think it does." She swallowed over the burn in her throat. "I'll check." She walked off to the spare room where she'd kept her laptop. She sat down at the desk, covered her face and cried.

"Hey, Jazz," Elliot said, "hang on a sec, I'm driving. Let me pull over." He signaled and moved into the far-right lane and pulled to a stop in front of an outdoor café. "What do you have for me?"

"Not as much as I would like. I checked your Dr.

Ettinger every which way but loose. Based on everything I've come up with he's a straight shooter. He's been running that clinic for just about ten years. Before that he was Chief of Staff at Methodist Hospital."

"Hmm, thanks, J."

"There is something else."

"What's that?"

"Prior to twenty years ago I can't find a scrap of anything on this guy. It's like he didn't exist."

"What?"

"I'm still checking but prior to 1984, the good doctor was a no-show."

Elliot frowned. "Keep checking, Jazz, and keep me posted."

"I sure will."

He disconnected the call. *Who are you, Dr. Ettinger?*

When Elliot got back to the apartment later that evening, he walked in on a ringing phone. It wasn't quite six. He didn't expect Ashley back until much later. She and Mia had a dinner meeting with a client. He tossed his jacket on the couch and walked into the kitchen, snatching up the phone on the fourth ring.

"Morgan residence," he said, and kind of liked the sound of it.

"Mr. Morgan?"

"Yes. Who is this?" He glanced at the caller ID and it showed Anonymous.

The caller cleared her throat. "It's Gail, from the adoption agency."

He pulled out his PDA from his jacket pocket, connected the USB cord to the phone and pressed record.

"Oh, hello. How are you?" He looked at the dial on his PDA and saw that it was recording. "Do you have news for us?"

"I may have a child for you and your wife."

"That's wonderful! This is the news we've been praying for," he said, bursting with feigned enthusiasm.

She cleared her throat again. "I was hoping that we could meet, privately, away from the office."

Bingo. Elliot felt the adrenaline rush through his veins. "Uh, a private meeting?"

"With you and your wife, of course."

"Of course. When did you want to meet?"

"Tomorrow evening. Eight o'clock at Bombay on East Seventy-second Street and Riverside Drive."

"I know the place."

"Good. I'll make reservations and see you and your wife at eight."

"Thank you. Thank you so much."

"Good night, Mr. Morgan."

"Good night."

The call disconnected and he turned off the recorder. This was it. He could feel it in every fiber of his being. Gail was going to make an offer, and once she did the trail had to lead back to the real source. He was hard-pressed to think that Gail Hastings was at the top of this particular food chain. No. It was someone else. That much he was sure of.

He was itching to share the news with Ashley and couldn't wait for her to get home. *Home.* His stomach jumped. He hadn't thought of anyplace as home in more than too many years.

Elliot pulled open the fridge and took out a bottle of Coors. What would it be like not to be in a pretend relationship with Ashley Temple, but in a real one? He twisted off the top and took a long, icy-cold swallow.

After their awkward and tense beginnings, they'd found a rhythm together, and not just in bed, that was an added plus. They found their rhythm in day-to-day life, doing for each other, looking out for each other, listening, supporting, laughing with each other.

He enjoyed her company. He looked forward to seeing her standing at the stove in the morning, and inhaling the scent of her shower gel at night. Over the weeks that they'd shared a life as a husband and wife, he'd come to embrace the idea of Ashley in his life, enjoying it. And it had become so easy and comfortable that it felt, natural, the way it should be.

When he thought of Ashley, it made him smile from the inside out, from her no-nonsense attitude to her unbelievable sensuality. She was smart, beautiful, funny, sexy and a damned good agent.

He sat down on the recliner, pressed the button on the arm that raised the leg rest.

And for all that was good and wonderful about the life he was living, he knew that it was temporary. They were actors in a play and soon they'd get their curtain call. If things moved in the direction he felt that they would, that call may come much sooner rather than later. Then he and Ashley would go back to the way it was before.

Something deep inside him twisted and he felt an emptiness inside. And he realized with sudden clarity that he didn't want "the way it was before." That realization scared him, scared him more than flying bullets, car bombs and threats of terrorism. Because he had no gadget, no protective gear, no retaliation to fight off feelings. He'd tried and for a long time he'd been successful. Until Ashley.

Elliot finished off his beer. He could almost see himself with Ashley for the long haul. But that wouldn't be fair to her. And he had no idea what he would do for a living if he stopped his line of work.

Humph, wishful thinking. He was certain that making a life with him was the last thing on Ashley's mind.

He felt the vibration of his cell phone inside his pants pocket. He pulled it out and checked the lighted screen. It was a text from Jasmine. *May have a line on that* other *project. Need to unravel some threads and let you know.* He halfway smiled. At least when he left her for good, he hoped to leave Ashley with some answers.

Chapter 17

When Ashley came in later that evening she was bubbling with excitement over the latest client that MT Management had landed, which was a new cable station that wanted to sponsor a virtual watch party of its launch in all of its markets across the country.

"It's an incredible opportunity," she enthused as she stepped out of her shoes and tucked them away in the closet that she and Elliot now shared. She pulled her hair away from her face with a headband that had magically appeared.

For a moment, Elliot was taken aback by her raw, natural beauty. Never one to wear makeup, her warm brown complexion was clear and glowed with vitality. Her large, luminous brown eyes sparkled with energy when she talked in concert with her slender fingers that fluttered and flowed, organizing the distribution of her narrative like a symphony conductor. Her body was a work of art and her smile could warm the coldest room. He was totally enchanted with her, thrilled by her, turned on by her and very much in love with her.

"So what do you think?" she asked, diving onto the bed and landing next to him, unceremoniously jolting him from his assessment of her.

His eyes danced over her for a moment. He stroked the curve of her jaw. "I think that there's not a better team out there that can do what you and Mia do. And they're damned lucky to get you," he said, searching every corner of his mind to piece together what she'd been talking about while he was daydreaming.

She rolled onto her back and giggled like a little girl. "MT Management is seriously in the big league. The sky is the limit."

Elliot braced himself on his elbow, leaned down and kissed her ever so tenderly. "Congratulations."

The rhythm of Ashley's breathing stuttered then sped up as she witnessed an outright look of lust in his eyes.

Elliot kissed her again while he lifted her top. "I want to make love to you," he said against the swell of her breasts, his voice laden with an emotion that he couldn't name. He could never tell her how he felt, what he was feeling about her. It wasn't fair. But he could show her. He could show her by the way he touched her, the way he kissed her lips, the way he got her wet enough to receive all of him, the way he moved inside her and held her on the brink until she could no longer bear the denial. Those things he could do. But he could never tell her what it all meant.

* * *

They lay together afterward beneath the soft light of the full moon. The evenings had grown warmer and the days longer as spring began to step aside for summer.

Elliot held her close, gently running his hand along the soft curve of her spine. "Got a call today."

"From who?" she asked, her voice heavy with sleep.

"Gail Hastings. She wants to meet us, privately."

Ashley blinked away her fatigue. She was fully awake now. She pushed herself into a semi-sitting position. "When did she call?"

"Earlier this evening."

"Why didn't you tell me?"

"I'd intended to but I got so caught up in your coup today and then…" He ran his thumb across her still-tender nipples. "You know I get distracted," he joked.

She swiped at his hand. "This is important."

He sat up. The sheet slid down to his waist. "I'm sorry. I know. This may be the break we've been waiting for. She sounded like she wants to make some kind of deal. We'll have to go the meeting and just play it by ear."

Ashley was bobbing her head in the semi-darkness. Her mind went fast-forward to finally cracking the case and finding out who was behind the abductions, and somewhere at the end of that rainbow she would find her sister.

"Her birthday is in two weeks," she said softly. "She would be twenty-three."

Elliot drew her close. She rested her head on his chest. "If Layla is out there, we'll find her. I promise you."

* * *

They went over all the details one more time before they headed out. Ashley would ask all the questions and Elliot would speak for both of them. They had to be sure to insist that money was no object. They had money and could get more.

Ashley had a minirecorder that looked like a cell phone inside her purse that she would activate as soon as conversation began. The digital device could record up to five hours before you had to upload the audio files to a computer.

"Ready?" Elliot asked.

Ashley angled her head and put her hand on her hip. "I'm supposed to be asking all the questions," she joked.

"Yes, dear," he tossed back. He put his arm around her waist. "Let's go."

The Bombay Lounge was a high-end, very expensive restaurant complete with authentic Indian food and decor located in the posh Upper East Side of Manhattan.

Ashley and Elliot arrived minutes before eight and were seated right away. Gail Hastings had already arrived. And so had Dr. Ettinger.

Elliot and Ashley, hand-in-hand, greeted Gail and the doctor and sat down at the round table.

"I'm so glad you could come," Gail began.

"Yes, we feel very confident that we can help you," Dr. Ettinger stated.

Ashley grabbed Elliot's hand and squeezed it. "You found a baby for us?" Her eyes widened with hope.

The answer was interrupted by the waiter who

came to take their order. Dr. Ettinger made some recommendations to Ashley and Elliot.

"We think we may have found the perfect baby for
you," Gail said once the waiter was gone.

Ashley's hands flew to her mouth. Her eyes filled
with emotion.

"We've gone over your entire profile, did a check on
your backgrounds and we have every reason to believe
that you will make ideal parents," Dr. Ettinger said.

Elliot used the opportunity to kiss Ashley. He turned
to Gail and her husband. "I told Ash that we finally
found the right place when we came to you."

"So what's the next step?" Ashley asked.

"I'm sure you're both aware that adoptions can generally take up to a year," Gail said, playing out each
word.

Elliot straightened in his seat. "But I thought you
said you had a baby for us."

Dr. Ettinger held up his hand. "What my wife is
saying is that for very select couples, couples that are
needy and deserving… Well, sometimes we can speed
things up."

Ashley ran her tongue across her lips. Her voice
lowered. "So what do we need to do…to help?"

"Speed is often costly," Dr. Ettinger stated.

Ashley looked at Elliot.

"I can't impress upon you enough that for us money
is no object," Elliot said. "Whatever it takes."

The waiter brought their drinks and the food was
right behind it.

Elliot was coiled as tight as a cobra ready to strike.
It took all of his training and strength of will not to
reach across the table, snatch the both of them by the

necks and shake all the answers out of them. Instead he concentrated on his meal, making small talk and sipping his drink.

When the dishes had been cleared away, Gail and Dr. Ettinger resumed the conversation as if discussing selling babies during dinner was bad manners.

"I won't beat around the bush. If you are truly interested, it will cost you $50,000 now and $50,000 upon delivery."

"How long is delivery going to take?" Ashley asked.

"No more than two weeks. Maybe sooner," Gail answered.

Ashley expelled a breath of relief. "Two weeks," she said, her voice shaky with excitement. "We've waited so long." Tears slid down her cheeks. She grabbed the white-linen napkin and dabbed at her eyes. "Sorry," she murmured. "Our dream is so close." She turned to Elliot. "Oh, honey…"

"You said $50,000. How do we work that out?" Elliot asked.

"We'll be in touch when we're sure about the baby. At that time we'll arrange to get the deposit. When we bring the baby we'll expect the balance. You'll be given all the papers to make it official."

The waiter reappeared with the check. Elliot went to take out his wallet.

"No, please, Mr. Morgan," Dr. Ettinger said. He put a black American Express card in the leather folder and handed it to the waiter.

"Can we drop you somewhere?" Gail asked.

"No, thank you—we drove," Elliot answered.

"When do you think we can expect to hear from you?" Ashley asked.

"Soon, I promise," Gail said, reaching across the table to cover Ashley's hand with her own.

Ashley nodded her head.

On the ride home Ashley and Elliot tossed kudos back and forth for their performances.

"You were totally on point with the questions. All of their responses will be used to nail them," Elliot said.

"You weren't so bad yourself, handsome." She squeezed his thigh. "The strong, take-charge husband. Perfect role for you."

He gave a mock bow as he pulled to a stop at the red light. "But I have to give it to you, Ash, the tears again were a real nice touch. How do you manage to cry on cue like that?"

Her brows flicked for a moment. "When I think about my parents and what they went through, how I felt…I imagine the pain that some other family will go through to make our dreams come true. Was Layla some desperate family's dream come true?" Her voice cracked. She lowered her head. "I'm sorry."

"You have no reason to apologize. It was insensitive of me." He took a quick glance at her. "I think we're finally on track. This may all be over soon, and hopefully we'll make a lot of families happy, including yours."

"And what about those families that will have to give up children they've grown to love and the children who love them?"

Elliot was silent. He had no answer.

The following morning they met with Jean and Bernard at The Cartel headquarters.

"Based on the information that you've provided, we're putting Dr. Ettinger and his wife under twenty-four hour surveillance," Jean said. "They could very well be getting these babies from mothers who are willingly giving them up for the right price. Either way, we'll get to the bottom of it."

"Any luck with the rest of the list?" Bernard asked.

Ashley shook her head. "Clean."

Jean nodded her head. "So for now, Happy Homes is our target." She closed the file on the desk. "Keep us posted."

Ashley and Elliot rose.

"Seems you two are getting along much better," Jean said, as she adjusted several stacks of paper on her desk.

Her comment froze them in place. They weren't sure if they should respond or ignore her.

Jean slipped her red-rimmed glasses from her nose. "Have a good day."

They practically ran out of the door.

"It's spooky how she knows things," Ashley whispered as they hurried out.

"Yeah, creepy. Her sixth sense is legendary," Elliot said, as they rounded the last flight of stairs onto the ground floor.

Jasmine was coming up from the basement as they walked to the front door.

"Hey, E, Ashley."

They turned to the sound of their names.

"Jazz," they said in unison.

"I'm glad I ran into you guys. I have some information on your case. I was going to take it up to Jean."

"What do you have?"

She handed over the file. "I'm almost 90 percent sure that Dr. Ettinger and Dr. Lester are the same person."

Chapter 18

Ashley and Elliot spent the rest of the afternoon going over every line of information that Jasmine had put together.

"When you put their files side by side they're practically identical," Elliot said, "from city of birth to professions. I mean there are a few variations, but nothing major."

"They can't be the same person, they look nothing alike."

"Nothing that a little nip and tuck couldn't cure. Same body types, complexion…" He turned to Ashley. "What's wrong?" he asked, seeing the strained look on her face.

"I don't know," she said, her voice drifting off. "Something is nagging me, but I can't put my finger on it."

Elliot gently massaged the back of Ashley's neck and she moaned in pleasure. "Put it out of your head for a while and it will come to you."

She closed her eyes and let Elliot's fingers loosen the tension in her body. "You're probably right. I'm overthinking this."

"Exactly. I'm going to take a hot shower and then check the videos. From the other locations."

"Do you think we should still pursue a hospital connection?" Ashley asked, stretching.

"Let's see what happens with Gail and the good doctor."

As Ashley lay in bed, all of the details that they'd been given by Jasmine ran around in disarray in her head. She was a person of detail and order, much like Mia. She firmly believed that for every endeavor there had to be a plan for a successful outcome.

She listened to Elliot's deep, even breathing and let it relax her and allow her mind to clear of all the stuff that was cluttering it and blocking what she needed to see.

One by one, she took the information that she had and lined it up like index cards on the white board of her mind: names, years, profession, affiliations, hospitals. Dr. Ettinger. Dr. Lester. Concentrate. What was she missing? The answer hung on the fringes of her consciousness. Her mother. Layla. She moved the cards around in her head.

Her stomach suddenly tensed. She jerked up in bed. Her heart hammered. Could it be? She eased out of bed and tiptoed to the front. Digging in her purse that she'd left on the couch, she took out her cell phone.

It was nearly 2:00 a.m. but her dad was a notorious insomniac. He'd be annoyed by the call, but he'd be awake. Her father picked up the phone on the first ring.

"Dad, it's Ashley."

"I guess it is. You're the only one to call me Dad."

"Dad, listen, I need you to try to remember something. Was Dr. Herman Lester the name of Mom's first doctor before she went to the specialist?"

"Hell, girl, I don't know. That was more than twenty years ago."

"Dad, I know. But please, think. It's important."

"Is this about Layla?" His voice rose in anxiety. "Is that what this is about? Why are you asking questions about that at this time? Why? You know how it upsets your mother."

Her heart started to break all over again when she heard the anguish in her father's voice. Her mother may have had the breakdown, but her dad suffered in many other ways. Not only had he lost a child, he'd lost the woman that he married.

"Dad, please. I'm sorry. I'm sorry. Look, we'll talk another time. Get some rest." She waited for him to say something and when he didn't she said good-night.

Totally shaken, she sat down on the couch, drew her knees to her chest and lowered her head. She wasn't sure how long she sat there, drifting in and out of sleep until the chirping of her cell phone snapped her fully awake. She shook her head to clear it. Calls this time of the night were never about good news, some part of her brain surmised. She snatched up the phone from the couch and frowned when she saw the number. She pressed Talk.

"Dad? Is something wrong? Is it Mom?"

"I went through the old bills and notes," he began. "I found one from a Dr. Lester."

Ashley's heart banged in her chest. "Is the first name Herman?"

"Just says Dr. H. Lester, Winston Medical Center. That's where your mother went…in the beginning. To the clinic."

Ashley's throat had tightened. She remembered going with her mother on her visits when she was first pregnant with Layla. She remembered sitting in the waiting room, looking at magazines with chubby-cheeked babies on the cover and women all around her in varying stages of pregnancy. But then her mother couldn't see Dr. Lester anymore, yes, that was his name, because her mother was high-risk.

Ashley could barely talk. "Thank you, Dad," she managed. "Please don't put that away. I may need it."

They said their goodbyes. Ashley's mind was on overdrive. The final piece of the puzzle was just out of her reach, but she knew she'd find it. She'd figure it out.

She walked back into the bedroom and sat down next to Elliot. He stirred, opened his eyes and squinted up at her.

"What're you doing up? What time is it?"

"Dr. Lester treated my mother."

He rubbed his eyes and sat up in the bed. "What? How do you know?"

"That's what was bugging me, the name. In the back of my mind. I couldn't figure how or why I thought I knew it." She went on to explain that she'd called her father and he'd found the bill from Dr. H. Lester.

"I don't remember seeing Winston Medical Center in the intel that we have."

"It wasn't. I know if I'd seen it I would have made the connection sooner."

"We'll get this info to Jazz in the morning and have her do a trace." He looked at her with a new admiration. "Have you been to sleep at all?"

"No." She breathed heavily and rested her head on his chest. He wrapped his arms around her and drew her close. "Try to get some rest."

"Some super spy you turned out to be," she teased, poking him lightly in the side. "You didn't even budge when I was tiptoeing around in here. I could have been an intruder."

"I figured I had a kick-ass Cartel sister in my bed who would make sure I was safe and sound," he said, nibbling on her neck.

She laughed and rolled on top of him to let him know just what a Cartel sister was capable of.

Elliot hung up the phone just as Ashley emerged from the bathroom wrapped from head to toe in towels.

"I just got off with Jasmine. She said she should have something for us in a couple of hours. I've been going over the video and the e-mails from all of the locations, including Happy Homes. There's nothing. Not a letter out of place. If there is anything going down, it's not happening at these locations."

"So what are you thinking?"

"If Gail and her husband are brokering babies they're doing it from someplace else, another office, their home...I don't know."

"I'm sure you're right, and it's obvious that whatever they're doing is shaky. Why not have us meet at the agency? Why take us to someplace private if everything was aboveboard?"

"Exactly." He ran his hand over the morning stubble on his chin and jaw. His cell phone rang beside him. He looked at the dial. It read Restricted. "Hello?"

"Mr. Morgan?"

"Yes, who is this?"

"This is Gail. I wanted to let you know that based on what we discussed we'd need the first part by the end of this week. Things are moving along much more quickly than we expected."

He stole a look at Ashley and mouthed "Gail. Uh, is tomorrow okay?"

"Of course. I'll be in touch with the arrangements." The call was disconnected.

Elliot dropped the phone onto the couch. "I need to get over to see Jean. We're going to need the first fifty grand by tomorrow."

"Give me fifteen minutes and I'll go with you."

He pulled her unceremoniously down onto his lap. "Don't you have a real job? Somebody has to work to pay the bills around here," he teased while wiggling his way under her towel.

She hopped up and snaked out of his grasp. "I actually do need to go into the office. We have tons of work to do with this new cable station account. Although, I'm sure Mia would understand if I came in later."

"Go on to the office. I'm not gonna run off with the loot like in the movies," he joked.

"Very funny. Okay. I guess you're right, and I don't want to leave Mia in the lurch." She started to walk off then looked back at him over her shoulder. "If you need me…just put your lips together and blow."

"Lauren Bacall ain't got nothing on you, baby," he chuckled.

She sashayed away to the rhythm of his whistling some unrecognizable tune.

"You'll be wearing a wire," Bernard was saying as he stacked the money into a plain black leather bag. "And we'll have some agents stationed nearby for surveillance."

"Women are so much more unobtrusive. We'll use Savannah and Danielle if necessary," Jean said.

"Not a problem," Bernard agreed, zipping up the bag. He handed it to Elliot. "You've done this a million times. You know the drill."

Elliot took the bag. "Walk in the park."

Gail had arranged to stop by Elliot and Ashley's apartment to pick up the money and drop off some paperwork.

"They're very cautious," Elliot was saying to Ashley as he hooked up a video camera above a piece of artwork in the living room. There were bugs all over the apartment to pick up even whispered conversation. But Elliot had a feeling that this exchange was going to be short and sweet. "They're not bringing us anywhere that can connect them to anything out of the ordinary. Coming here was an especially nice touch." He hopped down off the step stool and stood back to admire his handiwork. "Perfect."

"They should be here any minute," Ashley said.

"Yeah." He stepped up to her and wrapped his arm around her waist before swooping down for a quick kiss. "Ready?"

"Hmmm, hmm," she said against his lips and she had a sudden flash of what life would be like for her when this was over. How empty it would be. Suddenly she clung to him, surprising them both.

"What is it?" he asked, turning her face up to look at him.

She shook her head. "We're close," she said, instead of what was on her mind, the fact that this playacting they'd been doing had become real for her and how she was desperately, deeply in love with him, and she didn't know what she was going to do when he was no longer in her life. But of course she could never say that. They were adults, playing house and enjoying each other's company. No more. No less. He'd made it clear that his life was his job, a job that could take him to the ends of the earth at any given time for months on end. "This will all be over soon," she added, the double entendre having a special significance for her.

Elliot inhaled deeply and pressed her close to his chest. Yes, it will, he thought.

At nine o'clock Gail Hastings walked through their door. She'd come alone, which Elliot found significant. If anything were to go down, Gail would take the fall. He'd love to be a fly on the wall in their marriage. By nine-fifteen they had what appeared to be official documents and Gail was gone with the cash.

"The clock is now ticking," Elliot said as he locked the door behind her.

Chapter 19

"Elliot, it's Jasmine. I have some info on that side case that you asked me about," the message said. "I'm going to send the data to your PDA. Any questions, give me a call. Sorry it took so long. Seemed to be a rush on spying this week," she joked.

Elliot grinned. She must have called while they were making the exchange with Gail. While Ashley was on the phone in the bedroom with Mia, he went into the kitchen and booted up his PDA. Adrenaline rushed through his veins as he read the information. The overwhelming urge to kick down Gail and her husband's door had him shaking with rage, and he didn't want to rip up the seeds of hope that would never materialize because of something stupid that he did. He knew he had to keep himself in check. Overreaction could blow everything. This had to be done the right way down to the letter. But at some point he knew he was going to scramble the alphabet.

The next two weeks were like hell. The waiting was unbearable. They were so close to breaking the case wide open but it all hinged on that last phone call, the last meeting. The ball was in the other team's court.

And then the call came. They had a little girl. Three days old. They would bring the baby within the hour.

"They're playing this real close," Elliot said. "They're trying like hell to make sure that no one but them has time to make any moves."

"I'll call Bernard," Ashley said, shifting into action. "He needs to get someone here before they arrive." She was relieved when Bernard picked up on the second ring.

"Putting someone in the house at this point is too risky. They could easily run into each other in the lobby. Elliot is fully authorized to make an arrest. You keep the baby safe and Elliot can take care of the rest. We'll get social services over there as soon as Elliot throws on the cuffs."

Ashley hung up the phone. "Looks like we're on our own." She ran down to him what Bernard had said.

"Makes sense. You cool with this?"

She nodded.

"Good."

Elliot went into the bedroom and retrieved his gun from the top of the closet, checked the safety and tucked it into his waistband at the base of his spine then got his badge, which he hung around his neck, beneath his shirt.

Ashley watched his precision movements from the

doorway, the cold, almost-calculated look that descended across his features, the way his eyes darkened and his body tensed. This was who he was, what he did. There was a dangerous energy that radiated from him. And when he turned his head in her direction, she didn't recognize him. Her heart thundered. And then he smiled.

"They should be here any minute."

"Yes," she said, her voice barely above a whisper.

"Come on." He walked over to her, draped his arm around her shoulder. "Let's go sit down and pretend to be a happily married couple and snag these bastards."

They were seated at the kitchen table when the lobby bell rang. Elliot pushed back from the table. He went to the intercom, saw that it was Gail and the good doctor on the lobby cameras. He buzzed them in. He turned to Ashley as he removed his gun and checked it one last time.

Ashley swallowed. "Let's do this."

He leaned over and kissed her forehead. "It's gonna go down smooth as silk."

The front doorbell rang. Ashley opened it. Gail walked in first with her husband behind her. She was carrying a large tote bag with a flat bottom. She walked past them and gently placed the bag down on the couch. She reached down inside and took out the newborn baby girl wrapped in pink. She stood there with the baby in her arms.

"Do you have the money?" Dr. Ettinger asked.

Elliot went to the table and brought back the bag that held the balance of the hundred thousand dollars.

"Fifty thousand, just like you asked," he said.

Dr. Ettinger went to the bag and opened it. He lifted

several packs of wrapped bills and flipped through them. He turned to his wife and lifted his chin. Gail handed the baby to Ashley. Dr. Ettinger zipped up the bag.

"Our business is concluded. I'm sure you will be very happy."

"But you won't," Elliot said, pulling his weapon. "FBI. You're under arrest."

Gail screamed. Ashley clutched the baby.

Bernard and another agent burst through the door, grabbed the doctor and Gail, pinning them to the wall as they were read their rights. They'd been listening to everything from the microphone bud that they had in their ears. And while the Ettingers were busy selling a baby, the FBI was searching their apartment in Manhattan and their house on Long Island.

By the time the apartment was cleared and social services had come to take the baby, which they were told had been taken from Long Shore Hospital, Ashley was physically shaken.

"I need to go out for a while," Elliot said. "Some things I need to take care of. You gonna be okay?"

She felt numb. She nodded.

He looked at her for a long moment. "See you in a few hours."

Left alone, Ashley was tormented by the enormity of the past few hours, the past month. How could Gail and her husband live with themselves after what they'd done? She couldn't begin to imagine what would crawl out from beneath their rug once it was fully pulled. And for right now, she wouldn't. She curled up into a ball on the couch and cried.

* * *

Elliot worked with the search team for hours. By the time they were done they'd secured computers, files and journals. He was still sitting at the conference table at New York's FBI headquarters when Bernard came in bearing coffee.

"It's pretty clear that this Robert Ettinger is the mastermind behind a nationwide baby-selling ring. The bureau is lining up indictments for folks all over the city. You should be damned proud of yourself."

Elliot raised bleary eyes in Bernard's direction and briefly wondered how Bernard had managed to stay so pressed and unruffled after the night they'd had.

"Yeah," he said, the one word a testament to his exhaustion and his dilemma. He opened a file, compiled from information taken from the Ettinger house and what Jasmine had put together at his request, turned it around and showed it to Bernard.

Bernard slipped on his half-framed glasses, the only indicator of his age, and sat down. After several long moments, he slowly removed his glasses and set them beside the folder. "What are you going to do?"

Chapter 20

When Elliot dragged himself back to the apartment, it was eerily quiet. He walked through the rooms to his bedroom and immediately knew that something was wrong. All of Ashley's things were gone. He quickly retraced his steps and went down the hall to the other side of the apartment. He pushed open Ashley's door. Empty.

He felt as if he'd been kicked in the gut. The force of the realization that she was actually gone was so strong that it was physical. He turned in a slow circle, momentarily lost and off center. He gazed down at the file in his hand. Exhaustion gripped him one final time. He lowered himself onto the bed, supine, threw his arm across his eyes and begged for sleep.

Savannah, Danielle and Mia helped Ashley with the last of her things.

For Ashley, the decision to leave the apartment and

Elliot was more difficult than anything she'd ever done. Her insides felt raw as if they'd been gouged out with some sharp object. Her head pounded and she was sure that her heart was broken. But what choice did she have? It was better to leave now than to watch him walk away from her. That, she knew she would not be able to bear.

"You should have at least left him a note," Savannah was saying as she unzipped one of the suitcases.

"I don't know why you left at all," Danielle added. "You know you love the man, just work it out."

"It's not that simple, Dani. I can't just profess my love for a man who would just as soon hop on a plane to the jungles of the rain forest as make love to me."

Mia put her hands on her hips. "I have to agree, Ash. You won't know what's on the man's mind until you lay your cards on the table."

"You can't be any more hurt than you are now if he doesn't give you the answers you want to hear. But if you don't pose the questions you'll never know."

Ashley plopped down on the side of her bed and looked up into the three concerned faces of her girls. Deep inside she knew they were right. But she didn't think she could stand to hear him actually say that he didn't want to be with her.

"I can't deal with this right now," she finally said. "I need some sleep." She slowly stood and gathered the trio in her arms, kissing each cheek. "Thank you guys for everything. Ya'll don't have to go home, but you gotta leave here. I'm beat."

Mia snatched up her purse in mock indignation. "I've been kicked out of better places than this."

"No, you haven't," Danielle said, pushing her toward the door.

"Call me if you need to talk," Savannah whispered and finger-waved on her way out.

Ashley sunk back across the bed and in moments she'd drifted off into a troubled sleep.

The sound of ringing and banging permeated her dreams. She'd been running, pushing through a series of never-ending doors in search of the answers that would lead her to what happened to her sister twenty-three years ago. At first she imagined that the noise was the sound of the doors slamming shut behind her and her ringing bells to gain entry to the empty rooms. But it wasn't her dream.

Groaning, she blinked against the darkness and pulled herself up. She peered at the digital clock. It was after ten. She'd been asleep all day. Struggling, she got up and went to the door.

"Who is it?"

"Elliot. I need to talk to you."

Elliot! She looked down at what she had on; baggy, dingy sweatpants and a wrinkled T-shirt. Her hair felt like it was matted down on one side and she could feel the crust in her eyes.

"Come on, Ash. Open the door."

She wiped her eyes and ran her fingers through her hair. Reluctantly she pulled the door open and stood in the frame, blocking him from entering.

"Trust me, you don't look *that* bad," he said, hoping to tease a smile out of her.

The instant she opened the door, his whole world

shifted. There was suddenly daylight in the midst of his darkness. He felt a surge of possibility and an overwhelming desire to take her in his arms and never let her go. But of course he couldn't do that. The simple reality of her being back in her own apartment spoke volumes about everything. The case was over and so were they. That truth devastated him. But if this was what she wanted… He forced a smile.

She made a face and stepped aside. "What are you doing here?" she asked, walking behind him into her dual-purpose living and dining room.

"I have something you need to see. For the past couple of weeks, I've been feeding details to Jasmine."

Her heart began to race.

"Between what she found and what was pulled from the Ettinger's home, I've been working on putting this together all night and most of the day."

"Working…on what?"

He went into the inside jacket pocket of his FBI windbreaker and took out a rolled-up manila folder. He handed it to her. Her hand trembled as she reached out to take it.

Some time later she gazed up at him, her eyes teary from emotion and fatigue. "Do you think it's true?"

"I'm pretty sure," he said, nodding his head.

The tears fell freely now. "So, what do we do?" she asked, her voice breaking like a scratched CD.

"You need to decide what you want to do with the information, Ash…" He paused and sat down beside her. "Whatever you decide, I'll support you. I promise you that."

Ashley broke down and sobbed. He gathered her in his arms and held her, letting her release all the years of hurt, and guilt and loss. He knew that whatever decision she made it would change lives for better or worse.

Chapter 21

The campus of Brooklyn College was in full swing as students rushed from one building to the next and geared up for the Homecoming Weekend. Located in Brooklyn's Midwood section, the sprawling campus was one of the borough's crown jewels. They walked toward the graduate buildings and the President's office.

It had been ages since she'd walked the halls of a college campus, Ashley thought as she and Elliot navigated their way to the administrative offices. The closest she'd come to being back in school was on her last assignment where she posed as a high school student.

"Should be around the next corner," Elliot said, referring to the college president's office.

Ashley's heart thumbed in anticipation. She'd spent two weeks of sleepless nights debating about what was the right thing to do. It had been a painful, but thought-ful decision. She only hoped it was the right one. And during that two weeks when she'd wrestled with what to do, Elliot was there to support her, just like he'd promised.

Elliot opened the door to the outer office, and they stepped into the reception area.

An auburn-haired receptionist greeted them. "President Stevenson is waiting for you. You can go right in."

Elliot tapped lightly on the door and they walked into President Stevenson's office. The elegant gentle-man, surrounded by plaques and degrees, was seated behind an enormous cherrywood desk. The young woman, seated in front of his desk turned to look at them when they walked in, and Ashley's heart nearly stopped. They were her mother's eyes, wide and al-most see-through brown. Her knees wobbled and El-liot held her tight around her waist. The birthmark, a dark circle the size of a quarter, rested by her right ear, which she didn't bother to hide with her hair. She remembered asking her mother if the mark would go away. Her mother had hugged her and told her no, say-ing that birthmarks were little touches from God as He sent each of us out into the world.

President Stevenson rose from his plush high-backed leather seat. He extended his hand to Ashley and Elliot. "Please, have a seat." He waited for them to get settled. "Ms. Temple, Mr. Morgan, this is Sim-one McDonald. Simone, these are the people that I told you about." He cleared his throat. "My secretary can get you anything you need. I have a meeting." He walked past Simone and squeezed her shoulder before walking out and closing the door softly behind them.

After several awkward moments of silence, Ashley angled her chair toward Simone.

"You don't know me from the man in the moon," Ashley began, speaking softly and deliberately. She looked Simone directly in her eyes. "But I know you."

Over the next hour, Ashley held Simone's hand as she told her about the months leading up to her birth, her arrival and the agony when she disappeared. She told her about the toll that it took on their parents and on her.

"We've never forgotten you," Ashley said as she wiped away Simone's tears and then her own. "Never stopped wanting to find you and believing that you were out there somewhere."

"What's my real name?" Simone finally asked.

"Layla. Your name is Layla."

Bernard, Ashley, Jasmine, Jean and Elliot were gathered in Jean's office a week later for a debriefing.

"According to all the documents that have been confiscated there are more than eight hundred children that have been abducted by this network alone over the past twenty years," Jean said, the disgust that she felt evident in her tone. "I hope those S.O.B.s rot in jail. The devastation they've caused is incalculable. Unraveling this mess is going to take a while. And reconnecting the stolen children with their biological families...that is an even bigger nightmare." She took a long breath. "But the birth families deserve to know, they deserve some closure." She turned to Ashley. "How is Layla handling the news?"

"The DNA results came back." She turned to Elliot and smiled. He'd worked magic to push it through quickly. "She's definitely my sister. She wants to meet our parents. She's pretty much taken care of herself since she was eighteen. Her adoptive parents divorced when she was twelve and her mother died four years ago. Our road will be rough but certainly not as rough as other families. I'm planning to take her out to see them as soon as she finishes her thesis."

"Ettinger, or rather Herman Lester, had a smooth operation going," Elliot said. "He and his wife were not the only ones involved. We have indictments coming down for nearly a dozen more individuals. But I have to take my hat off to Jasmine for putting a lot of the pieces together."

Jasmine lowered her head. "Once I saw so many similarities between Dr. Ettinger and Dr. Lester, the time period and location and how one person ceased to exist and the other started, everything kinda fell into place from there."

"Excellent job, Jasmine," Jean said.

"I'll need everyone's final report in ten days. Try to do it as soon as possible as details tend to dim." She took off her glasses, a clear indication that the meeting was over.

Everyone stood and began to file out. Ashley was the last to leave. She waited until she was the only one in the room besides Jean.

"Forget something, Ashley?" Jean asked without looking up.

Ashley walked back over to Jean's desk. "I need to ask you something."

Jean glanced up.

"Did you know about my family situation? Is that why you assigned me to this case?"

"What's important is that the right people were chosen and the job was done." She waited a beat. "Anything else?"

Ashley pressed her lips together. "No. I guess not. Thank you." She walked toward the door and opened it.

"Oh, and Ashley..."

She turned partly around. "Yes."

"If you tell him how you feel, it will change your life."

Ashley's stomach did a three-sixty as she stared into Jean's all-knowing eyes, an instant before she slipped on her red-framed glasses and looked away.

Chapter 22

Ashley checked and rechecked the food. She'd looked in the mirror more in the past hour than she had in her entire lifetime. It had taken her nearly a week to get up the nerve and now she wished she had more time.

What if she was wrong? What if Jean was wrong? What if it was too late?

The bell rang and goose bumps ran up and down her arms. She took a long, deep, cleansing breath, squeezed her eyes shut for a moment then walked to the door.

When she saw Elliot standing on the other side, tall, dark, handsome, edible and looking at her as if he missed her as much as she missed him, she wondered why it had taken her so long.

She took his hand and gently pulled him inside. "Thanks for coming."

"I've never been one to turn down a free meal. And

from what I can remember…from our time together, you're a pretty good cook."

She stopped short and turned to him. The muscles in her throat worked up and down. "Do you think about us at all?"

His finger reached out and stroked her cheek. "All the time." The deep timbre of his voice reached inside to that empty place in her soul and filled it.

Her eyes glided over his face, recommitting every inch of it to memory.

"I love you, Ashley. I love you with all my heart. You gave me a reason to want to live again, really live life. To feel again, to want someone in my life that matters, who was there out of desire and not necessity. I've been going crazy these past weeks. I never knew how empty my life was until you weren't in it."

"I love you, Elliot Morgan," she said with all the eagerness and passion that had lived within her for months. "And I don't care if you want to travel to the moon. I want to be with you." There, she'd said it and she was certain that she'd never said anything more true.

He kissed her then—long, deep and sweet and she willingly gave of herself to him. The explosion of their need for each other made them dizzy with desire.

Elliot slowly broke the kiss, leaving Ashley trembling in his embrace. "Marry me, Ashley," he said in an almost urgent whisper. "Travel with me, wake with me, sleep with me, be my friend, my lover, my reflection." He dug in the front pocket of his jeans and took out a diamond ring set in white gold. He held it in front of her. "I didn't come for the free meal. I came to claim my woman."

Ashley's eyes filled with tears of absolute joy. "Yes, yes, yes."

She knew that the road ahead wouldn't be easy, but it would be full of excitement and adventure. With Elliot by her side, and her family united, there wasn't any challenge that she couldn't face.

As she rested in the warmth and security of Elliot's arms, she smiled and silently thanked Jean for knowing just what she needed.

* * * * *

Welcome to Club Babylon: where the A-list VIPs come to play...

BEYOND THE VELVET ROPE

TIFFANY ASHLEY

Club Babylon is the hottest club on the Miami strip, a magnet for major South Beach movers and shakers. And New York promoter Thandie Shaw is about to meet the biggest player of them all.

Babylon owner Elliot Richards is macho, arrogant and sexist—everything Thandie doesn't want in a boss or lover. He's also the most erotic man she's ever met. As he tries to seduce her into a world of intense passion, she knows it's too good to last...especially after she uncovers Elliot's explosive secrets.

A Club Babylon Novel

"This book combines humor, heat and great dialogue. The characters were so well written that I didn't want the book to end." —*Night Owl Romance* on *LOVE SCRIPT*

Available July 2014 wherever books are sold!

www.Harlequin.com

KPTA1340714

REQUEST YOUR FREE BOOKS!

2 FREE NOVELS PLUS 2 FREE GIFTS!

KIMANI
ROMANCE

Love's ultimate destination!